This excellent book is worthy of praise for several important reasons. The author stated early on that it is a book about the mental illness of bipolar disorder. As a retired psychology professor I found the author's coverage of the topic, well-informed and accurate. As an author myself, and an appreciator of good writing, I commend the high quality of the author's work. It is a challenging task to combine a thorough and balanced presentation of psychological material with the demands of writing an autobiography. This author has struck the perfect balance. And it is clear from the story of her life that she is supremely qualified to speak with a powerful voice about the ravages of mental illness. And beyond all of that, reading this book cannot help but influence the reader to share the author's ultimate emphasis on finding hope and meaning in the midst of the troubled waters of life."

Victor P. Garlock, Ph.D., Author of *Your Genius Within: Understanding Sleep, Dream Interpretation and Learning Self-Hypnosis*, Member of International Association for the Study of Dreams, and the National Guild of Hypnotists

You Showed Them We Aren't Trash

The true Story of a Pipeliner's Daughter

Beverly Ann Rider

You Showed Them We Aren't Trash
The true Story of a Pipeliner's Daughter

Third Edition 2025

ISBN 13: 978-1-952685-80-4

Cover photo by Frank Rider
Photos by Frank Rider
Wedding Photos on Page 189 by Duchess Thompson

Kitsap Publishing
Poulsbo, WA • USA

In Memory of Michael John Cloutier (1954-2023)

Mike served his country as submarine nuclear reactor operator, then as a Navy Officer, but his true purpose in life was met in the cause of the Rotary Youth Exchange Program. He lived to solve problems, taking care of people, computer systems and dogs.

Table of Contents

"If a story is not about the hearer he will not listen. And here I make a rule--a great and interesting story is about everyone or it will not last."

—John Steinbeck

Preface

"... the sins of the fathers shall be visited upon the children unto the third and fourth generation ..."

I have reason to believe that patterns of behavior are passed down from generation to generation. This behavior may exhibit itself in the breaking of a moral code, but more often than not it manifests itself in hurt and humiliation, and even in the form of mental illness. In my own family, I am aware of six generations whose behavior patterns have profoundly affected each succeeding generation. Now there is a seventh generation of children receiving behaviors passed to them.

I am the fourth generation of these seven. My father was a pipeliner, one who helped lay the oil and gas pipeline infrastructure across America. We lived in trailers and moved every month or two. If winter weather prevented working, we went to see family in Oklahoma until spring. By the time I started high school, I had moved 109 times to 25 states and changed schools 38 times.

Being a pipeline kid is not the point of this book. The subject of this book is bipolar disorder and the pain and chaos it produces. My father often had spells or tears, as we called them. These could last for months, followed by periods of calmer behavior. In my childhood, he would sometimes stick a gun in his mouth and threaten to kill himself or threaten others, or he would take Mother, with a gun pointed to her head, and drive around for hours. He wouldn't go to a doctor then, but in his later years, he was diagnosed with bipolar disorder.

In my own life, the year I turned forty, I was teaching an algebra class when a student threatened to kill me and reached into his jacket as to pull out a gun. I was especially frightened because elsewhere that week a school shooting with multiple fatalities had occurred.

My mind started unraveling and within days my family took me to the psychiatric emergency room at Vanderbilt Hospital. This mental breakdown became the first of multiple manic episodes. It was as though something was triggered in my brain, and if I were under severe stress or lost a lot of sleep, I began to exhibit signs of mania. These manic signs would evolve into a complete detachment from reality with hallucinations, severe paranoia, and other psychotic symptoms requiring medication.

Perhaps keeping a diary or journal would have been beneficial to me, but I've always wanted anything I wrote to be read by others. With this goal in mind, I began to write with the hope that my family, friends, and others could glean something to help them in their lives. I didn't just write from the heart, but also from the gut, as it was gut-wrenching for me to relive some of my experiences. I cried rivers of tears for many of the chapters I wrote—tears I had never shed at the time of the experiences. After a few months of writing, I realized it was I who was being helped. After finishing a chapter, I would feel a sense of release. The longer I wrote, the more I felt I could stand up and speak up for myself, things I'd been unable to do before.

As I neared the end of over two years of writing, a most remarkable thing happened. I realized I was no longer having even the earliest symptoms of going into a manic spell. It was as though reliving in a very deep way the pain I experienced as a child and pouring out on paper the sorrow from subsequent experiences had rewired my brain. I had taken the risk of opening up and sharing with others. It has transformed my life. I feel a sense of confidence and a wholeness and balance that I have never before known. Perhaps a doctor will say that the bipolar is in remission—that there is no cure. For me, to have to deal with mania every year for thirty years, and to now have over two years without even the slightest symptoms, is like a healing I never imagined.

Beverly Ann Rider, June 11, 2018

Acknowledgments

Throughout my life there have always been wonderful people at the right time helping me.

 Dr. Penne Laubenthal, English professor, saw potential in me that I didn't know was there. She encouraged me to edit my own book, saying this process would provide additional growth for me. There were those times when I was so low in spirit, and her wise words helped me in a very personal way.

My sister Sue checked on me frequently by telephone from California to monitor my mental health as I relived these many painful experiences. She is truly my sister/friend.

When my husband Buddy read the book, he reacted with these words, "While I'm not happy being portrayed as I was, it is the truth and I'm a grown up. I can accept it; it is the way I am." Without this blessing I would not have continued on toward a goal of publishing, as I was not trying to be vindictive or hurtful to him.

Mike Cloutier, my sister Sue's son, has devoted many hours proofreading the book and getting everything in shipshape. He is an amazing person. As a friend commented, "You are lucky to have him in the family and on your TEAM. What a supporter!"

I want to thank the following people for reading installments as I wrote them: Delle Brown; my college history professor, Dr. Bert Hayes and his wife Vickie; Cheryl Long; Henriette Parton; and my college psychology professor, Dr. Joe Slate. Thanks to Jon Garlock for helping me with computer skills and keeping the computer functioning.

Mother's Day Week and Some Hard Things

Mother's Day Week Phone Calls

As Mother's Day approached, I felt a bit sorry for myself. I always get a thoughtful gift from Linda and Tim chips in for it. His wife always sends a card and reminds him to call. My husband has never been one to acknowledge days—Mother's Day, birthdays, anniversaries, etc. Early in our marriage, I mentioned a little sadness because I didn't get a Happy Mother's Day greeting from him and he said, "You are not my mother." I wish I could say that I've grown used to that attitude and that it doesn't bother me at all, but I cannot. Much is more important in a relationship, so I dwell very little on it. This year I decided to do something very different for Mother's Day. I have a box of over 125 cards with contact information for people from my past. I decided to go through these and without dwelling on any certain one, if I had an impression to contact this person, I would set that card aside. At one point I dropped the box on the floor. Everything scattered, so the cards were in no particular order. At the end of this exercise, I had selected six people that I wanted to call.

The first person I called was the daughter of a dear friend of mine who passed last year on Easter. The previous week I had been thinking about an incident that happened during the daughter's college years. I brought it up, and we talked about it. She was home for Christmas and spending the night with a girlfriend across town. In the wee hours of the morning, she was brutally beaten and apparently left for dead. She was sleeping in her friend's bed, and the incident may have been intended for the friend. Over one hundred miles away in Tulsa (OK) her older sister awoke from a horrible dream that her little sister was trying to cross the railroad and was falling through the cracks, crying for help. She immediately started praying for her sister. Her mother awoke from a sound sleep and knew something was drastically wrong with her daughter and that she needed to get to her. The mother woke up the father, and they went to the house where their daughter was found in a pool of blood. There seems no doubt that if not for this intervention, she would have died. We talked about this, and I told her things her mother told me about this incident that she did not know. As the conversation progressed, she said that since she was very young, when around me, she always felt that I had a heightened sense of awareness of my surroundings. She asked if I were uncomfortable talking about this, and I told her that I was not.

Later that day she called me and told me how grateful she was for my call and that she considered me the person her mother would have said was her best friend. She felt her mother was sending her a Mother's Day message through me. She said, "If there were any person my mother would choose to send me a message, it would be you." Her mother, an English professor, had many opportunities for friends. As she recounted it, her mother was a very outgoing, friendly person (and she was definitely that), but she had few friends, and I was among those few. She told me that from a child, she would be in the background and listen to our conversations. As she was struggling for words, she said, "I would say that you and Mother had heightened cerebral conversations." I laughed and said, "'heightened cerebral conversations'—I want to use that." What a rewarding phone call for me. I had called to cheer her up for Mother's Day, but the call was wonderful for me in ways I will never forget.

The second call I made that day was to a most unlikely person, at least not one I would have chosen had it not been for the impression. Regina was a childhood friend with whom I had not talked in over fifteen years. Our fathers were welders on pipeline construction and helped lay many of the oil and natural gas pipelines that were laid in the '40s and '50s across America. Neither Gina nor I remember when we first met, but we must have been about six or seven years old. Duchess, a mutual friend, and I met in Dumas, Texas, at age five. The three of us were very good friends. Even though we moved every month or two, we were together and always hoping at each change of location to get in the same room in school.

When I was twelve, my dad left to go to work for one of the superintendents who had formed his own company, so the three of us were separated. Duchess and I remained close over the years, but it was about twenty-five years before I saw Gina again. When she saw me, Gina commented that I was slim and trim and still little Miss Proper, who was always so perfect and didn't get dirty even when we made mud-pies. That startled me. I had not known I was ever viewed this way, and to be truthful, the comments stung a little. A few years later I stopped again to see Gina. She had recently been seriously ill. Gina seemed cold and distant. Conversation was hard. I didn't know whether it was her health, or whether we just didn't have that much in common anymore. I sent Christmas cards a few years and made a call or two, but didn't remain in contact with her. Yet the impression came to call Gina. I called and she immediately said, "Friday, my little sister Joy dropped dead of a heart attack." Joy was Gina's only sibling. Gina told me over and over again how much my call meant to her at this time.

Gina and I talked about how most people thought we didn't get a good education because we moved around so much. We, however, got to experience geography—not just read about it. History lessons were often more real for us because we had been there. Yes, we were itinerants—here today and gone tomorrow. Our dads made good money when they were working (which was usually not in the winter), but the locals in a given town knew that some would skip out without paying bills. Rent was sky high for pipeliners, and often apartments were not available to them. Hence, most bought trailers to live in, and often we were parked in hastily built trailer camps. Back then, few trailers had bathrooms, so we had to share common facilities. Trailer trash was a name often applied to us.

Gina talked about how we had to part when my dad left to go to work for the new company. I shared with her how I handled the pain of having to leave her and Duchess. The new company was small, and there were no children my age. Some of the three moves we made that summer were not even spent in a trailer camp where there might have been some children with whom to become acquainted. We parked at the construction office at the job site and lived in our trailer there. I created a project to keep me busy. I decided to write to all forty-nine states and ask for travel literature from each state. I got so much mail that if something arrived at the office not clearly addressed, someone would mark on it, "must be for Frank Rider." I poured over these booklets and brochures and planned trips to places of interest in each state. I planned trips to EVERYTHING of interest—whether it was of natural or historical value. I would estimate the time I thought it would take to see each sight, the distance and travel time between the sights, and then figure the gas mileage, the cost of gas, food, and lodging. Talk about details—I filled two cardboard boxes with notebooks about vacation possibilities in the United States. So, from the age of twelve someone could name a state and I could tell you the sights to see in that state! Mother somehow found room for these boxes and stored them. Regretfully, in 1981, at the time of one of my moves, I broke down and threw them away.

Gina and I talked on. I had always wanted to play the accordion, and when I was five had asked for a toy one for Christmas. When I turned eight years, we lived in Fergus Falls, Minnesota, and my parents gave me eight accordion lessons for my birthday. During the next year when we moved to a new place, Mother would inquire as to whether or not there was an accordion teacher available. If so, I had a few more lessons. And so it went —sometimes yes, sometimes no. I recounted the time we were living in Fruita, Colorado. I had just turned nine. There was an accordion teacher in Grand Junction, ten miles away. There was also a television station with a talent show featuring children, and my new accordion teacher wanted to get me on the show. We did not have a television—there were only two TV sets in the trailer park of over fifty trailers. Everyone was excited that I was going to be on a TV show, so the two TVs were set outside in the park, and all the people were going to crowd around to see me on the show. I can see it all so vividly. I was playing two numbers, "What a Friend We Have in Jesus," and the Roy Rogers and Dale Evans song, "Open Up Your Heart and Let the Sunshine In." I did fine on the first song, but in the glare of the lights, midway through the second song, I glanced up and saw myself on a TV screen and got a severe case of stage fright! I didn't end the piece on a discordant note—I managed to finish the chord, but I brought things to a halt! The MC mentioned the piece had ended quickly. I piped immediately, "It was a short song!" He seemed fascinated by our lifestyle and asked me many questions. The stage fright hadn't gotten my tongue, so I talked on. In fact, in the thirty-minute show, my segment lasted about fifteen minutes instead of ten, thereby shortchanging the other two children a bit. I was mortified by all this! I was so sorry that I had let everybody down back at the trailer park. They were counting on me and so proud of me, but I had made a mess of things! When Mother and I got home, all of the people at the trailer camp were still around the TVs waiting on me. I immediately started apologizing for messing up the song. As I was lamenting, one woman spoke up and said, "That's all right, Beverly. You showed 'em we're not trash!"

How grateful I am for the defining moments in my life! It seems there has always been the right person at the right time there for me. I don't know the woman's name—maybe I never knew it—but I can see and hear her now, and I have never forgotten her words, "You showed 'em we're not trash!"

Tragedy in Red Oak

This was a chapter I intended to write much later in this project. There has been, however, a tragedy in the Red Oak, Oklahoma, area in my paternal granny and grandpa's house. This has prompted me to feel I should write about some painful things now. On Wednesday I had vertigo and had to stay in bed all day. Since I was too dizzy to read, about the only thing I could do was think, and I thought about some of those painful things in my childhood. On Thursday, my back was hurting (my back was injured in the car wreck we had on our honeymoon), so, for me, tension often settles there. When I made the decision to write this chapter, the pain left my back immediately. I took this as confirmation that I should write about this subject now.

Last weekend a little thirteen-year-old boy was buried, his parent's only son, the result of a needless tragedy. The two boys who now live in my grandparent's house were having a sleepover. As some of the invited guests arrived, they were looking at guns. As so often happens, the gun that was supposed to be unloaded, was, in fact, not. The visitor was struck in the shoulder. Though he was transported to the local hospital fifteen miles away and then sent on to a larger, better-equipped hospital, he bled to death. This affected me in a double way. I am deeply saddened for all involved. I was also saddened that it happened in my granny and grandpa's house—a house that knew so much trauma involving guns.

Guess I might as well start talking about my father now. My dad had a lot of good qualities, and I hope these will shine forth in future chapters in this book. Dad not only had some bad qualities, but he also had a mental illness. At times Dad had spells, as we called them. Sometimes we said, "Frank is on a tear." Today, there are words to describe the spells Dad had—words like manic-depressive and bipolar, but we didn't know anything about those words back then. We just knew something was wrong—so very wrong, and it was scary. My granny and grandpa have stood so many times in the living room of that home crying and begging my dad to go to Ft. Smith (AR) to seek medical help. Dad, of course, thought that there was nothing wrong with him.

When Dad had a spell, he always wanted it to involve guns. I don't know when Dad's first symptoms appeared, but they were definitely there during his first marriage. He was married to Eunie, and they had two children, Frankie Sue, ten years my senior, and John, eight and one-half years older than I. Even when John was a grown man, I have seen him put his head down between his legs, weeping, with these words, "Dad, I remember the time when you took us into the telephone booth and stuck a gun to our heads and called Mother on the phone and said if she didn't do 'such and such,' you were going to blow our brains out." Dad would sit there motionless and emotionless as far as one could tell. When Sue and I have discussed this, she will say, "Well, I remember the time Dad took us to the phone booth and took the gun in there and called Mother and had us talk to her and tell her that we were in there and that he had the gun and was going to kill us if she didn't do 'such and such,' but I don't remember him having it pointed at our heads." She will add, "And I'm a year and a half older than John, so I may remember it better." So, John remembers it that he had the gun pointed at his head, and Sue remembers it a bit differently. At this time they were living with Dad's parents in Oklahoma, while their mother, Eunie, was in California working. After this incident, Eunie decided she had better come back to Oklahoma and get those kids, and did so. Sue and John did not live with him anymore after that.

I remember things by pictures. I vividly can see pictures in my mind of incidents and hear (not audibly of course) the words spoken as well. I have always thought I remembered things accurately because of this ability. I have told my children about one of the times that Dad was on a tear and had a gun in his mouth threatening to kill himself. I was thirteen years old at the time. He was sitting in a chair, and I was down on my knees in front of him with my hands folded together in a position of prayer, crying and begging him, "Please don't kill yourself, Daddy. I love you, Daddy. I don't want you to kill yourself." Aunt Eunice, Dad's sister, got really upset and screamed, "Get outside, Frank. If you want to kill yourself, go outside so we don't have to clean up the mess!" Well, he did move outside, and the drama started out there. Lights went on up and down the block with people peeking out to see what was going on now. In today's world, somebody would have called the police, but it didn't happen then. I sometimes wondered if my children really believed all the things I told, but once, when they were probably in their teens, we were visiting Aunt Eunice. She told about this incident. When she finished, my children looked at each other wide-eyed, and my son Tim looked at his sister Linda and said, "That is exactly like Mother told it." It gave me a feeling of vindication that my memory was accurate, and I was glad that Aunt Eunice had retold it.

How many times have I hidden under the big dining table in that house where the boy has so recently died. Somehow, I felt the table would protect me if Dad decided to shoot in my direction. There are the times I was afraid to go to sleep at night and wondered if the next day people would be reading about my death in the newspaper. I would get out of bed and crawl under it—thinking in my childish mind that the bed would protect me. I would get so thirsty. If Dad were outside with a gun doing his threatening, sometimes I would crawl on my stomach from the bedroom to the kitchen for a drink of water—afraid to stand up for fear that he would shoot through the window.

So many times Dad would take Mother at gunpoint to the car to go for a ride. Granny and I would be hysterical, and she would get down on the floor and roll. She would cry, "I know he's going to kill her!" Often they were gone for hours, and we would be terrified that Mother was dead, until he would finally come back with her. In those days of my earlier childhood, we did not have telephones, so there was no calling the sheriff. Granny and Grandpa lived on a farm about three miles from town. Aunt Eunice lived just down the road, so she was often involved when some of this was going on.

When I was eight, it seemed like so many things happened. Sometimes I think I must pile so many things in that year—so many that some must have happened the year before or the year after. When I look at my list of our moves, I see we did live five months in Red Oak with Granny and Grandpa, so maybe a lot of things did happen that year. I would go to school on the school bus, and more often than not, by the afternoon I was throwing up. Mr. Bullard, the school custodian, would drive me back home. Granny went to the school and told the person to not let me go with Dad if he came and wanted to check me out of school—that she was afraid he would kill me.

That year Dad's spell seemed to last unusually long. He even went back to work in the spring and took Mother with him to Kansas, leaving me to stay with Granny and finish school that year. As I said, there were no telephones, but Mother wrote a letter, even if just a few lines, every day. If there were days the letters didn't come, we were worried. If two days went by with no word from Mother, Granny would again be terrified - -crying that Dad had probably killed her. Then, finally, a letter would come, and we'd know that once again, at least on that day, she was alive.

Now, one probably wonders why Mother didn't get out of all this. In years gone by, I have spent too many hours wondering this myself and analyzing and agonizing. I will say that Mother and Dad were often separated and filing for divorce—three years was the longest period I ever remember them not separated or filing for divorce; but when Dad would come down from his spell, Mother always took him back. I can tell you for sure, that his mother and his sister, Eunice, didn't want her to stay with him! So many times, Mother would say she was going to take me to California and get a job in a restaurant (she had worked in a restaurant for many years in California during the 1930s and then as a welder in the shipyards when World War II started). I often wondered why she didn't do this. It became a fantasy for which I longed. I will talk later about my healing process, but this is enough for now.

Hard Things

Once again I am deviating from writing about the calls I made Mother's Day week. I am not one to put off doing hard things—I'd rather get them over. This will probably be the hardest chapter I will write in this book, and I decided to do it now so that I could be free to write the many other things in my life. I am anxious to start doing just that.

One of the nicest things about writing about oneself is that you can choose the wording carefully, tell what you want and leave things unsaid that you feel shouldn't be put into written words. I know I don't have to write about this, and that I can change it or leave it out completely. To me, I believe the hardest part of this chapter is not revealing things about myself, but the fact that I know many people will read it who know nothing about the content. I dread writing for that reason. The people who know now—that's okay, but to put this into words for many to see, somehow feels like an exposing of myself for which I don't feel ready, and for which I may never be.

People who are labeled manic-depressive often have inappropriate sexual behavior, especially during an episode of mania. I am grateful that I don't have this problem. Whatever the reason, my dad's sexuality was abnormal, even when he wasn't having mental problems. Somehow, I don't feel I need the therapy of writing on this subject. Perhaps I do. I have never felt I let this subject define my life. Harder for me was the constant instability of dealing with Dad and the fear of his spells involving guns. I know, however, that this is part of my makeup, too. My story would be incomplete without addressing this issue, so I will.

In July 1991 I met with Dad's psychiatrist for the purpose of leading me into regression regarding the inappropriate sexual behavior of my father to me in infancy and early childhood. (Dad, due to inappropriate sexual behavior, was in the psychiatric ward of a hospital in Nashville, TN.) All of my life the pictures as memories flitted in and out, but this was from the toddler years, not earlier. In regression, I went back to about the age of five months. It was at this time I indicated this was enough—my agreement with the doctor had been that when I had enough I would say so. Did all of this bother me? No. It simply gave validity to those pictures in my memory and gave me a big sense of relief. My symptoms were so classic. It helped release so many things.

A few sentences ago, I just said going into regression did not bother me. Well, I came home and for about thirty minutes—that's all the time I felt I could spare in dealing with this matter—I sobbed. I cried for the little girl. By the afternoon, I was beginning to go into what could be described as a manic episode. I had to take care of Mother that afternoon and went next door to the trailer where she was living. A very interesting thing happened, and the whole event still amazes me. The television was on, and it seemed like there was so much static on the screen—if I moved a certain way the static would be so great that the picture would be off the screen, and there would just be static. The Oprah Winfrey Show was on. Sometimes, I was on the television screen and on her show talking about painful things in my life. Other times I was talking to large audiences about these things. If I moved to the right or left, the static would come back and completely cover the television screen. I had a powerful glimpse into the future—that we would have a lot of money, but that we would not be happy. There would be so much confusion, fights, husband and others drinking, etc. How horrible it all was! The amazing thing—it all came true! Every single bit of what I saw that afternoon came true except the part where I was on the Oprah Winfrey show and where I was speaking to large audiences. That has not happened—not yet anyway.

My daughter Linda was with me at the meeting with the psychiatrist and up at Mother's that afternoon. When Linda would pass by the television screen, I would ask her to move, because all of these revelations were coming through the TV screen, and I didn't want to miss any. She knew the content of the regression and became concerned about me. She called the doctor. She still gets mad to this day when his name is mentioned because he told her, "Your mother is okay. She is doing fine. She handles things extremely well." She told him I was NOT doing well at all! I did make it through the end of the day without coming apart emotionally or mentally, but I occasionally still ponder how accurate the revelations were that I had that afternoon.

Since my earliest memory, I had never wanted to touch my dad. I did not want him to hold me on his lap as a child—I was so scared of him. To have ever given him a hug even as an adult would have been revolting to me. This feeling never left me. When he was in the nursing home and I had to drive him to doctor's appointments, sometimes I would get sick and nearly throw up at the thought of having to be in the car alone with him. It would be such a relief to get the trip over and him back to the nursing home. This was a fear, I am sorry to say, that I never got over.

I remember one time that Dad and I needed to go from Tennessee to Oklahoma City to take care of some of the gas royalty business. Even with going in one day and staying with relatives in Red Oak, we were going to have to be spending overnight alone. My sister, Sue, and I talked about this on the phone, and she asked me what I was going to do. Money was not an object, and I know the simple thing would have been to have gotten separate rooms at the motel, but Dad would have thrown a fit at such wastefulness. I'm sorry, but I could never confront Dad, so I didn't consider that as an option. I told Sue that I had a plan—I just didn't intend to go to sleep. That night, with the best of intentions of staying awake, at some point in the wee hours of the morning, I drifted off to sleep. There was a sound. My body jerked so hard that I literally was raised up off the bed and fell in the floor. Even in sleep, the fear was that great. My dad had just gotten up to go to the bathroom—that was all.

As I said earlier, I would like to believe that I did not let this define my life, but Linda says that I was a cold mother. She has watched me with Eram, my little grandson, and says that I am so warm with him, giving him hugs, etc., things that she does not remember me doing with her and her brother.

Healing has been in stages. When I moved to South Carolina in 1995, I was forty-nine years of age. On a wall of photos in my office, I placed a picture of my dad and me, taken when I was about two. My dad was smiling, but I had the saddest little look on my face. I put this photo on the wall deliberately. Every time I walked in, I saw the picture. Hard as it was, I just made myself do it. It felt good when I could finally bear to look at this picture. It got easier and easier, and the twinges got less and less. In most of my childhood photos, I look very, very sad. Unfortunately, they depict what a lot of my childhood was—very, very sad. I don't know the psychology of this and guess I really don't care. These things have worked for me. I have a little antique child's sleigh in my bedroom filled with stuffed animals and dolls from my childhood, and it was a good feeling that at age fifty, I could begin to look at these toys with comfort—not pain. One is a Humpty Dumpty that I won at a circus to which my dad took me when I was about five. In the ticket drawing, three prizes were awarded. I was one of the lucky three. I can see the huge crowd now and see myself getting out of the seat to get my prize. I feel that is a capsule of what my life has been thus far—perhaps it was an omen—I have been so lucky; I won the prize. So many wonderful people have graced my life and have helped me at just the right time.

Yes, healing is a process. And sometimes the various ways this process unfolds surprises even me. When you think you are healed, something knocks you off your feet, and you know you have another step to take. A few years after my father's death, when I was in my late fifties and in the Catholic Church, if one did any volunteer work at the church, it was required that one take a class on how to recognize sexual abuse among minors. Though I had only shared my experience with regression among one friend and a few relatives, Harriet had become a very dear friend. Harriet was interested in my opinion since regression was used in many cases of sexual abuse where priests were involved. When it was announced that every volunteer would be required to take the class, Harriet told me she would go to the class session that I went to and be there for me in case I had problems with it. I assured her that, while that was kind, I would be just fine. I would have no problems at all attending the class—famous last words. I always like to sit at the front of a classroom, regardless of the subject. Well, when I got to the class, a lot of seats were already taken, but for some reason, I did not want to go toward the front where Harriet was sitting. I quietly slipped in a seat at the rear of the room beside a man and his wife whom I had met but didn't know well. The class consisted of a two and one-half hour movie specially made for the subject matter. Even now I am not sure I can explain why, but the moment—and I do mean the very moment—that the first scene and words appeared on the screen, I started shedding tears uncontrollably. I did not audibly disturb the class, but the tears quietly just flowed and flowed. As I didn't expect this, I did not bring extra tissues with me—I only had the two or three that I normally carry in my purse. Well, I quickly used mine, but the angel Marlene, sitting beside me, happened to have a whole box sitting on her desk. She would pass me a Kleenex; I would quickly soak it, and she would pass me another one. This went on and on for the whole hour and a half or so until the break in the movie. Guess I used practically her whole box. My desk was piled high with tissues. At the break, Marlene never bothered me— she never asked me any questions, did not ask if I wanted to talk to somebody or anything. She was just there with the Kleenex—I've said that always the right person is there at the right time in my life—and Marlene was certainly that person that day. As the class dispersed for a fifteen-minute break, Harriet saw me and asked how I was doing. I told her "Okay,"—that I wanted to go to the car alone, but I would be staying for the rest of the class. I went to the car and audibly sobbed for the duration of the break. As I saw the others gathering for the second segment of the movie, I came back in, sat down, and never shed another tear. Occasionally in my life, something triggers a few tears, and I spend brief moments crying for the little girl.

If someone asked me what has been the hardest thing I have ever done in my life, I would not hesitate—I would say, "taking my father's hand." When my father was ninety and a half years, he was nearing death in a nursing home in Oklahoma. My husband and children did not want me to go back, but I said, "He's my daddy, and I'm going!" One of the things I knew that I had to do was take him by the hand. Oh, how I dreaded this, but it was something I knew that I had to do for myself for what I thought would be my final healing step in these matters. As I was riding in the airplane on my way back to Oklahoma, my hands would break out in a sweat so dense that I would have to wipe them off to be able to hold something. I was so nervous that I didn't think to pray and ask for any help in this. I just kept telling myself, "Beverly, you've got to have the guts to do this." There was a rental car awaiting me at the airport, and as I drove to Poteau where he was, I was a wreck. I knew that the first thing I must do if he were still living when I got to the nursing home, was to take him by the hand. I knew if I didn't do this immediately, I would chicken out and not do it at all. Sooooo, you know what is said about one's worse fears usually never materializing. Well, that happened to me. I took his hand, and it wasn't bad at all. This frail hand just felt cold, that's all.

Dad lived a few days, and each time I held his hand, it got easier and easier. I spent the night before he died with him, much of the time holding his hand while I talked about his childhood and favorite grandfather and softly sang favorite hymns to him. The next morning Sue came to the nursing home; our cousin, Charlene, was there, and John and his wife, Janice, came a bit later. Within a few minutes of their arrival, as we were standing around talking, I looked up and said, "He's gone." I, who had never been able to touch my dad, was holding his hand when he drew his final breath.

The Remaining Calls of Mother's Day Week

Call number three was made to Louise, a young friend in England, the daughter of a good friend whom we had met in Saudi Arabia. She told me I had called the day before the second anniversary of her mother's death. Louise was so glad I had called and was in awe that I'd called the anniversary week of her mother's death.

Call number four was to the wife of Buddy's boss in Saudi. She had had a stroke and has been cared for at home for fourteen years. It was her caregiver who answered the phone. My call seemed so important to the sitter—she kept saying what a blessing the call was to her, and that she wished I lived nearby. It brought back many memories of the years I had cared for my own mother.

The final two calls that I was impressed to make the week of Mother's Day were to a brother and sister, Tim and Cheryl, my mother's nephew Guy's children. About fifteen years ago, I talked with Tim, but I had never talked with Cheryl since the last time I saw her when I was eleven years old. At that time, we were all living in Oklahoma. Their mother left the children and their father and went to Texas. Cheryl was nine, Phillip Kevin was six, and Timothy was three. Guy brought them to my mother for care.

There were only two times in my school days that I remember ever being reprimanded, and the following is one of those times. We lived several blocks from the school, and it was my responsibility to see that the children got to school okay. Phillip was a very quiet child and kept his emotions inside, so he walked obediently. On most mornings, Cheryl cried all of our walk. She would cry for her mother, wailing, "I want my mother; I don't care if she doesn't want me. I love my mother; I don't care if she doesn't love me." If I didn't hold her hand tightly, she would break loose and run back toward the trailer where we lived. One morning we got on the school grounds with Cheryl, as usual, crying her eyes out for her mother. Somehow she got loose from me and started running. I ran after her, knowing if I could get her to her classroom, she would settle down. A teacher saw me breaking the school rule of not running on school grounds, and he took me to the office and scolded me. I tried to offer an explanation of the situation, but that didn't matter—I had broken the rule.

The three children lived with us for several months, and it was the only time that I got to feel as though I had brothers and sisters. Then Dad had one of his spells, and other arrangements had to be made. The children went to a nearby town to live a few weeks with a grandmother and then later to live with their mother's sister. I named my son Timothy Kevin after Phillip and Tim.

Though I was able to contact Tim by phone once, I did not have Cheryl's correct married name and had never talked to her. The last address I had for Tim was in Hobbs, New Mexico. I was able to contact him. My son and family were living nearby at the time, and on a visit to them, we met Tim and his wife. What a wonderful reunion we had! Everybody was very frank about their lives—the good and the bad. He had no idea he had a namesake. As my son Tim and grandson Eram were there, my cousin Tim commented that if Eram had been named Tim, we'd have three Tim's in the room. I explained that Eram was named after my grandfather—Tim's great-grandfather. It seemed unreal, but he had no knowledge of his grandfather's nor his great-grandfather's name. It was the first time it became clear to me how little the role Guy had played in his life. The fact is that Tim, in his childhood or adulthood, seldom saw or heard from his dad. Tim and his wife were planning to go to Oklahoma to visit Phillip the week Phillip committed suicide. They went to his funeral instead. Tim has had his problems, not only emotional but physical (cancer years ago that had a poor prognosis, among other things). It is chilling to think of growing up rejected by both a mother and a father! That Tim is doing well now is a testament to pure guts and determination, and I admire him for sure.

Tim told me that Cheryl is indeed alive and living in Midland, Texas. We spoke by phone. Though I was close enough to visit her, she had just finished surgery for ovarian cancer and was undergoing chemotherapy. We have talked many times by phone since and do plan to meet.

This completes the calls I felt impressed to make the week of Mother's Day. How glad I am for each one!

My Childhood

Thoughts – Email from Dr. Slate

I received this email from Dr. Slate December 6, 2014:

Hi Beverly,

It is always a pleasure hearing from you.

I can certainly relate to what you are experiencing at this time. In my writing, I often find it is necessary to "strategically withdraw," probably due to stress and perhaps mental fatigue or so-called "writer's block." You will work through this, and after that, your writing will be even better than before.

I wish you a most enjoyable holiday season!

Enjoy!

Joe

My answer:

Hi Joe,

Thanks so much for this email. These words of encouragement have really helped me. I seemed to be slipping into a depression—as we know, it's usually mania that's my problem—not depression. I keep thinking I will be getting to some writing that will be fun and uplifting. I know I will, but seems like every topic I think about has so much sadness in it. I want to write so badly, but my memories really get to the surface, and I'll remember every detail, where I was sitting when a certain thing was said, what direction I was facing and on and on, and this happening fifty or sixty plus years ago does not change a thing.

Surely, most people out there do not think like this. Today, I stayed in my housecoat until nearly four o'clock and in bed a great deal of the time. I decided I better get hold of myself, so I got up, dressed and went by myself to the Cracker Barrel and ate—I had even forgotten to eat lunch. I feel much better.

Christmas is coming and there has been so much sadness in my life about this. There has been happiness, too, but working through the sadness is necessary. It is also part of my story. I wasn't even going to put up Christmas decorations but decided to invite some people for a meal, so I would make myself get out some decorations. I'm going to put on some nice Christmas music and make out my Christmas card list.

Thanks again.

Beverly

Christmastime

With a novel, the author can be creative and achieve poetic justice by weaving pathos with enough uplifting material to continually engage the reader. A person writing an autobiography has no such liberty, in my opinion, unless he keeps the reader at arm's length and carefully sifts through the material of his life. While there will always be some sifting going on, there is no way I'm trying to write in such manner. I would like to say that I do not feel I am writing from the heart, but from the gut. A lot of what I've written so far has been gut-wrenching for me. Let me clarify further. My primary objective is to write that there may be something for members of my extended family—even those yet unborn—to glean and help them in times of deep introspection to cope with life and facilitate growth. A secondary purpose is already unfolding. It is a remarkable cleansing experience for me, and I am continually amazed at the insight I am getting into difficult periods in my life. If there are others out there who may read my words and be helped in their lives, no tear I shed while writing will be in vain.

For almost fifty-five years now, Christmas time has not held the joy it should have for me. When I was a little girl, my family always made Christmas a nice celebration. Christmas was always a favorite time for my dad. As I've mentioned previously, we lived in various parts of the United States where Dad worked on pipeline construction. If we were living in a cold climate and the job was going to be shut down for the winter, he always wanted to make sure he got to finish in time to be home for Christmas. Thus, many of my childhood Christmases were spent at my paternal granny and grandpa's farm in southeastern Oklahoma. On Christmas Eve (and not one day before), Grandpa and I would go into the woods to cut a Christmas tree. I loved my grandpa dearly, so this is a special memory. I don't remember Granny having any

Christmas ornaments that she used from year to year, but perhaps she did. She would pop a lot of corn, and we would take needle and thread and make long strings of popped corn to wind around the tree. We took catalogs and cut the pages into strips. Granny would make paste from flour and water, and we would make paper chains to put on the tree. Granny was a seamstress and sewed for the public, consequently, she had a lot of empty wooden thread spools which we also used for decorations. Granny would make divinity and peanut brittle during the day, and Christmas Eve night we would eat that delicious homemade candy and some of the popcorn while we decorated the tree. Aunt Eunice and Uncle Charles and their daughter Charlene lived just down the road, so they were always there, too. On New Year's Day, after our meal of black-eyed peas, hog jowl, and cherry pie, we would take down the tree.

My great-aunt Francis, Grandpa's older sister, lived at Wilburton, about seventeen miles from Granny and Grandpa. She was a widow and her two sons lived out on the West Coast, so she spent her holidays with us. We didn't have telephones then, so a week or so before any holiday, she would write a letter asking the time and day that someone would be up to get her. Her job was to make the fruit salad and the homemade yeast rolls. Though my mother could do a great job with those items, too, Aunt Francis felt her presence was absolutely essential to make the fruit salad and bread, and she wanted to get there in plenty of time for this.

If it were not possible, such as a job in a more southern clime, to get to Oklahoma for Christmas, Mother always put up a Christmas tree in our little trailer. The year I was five, at Christmas time we were living in Dumas, Texas, a small town in the panhandle. The dearest memory I have of my father was from that Christmas. I must have been a very unusual child, for I never told a single person what I wanted for Christmas, and I guess nobody asked. On Christmas Eve, I wrote a letter to Santa and put out cookies and milk for him to eat and drink. In the letter, I asked for one item—a toy accordion. Mother had bought me a doll and other gifts; but, as she told me years later, my dad ate the cookies, drank the milk, and put on his clothes to go out to try to find me a toy accordion. Now, as I have said, Dumas was a small town, and stores didn't stay open late like they do now. It seems almost like the song, "Scarlet Ribbons," but Dad saw a light on in a drug store. The door was open. He went inside, and there was a toy accordion. On Christmas morn, there was my toy accordion just as I had faith that it would be.

Tears are streaming down my face as I write this. Every Christmas since my first child was born fifty years ago, with this memory is associated such pain. You see, my husband Buddy would not let us celebrate Christmas, so I never got to pass down the joy that I had at Christmas time. It seems that all that pain is wrapped up in that toy accordion. We could not have a Christmas tree. I could not buy Christmas gifts for the children, and I had to caution them not to say anything at school that could hurt other children. At the time we married Buddy was a Free Will Baptist preacher. Though it is a very fundamental church, the church did believe in observing Christmas. Buddy's mother, however, did not attend any church but listened faithfully to a radio preacher, Herbert W. Armstrong. He preached that celebrating Christmas, Easter, and individual birthdays was all pagan and very sinful. Buddy, of course, was greatly influenced by his mother's beliefs and became very confused. When we moved to Athens, Alabama, in 1970 and Buddy enrolled in Athens University, then a Methodist school, he got exposed to a wider and more moderate religious system. He then relaxed his ban and allowed us to celebrate Christmas. By that time, however, Tim was ten and Linda seven, so it was too late for early formation of precious Christmas memories. To this day, neither of them is very enthused about Christmas. When I was visiting Tim and family this Thanksgiving, his wife mentioned this, and I told her this story.

Buddy and I did not have a conventional courtship. He attended and often preached at the church my father attended in Red Oak, Oklahoma. My father liked him and told me that he could be my boyfriend, but I could have no other. So, Buddy was often at our house. He would come by after work and eat supper with us. I was so eager to be wanted and accepted by him that when Christmas time rolled around, I asked my mother to not put up a Christmas tree and have no decorations. In fact, I begged her—saying he might be offended and quit coming. My mother reluctantly complied with my entreaties. In my later years I feel very guilty about this and want to say, "Mother, I'm so very, very sorry that I asked this of you." But then, I also want to add, "Mother, I wish so much that you had not complied with my pleadings."

Earlier, I mentioned Aunt Francis. Aunt Francis always spent many hours on her homemade gifts making sure every person had something. She was not talented like my grandmother and could not sew very well. Gifts from her represented her love for each of us and needed to be accepted as such. She made me two Santas, each very different. As I write, I can see them both so clearly. They were made from red socks. One could even say one was a Santa Claus and stuffed so full and roly-poly, with white looped yarn around the fat waist. The other was more like a Father Christmas with black leather boots and belt. One day, when my children were small, I was cleaning out a closet and decided that, since I could not display them, I might as well give them away. Never a Christmas passes when I decorate for Christmas that I don't see those two Santas and long to have them.

I have often told the above to people, especially the painful part about the toy accordion being the dearest memory I have of my father, adding with deep hurt, and yes, even bitterness, that Buddy took that from me. In the wee hours this morning, I awoke and had a breakthrough that I've never had before. It was that, and the first time it has ever occurred to me in this way, "No, Buddy did not 'take' this from me. I allowed it to happen." Okay, so I've said it exactly the way psychologists and psychiatrists say one should say it—"I allowed it to happen." So, where does one go from here? Will writing all of this down, and yes, having the breakthrough in my choice of words change things? I don't know. Will this be a beginning of an ease of my pain? I don't know. It remains to be seen. This I know. As I said when I was writing the previous page, tears are streaming down my face. I was fourteen years old when I made my requests to Mother. As anybody who reads this can see, I was a very wounded soul. Is accepting my part in all of this going to be the beginning of healing? As is often repeated, "Time will tell." Right now, I can tell no difference.

Places

One of the things that has bothered me a great deal about my writing so far concerns the fact that every time I start to write, it usually seems so sad. As a cousin said when I first started writing, "Beverly, don't just write about the sad things; write about the happy things, because nobody will want or can stand to only read all that sad stuff." I have always wanted the book of my life to be balanced. So far, my writing hasn't been very balanced. As I think about my childhood memories, I dig and dig for something happy. I have read that even if your childhood memories are very sad, you should keep on digging, and you will find that gold nugget. The Christmas present my father got for me when I was five is my gold nugget, but, of course, from adulthood, I have let that memory be marred by sadness, too.

Before I start a chapter about other childhood memories, I want to share something which I'm putting in an appendix at the end of the book that illustrates a big part of my life. In 1974, when Mother was sixty-six years old, I asked her to tell me all the places where we had lived. Recently, a friend asked me if my mother was extremely intelligent. I answered, "I don't know. Honestly, I have never thought about it." I still don't know the answer to that question, but I do know this—WOW, did she ever have a memory! I can remember so well the afternoon I asked Mother to tell me all the places where we had lived. Beginning with entry #1 until entry #109, Mother started slowly and deliberately telling me where we lived and how long we lived there. I know that some of the years will add up to a bit less or more than a strict twelve months, but that is, of course, because she didn't have exact dates in her mind. She sat in a chair and you could see her mind working. We spent a good portion of an afternoon, as I sat on the couch and recorded it just as this is written. The friend looking at these pages blurted out,

"Nobody could remember like this!" Well, I couldn't, but Mother did!

Having this paper will be a bit of help to me to more precisely attach an age to a memory, but I realize, of course, that this is not of great importance. It is certainly nice to have, though. The first thing most people think when seeing this or hearing of the many moves I have made is how unstable my life has been. Yes, psychologists also want to make something of it. But I can tell you for sure and in no uncertain terms, that all this moving was the most stable thing in my childhood! The instability occurred when Dad didn't come in from work on a weekend, and we cleaned the car out and found women's underwear. It occurred, it sometimes seems like, on an almost daily basis when Mother punctuated a sentence with, "If we are still here . . . tomorrow or next week or whenever . . . maybe such and such will occur . . . " I am not talking about the physical presence of that location, but the meaning that—if we are still with Dad, if he hasn't taken off with someone, if he hasn't thrown us out to go back to Granny and Grandpa, etc.

So, all this constant moving was a VERY HAPPY memory. I loved it. I loved going to new places and seeing new things. Changing schools was no problem. I didn't dread this one bit. It didn't matter where or how many times in a year we moved, I knew I'd be making A's, so there would be no apprehension there. When I'd be sitting at my desk and see somebody's mother that I knew walking down the hall, I'd know she was coming to check her child out of school for the next move. I'd be so excited and hope my mother would be coming soon to check me out. You see, Dad was the utility welder on the pipeline, which meant he welded the broken parts of the equipment that broke down. There were usually two utility welders, and one had to be at the new location and one at the old. So, we were either the first to get to move or the last. Far too often to suit me, Dad would be the last to leave.

No doubt all this constant moving has made me a very adaptable person. It has also made me eager to try new things—there's not much fear in me for the new. I love to travel, with somebody, by myself, or just whatever it takes. "Go" is in the blood. Alone, I have made many trips to Europe, as well as stopped in and out of various countries when traveling back and forth from the Middle East. A good friend, who lives in Oklahoma, summed me up like this. She wanted to go to Dallas, Texas, for the weekend, and her husband was concerned that they didn't have hotel reservations. She said, "If Beverly can get on a plane and fly to Europe without a hotel reservation, SURELY we can go to Dallas!"

Memories from the Early Years

At long last, I am sitting down to write about my earliest memories. Whether some of them were at the age of two or three really does not matter and I know this. Because of having my mother's list of places and dates of where we lived, however, there are some that I can accurately date, and I will do so when I can. My earliest memories, both the ones I can date and the ones I can't, are either very sad or very frightening. I cannot help this. I have often tried to rake the bottom of the barrel, but I still come up with sadness. So be it.

When I was three years and three months old, we were living near Kansas City, Missouri, and I can date a memory with accuracy. We lived in an 18-foot trailer that was parked on top of a high hill. The wind was blowing that night, September 8, 1949, and there came a knock at the door. It was a policeman, and he had a telegram for my mother. Her father had passed away that day back in Oklahoma. When he handed her the paper, Mother started sobbing. I remember this so clearly. The next thing I remember is Mother and I boarding a bus to go back to the funeral. We were at the door of the bus and had to climb those tall metal steps. I did not want anyone holding my hand as we went up the steps. I wanted to do it by myself. Mother let me. I can see that little girl with the blonde Shirley Temple curls so distinctly taking those giant steps. I did make it to the top all by myself. That is the last thing I remember about this. I do not remember the bus ride, the funeral, any of the people nor anything else about this occasion. I have no memories at all of this grandfather.

There is much that I can remember about the next memory that I can accurately date. We were getting ready to leave Missouri, after having lived there about four months. I had two dolls which I had named Sally Jane and Cynthia Sue. They were my treasures. Mother and

Granny and Aunt Eunice had made clothes for them. I played with them every day. I have a photo taken on my second birthday, and Sally Jane is sitting on the shelf behind me. I must have gotten Cynthia Sue later because she is not in the picture. Dad was preparing the trailer readying it for moving, unhooking the water, electricity, hooking the trailer to the truck, etc. Several of the kids from the trailer park had come to stand around and watch. Dad gruffly said, "These kids don't have any toys. Go into the house and get your dolls and give them to them." I guess kids back then didn't defy their parents very often. I know that I didn't, that's for sure. A broken-hearted little girl went in and got her two most prized possessions and gave them to the kids. I so vividly remember thinking, "Daddy hasn't thought about the dolls' clothes. I'm not going to remind him, or he will make me give them, too." Guess I didn't follow the Biblical admonition "when asked to give a coat give the cloak, also." I can remember the guilt that I felt in withholding this information from my dad. Tears are streaming down my face as I write about this. I continually think I'm through writing all the hard stuff—that I will not need to shed any more tears in my writing, but, alas, thus it doesn't seem to be so. Well, within the hour, as we continued to get ready to leave, I was playing by the ditch, and there were Sally Jane and Cynthia Sue with their arms and legs and head torn off just thrown in the ditch. I remember thinking, "No wonder these kids don't have any toys; they don't take care of them." But I also remember the pain I felt at having to see my precious dolls lying torn apart and having to leave them in the ditch. In the things from my childhood that I have saved, I have those doll clothes wrapped up in a little pillowcase, stored in a box under the bed upstairs. Occasionally, maybe every five or six years or so, I will go through and handle the little clothes and remember Sally Jane and Cynthia Sue and how dearly I loved them.

When Christmas came around that year, and we went back to Oklahoma, guess I was still whining about the dolls. Aunt Eunice got so mad about Dad making me give up my dolls. Granny bought me a new doll the same size as those I had to give away, and Aunt Eunice crocheted a lovely dress, coat, cap, and underclothes for my new Christmas doll. I still have this doll dressed in those clothes displayed on a piece of furniture in my upstairs office. My family were not huggers and didn't go around telling you they loved you, but when I look at that doll, I know she represents the love that my grandmother and Aunt Eunice had for me. Though I remember the names Sally Jane and Cynthia Sue so well, I have no idea what this doll's name is. I cannot even remember ever knowing the name of the doll.

Though we lived in an 18-foot trailer with no bathroom, and Mother bought most of our clothes at the Salvation Army and rummage sales, Dad decided he wanted to buy an airplane and learn to fly (yes, he bought the airplane first and then learned to fly it). To the outside world, I guess this gave the appearance that we were rich. After all, when we would go back to Red Oak, there was no one around who owned an airplane or maybe even thought about owning one, and Dad was quite the hero. We were living in Wyoming, and I was two when Dad got his plane. My early memories of this plane are horrible. Mother, Dad, and I would drive out to the airport, whichever one happened to be closest to where we lived, and Dad would take us for a ride. Instead of letting us get in the plane and then start the engine, he would have Mother get in the plane, then start the engine and make me walk under the propeller. Now, when I think back on this and look at planes, I think, "Surely, he didn't make me walk under the propeller," though I guess it was far enough off the ground that it wouldn't have killed a toddler. Nevertheless, the way I remember it, I had to walk UNDER the propeller after he had started the engine. Even if, instead, I was just walking under the wing and beside the propeller, the noise of the engine and this propeller turning was extremely frightening! I would start crying until it turned into screaming. Mother would ask Dad not to make me do this—to let us get in the plane before he started the engine, but he refused. He would say (maybe it's okay to use the word scream), "I'm teaching her to be strong—to be brave." It goes without saying that one didn't cross Dad. This happened over and over again. I was scared to death of that plane, and it took many years before I found any pleasure in riding in it. By that time, Dad had decided to sell it, so my memories of Dad and the plane were not good, to put it mildly. I do feel I am a strong person—but not very brave. Possibly having to endure such frightening experiences played a part in this. I really don't know.

Another of my earliest memories when I was two, also involved the plane in an indirect way. We had gone to the airport to take Dad to fly somewhere—quite possibly to our next place to move. We had a 1946 Ford truck. This was not a pickup. It was a full-blown truck with welding machine, etc. on it (this was Dad's work truck—we did not have a separate car). Well, we let Dad off to fly in the airplane, and Mother and I were to go back to wherever we lived in the trailer. We could not get the passenger side window rolled up. It was in the middle of a bitterly cold Wyoming winter. Since Mother could not get the window rolled up, all we could do was drive on. As I write, I can see that little girl huddled as close to Mother as I could get, while that bitter, icy cold wind, mixed with rain and snow, blew in. Not only was I very cold, I was also very scared! What a memory—this ride seemed to take forever, and we did have to go many miles!

Writing about my dolls has been very draining for me. Even though I have told this story many times in my life, I don't believe I have ever cried about it. Perhaps this is what I needed to do—just go into this memory—not keep it at arms' length in my telling of it—but just experience it and let myself cry about it. Perhaps I'm beginning to grasp why writing my life story will be so cathartic.

I am very fatigued. I will save other early memories for writing another time—hopefully, tomorrow.

Email from Dr. Slate

I received this email from Dr. Slate on Tuesday, January 27, 2015.

Hi Beverly,

I'm amazed at your memory for details! I am greatly impressed with your recall of those early experiences. Our early experiences, according to psychologists, are critical because of their capacity to shape our lifestyle. Rather than excess baggage, they can become positive motivators that propel us always forward.

I try always to keep in mind that, while the past is ours, we live in the "now". Within that context, the past becomes a growth resource that can both enrich and empower our lives.

Thank you for sharing these early experiences!

Best.

Joe

More Memories from the Early Years

When I was four years old, we lived in several towns in North Carolina, about one month in each place, and in South Carolina and Virginia. While we were in North Carolina, I can remember playing with my brother creating roads, a river, a lake, etc. for our toy cars and trucks. This is where I first learned catfish have horns. We were very detailed in our building project, even having some live little catfish. You know what happened. I picked one up, and it stuck its horn in my hand. OOOOhhhh, the pain! No wonder I wouldn't forget that! After this summer, I don't ever remember John coming for the whole summer. He would have been a teenager and probably got jobs. I can barely remember Sue being with us. She came that summer we were in the Carolinas. She got really mad at Dad and said she was leaving and would never be back. She made good on that promise. We visited Sue and John in California for a week or so every few years, but it wasn't until adulthood that we developed a true familial relationship.

It was in North Carolina the year I was four that we got a bigger trailer—a 27', including the hitch (minus the hitch left it at a bit less than 24'). It still didn't have a bathroom but was so much bigger and nicer than our 18' (minus the hitch made that one a few inches less than 15'). I well remember that day! This one had three separate rooms— tiny though they were. We often had people living with us, as Dad was always willing to help somebody from back home get a job on the pipeline, and they usually couldn't get a place to stay. Because of usually having someone extra, I couldn't sleep on the couch. If the weather was warm enough, I slept on quilts on the floor, but in the winter, Mother put up three green wooden folding chairs at night and placed quilts on them. Long before morning got there, the chairs were sliding apart—most uncomfortable! I would beg to just sleep on the floor. It was so much more comfortable, but Mother was afraid I would get cold.

Late in my fourth year, my mother's mother came to visit. We were in Tennessee at that time, and it is the only time she ever visited us. Mother always called her Mamma, and I did, too. She was a large woman. I remember that we went to Rock City in Chattanooga. There are three things that stand out about that trip. One is Mamma trying to get through the Fat Man's Squeeze. The second is fond memories of the caverns with the nursery rhyme characters. The third, unfortunately, is another scary memory. It is Dad MAKING me walk out on the swinging bridge with him shaking it. He made me stand in the middle while he took my picture. I begged him not to make me do this, but you know the answer by now—it was to make me brave. I will tell you that the ravine I was standing over seemed humongous! I was scared of heights, and it seemed such a long, long way down! All of my life I carried this memory of being so scared of having to stand over this deep canyon. When, as an adult, we moved to Alabama, and I took my own children to Rock City, I couldn't believe how this swinging bridge was almost nothing. It wasn't very far off the ground at all!

Another memory at age four was visiting a friend of Dad's, Preacher Kemp. We were living in Wharton, Texas. They lived in a real house near Houston. It was probably only a four-room house, but it seemed so big to me. Outside of Granny's and Aunt Eunice's, it is the only house up to that time in which I can remember being. We got to spend the night, and I slept in a real bed. When we visited Granny and Grandpa's, we were usually in our trailer, so I didn't sleep in a real bed. For supper that night, Mrs. Kemp cooked noodles and put a can of cream of chicken soup in them. Mother had never fixed anything like that, and I was enamored with that dish. Mother started fixing this dish, and, for me, it became a comfort food with wonderful memories attached.

Dad took Bro. Kemp on his first airplane ride and it sparked within him a strong desire to fly. Later, he started taking lessons. On the day that he would be in complete control of his first landing, but with the instructor still by his side, Bro. Kemp evidently froze at the last moment and crashed the plane into the ground, killing both his instructor and himself. The day Dad got the word, he said he would never fly his plane again. He immediately put the plane up for sale. We were living in New Mexico at the time. I was now seven years old, had gotten over my fear of flying, and was just beginning to enjoy riding in the airplane.

When Dad was in his late seventies, one day I was talking to him and asking him questions about his life. I asked him if there was anything in his life that he would do differently—anything he regretted. He said, "Yes. There is one thing. I regret ever buying an airplane. There is no telling how many people I caused to go to hell over owning that airplane."

At age four, I received one of the two dogs I had as pets. These memories are more of the sad ones. We got a little black cocker spaniel puppy that I named Peggy. Mother took her for shots, spaying, etc.; but, unfortunately, she did not have distemper shots. We were at Granny's, and she showed the symptoms of distemper. Dad said, "I've got to kill that dog." He got a gun and went outside. I was standing in the middle of the living room in Granny's house waiting for it to happen. He pulled the trigger, the puppy gave one loud yelp, and then there was silence. I had only had her for a few weeks.

Mother noted in my baby book that I was given the second puppy on September 21, 1951, in Monroe, Louisiana. I was five by then. She was another cocker spaniel—a tan one that I named Ginger. Mother made sure that Ginger had distemper shots along with her other shots. We got her just before we left to go to Tulsa, Oklahoma, for a short job, so about all she'd known was to ride in a car. We stopped by Granny's. Mother, Dad, and I were getting in the car to go up to see Mother's mother in Wilburton. Ginger wanted to go, too. I begged to take her, but Dad said, "No." As he backed out, Ginger was following the car, and he ran over her and crushed her little body. We got out of the car, and I watched as her little body writhed and died. Surely we buried her, but I don't remember taking time for that. We got back in the car, and I was sitting in the back seat crying. I asked Mother if dogs went to heaven. Mother started to say something in a round-about way in the affirmative, but Dad screamed, "Don't be telling her a bunch of lies!" He turned around and told me that "No, dogs don't go to heaven," and to "shut up crying, or I will slap your face."

I, unfortunately, did not have much better luck with cats. It was very hard to be moving around so much and living in trailer parks and have any kind of pet. I got a cat that got poisoned, and I can remember the thud against the metal trailer as the cat was trying to get home after eating the poison. It died within minutes. I had an orange cat that I named Taffy, who would suck a doll bottle, but something happened to her, too. Even now, I don't feel a closeness to pets, and I know these experiences are the reason why.

The Christmas I was four, we went back to Oklahoma for the holidays. At the country church near Granny and Grandpa's, the members sponsored what was called a "Christmas Tree." The Christmas Tree was always held at night and was a community event— not restricted to church members. Candy and fruit were put in brown paper sacks and handed out; and as everyone looked forward to getting their sack, it was a well-attended event. Mother was in a little play/skit at this one. As the church was full, I was told I would have to sit on Daddy's lap. As I've stated previously, I never wanted to be near my dad, to touch or be touched by him. Well, when Mother got up from the seat to go to the front for the performance, I started to cry and beg not to be left with Dad. Things went from bad to worse. I wasn't just scared—I became terrified at the prospect of having to sit on his lap. My dad took me outside down by the well (an old-fashioned kind with hand-pump to raise the water) to give me some hickory tea. He started whipping me, and did he ever mean business! Another man was outside taking a smoke break and witnessed the whole thing. He very approvingly commented that Frank believed in following the Biblical admonition to "not spare the rod and spoil the child." Even when I was an adult, this person would tell, in my presence, about this event and voice his admiration that my dad "bent the twig before it grew into the tree."

For Christmas that year, Mother bought me a Horseman baby doll. It was about the size of a real newborn. She handmade a layette for it: blanket, gowns, etc. The material was yellow flannel, and she crocheted around all the edges with orange yarn. We had a sliding pocket door between the little kitchen and bedroom in our trailer. I remember Mother would often have the door closed when I came in. She was back in the bedroom making the doll layette and wanted it to be a surprise for me. She bought a doll bed from a man who made nice ones out of oak. There are so many things from the year four onward that I remember that I will stop with these memories. It could all get boring very, very quickly.

The Middle Years

When I was seven, we lived in Midland, Texas, for a couple months. From Midland, we moved to Eunice, New Mexico, and it was from there that we went to Carlsbad Caverns. WOW! Do I ever have memories of that visit! It made such an impression on me that I carried pictures of those caverns in my mind from that day onward. I was eager for my children to be able to experience that wonder, but it was not until October 2009 that I had the opportunity to revisit Carlsbad. We had traded motorhomes, and we spent the maiden voyage in this one in Colorado and New Mexico, arriving back in Oklahoma in time for my uncle Virgil's 100th birthday party. I wanted to see the caverns thoroughly, so I booked an additional tour rather than just take the general tour that comes with the entrance fee. We did the extra tour first. The longer we were on the tour the more disappointed I became. I kept telling Buddy and Linda that, though it was beautiful, it was not like I remembered it. I was beginning to wonder if, as a child of seven, I had been so impressed that I had some exaggerated pictures in my mind. After a rest, we started on the second tour—the general one that everybody does. I hadn't gone far when THERE IT WAS—just like the pictures in my mind! The farther we went, the more excited I became. So, I had remembered it accurately after all!

It is with fondness that I recall the two months (still second grade) that we lived near La Platte, Nebraska. We lived in a trailer park up on a bare windswept hill, in a setting just like those that South Dakota artist Harvey Dunn captures in his prairie paintings. It was there that I had the wonderful privilege of attending a two-room country school, and I never miss an opportunity to tell people how good I think they are. The school was within walking distance of the trailer park, so each morning I carried my lunch pail and trudged up the hill. The teachers knew we pipeline kids wouldn't be there long, so they didn't want to order extra books. When they didn't have second-grade books for some of the subjects, they just gave me third-grade books instead. I got to sit with the third-grade kids for the recitations; and with older children helping younger children as they do in that setting, I did not have one bit of trouble keeping up. When we recently visited a museum park in Fredericksburg, Texas, and went in a one-room schoolhouse, my little grandson Eram said, "Grandma, I'd like to go to a school like this. Did you ever go to a school like this?" It was neat to be able to share that wonderful memory.

These good times, unfortunately, didn't last long, as Dad kicked Mother and me out again while he ran off with somebody else. Mother's mother, Mamma, had been diagnosed with cancer, so this time we went to stay with her in Wilburton, about sixteen miles from Granny and Grandpa. Mother spent this time caring for her mother. Mamma was in bed most of the time, but she usually came to the table for meals. That's about all I remember about her. The first-grade teacher at Red Oak lived in Wilburton, so arrangements were made for me to ride back and forth with her to school in Red Oak, where I at least knew some of the kids.

School finished in about two months or so, and Dad's latest was over, so he came back and took Mother and me to Fergus Falls, Minnesota, where he was then working. It was there I met another of my life-long friends, Esther. Her father joined the pipeline, and she and her mother and brother started moving along with us. Esther was a smart girl who did not have any trouble adjusting to going to several schools a year. In moving so often, many people immediately wonder about friendships and think I must not have had the privilege of cultivating many. This is definitely not true. I had the opportunity of meeting people of many diverse backgrounds, religious affiliations, etc.—far more so than I ever would have by living in one or two places during my childhood.

It was in Fergus Falls that I had my eighth birthday. Remember how much I wanted the little toy accordion for my fifth Christmas? I would have preferred to study piano, but since that was impossible, the accordion was the next best thing. At least it had a keyboard. It was I who initiated these things, and my mother and dad went along with my requests. They gave me eight accordion lessons for my eighth birthday. I still have the little pair of screw-on accordion earrings that I received from the music studio for successfully completing my coursework. When we would move somewhere, Mother would get out and see if there was anybody in whatever little town it was that could/would give accordion lessons. From looking at Mother's list of places, looks like about two months or so was all we lived in Fergus Falls,—but enough time for me to finish the eight lessons.

While we were in Fergus Falls, we received joyous news from California that Sue had had a baby boy, Michael. I remember the day so well! I was now an aunt!

From Minnesota, we moved to several towns in Kansas. Wherever we moved, Dad always asked around if there were any sights for us to see nearby. On Sundays, we always went to church, but in the afternoon we would drive to see whatever, if anything, was available— be it a natural wonder, historic house, museum, etc. As I have previously stated in another letter, I got my history and geography lessons first hand. By the time I was eight, I was seeking out the places on my own. Shortly after we moved to a new place, I would have Mother take me to the local Chamber of Commerce, where I could get the sight-seeing literature. I was always interested in famous people's homes. Mother and Dad didn't much care for this but would take me and wait in the car while I went through and learned more about the author, inventor, or another historical figure who was born or grew up there. A few years ago, when a tornado hit Greensburg, Kansas, I immediately thought about the day I went to the Chamber of Commerce and got literature on the largest hand-dug well in the U.S, which was in Greensburg.

And yes, the reporters even mentioned this hand-dug well in the news broadcast about the tornado.

The year I turned eight became so traumatic. I remember it as one of my worst years ever. After work ended in Kansas, we went back to Red Oak and were there for five or six months. Soon after arriving, I started taking accordion lessons from a woman in Wilburton. There was a student recital, and for this recital, Dad bought me a beautiful pink lace dress with tiers of the lace all down the skirt. He paid ten dollars for it—an enormous sum for a child's dress back in the fifties. So distinctly I can see myself in this beautiful dress playing the accordion at that recital. Unfortunately, Dad became enamored with the accordion teacher. Mother and I lived in our trailer out by Granny and Grandpa's house, and this became another year that Mother and Dad were getting a divorce. Granny would get me up early in the morning to go to Wilburton to see Dad's car at this woman's house, so, that if need be, I would be able to testify to this fact in court. Dad was especially bad with the guns and threats this year. Granny went to the school to alert the authorities that Dad was on one of his tears and to ask them not to let me go with him if he came to school and wanted to check me out. She expressed her fear that he might become so unwound and kill me. Granny and Aunt Eunice supported Mother wholeheartedly and begged and begged her to stick with getting a divorce. Mother just couldn't stick with it. She always took Dad back when he decided to come back. This really upset Granny and Aunt Eunice.

The first occasion during my school years that I was reprimanded in class occurred during this time when I was in the third grade in Red Oak. It was a simple thing really, but I was so fragile that year. Barbara was a neighbor girl who lived just down the road from Granny, and, after school the next day, I was going to ride the school bus on down to her house. I wrote her a note in class and passed it to her. The teacher saw this and got the note and read it aloud to the class. I was only asking Barbara if she wanted me to bring my doll. That's all. But, oh, how mortified I was!

It was just after I turned nine, while we were living in Fruita, Colorado, that we got our third trailer. Dad had made arrangements to buy a new 37' Spartan, the best brand trailer ever made—conceived by Howard Hughes to use up the post-war aluminum left from building aircraft in the war. It had two bedrooms (I would finally have my own bed to sleep in), and a bathroom with a tub! Mother and I were so excited when the day arrived to go get it. What a disappointing ending that day held! Dad was going to finance it, but after looking over the paperwork and calculating the interest he would have to pay, he backed out on the deal. Mother and I reluctantly went back to our smaller trailer. Soon, though, Dad did buy another trailer, but it was a not very well cared for used 35'. It did have two bedrooms and a tiny bathroom with a tin shower—not a nice tub like the Spartan. Oh well, it was a lot better than what we had and did serve us well enough until Dad had a small house built in Red Oak during my high school years.

From Fruita, we moved to Moab, Utah. This was during the boom years of the uranium mining there. There were simply not enough school facilities for all the people moving in, so school was held in two shifts. One had to get up and be at school by 7 a.m. for the first shift, which lasted until about 1 p.m. or so. Then a few weeks later one got to attend during the second shift, which meant not getting home until after dark. Somehow, I don't think my education suffered one bit for these inconveniences.

One of the neat things about Moab was riding around the countryside and seeing the arches in what is now Arches National Park. I haven't been back since the area achieved national park status, but I do remember the beauty. Next month, our son is being transferred nearby, so, when I visit his family, I hope to go see it again.

It was at Moab that something happened that made a lasting impression on me. One day Mother and I were in a grocery store, and for some reason, the store manager's name was mentioned. Mother said, "I wonder if that's Julian Joseph." She asked for him by name; and I can remember him telling her that when he was told somebody wanted to see Julian, he said, "It must be somebody from back home. Nobody ever calls me Julian." You see, as Mother explained it, Julian was a Jew who had married a Gentile. His family had completely disowned him. He seemed overjoyed to see Mother—a link to his past in Oklahoma. At that age of nine, I remember feeling so very sad about that whole situation.

After a couple months in Kansas, it was while we were in Lamesa, Texas, while I was yet nine, that my maternal grandmother died. I can see Mother now as she came to my room at school and stood by the door crying, with the teacher comforting her. She was checking me out, so we could head back to Oklahoma for the funeral.

The end of the fourth grade saw us in Aztec, New Mexico. My pipeline girlfriends and I still talk about our school there. It was a rural area, but there was a trailer park within walking distance of the school. It was during the period of U.S. history when the Indian children were taken from the reservations and forced to go to boarding schools during the school year. As you can imagine, there was, for good reason, a lot of resentment. Some of the boys, especially, were really mean. They would go out at recess and get spikes from tractor parts nearby and come in and punch holes in the desks. Our cute little blonde teacher was scared to death of them. Her fear really showed. She would go down and get the principal to come give a talk, but his order didn't last much longer than it took for him to close the door and start back to his office. We had to grab our lunch and carry it with us to the front if we even wanted to ask the teacher a question; otherwise, it wouldn't be there when we got back to our seat. Our poor, scared teacher got married, and with that, she left. I bet she was one happy bride!

Whatever one learns in the fifth grade, I always laugh and say, "I never learned it." I only went for about one month in the fifth grade.

We were in Edmond, Oklahoma, and were getting ready to move to Nebraska. How well I remember this day, too, and for good reason. Mother had come to check me out of school for my next move. I was present while the teacher had a talk with Mother. The teacher told Mother that she thought I should skip the fifth grade and move on to the sixth. She went on to say that she did not believe in holding a child back. The teacher said that she couldn't do it herself, but she advised Mother to turn the five into a six on the paperwork she would be giving her. I remember her words to Mother so well. She said, "As often as you folks move around, her records will never catch up with her." How true those words were. By the time my school records were requested and arrived at a new school, we had always moved on to the next place.

On my first day of school in Fremont, Nebraska, now a sixth grader, I was just a bit nervous. I can see myself in the classroom. I was seated on the far right aisle, about mid-way back. I had made it fine until our math lesson. These kids were using double digits for the divisor, and I had only used a single digit divisor. My thoughts were, "Maybe the teacher back in Oklahoma did not know what she was talking about. Maybe I don't belong in the sixth grade, after all." Well, I went home that evening and figured out how to divide by a two digit number. It wasn't hard at all. So, the next day I went back to school confident that I would do just fine in the sixth grade.

I will mention one other memory from the sixth grade. We spent a couple months or so in Gallup, New Mexico. This was another experience with Indian (in this case, Navajo) children being forced by the U.S. government to leave the reservation and be schooled in town. Things were always especially bad after the kids had been allowed to go home for a holiday such as Christmas. I was the only white girl in my class (there was one little red-headed white boy, but we never talked). The children were forbidden by law to speak Navajo in class or on the playground. When some were called on to read aloud, they would read in Navaho, anyway. This was true in normal speaking, also. It was hard to break their strong will. When we had recess, I would stand outside with no one to play with. The girls would point at me and speak in Navajo, so I felt they were making fun of me. While I usually had the two or three girls my age that traveled with us on the pipeline, there they had been put in different classrooms than I, and, consequently, had their recesses at a different time. With reflection now, I think how terribly cruel this whole policy was for these Indian children. My feeling of loneliness was nothing compared with the ordeal they were having to experience. They had to be away from their families for months at a time, eating strange food, speaking a strange tongue, being forced to endure strange customs, not to mention having strange living accommodations, too.

From my middle years, I will choose just one more memory about which to write. This occurred while we lived in St. Anne, Illinois, and I was in the eighth grade. That year Dad had left the regular group of pipeliners with whom we traveled, so I was on my own with none of my friends. I had met a girl in my class at school who also lived in the trailer court where we lived. She invited me to her home for a visit. I was at the age where I didn't know whether or not I should be playing with dolls, but I still kept one on my bed. She didn't seem the least uncomfortable about the situation and asked me to bring my doll. It was a relief to me that I didn't have to bring up the subject. While she lived in the trailer court, she didn't live in a trailer—she lived in a railroad boxcar. When I got to her home, I was so excited. This boxcar, with its high ceilings, seemed so huge compared to our little trailer. I just loved it. She had her own real room—not just a bed that was sandwiched in a middle hall like mine was. It was with so much excitement that I eagerly arrived home to tell Mother about this wonderful boxcar for a home! When I tried to describe it and exclaimed my wish for her to be able to see it, too, Mother said, "I have seen them. I have wanted a boxcar for a home, too." What a special moment between my mother and me. It was the first time in my life I ever remember my mother expressing that she wanted anything.

Reunion with Cousin

The past few weeks have been a period of tremendous personal growth for me, but with this growth has come great pain. It seems like that is the way it always is for me—it takes pain before growth. Maybe that is the way growth always is. I have always struggled with a lack of self-worth or low self-esteem or whatever terminology one chooses to use. Certainly, I am no longer the young girl who would often hold her head down looking at her lap when she talked to someone, though, even now I often have to consciously tell myself to look at someone when I talk. Ah yes, I am tremendously better than I used to be, but it seems growth is a life-long experience!

Even good stress has to be processed. I have had a reunion with my cousin, Cheryl, whom I talked about in my writing of the Mother's Day week calls. What a gift she gave me in thinking about my mother and her behavioral patterns. Certainly, a paradigm shift in my thinking occurred. I hadn't seen Cheryl since I was eleven, and she was nine. When I saw her, I said, "Oh, Cheryl, I would have known you if you were walking down the street. Your features are the same."

Her first words to me were, "Beverly, I can see your mother in you." And then she said, "She was the kindest person I ever met." I told her that I had never heard a person say otherwise.

We talked about how Dad used to take Mother at gunpoint and ride around for hours, as I've related earlier. I talked about the breakthrough I had while in therapy when I stated that I realized Mother was so passive that she couldn't offer me the protection that I felt I needed. Cheryl never hesitated one second, but said, "If she hadn't have been passive, she wouldn't have lived to have raised you." What an amazing gift! I have never had a psychologist, a psychiatrist, or a friend ever say this to me. That incredible insight could have only come from the mouth of one who has known and survived the rejection of both Mother and Father! Maybe you can't even imagine the peace, and yes, the euphoria that I experienced! I talked with a cousin, my sister, and my best friend—they all concurred that if Mother hadn't been so passive, Dad probably would have killed her, but they hadn't thought of looking at it this way before, either.

I have SEVERAL MAJOR stressful situations to deal with now, and I want to be careful. I know that it is in times like this that I could make tragic blunders in my life, not to speak of going into a manic spell. Next month it will be eight years since I've had to take medicine for mania. I feel stronger and have more insight than ever, but I need to be very, very careful.

My sister has said, "In your writing, it comes across that you loved Dad. I don't see how. The only thing good he ever did for us was to give us money." When did I, consciously or unconsciously, decide to love my dad? I'm not for sure. After all, he was my daddy. I can tell you this. It was long before I remember him sticking a gun in his mouth threatening to kill himself while I pleaded, "Please don't kill yourself, Daddy, I love you." Nobody would disagree on whether or not we are supposed to love ourselves. That's even one of the most quoted Bible verses, "Love thy neighbor as thyself." Loving thyself comes first. Loving me has been something very hard to do. Oh yes, now that I've had sixty-eight years of trying, I am a lot better at this than I used to be. How could I love myself if I did not love my dad? Fifty percent of the genes in my body come from my dad. I am so like him in many ways. When I mention to some of my paternal relatives, "Oh, I get this or that trait from my dad," immediately I am bombarded with, 'Oh, Beverly, you are NOT like your dad.'" Baloney! The older I get, the more I even sneeze like my dad, and everybody in my house laughs with me. I am very comfortable being like my dad, though I'm certainly thankful that I have fifty percent of my mother's genes in me, too. I know that a great deal of the way I think—my very mind—comes from my dad. The very pictures that I can lay out in my mind—that's a Dad trait.   With being like my dad comes responsibility. I have to be on guard for the traits that crop up that are not the most desirable, also. When our friend Ellen was recently here, and we were discussing her memories of my parents, she said, "Beverly, you got the best of both your mother and father." I replied, "That's what I've hoped for a very long time, but it's good to hear it expressed by someone else!"

Early Teen Years

My high school days began in Elgin, Illinois, where I went for nine weeks. There I met Donna, who invited me to her home. In our various locales, Donna is the first person that I ever remember inviting me to a traditional stick-built home. What a special person I felt she and her parents were. Though we shared only a French class for nine weeks, Donna and I wrote to each other throughout our high school days. I have not yet had the privilege of seeing her since then, but for fifty-five years now, we have never missed a Christmas exchanging cards. She sends me a hand-written letter each Christmas season telling me of her year and her travels. We share a love of travel, and she has circumnavigated the globe.

School officials at Red Oak had told me that if I wanted to be valedictorian when I graduated high school, I would have to attend all of my high school years in Red Oak. They didn't care how many A's I had—if I traveled from school to school, I would be denied the honor. This was important to me—yes, too much so, no doubt, but I guess it's how I identified myself. We came back to Red Oak from Illinois, and I finished the first semester of high school there. When Dad went away to work, I stayed some with Granny or Aunt Eunice so that I could go to school in Red Oak. Dad was beginning to get money from his mineral interest, so he didn't have to work as much as he used to. He had a small house, 864 sq. ft., which seemed BIG to mother and me, built in Red Oak.

I am beginning to struggle writing this part of my life, too. I keep thinking that I am finished with all the hard stuff, but things just seem to come up that I need to write about. I wonder when this will end.

My dad would not let me attend parties that my classmates gave. Linda, who became my best friend in life, lived just down the street two short blocks from us. She was giving a party, and all of the kids in our class were invited. Because there would be records played of what I guess would be called be-bop music, I could not attend. I remember sitting on the porch listening to the music and wishing I could be there with the others. Not only can I not ever remember saying, "Everybody else will be there," I cannot remember ever having a thought to say something like this. These kinds of phrases were not only NOT in my vocabulary to Dad, they were just not in my thoughts either.

There is only one party I ever remember attending. It was a Sunday school party, and the end result was not good. Mignon and Mary were good friends of Dad's, owners of the local grocery store. Dad had not come in that weekend (we didn't know for sure where he was), and after church that night, Mary invited me to her house for a party for her training union class. I can remember Mother and Granny discussing whether I should be allowed to go, and they came up with the consensus that it should be okay. I was very apprehensive knowing we hadn't asked Dad. All the kids were sitting on the floor—I can even remember the game we were playing and the direction I was facing, and there came a knock at the door. I knew it was my mother. It was. She was upset and said Dad had come home. He was really mad, and I had to come home immediately. I can remember getting in the car. Strange—I can remember all these details, but I have no idea what happened when we got home.

In November 1960 my grandpa died. He was a very quiet man—a man of few words—someone I admired and loved very much. He had had a stroke several days before, and his death was not unexpected. I was at the school having a piano lesson, and Mother came to me and said Grandpa was not expected to last long. We left immediately, and though it was only three and a half miles to their house, he was already dead when we got there. As we walked in the door, I saw the sheet had been drawn up over him as he lay on the bed, and I started to quietly cry. BOY, did my dad ever jump all over me! He started screaming and said, "Shut up that crying. He is in a better place and you shouldn't want him back." Well, I did quit crying immediately. Now, I know the story sounds harsh, but this training in self-control was very beneficial for a new role I was about to begin.

In the early sixties, if canned music was used at funerals in other parts of America, it hadn't yet reached Red Oak. I was selected to sing with our high school and junior high principals, Mr. Rutledge and Mr. Kitchens, as a trio to provide music for funerals. There were times when one or the other was not available, and then we were a duet. Most of the time, though, the three of us provided the music for almost all of the funerals conducted in Red Oak. What a sobering and beneficial experience it was for a young girl to see so much of the sadness of life. Most funerals were held at 2 p.m., and around one o'clock the voice would come over the loudspeaker in our classroom, "It's time for Beverly Rider to come to the office." School let out at 3:30, so I wouldn't be returning to school. Sometimes some of the kids would, in a wee bit of a jealous tone, say, "Oh, Beverly's getting out of school again." How could they have known what some of my afternoons were like?

Since many people from our area had migrated to other states, especially to California during the depression of the '30s, there were a lot of funerals for people who were brought home to be buried. So, often as not, I wouldn't even know the deceased. For such a small town, though, there were an awful lot of tragedies among the people I did know. Because this service to the community played such an important part in my high school years, I do want to talk about some of them. Normally, we sat in the choir loft at the front of the church facing the congregation for the entire service, not just for the singing, so self-control was a tremendous asset. Guess I pretty much believe that whatever happens to us in life prepares us for the next thing, and that thing prepares us for the next, etc. I've always thought that being able to sit and look at so much grief without showing emotion was an important attribute that I had. One of the saddest funerals I sang at was for a little toddler who had drunk cow dip (poison mixed in tanks of water to dip cattle to kill flies and other insects that landed on them). This little guy had been such a wanted child. His parents had been married for many years—I guess ten or more —without being able to conceive, so what a joy he was to them. When the smell on the little boy's breath gave way to the discovery of what he had done, his parents started for the hospital; but, with his mother cradling him in her arms, his little body writhed one last time, and he died before they ever got there. To add to this tragedy, the grandfather, who had sat the jug of cow dip on the porch by the back door of the house, was known as a drinker of alcohol. Some of the locals cruelly said, "Well, picking up a jug and drinking from it was what the little feller had seen." Without shedding a tear, I listened to a broken-hearted mother crying out over and over again, "Please God, cover him up tonight. He kicks the covers off, and he gets cold." I watched a devastated grandpa blaming himself. Yes, I sat there without shedding a tear, but I can tell you that in the years since, whenever I think of this, I shed many a tear—even some as I now write.

In just a few short months, a cousin of the above father (same grandparents) buried a little baby, their first child, of crib death. The mother had to be carried out of the church. Yes, I've watched little boys, far too young to have to face this kind of grief, crying for their mommy "in heaven." This September, when I attended the celebration for my best friend's husband's eightieth birthday, I sat beside a mother who had buried her little girl who had died from drowning. The father had taken her to the pool and was on watch, but in a split second, life can be forevermore altered. They were living in California at the time, but they brought their little girl home to Red Oak to be buried. As I so recently sat beside this mother, I wondered if, in her grief at the time, she even knew it was I who sang at her child's funeral. We didn't speak of it, but I remembered.

Courtship and Marriage is Next

Courtship

One day in May 1960 I can remember sitting in Mrs. Westover's English class; I was sitting in the front row and one row to the right of the teacher's desk. I was doing a bit of daydreaming about a young man who attended the church where we were going at the time. It was just before school was out for my freshman year, and in two or three weeks I would be fourteen years old. My classmates were a year older than I and most had begun dating. At this point, my dad had not allowed me to date. This young man, age twenty-four, was a preacher, and my dad liked him a lot. He was not the pastor of the church, but attended there often and was allowed to preach frequently. Dad started inviting him to our house for Sunday dinner and other meals. Dad told me I could start riding back and forth to church with him. In fact, Dad told me I could go with him but not with anybody else. I was very pleased and eager to do this. His name was Buddy.

Dad soon allowed us to ride together alone over to visit Buddy's parents, who lived eight miles in the country. There were two routes to get there. Each was about the same in distance. Often, if we took one route, Dad took the other route and was waiting when we arrived to make sure we went straight there.

Buddy was good friends with Bill Daniel, a fellow preacher, and his wife Marie, who were my parents' ages. They lived in Wilburton, thirteen miles away. Dad began to let us drive up to visit with them. Most of the visits consisted of Buddy and Bill discussing the Bible. I liked Marie and talked with her some, but guess I was really mostly a spectator. On a few occasions, we went to Mr. and Mrs. Johnson's house. Mrs. Johnson was a childhood friend of my mother's, and

Mr. Johnson was a retired school teacher. He loved to go to singing conventions—gatherings where one sang religious songs. When we went to their house, I played the piano, and we sang these singing convention songs. The songs were generally of just a few different tunes with similar words as far as I was concerned and were very boring to me. Mr. and Mrs. Johnson were very nice people, though, and it was a treat to be able to get out and do anything. They soon moved to another part of the state to be near Mr. Johnson's son, so those outings ended.

As I remember it, except for one occasion, this consisted of our dating. Dad did not allow me to go to movies. One time Buddy and I did an unpardonable thing. Dad left to go to Louisiana on some mineral interest business, and we decided we would like to go to a movie in McAlester. Mother was scared but decided to let us do it. We were sitting in this movie, Alfred Hitchcock's *"The Birds,"* and I was miserable. It didn't take me but a few minutes to decide that what we had done was definitely not worth it. What if something happened and Dad came back home? I asked Buddy to leave, and we did. Am I ever glad that we left! Dad had not come back, but when we got home, Mother was walking the floor and crying hysterically. She, like I, got afraid that maybe Dad would turn around and come back.

Buddy and I had been going together for about a year and a half when Dad got Buddy a job with him on a pipeline being built in Wisconsin. As I related in an earlier chapter, I stayed with Granny or Aunt Eunice when Dad and Mother were gone, so that I could go to school in Red Oak. I asked Buddy to write every day that was practical, and I would do the same. I asked him to just throw my letters in his suitcase so they could be saved, and that I would save mine from him. In 2013 I reread these letters for the first time since they were written fifty-two years before. This was the year of Buddy's and my 50th Wedding Anniversary, and we were making a motorhome trip to Wyoming to visit our son and family. I decided it would be neat to read them aloud to Buddy as we journeyed. It didn't turn out to be such a neat thing after all. The more I read, the madder I got! I could not believe Buddy had talked me out of doing several things I wanted to do. I thought I had made these decisions entirely on my own. At one point, Buddy said, "I think you've done enough letter reading." I answered, "No, I have not. I am going to read every single one, and you're going to listen!" Well, I finished the letters and put them away. When I started writing this book, I knew I would want to use portions of these old letters when I wrote about our courtship.

These letters brought back memories of things forgotten, such as my teaching typing classes while our teacher worked on a play that another grade would be presenting. I wrote, "Everyone has been asking me if I am going to be a business education teacher." Buddy wrote back that I didn't need a college education; he could make us a living. In another, I said, "A lady is going to come down to the school tomorrow to see who all wants to take piano lessons. I intend to start taking them again." He discouraged this and said I played well already, so I did not sign up to take more. In one letter he said, "From now on, anytime you wish, you may wear your high heels. I mean out with me." There were several references to commitments of marriage that were made even as early as July 1960 after I had just turned fourteen on May 28. We had probably been going together no more than six weeks. It is certainly with a touch of sadness that I read these letters.

When I was small we were sometimes through Nevada, and back then silver dollars were very frequently used as a medium of exchange. I had collected twenty-two that were from the 1800s. As a teenager, I considered the collection my prized possession. Granny and Mother had always told me to hang on to them. One day when Buddy was at our house and we were talking about these silver dollars, he asked me to give them to him. I did not want to. I was actually very torn as to what to do. I wanted to follow Granny's and Mother's advice to never part with them, but Buddy told me if I didn't give them to him, he would leave and never come back. They were so important to me that I still refused, and he got up and left. After he had walked out the door and driven away, I started crying uncontrollably. I went in and got out the silver dollars to give to him. Mother did say to me, "Beverly, he is a grown man, and you are just a young girl. He shouldn't do that to you." In a few minutes, his car pulled back up, and he got out. I was standing by the door with the silver dollars in my hand. As he came in the door, I handed them to him. He said, "Beverly, I don't want your silver dollars. I just wanted to see what you'd do." I can tell you that that sort of thing happened way too often in our early married life. Buddy would say cruel things; I would cry, then he would apologize and say, "I don't know what's wrong with me. There is something in me that wants to see you hurt, and after I've hurt you, I'm sorry."

This next incident has affected me for most of my adult life. Buddy and I were sitting watching a Miss Fort Smith (AR) beauty pageant on television. There was one girl that I thought was so beautiful, and I especially liked her. I made some comment to the effect that I wished I looked like she did. Buddy turned to me and said, "Beverly, you could never be beautiful, your nose is too big for your face." When I expressed that the comment hurt me, he said, "Well, I'm just telling you the truth. You do want me to be honest, don't you?" I said that I did. I had never thought about how my nose looked. I always had my nose in a book, not a mirror. But from that day forward, every time I looked in a mirror I worried about my nose. I wish I could say I was a better person than one who was so concerned about looks, but it's only been in the last few years that I've been able to overcome that comment; and then, maybe in a way, I haven't even yet. For over fifty years I let that comment define my life.

Wedding and More

Our school baccalaureate was always scheduled on Mother's Day, as Mr. Collins, our superintendent, felt it was such a fitting time for mothers to see their children complete such a milestone in life. Our commencement activities were always the following Friday. I graduated on May 17, turned seventeen on May 28, and married on June 15, 1963. Guess I could be described as the teacher's pet for many of my teachers, but probably none more so than for Mrs. Westover. After graduation ceremonies, Mrs. Westover, even though people were still around, put her arms around my neck and broke down and started crying. She said, "I know I shouldn't do this, but I want you to know that so many times I have looked out at you and wished I could adopt you." What a touching moment to feel so loved. Mrs. Westover had two lovely daughters, one just a bit younger than I, but a heart that included me, too.

Granny had decided she wanted to move to town and sell the house and farm where she and Grandpa had lived. When all three of their children were in their early married lives (the 1940s) Granny and Grandpa had divided some of their property so as to help each child when they felt each needed it most. They gave some land to Alice and Eunice and helped them build houses. As my dad was interested in mechanics and welding, they gave him a sum of money. This furnished seed money to buy a welding machine and eventually open a garage/welding shop. Well, when Granny wanted to sell the family farm and move to town, Dad objected. He used the Old Testament teaching that the "eldest son inherited a double portion." Dad did not want Granny to sell, and he wanted the farm eventually. He and Granny had a major falling out. As usually happens in family disputes, innocent parties are often hurt, too. One day near my graduation, I came out of the grocery store, and in our parked car was a large clear plastic bag filled with Tupperware, some of which I still have. Granny was selling Tupperware at the time. As a graduation gift, she had given me a nice amount of these excellent items. Perhaps finding this should have been a clue, but I had no idea of what was to come.

It has been my stated goal, at least from the time of my teen years, that it was my desire to strive to live so that I had no regrets in life. While so far I can say that I have no major regrets, guess no one could get by without having some minor ones. One of those which sometimes surfaces is that I wished I had made a floor length dress for my wedding. Dad was getting quite a tidy sum from the royalty by now, but he wasn't about to waste money on a wedding. Among my wedding keepsakes, I have some receipts and a detailed list of my wedding expenses.

Including gifts for the attendants, flowers, and other items, the expenses for my wedding totaled $91.28. The following list provides some examples of the expenses:

$1.53— for Bride's Keepsake Book

.75— material for veil

1.60— invitations (I used notepaper and handwrote my invitations) and stamps for mailing

3.00— ingredients for punch

3.00— announcement for newspaper and newspapers

10.00—wedding cake (as with Granny and Grandpa's Golden Wedding Anniversary, we ordered the cake, and it came down on the bread truck from McAlester, fifty miles away)

11.20—wedding dress

For the $11.20 spent on my wedding dress, a white knee-length dress marketed as a graduation dress, I could have bought the material and made a lovely floor length wedding dress. I still have the pages from the Montgomery Ward catalog of the dress I really wanted. It was a beautiful creation costing $35.98, but Dad certainly wasn't going to pay for something that extravagant. This dress was easily within my sewing skills, as I have made many of my own clothes from the time I turned twelve and could have made this dress for around $10.00 to $12.00. I am ashamed of this attitude now, but I would not consider a homemade wedding dress.

During my growing-up years, Mother either bought my clothes at the Salvation Army, rummage sales, or she or Granny made them. While Granny was an expert seamstress, Mother's sewing skills always turned out clothes that looked homemade. Yes, as most of my peers, I have worn many flour sack and feed sack dresses. For those who may read this and not understand the term, fifty pound sacks of flour and feed for chickens came in cotton sacks with colorful floral designs. One used the flour and the feed and then used the sack. For my wedding, I wanted a bought dress.

What a day! We were having the reception in our front yard, where Dad also had his welding machine and a metal grinding table set up. As someone commented at the reception, "Surely Frank could have moved this stuff for Beverly's wedding." To add to the stress, somebody came to Dad to have a welding job done, and Dad worked several hours doing this. As the time neared for me to leave for the church, Dad was still working on this project. He had been part of the rehearsal the night before, so I thought that he surely was coming, but I was really nervous and beginning to wonder if Dad would ever tell the customer that he needed to get ready for a wedding, or maybe if he was even coming at all. Dad finally showed up to walk me down the aisle.

As I stood at the church door and looked in, the scene I saw remains among the most painful scenes of my life. The custom of the bride's friends and family seated on the left and the groom's friends and family seated on the right remains to me most cruel. I looked in, and Buddy's side was comfortably full. He was pastoring a nearby rural church at the time, and many of the church members came and sat on his side. My side had so few. There were a few classmates and family friends, and my cousin Charlene and her little girl, Carla, had come, but Granny and Aunt Eunice were not there. I stood for a moment and bit my tongue until it nearly bled to keep from bursting into tears. As I was walking down the aisle, someone audibly said, "Beverly, smile, look happy." I was numb for the remainder of the ceremony.

Dad was the photographer. Photography was one of his hobbies, and Dad took his hobbies very seriously. He bought the finest equipment, read extensively, took classes on developing and enlarging pictures, etc. We probably spent close to thirty minutes after the ceremony taking pictures. When we got to the house and Dad noticed he was able to take more pictures than normal for a roll of film, he opened the camera to find the film had not gotten wound on the camera properly. (Thank goodness for Duchess and her little Brownie camera!) Dad had taken one photo with his Polaroid camera, and we used this one for the newspaper. When I look at it, it reminds me of Grant Wood's *"American Gothic"* that was often on the back of cereal boxes. I still looked like I was ready to burst into tears.

Somehow I stumbled through the act of being gracious at the small reception. We were planning to go to New Orleans and the Gulf Coast on our wedding trip. Duchess, my childhood friend from pipeline days, had come on the bus from Texas to be Maid of Honor at the wedding. In order to help save on her expenses, Buddy and I volunteered to drive her to the bus station in Dallas, so she would have a short ride home. As we started toward McAlester, I remembered that I had forgotten to bring my Brownie camera and would have no photos of our wedding trip. It seems like a small thing, but I started sobbing. We turned around and retrieved the camera. Granny always said that it was bad luck to cry on your wedding day. I certainly cried on mine.

We enjoyed the winding River Road with its plantations as we drove into New Orleans. We went on to the Gulf Coast of Alabama and

Mississippi and even had a picture taken at the "Welcome to Florida" sign before turning north to Vicksburg, Mississippi, where we toured the battlefield park. Late Thursday afternoon we drove through rain-soaked streets of Malvern, Arkansas, where, in places, deep water had accumulated. We should have spent the night there and did discuss it, but, after the fact, we all have 20/20 vision. When anyone teases us about taking a "second honeymoon," I quickly say, "I hope not." The following is an excerpt from an article in a Hot Springs, Arkansas, newspaper:

Mrs. Beverly Ann Biggs, route one, Red Oak, Okla., received lacerations to her face, feet, and legs when the car which was driven by her husband, Buddy R. Biggs, struck a bridge about 17 miles west of Hot Springs on Highway 270 during a rainstorm early Thursday night, the Garland County Sheriff's Office reported.

Buddy had gotten out of the lane and accelerated to pass another car when he saw a curve and a bridge up ahead. He applied the brakes, but they were wet from being in water up to our floorboard; and we hydroplaned, slamming the car into a concrete bridge barrier. The car went through the barrier and was partially hanging over the bridge. There were no seatbelts in the car, and my face went through the windshield. Among other things, two of my front teeth were knocked out. I was sitting at a slight angle and my back was winched, causing some problems that I live with today.

Among the cars that started stopping, I don't believe there was a gawker among any of the people in them. Some quickly decided I better be removed from the car because it was in danger of going on over the bridge. I was placed on the ground. It had started raining a bit again, and some passer-by threw out a cloth raincoat to cover me. I was losing so much blood that it was quickly decided that time was of the essence and that it was imperative to get me to a hospital as soon as possible. I'm forever thankful that nobody seemed to give any thought to the possibility of being sued for breaking the rule about not moving an accident victim. A woman with a brand new 1963 Buick volunteered to start toward Hot Springs with me. I was lying in the back seat and gushing blood all over her brand new car. Buddy kept talking about it and how it was so new; I kept apologizing and saying I was so sorry for ruining her car, and she kept saying it didn't matter. Maybe no more than a mile or so away there was a little country store, and she pulled in. The storekeeper called an ambulance and gave the description of the car. We left the store, and somewhere between Mt. Ida and Hot Springs, Arkansas, we met the ambulance and I was transferred for the wildest ride of my life (and I've had some pretty wild ones with taxi drivers in Saudi Arabia). The siren was screaming, and Buddy kept begging the ambulance driver to slow down, saying, "I'm afraid we're going to have another wreck." The memory does play tricks on one. If I didn't have the news article to read, I would have certainly said, with the siren screaming all the way, that it was a lot farther than seventeen miles from the wreck to the hospital.

I'm not sure what being in shock is like, but a nurse commented to the doctor who was working on me that I was in shock from the blood loss. I heard everything that was being said, so if you can be in shock and still know everything, perhaps I was. My body was placed on ice—I DO mean my whole body—my head, my neck, etc., completely to my feet. In a day or so, I begged to have some of these ice packs removed. The answer was always "No." I was told that this was for internal bleeding. With every change of nurses, I would ask if I could at least have my head and neck off the ice. Sometimes one would check with the doctor, but the report back was always that the best they could do was crush the ice in smaller pieces for my head and neck. There was an intercom system in the hospital, and at news time, a nurse would sometimes peek in and say, "They are talking about you now." I can remember the talk about the young bride on her honeymoon, and the description would often end with, "She is reported to be resting comfortably at St. Joseph Hospital." Bits and pieces of glass continued to work their way out of my mouth and gums. I would think, "So much for the media. How could I be 'resting comfortably' with my body on ice?" I could not even turn over.

My head was completely covered with a big bandage. The only holes were for my mouth, my nose, and my left eye—my right eye area had twenty-two stitches in it. I had to tilt my head to one side to be able to look through the small slit in the bandage. When my dad and mother arrived, Dad took pictures of the car and of the day I left the hospital, but he did not take one with my head in a bandage. I'm surprised, because he usually took pictures of everything. I would like to have a paper photo, though I have the picture in my mind. Amazing—that's all I can say about my mother's composure the first time she saw me. How Mother stood there with no outward emotion as she looked at her only living child with her head and face completely bandaged, is incredible to me. How she must have inwardly wondered what my face looked like. Maybe, just as I was, she was so relieved that I was alive that it didn't matter. She told me that on the way to Arkansas to the hospital that she had begged Dad not to get on to Buddy for driving too fast.

Numerous times I had asked nurses if I could see a mirror. That request, as with ice pack removal, was always denied. In fact, I was told that it was even written on my chart that I was to see no mirror. As soon as I had Mother to myself, I asked her for a mirror. I told her I knew I was not supposed to see one, but that she knew me well enough to know I wasn't going to get hysterical. I was so grateful to be alive! What I looked like under the bandages really didn't matter. So, Mother got out a mirror, and I had a look. I had the opportunity at this young age to know that we really are only a heartbeat away from death. Things can be going along great one minute, and in the next one, life can be forever changed. I can assure you that I've never forgotten that lesson.

The day that the doctor removed my bandages, he stepped backward a full step and exclaimed excitedly, "The healing powers of the young! This is like a miracle! You are going to be all right!" He was standing at the right side of the bed, and he took my hand. He continued, "When they brought you in here, I took one look at you and thought, 'Here's a pretty young girl ruined for life.'" That is the first time in my life that I can ever remember hearing the word pretty associated with my name. The doctor said that the tendons in my right eye had been cut; and the night I was brought in, as he worked with me, he didn't think I'd ever be able to keep my eyelid open. The top of my nose had been cut in a horseshoe shape and was peeled back—I had seventeen stitches in my nose. He had thought that I would always have a hump on my nose. So clearly I remember him, with deep emotion, saying, "I tried so hard with you." When I got to see a mirror the next time, I really had to just take the good doctor's word for it. He could surely see beyond what I could see. I thought I looked horrible. But still, it really didn't matter. I remain thankful to this day that I had such a caring, careful, skilled, emergency room doctor.

When I tell about this wreck and the cuts on my face, etc., some people may wonder if I'm exaggerating a bit. After all, when one looks at me, these scars aren't apparent. Last year I had a small area appear on my nose that I thought should be professionally checked. The doctor was examining this place and abruptly said, "You have scars on your face. I can see them through this ten-power loop." I said, "Yes," and told him the story. He explained to me that looking through these loops is even better than looking through a 10-power magnifying glass. Somehow the loop allows one to see deeper into the skin. This reminded me again of how truly blessed I was on that rainy night fifty-two years ago.

In an untold number of ways, writing this book has been so good for me—more so than I could have possibly imagined. It does seem that in every chapter I have the pain to deal with, and yes, I shed a few tears. After the initial sobbing on my wedding day, I can never remember shedding a tear about anything I have written in this chapter. As I write, however, there are times I stop and cry. Yes, I remember. I remember and write details. After completing the writing, of course, I still remember, but it seems I let go of the pain—pain that I didn't even know I carried. In addition, because of the writing, I am opening up to people and talking about things I have never brought up before. These people can and do give clarification on these matters that I have buried deep inside. Just before starting this chapter, I told my cousin Charlene how it hurt that she and Granny and Aunt Eunice did not come to see me when I got home from the hospital. She replied, "Beverly, as soon as word came that you had been in a car wreck, the whole church banded together and started praying for you." I had never known this. What a comforting thought!

I want to mention those, unknown to me, who visited me in the hospital. These people have remained in my thoughts to the present day. There were three—one was a lady from town who told me she had read about me in the newspaper and wanted to come visit me. Though I'd registered as a Baptist and was in a Catholic hospital, it was a Methodist minister who told me he'd heard about me on the radio and wanted to come. It is with comfort that I have thought of this kind man down through the years. The lady that brought me to meet the ambulance came. I can remember her saying, "I wanted to see how you are." I have never been able to remember anything else about the conversation. It seems like I asked her about the car, but I'm not sure. Surely I thanked her again, but I'm not sure. After I returned home, Mother suggested we send her a little gift. I not only did not have her address, but I didn't know her name. Many people weave in and out of our paths in life. Down through the years, I have often thought of this kind, generous lady who was such an important part of my life. I think of her with a touch of sadness and regret. She was the person who may have been most responsible for saving my life, and I don't even know her name.

Remarkable

A most remarkable thing, in my view, has happened. For almost thirty years, since my mental breakdown at age forty, when I've been under extreme stress, I start losing a lot of sleep. This escalates into developing manic tendencies, and often into full-blown manic episodes. When this happens, I develop most of the symptoms of severe mania, have to be under the care of a psychiatrist and take prescription medicine. I have been told by several psychiatrists that I should be permanently on this type of medicine—medicine for bipolar disorder. I have always refused to accept this prognosis, and as soon as I came down from the manic high, I would begin to wean myself from the medicine. As the years have gone by, instead of getting worse, as has been predicted, I have actually gotten better and better in being able to sense when a manic episode is developing. Many times when the symptoms are developing, I go to bed in order to get as much rest as possible and to sleep whenever I can—be it night or day. As part of my regular routine, I try to eat at proper times, as hunger seems to affect me greatly. As I said earlier, it has been over eight years since I have taken any medicine. I know the tendency is still there, and many times I have to get in my prevention mode.

During this past month, I have been under such severe stress from several sources that I know in times past it would have brought on a full-blown manic episode. As this involves both of my children as well as Buddy, it is not appropriate for my book to give details. Now, I was guilty of bringing a small portion of this on me, but in the main, I was right, and I knew it. Because of the strength, self-worth, etc. I have acquired in the course of writing, I was able to stand my ground. I believe everyone was waiting for me to fall off the cliff. This would have been my normal pattern. Though I attribute most of the strength to having completed a lot of writing about my life, I did talk to a few trusted friends and relatives. This has also helped diffuse my mental anxieties. I think the word empowered is overused; therefore, I seldom use it. In this case, I will tell you that I really feel empowered more than I ever have in my life.

I have known from past studies that many psychologists and psychiatrists believe that most, if not all, mental illnesses are caused from unresolved anger. In my particular case, I now believe this is true. When I finally developed enough strength to stand up for myself and my convictions, I came through it and then realized I didn't have to go off into a manic spell. Now, of course, I never deliberately went off into a manic episode. It's just that I now believe that this is a coping mechanism that when my brain got overloaded, the end result was a manic spell. It's actually really very, very sad. Certainly, the genetic tendencies are there, as members of my extended family have had the same problem, but I NO LONGER feel that I have to be controlled by this. For me, this no longer has to be the end result of extreme stress. I feel like a new person! I feel a wholeness that I've never felt before!

In writing chronologically, I am now at the point to begin writing of my marriage. I have dreaded getting to this point. It has been my sincere desire not to hurt anyone with my writing, and if I write some of which I feel I should relate, that will most likely hurt Buddy. As I have said before, Buddy is NOT happy that I'm writing! He has not read one word that I've written, even of things that I've offered to let him read, and has yet again said even this week that he didn't know if he ever would. He appears to feel very threatened and has cautioned me that he hopes I will be fair. So be it. The writing so far has helped me so much that I believe I should continue to write from the heart—it should be from the heart now, and not from the gut—as I've said some of my writing has been.

The First Seven Years

As I begin to write about another difficult period in my life, I am well aware that these things are told from my perspective. Another might see them differently, at least when opinions surface rather than writing just facts. For a long while, I have dreaded starting this chapter. After much contemplation, I arrived at the conclusion that to not put down things I remember that have bothered me a great deal would add a false note to my writing. It also would not benefit me as my previous writing has done. Perhaps I can find healing for this period of my life, too.

In many ways, I was far advanced for my years, even for the 1960s. There was, however, much about me that was very immature. Since I had not been allowed to have a normal dating period, I looked forward to being married, so Buddy and I could go to Ft. Smith on a date and stay out as late as we wanted. Perhaps it was because of the car wreck, or perhaps it was the reality of being married and soon realizing there wasn't enough money, but the date to Ft. Smith never happened.

From the hospital, I came to my parents' house to be cared for while I recovered from the car wreck. My right leg had been injured, and I walked on crutches. When I was able, Buddy and I moved out into the trailer that I had grown up in from the time I was nine until Dad built the house in 1960. I invited Buddy's mother to go with me on my first grocery shopping trip. This gesture caused me to emotionally distance myself from her. She came back and said to other family members, and the word was passed to me quickly, "My poor son, he will never have anything—that woman he has married will keep him in the poorhouse." She was very upset that I'd spent so much money on food. To stock our kitchen, I had purchased 104 items for a total of $37.12, including the 2% sales tax. I never said anything in defense—no need. I did invite her for other outings, but it was hard for me to relate to a woman who would not even eat in a restaurant. If we went somewhere and were out at lunchtime, I would have to bring her a hamburger to the car.

Several girls in the area were getting married in the few weeks after school was out, and it was the custom for teachers and friends (it would have been considered horrible etiquette back then for a relative to be a host) to give bridal showers for each. I was told that I wouldn't be left out, but it was thought that because there had been several showers recently, it would be better if a shower for me was given after the wedding rather than before. I wanted to have my front teeth partial, so my shower was on August 15, two months after the wedding. Charlene attended and brought her little girls, Glenda and Carla. Aunt Eunice came, too. Granny did not. Clearly, there was something wrong. Instead of seeking her out and trying to find out if it were something more than her problems with Dad, I just accepted the hurt.

Guess I can really relate to the young teenage girls out there, though pregnant and unmarried and not mature enough to be mothers, who say, "I wanted a baby. I wanted a baby to love." Though I was seventeen and married, I wanted a baby very badly, and the seven months I waited until I found out I was pregnant were a very long time for me. In fact, I had already started worrying that maybe something was wrong with me—that I might never be able to have children. I can remember when Planned Parenthood was not all about contraceptives and abortion clinics. They provided literature with suggestions for those trying to conceive, and I ordered some of that literature. So, I can identify, too, with those who want a child so badly and struggle with being able to conceive.

From high school days, my best friend in life has been Linda Brewer Kitchens. I told her that if I had a little girl, I would name the baby after her. The baby was due September 6. Linda and her mother, Leona, were visiting me the evening of September 1. Mrs. Brewer commented that I seemed tired, and the talk was that Linda's birthday was September 2—maybe I'd have the baby a few days early. In the early morning hours, my labor pains started, and we went to McAlester to the hospital, where Tim was born on September 2, at 9:46 a.m. Linda has often made the comment, "How many friends would have their baby for your birthday gift?"

When we first married, Buddy was working for Field's Hardware for $35 per week. He had also started trading cars on the side and quickly quit his job at the hardware store to trade cars full time. He gave me $20 per week for the household expenses, including the electric bill. I knew he was in debt when we married but didn't know how much. He always said money was tight, and I never saw any records of his car business. We did not own a car for ourselves, but just drove whatever he had bought at the moment to resell. This meant, of course, that there were days I did not have a vehicle to drive. We, however, made it okay with this arrangement.

Granny had built her house in town and lived just one block south of us. Living in a little town of 500 people, it's surprising that we didn't see each other more often. One day when Tim was just two or three months old, I was walking from town and pushing him in a stroller. Granny had never seen him. All of a sudden I looked and Granny was walking on the same sidewalk. When we met, she really didn't look at Tim, but paused long enough to say to me, "Beverly, if you don't get that baby out of this wind, he's going to have the colic." That is all. I went home and did something I deeply regret to this day. I got a stuffed doll and some other things (how I would love to have them now, especially the doll) that Granny had made for me and put them in a sack to give away. Sally Jane and Cynthia Sue's doll clothes were packed away, and, fortunately, I didn't find them and give them away, also. I felt that if Granny didn't want to have any more to do with me, regardless of the reason, I didn't want these things to remind me of the pain.

When Tim was around eighteen months old, we were visiting a brother of Buddy's who lived in the countryside a few miles away. Tim was playing on the floor with some pillows that had been on the couch.

At one point, Buddy told Tim to put them up. Tim did not. Buddy told him again, but Tim kept playing with the pillows. This happened yet a third time. Buddy was furious and went over and started whipping Tim, saying that he had to "get control of him now," "break him of disobedience once and for all," etc. He did not just whip Tim on his buttocks but whipped him on his back, especially the small of the back, so hard that blood came to the stripes. For my part, I just sat there not knowing what to do. I was scared, very scared. This same brother had been known to get mad at his wife and throw her across the room into a wall, and I knew this. I knew that Buddy's folks really didn't like me very much, and I was really afraid of Buddy and wondered if a big brawl would break out if I interfered. Surely I wouldn't have kept sitting there, but Tim did comply, and the whipping/beating ended. (I can tell you that Tim remembers this, with great pain, to this day and refuses to use even small spankings to discipline his own son.) This is what I did. We went home, and the next day I got out my camera and took several pictures of the wounds on his back. I made an appointment with the doctor that I used in McAlester. I took Tim and the pictures to the doctor. I asked him if there was any medicine I could get to put on the places so they would heal faster. He gave me a stern look and said there was not. I told him my mother was coming in a few days, and when she changed Tim's diaper, if she saw this, she would be furious. I told the doctor I was leaving some of the pictures which I wanted to be kept in Tim's folder. I also wanted a complete description written on his chart. Now, I'm sure that in today's world, the doctor would have probably turned the whole thing over to the authorities, but back then, he did not do this. I made sure the doctor knew exactly my intentions. I did this because if this is the kind of father Buddy was going to be, I would not stay in the marriage. If I went to court for a divorce, it wasn't going to be a "he said," "she said," situation. I would have proof. There would be no hearsay. I wanted it as ironclad as I could get it, so that, hopefully, Buddy would not be allowed unsupervised visitation rights. Granted, I was too much of a doormat and too scared to do anything as the event occurred, but I sure wasn't about to give it a pass, either.

In spite of the fact that Buddy emphasized so much that he did not believe in divorce, and no one at that time in his family had ever gotten a divorce, if Buddy had kept up this behavior, I believe I know myself well enough that I would have gotten out. Now, you may wonder if Buddy ever did such a thing again, and I have to answer, "Yes," but he didn't bring the blood the next time. The next incident occurred several months after Tim had turned two. Down at the end of a lane from us, a little elderly lady lived alone. She was from France and had been a World War I bride. Mrs. Gentry had two sons, but they lived elsewhere in the state. She had never assimilated into our culture well and could not speak English without a heavy accent. Because of these barriers, no one went to visit her. I started going down each day to check on her. Every Saturday, with Tim in tow, I would go down and take Mrs. Gentry to town to buy her groceries. Even at such a young age, Tim had an ear for languages and could understand Mrs. Gentry better than I could. He loved to sit and talk with her. Now Tim had been told not to wander off by himself, but on one afternoon, when I checked on him, he was nowhere to be found. Buddy and Mother were both at the house. After calling for him, we decided to check to see if he was at Mrs. Gentry's. Sure enough, he was there. Well, Buddy gave him the second and last really hard whipping. My mother was furious, and it did get stopped before it became as bad as the other one. There have been many occasions when Tim has, with great pain, brought up the whipping his dad gave him. I have often wondered if it is this whipping he remembers, but since I can remember things before I was two, perhaps, Tim, indeed, does remember that first really horrible whipping.

On occasion, during these early years, Buddy would sometimes threaten me by saying if I ever divorced him, he would kidnap the children, take them somewhere where I could never find them, and I would never see them again. This was, I will admit, a deep-seated fear that I had.

At the period in my life when Tim was around two, I went through a period of fantasizing. This was not just some casual daydreaming that happened at various periods in the day. I literally pretended I was someone else. I had a different name, a different husband, lived in a different place, etc., and often lived this roll for days at a time. Sometimes my actions were such that Buddy noticed a difference and would comment that I seemed to be living in a dream world. I was really miserable, and this was a definite coping mechanism for me to escape and get through that time of my life. This lasted several months, but, for no apparent reason, eventually subsided. I have never had the need to do this at any other stage of my life.

It was very obvious to me that I knew nothing about parenting, so when I was pregnant with Tim, I bought two books. One was Dr. Spock's famous book, and the other was a Better Homes and Garden's baby book that was about half a writing on parenting and the other half a record-keeping book of baby's early years. This was another area of criticism from Buddy's mother. When Mrs. Biggs would bring a family friend to visit and see the new baby, she pointed out to them with disdain that I was raising my child by the book. This was definitely not true. I was only reading for guidelines and no way did I follow everything I read. There were many things of value to me, however, that I did incorporate. While I never had an audible disagreement with any member of Buddy's family, I always felt that I was certainly not the person they would have chosen for a wife for him.

It was during this period that Buddy wanted to go out to California to the college that the radio evangelist, Herbert W. Armstrong founded. Buddy was never really comfortable with the doctrines of the Free Will Baptist Church, of which he was a minister. His mother did not attend church but listened to Herbert Armstrong on the radio, so Buddy had been exposed to his teachings for many years. He ordered many books from this organization. Buddy was constantly confused with the disparity in the two sets of teachings. I read some of the books, and the doctrines were so strange that I was frightened. Again, I wondered if I could stay in the marriage with Buddy if he did take us to California to this college. It was a great blessing and relief, to me anyway, that we never even came close to having the money to act on his desires. I will add, though, that Armstrong had a book on child rearing that I added to my collection. Again, I didn't agree with everything in the book but did find some very useful suggestions—things I may have never thought of on my own.

My preference would have been to have a second child at about the time Tim was two, but it didn't happen. After about six months of trying, I, again, resorted to the suggestions in the Planned Parenthood literature. So, Tim lacks a month and a half being three years older than Linda.

A few months after I became pregnant with Linda, a most wonderful thing happened! There was a knock at the door, and when I opened it, there stood my granny! She had some homemade diapers in her hand and said, "Beverly, I heard you are going to have another baby." I said, "Yes, that is true." She replied, "I got some knit scraps from the mill in McAlester, and I made these diapers for you." Of course, I immediately invited her in. I was sitting on the couch folding clothes, and she started helping me. I had dishes in the sink, and she went over and started washing them. Granny picked up our relationship like nothing had ever happened. It was months later I found out that her problem with me had been that she had gotten a letter from Dad during their initial disagreement where he told her he had a vision of her in hell, and Granny thought I had typed it for him. Everyone knew that I did a lot of secretarial work for Dad, helping him in his gas royalty business. I had not typed this letter. It had several typographical errors, and I pointed out to Granny that no way would a letter I typed be filled with so many mistakes. In fact, I told her that I, too, had gotten a similar letter from him at about the same time. So, our estrangement of over four years was over. Too bad that back in 1963 there hadn't been more communication instead of assumptions on both our parts. Though we had a good relationship for the rest of her life, I will say that there remains just a tiny bit of sadness, or maybe it's an emotion for which I don't even know the word, but things were never quite one-hundred percent the same. Yes, maybe ninety-eight percent, but not one-hundred percent. Anyone who reads my earlier chapters knows that Granny was one of the most important people in my life, and I did not have her for over four years.

With maturity in so many areas so far beyond my years, it is with a touch of sadness that I relate how childlike I really was. I wanted a little girl so badly. Yes, I know if I'd had another boy, I would have loved him just as much, yet I wanted a little girl for whom I could make dresses—a little girl for whom I could buy dolls and make doll clothes. Buddy's mother, using folklore, said since I was carrying the baby low, I would have another boy. This bothered me greatly, so about a month before Linda was due, I prayed for a little girl. When I confessed to Buddy that I had done this, he was very annoyed. He said, "Beverly, surely you don't believe that God would change that baby at this late date." Meekly, I replied that I did. Somehow, in my childlike mind, I felt if I gave away things that were important to me in my childhood, my prayer would be answered. If I didn't give away these toys, I believed it would not. I gathered up my little oak doll bed that Mother had the old man in North Carolina make for the Christmas when I was four, my little wringer washing machine, my toy sewing machine, some dolls, and other little girl items. Against Mother's soft protests, I took them to my cousins in Wilburton for their children, who didn't have many toys.

Almost three weeks before the baby was due, once again, in the middle of the night (Buddy was not happy) my labor pains started, and we drove to McAlester. Buddy was heavily involved in trading cars and had an agreement to get a vehicle from a dealer that day, so this came at an inconvenient time for him. Maybe because she really wasn't full term, but it took me longer to deliver her. She was born at ten minutes after 12 Noon. When I awakened from the anesthesia, Buddy was not there. When I asked to see him, one of the elderly nuns in the hospital was very angry at him and said, "I've never seen a more unconcerned father in my life." It seems he had actually waited until the baby was born but had immediately left to go pick up his vehicle. Mother had Tim at their place on Lake Eufaula. There was nobody at the hospital that I knew. My regular doctor was on vacation. The substitute came and asked me some questions regarding the possibility that I was mixed up on the due date, as he didn't feel she looked like an eight-month-plus baby. He felt she was more premature. I told him the dates were correct. I asked if she were okay and was told that she was fine, but had been placed in an incubator—that they would bring her to me later. I was so disappointed that Buddy hadn't stayed. The nurses would bring the other lady's babies into the ward where I was, but mine was never brought. I began to wonder if something was wrong with her—something that was being kept from me. On occasion, I would quietly ask if she were okay and if I could see her. Somehow in the shuffle, this never happened. Maybe it's hard to believe, but I was just so meek that the next day I still hadn't seen her and hadn't made an issue of it. I just quietly wondered and kept the fear inside. Finally, I saw the nun I'd spoken with the day she was born, and she was horrified that I had not yet seen my baby. She immediately brought her to me, and I removed the blanket to count her fingers and toes.

As Linda was going to be kept in an incubator for several days, the doctor said, in order to save costs, that I could be released. The following day Mother came from Eufaula and took me there to recuperate and await Linda's dismissal. I did contact Buddy and ask him to come take me to the hospital on a Sunday afternoon to see her. He couldn't see the point and said she was getting the best of care, but reluctantly complied. Buddy's behavior surrounding the time of Linda's birth was something I had a hard time dealing with for many years. These things that would have meant so much to me just did not seem important to him.

Buddy opened up a salvage yard and a garage in addition to trading cars. He regularly went to car auctions in Ft. Smith, Arkansas; Springfield, Missouri; and Dallas, Texas. This meant he would often not get home until the wee hours of the morning. For a couple years, he was preaching on Sundays at a church in Antlers, Oklahoma, about eighty miles away. This was often the only time that the kids and I together got to see Buddy. We usually spent the drive down there with me reading to Buddy the Bible scriptures he wanted to be read as he prepared his sermons. I can remember those Sundays as being very hard, as I prepared the things necessary to take for one and then two children for the day. It was also hard being in someone's home for the afternoon and being concerned that the children did not disturb others or bother anything. Then there was the long drive home after church at night. It was, however, an outing for me and our chance to be with Buddy, so, except for Linda's birth, I don't remember missing any Sundays.

From the time Linda came home from the hospital, she was crazy about Buddy. Very early, when he walked across the room, her eyes would follow him. When she was taking her bottle, she would stop and look at him. When she learned to smile, imagine how her face would light up when he was in view, but he was just not home very much for the kids' early years. One of the things I most disliked about these Oklahoma years was that even when Buddy had the opportunity to be home at night, he chose to go with his friends to play dominoes, checkers, and other games. Every night of the week there were some of these gatherings. In order to entice the group to our house, I would bake cookies and other goodies, but that didn't last long as they didn't like the noise of small children, and our house was very small (we moved in to Dad and Mother's house when they moved to the house on Lake Eufaula before Linda was born). I tried to talk to Buddy about this, but he said because he had so much stress and was gone a lot, he needed to do this to be able to relax and get his mind off his problems. If he had some free time during the day, he spent it fishing. He even used to laugh and tell people that there would be many months at a time when he threw a hook in the water every day of the week except Sundays, and even a few times on Sundays. I resented that he wouldn't spend time with Tim, Linda, and me.

Buddy continued to have more and more financial difficulties. It is probably just as well that I didn't know the extent of it, as I would have been horrified. We left Oklahoma in July 1968 owing over $30,000, plus interest, (this would easily be $300,000 plus in today's value) to MANY different sources—banks, business establishments, relatives, and friends. Buddy was advised that he should just declare bankruptcy, that there was no way he would ever be able to pay that amount back. He said, "I'll pay it back, or I will die, whichever comes first." Dad got Buddy a job as welder's helper on a pipeline in Wisconsin, so we moved there for a few months. After this job, Dad taught Buddy to weld and got him in the union as a pipefitter. We then went to Springdale, Arkansas, where he had his first job with full journeyman union wages. Take-home pay was still less than $200 a week—it was in Alabama in the early '70s before he made that much—but it was good money for that time period. We, however, tried to take so much of his salary to pay off the debt that we lived in Dad's 19' camper trailer. We did not have electricity, as we did not take enough money out to pay the electric deposit. The RV style dual refrigerator had malfunctioned, and Dad had replaced it with an electric refrigerator; therefore, we had no refrigerator either, and used an ice chest which we kept in the middle of the floor. This also meant we went to bed at dark. It was summer, but we weren't used to AC anyway. I can remember going to church and being so embarrassed and trying to avoid answering when people asked where we lived. I certainly did not want any surprise company. This did not happen but a few times, but I can remember visiting neighbors, them offering to fill Linda's bottle with milk, then taking her home and giving her some water, so I could save the milk for later. There were those times when I thought I had carefully figured the amount of money to spend at the grocery store and still would come up a few cents short. So, I know the feeling that comes when someone offers to make up the difference, and for over forty years I have been able to pass those kind gestures to others.

It was during this stay in Arkansas when I was twenty-two years old that I had a horrible bout of deep depression. I could be standing at the sink doing dishes or cooking or whatever, and all of a sudden, for no apparent reason, I would just sink to the floor and break into uncontrollable sobs. This went on for a few weeks, and Buddy decided it would be better if he brought the children and me back to Red Oak to live. It wouldn't have occurred to any of us that I may need to see a doctor for depression. I'm not for sure we even used the term. We did come back, and Mother came and took the kids to her place for a while. I stayed alone in Dad and Mother's house, and Buddy came in on weekends. For his part, he lived mostly on a can of sardines and some cheese for the day. I pretty much stayed in bed and didn't get up to shower or dress except for the weekend when I knew Buddy would be coming in. Sometimes Leona Brewer, Linda's mother, would bring me food. After a few weeks, these symptoms subsided. It was, however, during this time that I first started rehashing things that I had gone through as a child. I would lie on the bed and start from my earliest memories and go over every detail in chronological order. It would sometimes take three days to complete this. Unfortunately, this started a pattern for me that lasted for years. When I had something happen that would deeply hurt me, I would go to bed and start going through the list, remembering in great detail each thing that was done or said.

After a few months, Buddy's job in Arkansas ended, and he was sent to work on the construction of a carpet plant in Wilburton, only fourteen miles away from Red Oak. I started giving some piano lessons for the months we continued living in Red Oak. When I went back to Red Oak for my 50th class reunion and alumni banquet, I was surprised at the people who came to me and said I was the first person who had introduced them to music and the piano. Believe me, this is only one of the many things I have done in life for which I was not really qualified. I even thought of this lack of qualification when I read the letters I wrote to Buddy during our courtship where I had been teaching the typing classes while our teacher was directing students for a high school play.

It was with much joy, but also a touch of sadness, that Buddy, when the job at the carpet plant finished, was told he could go to a job in Fernandina Beach, Florida. I was overjoyed that we could travel as I had done as a child. We could have normal hours for eating together, and Buddy would be home at regular times. For as long as we lived in Red Oak, he spent a lot of time with his friends, hunting quail, fishing, and playing games at night. The sadness came because we would be leaving our friends and family. Linda Brewer's mother, Leona, took it especially hard—she felt she was losing two of her grandkids. Oliver, Linda's dad, was the banker in town, and we owed him so much money, I'm sure he had mixed emotions.

Some of our best memories of these years involved being with our friends, the Brewers and Morgans. The Morgan's daughter Ellen shared a September 2 birthday with Linda Brewer and our Tim, and we usually gathered for a cookout together. Though Buddy would not let us celebrate Christmas because of the Armstrong teachings, he did not object to us having birthday gatherings—even though Armstrong didn't approve of that, either.

In the spring of 1970, we loaded our few possessions in the trunk of a car, thinking we would be gone a few months. As it turned out, we never returned to Oklahoma, except for visits of a week or two at a time.

Our first few weeks in Florida were miserable for me. In trying to use most of Buddy's salary for paying debts, we rented a small cabin in what had been an old-fashioned tourist court. There were no white people living there. It was very dilapidated. The bathroom had a huge hole in the floor that someone could have stuck their whole leg through. Buddy repaired that, but the worst part was the roaches. I didn't know roaches built nests, but there were nests close to the size of basketballs behind the refrigerator and cook stove. They crawled inside the refrigerator, were in the cabinets crawling in the pots and pans and dishes—I had to wash everything just before I cooked or we ate. They fell from the ceiling on the bed at night. Linda, who was not yet three, remembers them vividly. I began to get nauseous and could not eat much. I even became ill for a day or so trying to spray for them. It was apparent we had to make other arrangements. Even though we owed Mr. Brewer so much money, we called, explained the situation, and asked if we could borrow a thousand dollars to buy a trailer, and pay it back at $100 per month. Being the good person to us that he was, he never hesitated. We looked in the newspaper and found one advertised for a thousand dollars. As we went to look at it, from far off I recognized the brand, and said, "Oh it's a Hicks. I always liked that brand." As a child, I had spent hours drawing all the different brands of trailers in great detail, so I certainly knew brands. This trailer was from the '50s. Hicks trailers had been painted in pretty colors, but someone had recently painted this one all silver—guess they were trying to make a "Spartan" out of it. Never mind, it had been really well cared for inside. It was 36' long (incl. hitch), had two bedrooms (one with bunks), a bathroom with a small tub, and those beautiful knotty pine cabinets for which Hicks trailers were famous.

It seems no small miracle to me that I managed to transfer our belongings without transferring roaches, too, but the miracle happened. Memories of life in Fernandina Beach are most fond. Every Friday after supper, we went to the ocean, and Buddy played with the children on Saturday, too. It seemed like we were a real family, the kind I had always imagined and for which I had longed.

There is one thing that happened when we were in Florida that Buddy and I both have told many times over the years. As I've related, we really lived on a tight budget, sending all the money we possibly could to pay debts. By this careful budgeting, we hoped to be able to pay out in five years. The church we started attending was without a pastor, and Buddy was asked to fill in until they acquired one. Buddy only had one suit, which he wore Sunday after Sunday. It finally was getting thread-bare, and at a conference we attended, a whole seam came undone on the pants. I was, fortunately, carrying a pack of safety pins in my purse. One morning I was sitting in the laundromat doing my clothes and picked up the newspaper lying on a chair. I glanced at the sale sheets and saw a big ad for a major department store in Jacksonville, about thirty miles away. The advertisement was for men's 100% silk suits for $10. I looked in my billfold, and I had only $10. I glanced at my watch and thought, "I've got just enough time to finish this load and drive to Jacksonville and get one of these suits soon after the store opens." Now, I had never been in downtown Jacksonville, but that didn't stop me. With kids in tow, I loaded wet laundry in the car, and we took off. I had no idea where this department store was other than having the address from the newspaper ad. As I drove into Jacksonville and looked up, I was on the correct street. I soon arrived at the store, and there was a parking space available right at the front door! The store was just opening. I quickly asked where the men's department was and followed the rushing crowd. By the time I got there, the room was filled with people all after this terrific bargain. Within a minute or so, an employee came with a newspaper in hand

and said she had an announcement to make. She said there had been a misprint in the ad for men's suits. She said these suits were supposed to be on sale for $100, NOT $10, but because of the ad having been published, the store would honor it by offering ten silk suits for $10 to the first ten people in line. That was all that would be sold for that price. People began scrambling for suits. I was standing next to a rack of suits, and I reached for one. It was a 36 short, which was exactly Buddy's size! I rushed to get in the line, which by now had four or five people. As each person paid, she said, "$10.40," and I realized I had forgotten about the sales tax. As I frantically looked in my coin section, all I had was fourteen cents. She quickly got to me and was very impatient as I explained I didn't have enough money. She rudely said, "Get out of line! Next," and started ringing up somebody else. With a crestfallen face, about ready to burst into tears, I turned around to see a person from the back of the room—with no suit—pushing her way through the crowd. She shoved the money in my hand and said, "I wouldn't see that girl miss getting a suit over twenty-six cents." I asked for the woman's address so I could send her the money, but she declined my offer saying, "No, when you have the opportunity, just pass it along." Every time one of these opportunities comes my way, I remember her words and that magical day in Jacksonville. By the way, after all these years, Buddy still has that beautiful black, pinstripe, silk suit.

There is one last event I want to mention before I close this chapter on our first seven years. Just in time for Tim to start first grade, we moved to White Springs, Florida, within hearing distance of the carillon bells daily ringing out Stephen Foster's songs at the Suwannee River State Park. We had not had any black people in Red Oak, so we were a bit nervous to find out that he had been assigned to a black teacher. What a wonderful lady! As I left an apprehensive little boy for his first day of school and walked down the steps, all at once, to my surprise, it came to me that while meeting and talking with her, it hadn't even occurred to me that she was black!

In November Buddy's job ended in White Springs, and he was assigned to a job at Brown's Ferry Nuclear Plant in Athens, Alabama. We had had such a wonderful eight months in Florida. With Buddy pulling the trailer with the truck and me following behind in the car, tears were streaming down my face as we crossed the Florida line into Georgia. Little did I know what awaited us—that the very best years of our marriage would be spent in Athens, Alabama.

Writing and Handling Stress

Perhaps I will not leave in this chapter when I compile the letters for a book. I have debated quite a while on whether or not to write on this topic. Since I have been dealing with this current stress for a while, it may be better to write it down in the hope that I can deal with it better in the future. Buddy has a lot of anger inside, and sometimes it develops into rage. During the years that he drank heavily, it usually occurred on a daily basis. The lighthearted statements that the reason we have lived together for so long is "because he was gone most of the time" does have some validity, as humor always does. When Buddy quit drinking twelve years ago, his attitude was so much better that I failed to understand he still hadn't really dealt with the anger inside.

In the past several months I have noticed that Buddy's judgment is not what it used to be. This inability to deal with anger is surfacing more now. Buddy still likes to work outside with repairing tractors and farm implements. He cannot remember how to repair a lot of the things that he used to, so he has hired some part-time help to get the tractors fixed that he has now. When working in the shop, he gets angry and throws tools, hits the tractors, and screams at the dog that he is going to bash his head in (though he loves the dog very much). A couple weeks ago he left his billfold in his pants pocket and put them in the washing machine. When he realized this, we stopped the machine, and he retrieved it. Even though the crisis was over, he doubled up his fists and ran at the washing machine. I said, "Buddy, don't be angry at the washing machine. It is not the washing machine's fault—it is an inanimate object."

Tim bought a used $20,000 excavator, and Buddy has a lot of fun with it. A man from an equipment dealership called and said he would be up to look at the excavator. When I inquired, I found Buddy wanted to trade it for a $50,000 one. I called Tim and asked him if this was something he had agreed to. Tim said his dad had called him that morning, and that he had told his dad he did not wish to buy a better one at this time. Well, Buddy was going to let the man come anyway, and I explained to him that this was not right. The man would be taking time and using money for gas when Buddy knew he was not going to be trading. Buddy got mad, but reluctantly called the man and canceled. The next morning, Buddy was on the phone with someone else about an excavator. When he finished the conversation, I came into the room and asked Buddy to please leave Tim alone about buying another excavator. Buddy doubled up his fists, rose up out of the chair and screamed, "What am I going to have to do to get you to SHUT UP—RAP YOU UPSIDE THE HEAD LIKE A MULE?" I immediately left the room, so as to not provoke him further.

While Buddy has never actually hit me, back nearly thirty years ago when I was in therapy after the mental breakdown, he did grab my arm once and put bruises of his handprint that stayed for over a week. At the time of this incident, in addition, he knocked out the bedroom window. During that period, Tim did come between him and me a few times and say, "You had better not hit her." So, I know Buddy is capable of violence, and while he is in that instant of rage, had better not be provoked. I always immediately get out of the way. I will tell you, however, that while I know how to handle this, with this current behavior, I was a bit down later in the day and realized why. After an outburst, Buddy always gets extremely meek, but I feel no compassion at that time. In times past I have always let these things pass, but decided this time not to do so. Buddy is certainly not senile, so he knows well what he is doing. The following night, in a calm, but firm manner, I brought up the subject. He, of course, immediately started to put the blame on me. I said I would not accept this and pointed out that these outbursts are not just directed at me. I mentioned the washing machine, the tools, the tractors, the dog, etc. He then started talking about how I have changed in recent months. Yes, I have changed. I didn't point out at that moment that he has not. Buddy is the same person who told me before we were married about the time he was on his way to a preaching appointment and had some car trouble. He said he pulled to the side of the road, and because he couldn't get the car hood latch released, got up on top of the hood and stomped it in. After fixing the problem, he continued on to his preaching assignment.

In spite of therapy with both psychologists and psychiatrists, I had never really confronted him like I did with this current incident. Again, I'm going to attribute a lot of this change to the benefits I am gaining through writing. I feel a sense of empowerment. I, however, must point out that I was VERY stressed. In fact, within a day or so, my back was really bothering me, as it often does when I get under stress. For sure, the stress of confronting him was a whole lot worse than the stress I felt in my "just getting out of the way." Interestingly, Buddy has been quite a bit nicer since the incident. While I am under no illusion that this better behavior will last indefinitely, I feel confident that when the next occasion arises, I will stand my ground just as I did this time. I believe that the next time it will be a whole lot easier! Perhaps putting all of this down on paper will help make it so!

The Athens Years

We arrived in Athens, Alabama, where Buddy would be working on the Brown's Ferry Nuclear Plant. When we got the little silver Hicks paid for, it looked like we could stay in Athens for a while, so we decided to upgrade to a larger trailer. As these wonderful opportunities have always happened at just the right time, within the week of our decision, an ad appeared in the Huntsville paper for a used 10' X 50' Windsor for $2500. When I was a teenager, my mother and I visited pipeline friends from my childhood who lived in Illinois. When we visited in their home, I was so taken with the beautiful walnut cabinets in their kitchen. From that day, I had wanted to someday have a kitchen of walnut cabinets. The Windsor brand was one of the three best brands of the larger ten feet wide trailers on the market. As soon as I saw the ad, I remembered that the Windsor was the brand that had kitchen cabinets of walnut. Was I ever excited! This Windsor floor plan was a front kitchen model, so I had more of those beautiful cabinets than were available with different floor plans. Since we had paid $1,000 for the Hicks, we placed an ad for it at that amount, and within the week it was sold.

We had arrived in November 1970 and in December I happened to be listening to the radio—something I seldom did. There was an advertisement for a Hebrew class being taught at the local college—Athens College, then owned by the Methodist Church (it was transferred to the state the year I graduated and is now Athens University). When I mentioned this to Buddy, he was extremely interested. Before he became a minister, he had gone a year and a half to Eastern A&M College in Wilburton, Oklahoma. Buddy enrolled in the night Hebrew class taught by Dr. Bert Hayes and was enthused about this opportunity. The following semester, Buddy decided to take three classes and changed his work schedule to the night shift so he could take some day classes. Before long, it became Buddy's goal to complete a B.A. degree. For about a year, he pastored a Free Will Baptist Church in the Hanceville, Alabama, area, but it quickly became apparent that it was too hard to do so many things. That is the last church that Buddy pastored. Buddy completed the requirements for his degree and graduated in 1974.

When I graduated from high school, I had received college scholarships for various achievements but did not use them. Honestly, when Buddy started to school, I can't really say at that time that I ever intended to go to college—I wasn't thinking past being a stay-at-home mother, which I truly enjoyed. Soon I was typing papers for Buddy, and, as he admits, making some corrections, when I caught the enthusiasm for going to college myself. I took a Music Appreciation class and then decided that I would like to go full time and pursue a degree. At this point, too, I was a little more practical and realized if something happened to Buddy, I was in no position to make a decent living for the children. My dad had come to work at Brown's Ferry, also. He had found a used Spartan trailer, bought it, and he and Mother moved next to us. In 1973 Linda started first grade, and with Mother there to help out with the kids, I started to college. Though it was ten years later, I was like many who enter college right after high school graduation and don't know what they want to major in. I knew I wanted to prepare to be a high school teacher, but I wanted to major in everything. I first decided on business and music, but found the business a bit boring and dropped out of those classes during the first couple weeks. The music studies were wonderful, but I spent so much time in the music lab—trying to be the perfectionist—that I decided this major was going to require much more time than I felt, being a wife and mother, I had to give. I only stayed with those classes for one semester.

It was during this semester that I received the nicest compliment I feel I have ever received, all because of the way it was given. I was enrolled in an Introduction to Education class under Dr. Robert Murphree. As I normally do, I sat at the front of the class. We had a test with discussion questions, and, again, as I normally do, I wrote until the dismissal bell rang. Well, at the next class session, Dr. Murphree started talking about students who studied all the time and wrote and wrote when answering questions. For sure, whether or not there were others who fit his description, he was talking about me, and he let it be known he was not pleased. A few days later, with my children in tow, I was going into a local store as he was coming out, and we exchanged greetings. At the next class session, he was friendlier toward me, so I thought, "I guess he realizes I have a family—that I don't study ALL the time." I was taking Voice and singing in the college chorus and was chosen to sing a solo part in the Christmas program. At the next class session after this program, Dr. Murphree came into the classroom, looked at me, then at the class, and said, "I was at the Christmas program, and when Beverly started singing, I wanted to jump up and say, 'That's my student! I didn't know she could do that!'" This was done in such a public way, and I felt just wonderful! He went on to talk about compliments and how to give them. I can tell you that the demonstration he gave on how to give compliments remains a dear memory to me. A few months ago, my psychology professor, Dr. Slate, told me of Dr. Murphree's recent death. I told him about this, and Dr. Slate asked me if I had thanked him. I had to reply, "No." I'm sorry to say that I never even thought of telling him, "Thank you." The truth of the matter is—I didn't know how to properly receive a compliment—and still fall short in this area. Often, I just feel uncomfortable and feel somehow that I don't deserve it. It is my belief that Dr. Murphree does now know how much I appreciated him and the compliment that he gave.

Mr. Fowler, the music instructor and my voice teacher, asked me if I would sing a solo each Sunday at the First United Methodist Church in Athens, where he was director of music. The pay would be ten dollars each Sunday. This seemed like a lot of money for just singing a song on

Sunday. Today, I think back about my reaction to this opportunity—I felt it would be somehow wrong to accept money for singing in church, so I declined. How much I have changed. There's a part of me that says, "I wish I had continued with the voice lessons and accepted the position to sing." That the professor thought my potential was good enough to become a paid soloist remains a lovely thought to me.

What a wonderful change the people we met at Athens College made in our lives! Buddy soon took a religion class under Dr. Charles West. The subject came up that his daughter, Charlotte, age nine, was taking French. It came about that our son, Tim, age six, wanted to take French under Charlotte. These weekly lessons were arranged, with Charlotte earning her fifty cents or dollar for teaching. It wasn't long before we discovered that Tim was more interested in playing with her brother Philip, also age six, than he was in learning French. Charlotte's French lessons were the seed for a wonderful family friendship that has lasted for generations down to the present time. Philip remains Tim's earliest childhood friend with whom he is still in contact. I have letters that Dr. West wrote to Buddy while Buddy was in Saudi Arabia. Our families visited each other across state lines and had numerous outings together. We always visited our Athens friends when we came in from Saudi, and while I was in the U.S. and Buddy in Saudi, I would often go down from Tennessee and see his wife, Marion.

It is with fondness I remember taking our tent camping trailer to the Outer Banks of North Carolina with Linda, Tim, and Philip helping me set up the camper. Tim wanted to go hang gliding on Kill Devil Hill but was a couple pounds short of the required weight. We went out to eat and did he ever stuff himself! With adding sand to his shoes before he got back on the scales, he barely qualified. Philip wanted to hang glide so badly! In spite of numerous begging calls to his mother, she wouldn't give permission. Philip teases me to this day about how he has never forgiven me for not letting him go ahead and hang glide.

Among other trips, Philip went with us to Oklahoma, for a vacation of fishing and visiting with our relatives there.

With the grace of the Southern lady that she was, Marion always promoted women's rights. Once Tim bought her a quartz paperweight that was engraved "A woman's place is in the house . . . and in the Senate." Did she ever enjoy that! It went with her at every move she made. In her later years when time had stolen much of her memory, Charlotte cared for her. On our last visit to see Marion, at her bedside table, there was the paperweight. Even though Buddy and I were not sure Marion recognized us, Charlotte told us she talked about us after we had gone. A few months later, just days before her death, Marion wrote me a letter, and Charlotte gave it to me at the funeral. Those few halting lines were Marion's last writing.

What a difference that radio advertisement for Hebrew classes made in our lives! Buddy went on to take two years of Hebrew under Dr. Bert Hayes. He and his family became our good friends, also. Later, we went on camping trips together to the Alabama Gulf for the beach and deep sea fishing and to lovely parks in North Alabama. In 1979 Buddy came in from Saudi Arabia for surgery. We had some business to conduct in Oklahoma, and, as Buddy was unable to drive, Bert drove us back there. I was looking through some old letters the children had written when we were apart, and in one from Tim, practically every other sentence was about Dr. Hayes and his flying lessons and about his promise to fly up to Tennessee—a promise he kept—to see Tim. What a wonderful friend he has been down through the years!

We lived in Oakwood about a year and then moved our trailer to the beautiful site of an old cotton plantation in the Ripley community. The plantation house had burned many years before, and four lovely trailer spaces were made under those ancient trees where the house had been. When Buddy and I bought the Windsor, we slept on a couch hide-a-bed and gave Tim and Linda each a bedroom. After about a year, this couch seemed very uncomfortable. We found a beautiful 45'

Spartan with front and rear bedrooms—so at last, I got my "Spartan." We attached the two trailers together with a small walk-thru hall. One trailer faced one way, and the other faced the opposite. Buddy and I now had a bedroom, and he had a quiet place to study. How humorous the pictures of this arrangement are! There were so many dear people associated with Athens College. When Buddy's mother passed away in Oklahoma, our first visitors after we returned were Dr. Dan Jones and his wife, Mary Louise. Over the years, I have often wondered what they thought of our living arrangements, but they treated us with such respect. I often think of those fine people who truly did not judge people by the possessions they had. They were among the many fine people we met at Athens that were part of a moderate religious denomination, the Methodist Church. Though, in her later life, my maternal grandmother had converted from the Catholic Church to the Methodist Church, and my paternal grandparents had been Methodists until a Baptist Church, the only church in the rural area where they lived, was built, most of my exposure in life had been to people in very fundamental churches. Buddy's experiences had pretty much been with people in fundamental churches or who were in no church at all. To be exposed to a moderate way of thinking was good for our family. As I stated in the chapter on Christmas, it was after attending Athens College that Buddy first allowed us to celebrate Christmas.

What an opportunity to have had the privilege of attending Athens College! Surely, there was a monopoly of the most remarkable people in the world on the faculty there! Dr. Slate was one of them. For my whole life, the right people have come into it at the right time. How grateful I am for his friendship and wise counsel over so many years. Sometimes I sat in his office so broken I wondered how I could go on, but I always left with a new lease on life. It has been forty-two years since I first sat in a psychology class under his instruction. Even now, as I write these chapters that he so graciously volunteered to read, he is such a help to me. His thoughtful comments and words of encouragement are so appreciated. Sometimes I am almost overwhelmed at the marvelous way my life has unfolded. No way, not for one moment, do I believe it is all just by chance.

Allowing one to acquire college credit for knowledge gained outside the classroom was another opportunity for me. Because of Athens being a part of the College Level Examination Program (CLEP tests), I was able to get two years of college credit through testing. I took three years of classroom instruction in two years, thereby receiving five years of college course credits in the two years (I went the summer session between the two years). I made A's in all classes and completed three majors and a minor, thus qualifying me to teach four subjects at the high school level. The majors were History, English, Social Science, with the minor in Psychology. Ten years later I went back to college and added Mathematics to my high school teaching certification, plus got a business degree. Guess I still could have been that Business Education teacher that my high school classmates asked me if I intended to be.

A few years after I graduated from Athens, for a time, I felt a bit guilty about taking the CLEP tests. I felt I really didn't know the subject matter very well for which I had taken the tests. The tests were really designed for people who had learned the material through life experiences, including reading, etc. With taking care of the children, I really hadn't spent much time reading the classics of American and British literature and other subjects for which I was being tested. About two weeks or so before a test date, I would get the textbooks for the appropriate subject and go through them—usually, I did this during the break we had between semesters. I would read the books once and underline what I thought was important. Then I would go through and read what I had underlined. I usually tried to scan the main points again. Since I had the ability to picture in my mind and pull up the various pages, as I read the test questions, I would flip the pages in my mind. I never concerned myself with page numbers or even noticed them, but I could look at the whole page and know whether the answer was on the left page or the right page of the book, at the top or bottom of the page, which column it was to be found, etc. I know I don't understand how I could do this, but the fact is that I could. This ability allowed me to make in the 90's on all of the tests except Math. I had a general mathematics course in the ninth grade and geometry in the tenth. At that time, the high school I attended did not yet offer any algebra. So, I dreaded taking the math test; however, I bought the textbook for the degree requirements for college-level math and started teaching myself this subject. I made seventy-seven on the math test, which allowed me to get credit for the college math requirement. While normally I would be mortified to make seventy-seven on any subject, as I look back, I feel it was quite an accomplishment to be able to teach myself this subject in the few weeks that I had to give.

Well now, you may be wondering why I said that later I felt a bit guilty about getting credit for taking CLEP tests. It was a few years after graduating that I became aware that not everybody's brain uses pictures to process information. When I found this out, I felt that somehow it was like I had cheated on the tests. When I was in high school, my American history teacher, Mr. Gillespie, had said in front of the whole class, "Miss Rider, you have answered the essay questions exactly as the wording in the text. If you hadn't been sitting directly in front of me with me watching you, I would have thought you cheated." I do remember the school superintendent, Mr. Collins, saying that I had a photographic mind. I really did not think much about it at the time—I really didn't know what that was. Never mind, I didn't feel guilty very long. I was just grateful that I could get my bachelor's degree in two years. I saved not only time but money, too!

When I was a little girl, I used to sit out under the big oak tree in my granny's yard and daydream about traveling around the world. She would say, "Beverly, there's a lot to see in this country. Isn't the good ole U.S.A. good enough for you?" I would answer, "Yes, but . . ." I wanted to see the rest of the world, too. Even during my senior year of high school for our yearbook, as each was asked their dreams for the future, I wrote that I wanted to be a high school history teacher, but that my biggest desire was to travel around the world. Up to this point in my life, that dream was seemingly forever shoved in the background. Then a most wonderful thing happened! Our Western Civilization professor, Dr. Caudle, and the head of the art department, Mr. Johnson, jointly planned a month-long trip to Europe for students to study Renaissance history and art. Mother was glad to keep the children, and Buddy graciously agreed and paid for me to go. For me, what a dream come true!

When I tell friends I'm writing my life story, they immediately think I am going to tell of my travels and indicate they want to hear about them. Quickly, I assure them that I am not writing a travelogue, but I am more than ready to share thoughts about this wonderful trip. I always give credit to Dr. Caudle for teaching me how to travel. I feel she helped me be a traveler, not a tourist. She had made several trips to Europe with Arthur Frommer's book, *Europe on Five Dollars a Day*, in tow. In December of 1974, inflation required that we use *Europe on Ten Dollars a Day*. I still have my well-marked copy with which to reminisce. Excitement floods my soul as I think of a week spent in Rome, a week in Florence, days in Venice, Paris, Strasburg, Zurich, Munich, Luxemburg, train rides beside the castles of the Rhine, the Swiss Alps covered in snow, the Italian countryside, and traveling Icelandair and landing in Reykjavik, Iceland, in the middle of a huge snowstorm. Though it's been over forty years ago, the pictures in my mind are as vivid as though it were yesterday! We were a group of about fifteen or so. Dr. Caudle had booked us in pensiones and bed and breakfast places where we could be accommodated. Ah, for me, it became the REAL way to travel. Luxurious hotels don't hold an allure for me. I much prefer to meet the locals. It's amazing how much one can learn and communicate even if one does not know the local language.

Some who get to know me have described me as being an intense person. I take that as a compliment, though it's not always intended that way. I DO feel things very, very deeply and very strongly, so I choose to use the word intense in that manner. Oh, I remember the night we all went to the opera house in Strasburg, my first live art music performance, and saw Johann Strauss's *"Die Fledermaus."* The walk in the gently falling snow to and from the opera house added to this enchanted evening. I sat transfixed with the orchestra, the music, the vocals, the impeccably dressed crowd, the beauty of the building— just everything! Then there was Florence, certainly one of my favorite cities in all of Europe. When we had a week in one place, we were given a free day to do whatever we wished. Most of the others went shopping, but as I was accustomed to doing things alone, I went off on my own to touch and feel the art of Florence—statues that just line the streets.

When we had our week in Rome, again, alone, I went back to the Vatican Art Museums to stand and weep at Michelangelo's *Pieta* and other works of art. It was this day that I did something I now view as very foolish. I decided to walk out on the Appian Way, that famous ancient Roman road I had read of so often. I don't know how many miles I walked, but I found myself completely out of town and in deserted countryside. There was nobody in sight, and I was immersed in solitude when I realized somebody was coming up behind me. It was a young American man who overtook me and started a conversation. I became scared. Nobody in our group had any idea where I was going—I hadn't even planned the day myself. I became fearful this man might rape me—maybe even kill me—and nobody would have a clue as to where I was. Quickly, I made the decision to head back to the city, and he followed along with me the whole way. Fortunately for me, we just had a pleasant conversation about history and our visit to Rome.

All of my life, when I am really stressed, I tend to lose my appetite.

This trip had an overwhelming effect on me! While it was good stress, to be sure, it WAS very stressful! It's hard for me to put into words the enormous emotions I had about the wonderful experiences I was having, and, how in my life, such a short time before this trip, it would have seemed an impossible dream. So . . . I wasn't eating much. At one point, Dr. Caudle took me aside and asked if I had enough money for food. She offered to loan me some money if I needed it. While I did have to budget carefully, I did assure her that I had enough money to buy adequate food. Perhaps she and Professor Johnson had privately discussed things about me, perhaps not. I guess it was in Rome, however, that Mr. Johnson took me aside and said, "Beverly, it is a pleasure to see you so touched by great art. I, too, can stand and weep before great works of art, but—to not eat?!" What could I do but offer a feeble explanation of something I could not myself put into words—just an oft-used, "You wouldn't understand."

Our last few months in Athens found me doing my practice teaching. Out of my majors, I chose to do it in History. That is the only time I've taught History, but it was enough that I can say I fulfilled the dream I wrote for my senior yearbook. It was such a wonderful experience! My supervising teacher quickly decided I was capable of handling the classes and chose to take time off and use many days she had built up for paid leave. I was teaching American History to high school juniors and was it ever fun! In my education classes at Athens, I was taught the importance of keeping something interesting by using different methods to achieve goals. I tried to do something different every day of the week. We would write plays about events in our history and enact them. The students would get so interested they would even carry it further than I intended—even wanting to dress the parts. I had the students interview their grandparents or other elderly relatives and friends about various subjects as they came up. We had guest speakers, films, and show and tell days among many other things. Toward the end of the semester, the teacher had a talk with me. She asked me if I wanted a job teaching at Athens High School. I told her that we were leaving in the summer to accept jobs teaching part-time at a religious college in Oklahoma. She named a certain girl and asked me if I really knew who she was and what she was doing. I replied, "No." She said, "Well, she is taking a petition throughout the school asking kids to sign that they want to hire you for next year." She continued, "Her father is on the school board, so I wanted to tell you that if you want a job here, you can probably have it."

After those wonderful years in Athens, a new adventure was about to begin!

Oklahoma and Tennessee

Buddy and I accepted part-time teaching positions at Hillsdale Free Will Baptist College in Moore, Oklahoma, so in August 1975 we sold the Windsor and hooked on the Spartan and moved to Oklahoma. As his dad had done before him, my dad divided some of his property among his three children, so they could benefit when it was most needed. Dad had a contract for sale with owner financing on the house on Lake Eufaula. That is the portion he gave me. He gave Sue the house in Red Oak and John some land in the country to try to make things as fair as possible. We didn't live in the Spartan long. With the payments coming in from the sale of the Lake Eufaula house, we used them as collateral to buy a small house with 10 acres in Newcastle, Oklahoma, near Moore. The house wasn't much by today's standards—it had originally been three small rooms, but a couple more small ones had been added in recent years. Underneath the two-room addition there was a one-room basement/storm shelter, so needed there in tornado alley. The layout was the living room, the kitchen, the dining area, two bedrooms, a bath, and the utility room. This time it was Tim who slept on the couch, as Buddy and I took one of the bedrooms. Linda's room was only big enough for a twin bed, but she had her privacy.

Buddy taught New Testament and Pauline Epistles, and I taught Classical Literature and Humanities. As we just had Bachelor degrees, the understanding was that if we were hired the following year, we would need to begin studies toward advanced degrees. Though I surely wasn't really qualified to be teaching at the college level, I sought permission from Dr. Hayes to use some of the test questions he had used in the Classical Literature class I'd had under his instruction. He, of course, was glad to help out. Since I had majored in English and History, and had taken courses in Art History and Music, I loved teaching these subjects from the integrated perspective, and in the Humanities course, I could do just that. As I wanted to be able to teach totally without notes, I studied far more than the students. I was really in my element, though, and am happy to say that many students, among them preachers much older than I, who had complained to the administration about not seeing the relevance of Humanities as a required class, came to me at the end of the year with a complete change of heart. For their appreciation, the class gave me tickets to the Oklahoma City Symphony, so I introduced our children to the excitement of listening to live art music.

Buddy did not enjoy the classroom setting as much as I and applied for a job in Saudi Arabia. He was accepted and left for this job near the beginning of May. It was arranged for me to administer the final exams for his classes. The administration offered me a job to teach at Hillsdale the following year, but I declined. To teach at Hillsdale, I had signed a document stating I would not attend movies, I would never wear shorts, I would never wear slacks outside of the home, I would not swim in mixed company, etc. While it was not an issue for me to sign this document, and I kept the requirements faithfully, I was beginning to not want to be confined to such narrow thinking. Previously, Buddy had imposed similar requirements on our family, but during his time at Athens College, he began to soften a bit. I elected to move to Hartsville, Tennessee, where my parents had moved at the close of Dad's job at Brown's Ferry.

We advertised our house for sale, and it sold within the week. I used the Spartan for storage, had it moved to Red Oak, and the children and I moved to Tennessee. We only had to stay with my parents briefly, as a most marvelous thing happened—as they often do! My cousin Charlene and her son Lyle came for a visit. We all took our little pop-up tent camper and went to the Smokies for a vacation. I was sitting in the laundry reading the newspaper (sounds familiar, eh?), and there was an ad for a 12' X 68' three bedroom, 1 ½ bath Vindale mobile home with an expanded living room (large slide-out at this area of the plan). Along with the Windsor, it was another of the three best brands of mobile homes on the market. While we had lived in Athens, I had looked at new ones on a dealer lot and dreamed. They cost over $10,000, but, never-the-less, I got a copy of the advertising brochure, chose the plan I would like, and saved the literature. To this day, I still have the brochure. The mobile home was only a few years old and immaculate—the same plan I had marked in the literature! I bought it for $4,900.

How exciting! One of the things I really liked about these larger Vindales, in addition to their beautiful solid pecan paneling, was the fact that they did not have built-in furniture like most mobile homes. It meant I could pick and choose furniture just like I would get to for a real house. When we moved in the little house in Newcastle, Oklahoma, Buddy had said I could take $1,000 and buy furniture. I wanted to buy antiques, so I promptly went out and bought some antiques that were practically worthless. When I went to the library (after the fact) to check out my purchases, I quickly became aware that I had better study—buying antiques was not for amateurs. So, when I moved to Tennessee and got my second chance, being the thorough person that I am, I launched a year-long study into nothing but antique books. I wasn't willing to buy something just because I liked it—I wanted it to meet certain criteria. How neat to be living in such a wonderful old state. We lived near the Kentucky line, so I had two old states to explore for purchases. It became a wonderful, satisfying hobby. Soon I had furnished the Vindale with eighteenth and early nineteenth-century cherry, maple, and walnut pieces. In fact, when I wanted to add them to my insurance, as the furniture was worth more than the trailer at that point, the request was denied. I couldn't insure antiques, jewelry, etc. and be living in a trailer.

When September rolled around, and it was time for Buddy's first leave, we decided to go to England for three weeks. At that time, there were tax advantages for staying out of the U.S. for a required amount of time, so we decided to do this for the first year and use the tax savings to more than pay for our trips. The children and I met Buddy—with a copy of Frommer's guidebook in tow—in London. We rented a car and spent three weeks traveling around England, and, as luck would have it, Fluor, the company Buddy worked for, was delayed in acquiring his visa back to Saudi. So, we had another three weeks to wait for the visa and thus added Scotland and Wales to our itinerary. Buddy's expense allowance was for nice hotels and restaurants, but with us staying in farmhouses, bed and breakfasts, and eating where the locals ate, we had money to completely pay for the trip for all four of us without even having to dip into our tax savings.

One of our favorite family memories of this wonderful trip to the British Isles comes from the Cotswolds in a little village called Stow-in-the-Wold. It was nearing eventide, and we were on the lookout for the little handmade B & B signs that would be posted on the side of farmhouse roads. One appeared. Upon inquiry, the farmer told us that he was already full for the night. We, of course, asked if he knew where we might get accommodation. He said, "My mum does B & B's in the village, but she is already closed for the season." He hesitated, but then said, "Mum just can't turn away children, though, so I'll ring her and see if she will accommodate you." "Mum" took us into her tiny, cream-colored stone cottage, typical of those for which this area is so famous. What a night to remember!! She had been a nurse and had served in India and other parts of the British Empire. What a Rudyard Kipling! Tim and Linda sat wide-eyed until the late hours of the night listening to her riveting stories of World War II. She was present at the bombing of Coventry and made that history lesson come alive with her first-hand account. When days later we visited the bombed-out shell of the Coventry Cathedral, our thoughts took on such personal meaning.

This lady had no refrigerator; she kept her milk, butter, eggs, etc. in a cellar behind her house. She set up a card table in the tiny living room and brought us the same breakfast we had each morning in England—rashers of bacon, fried eggs, toast, and stewed tomatoes with sometimes a spoon of pork and beans added to the plate. Up to now, most of our tomatoes had been canned, or tinned, as the British would say. Though my dad enjoyed sliced tomatoes when they were in season for breakfast, it was not a normal breakfast food for us, and, quite frankly, we were pretty tired of them by this time in our trip. Our hostess assured us that we were in for a treat. She happily announced, "I knew you would want your stewed tomatoes, and I didn't have any, so I rang up my son to have him bring up some from the farm." We all looked at each other with a carefully placed sigh. Each plate had a lovely, small freshly stewed tomato on it. Tim and I ate ours, but as soon as our proprietor left the room, Buddy and Linda asked me to put their tomatoes, with skin still intact, in my purse. The lady came back in the room and was so pleased to find the tomatoes gone that she quickly said, "I'm so glad you are enjoying the tomatoes. I'll bring you some more." Tim, who did not like tomatoes at all, quietly ate his, but this time—it had seemed too late to refuse her—my tomato joined Buddy's and Linda's in my purse. Our hostess was so happy that her efforts had not been in vain that she brought us yet a third serving of tomatoes. Tim, yet again, ate his tomato, with the other three going in my purse. Well, by now, I REALLY needed to handle my purse with tender, loving care. As it came time to leave, along with the goodbyes, there were warm hugs all around. Yes, my purse was on my arm. As we drove away and reached the end of the block, it was with great trepidation that I slowly opened my purse. How the tomatoes had survived the hugs is beyond me, but every tomato was still intact. None of us wanted to hurt the grandmother's feelings, but it was Tim, even though he disliked tomatoes at any meal, who expressed in deed as well as words, "I wouldn't have wanted to hurt her feelings for anything in the world."

In January, it was time for Buddy to have another leave. We thought it would be better not to ask to again take the kids out of regular school for this alternative education, so Buddy and I decided to meet in Spain without the children. As it turned out, for the three weeks I was gone, it had snowed so much back in Tennessee the children were out of school most of the time anyway. Who knew? Buddy and I crisscrossed Spain by public bus and train transportation. As always, I tried to include as much as possible in the trip—Madrid, Toledo, Segovia, Avila, Sevilla, Cordoba, Granada, etc., again staying at small pensiones and bed and breakfasts. If Buddy got tired of being dragged to history and art museums, historical sites, and to see grand architecture, he would stay in the room and rest, and I would do it alone.

By ship, we crossed the Straits of Gibraltar to Morocco and spent a couple nights in Tangier. As I look back on my life and think of the things I wish I could do over—things I deeply regret—an event in Morocco comes to mind. We hired a car and driver along with a guide to take us to the countryside and the beautiful coastline of Morocco. Now, of course, guides always want to take you to special shops where they get a commission on your purchases. Yes, I was fascinated with a beautiful caftan as well as other things which I did not need and had spent a fair amount of money. I'm not particularly fond of bargaining to establish the price of something and had not only grown tired of it but was leery of offering almost any price or the article in question would be considered sold. Once, for my first offer, I offered one-eighth the asking price for a coverlet which I didn't particularly want anyway and had hardly got the words out of my mouth when it was considered sold. I was in this frame of mind when, on our ride in the countryside, we happened on some children selling items they had made. One boy, probably about ten years of age, had made a little guitar-like musical instrument from a turtle shell, sticks, seashells and other things. I was quite taken with it and wanted to buy it. He probably started out with an asking price far beyond what he expected to get, but as we bargained back and forth several times, he did seem genuinely disappointed when he accepted my final offer. I carefully hand-carried this little instrument throughout the rest of our visit to Morocco and Spain. As Buddy and I were at the airport with me flying to the States and him back to Saudi Arabia, I had the instrument in my hand. I was burdened with too much luggage—even hand luggage—that's for sure, and Buddy offered to take the guitar back with him. He assured me he would be careful with it and bring it with him the next time he came home. He hung it on a wall in his room, and, as luck would have it, someone else took a fancy to it and stole it from his room. Perhaps it seems silly, but I've often thought of the look on the young boy's face as I bought the little hand-made instrument, and felt that somehow if I hadn't bargained so much with him, maybe I would still have it. That very day I bought it after we had pulled away, I was filled with regret. Here I was over in a country and spending in shops far more than the shop owners were often expecting to get, and yet I bargained with a little boy over a few cents.

In the early fall, Buddy needed a medical procedure and came to Canada to have it done. The children and I drove up to meet him in Toronto and had a great time driving through the countryside to Montreal, from where he flew back to Saudi. While on that trip, we all rode "The Polar Bear Express" train to Moosonee in the Arctic Circle, and visited the Dionne Quintuplet Birthplace in Quebec, among other things. Buddy and the children did quite a bit of successful fishing, and, for a few days, we enjoyed cookouts with a couple we met at the cabins where we stayed. We corresponded with this couple down through the years, through their divorce and other hardships of life, until there was one year that I no longer heard from the lady. It is with a touch of sadness that I wonder what happened to her.

When Buddy went to Saudi Arabia, I, like many others, often asked, "What's it like? Tell me what it's like." His answer to others as well as to me was always the same, "There's no way I can tell you what it's like. You would just have to see it for yourself!" How badly I wanted to do just that! Only a very small percentage of expatriates who worked in

Saudi had their families there. Though it was considered very unlikely, through Buddy's exceptional ability and advancement, soon after the children and I arrived home from Canada, via a detour of the highlights of New England, paperwork arrived for our preparation to join Buddy in Saudi Arabia. Another wistful dream had come true!

My Years in the Middle East

Saudi Years – The First Week

Sunday night, September 25, 1977, a 747 jumbo airliner landed at the airport in Dhahran, Saudi Arabia. Tim, who had turned thirteen that month, Linda, who was ten, and I, age thirty-one, stepped off that plane into a blast of heat and humidity that I, with experience of the heat and humidity of the summers in my native Oklahoma, had never before felt. By the time we had cleared customs, six other 747 jumbo jets had landed from various parts of the world. There was no luggage carousel. We just entered a huge room where people were throwing luggage from all these planes into one big heap. This pyramid quickly became much higher than my head. Welcome to Saudi Arabia!

Eventually, we found our own luggage. Tim and Linda's suitcases were intact, but mine, a large Samsonite hard side, had literally come apart at the seams. According to Fluor's inaccurate preparation information packet, even shampoo and toothpaste were hard to come by in the remote location to which we were going; therefore, I had certainly over-packed. I carried the two pieces of my luggage out to Buddy with items spilling out as I made my way through the throngs of people. Did all of this really matter? Not at all. I was way too excited about the newest adventure of my life!

The children and I had spent three days in Amsterdam on the way over. Fluor provided ten percent of the cost of airline tickets for spending money. With my experience traveling inexpensively, I was able to use this money to pay for our little break, and I felt it was fun to be able to do so. We stayed on the top floor of an old canal house with no elevator—getting our luggage up and down the stairs stands out in my memory—but, oh, the view! We went to art museums and the Anne

Frank House, then took a boat out to seaside towns to see the Dutch windmills. With memories of *Hans Brinker* in our heads, we rode in canal boats, wishing the canals had been frozen so that we could have seen the people ice skating. These were the types of short breaks I tried to do each time we came in and out of Saudi.

Our newest home was called 'Udhailiyah. It was a construction camp of about fifty families. We lived in structures that were more like plain, but well-built, double-wide mobile homes. There were two models—a two-bedroom plan for those couples who had zero or one child and a four bedroom model for those who had more than one child. Several hundred men on single status lived in a separate section of this camp, also. There was a very tall chain link fence with barbed wire at the top surrounding the camp, and we entered and exited through a guarded gate. Even though we were in our own little enclave, there were rules to follow—especially for the women. We were not allowed to wear shorts outside our houses, though we could wear slacks in the camp. There was an Olympic size swimming pool, but the women had certain days when we could swim, and the men had others. There were no movie theatres in Saudi Arabia, but in the camp, there was a large room with a projector where a limited number of movies would be shown. A lot of women had trouble adjusting to these rules, but they were not a problem for me. After all, it had only been a couple years since I had signed a paper that I would abide by very similar rules. The rules got a bit more rigorous when we left the camp. I have often been asked if I had to wear a veil. Western women in the Riyadh area and in the western provinces had to wear one, but here in the Eastern Province, it was not a requirement. When we left the camp, however, we did have to wear loose fitting clothes that covered our arms and our legs. Women are not allowed to drive cars in Saudi Arabia, so the company provided various means of transportation, depending on one's needs.

There was a cafeteria in the camp for feeding the men on single status.

Families were allowed to eat there if they paid for their meals. That is where we ate the first couple days after our arrival, as Buddy had just gotten possession of the house and had no food in stock. Two days a week the Arabian American Oil Company (Aramco) provided a bus for shopping in our nearest town, the city of Hofuf, about forty miles away. There was a small one-room commissary at the camp, but it had a very limited supply of food. I was eager to get on that bus, not only to get groceries but to experience life in Arabia.

Hofuf, along with Damascus, Syria, is considered one of the oldest continuous settlements in the world. Arriving there did seem like a time warp. Was this a movie set or a real-life scene from the Old Testament? Donkeys pulled carts in the street. Huge shallow baskets about three feet across were mounded with spices that fueled the air with exotic aromas. Gold chains hung in draperies, and gold bangles and pendants filled baskets waiting to be scooped up and put on a scale to be weighed for would be purchasers. There was a huge mud fort that had been built in Ottoman times, about 500 years before. In the center of town was a small park with an elevated iron cage-like structure. I was quickly informed that this was the place where beheadings and stonings took place. In the meat markets, chickens and lambs and goats hung openly, with the accompanying swarms of flies. I was sickened. The fruit and vegetable markets, likewise, had more than enough flies. Ladies from the camp took me to the best grocery store, a small one-room place maybe 15' X 30'. A thick layer of dust covered the canned goods. Rats were hopping like kangaroos—I later learned they were actually called kangaroo rats. I didn't know whether to look up or straight ahead or concentrate on my feet. There was an old chest type deep freezer like one my granny kept on her back porch when I was a child, only this one was a lot more rusted than Granny's. I looked in. There were three pieces of meat, poorly wrapped with torn coverings exposing the white freezer burn of the contents. I walked around, then finally chose the least obnoxious piece of meat, picked out a couple cans of vegetables, and made my way to the check-out counter. As I laid the items down, at that VERY INSTANT, from outside came the loud chanting of the muezzin. The store clerk said, "Sorry, we do not sell in time of pray."

"Time of pray" for us ladies meant it was time to make our way back to the bus to be taken back to our camp at 'Udhailiyah. It was a first for me all right—the first time I had ever gone grocery shopping and returned with nothing! When Buddy came in from work that night, he quickly inquired, "What's for supper?" After a brief description of my shopping choices, I hesitantly replied, "Well, I've decided we will just eat in the cafeteria." To understate the situation, in a heightened audible tone, Buddy said, "I did not go through all I've done to get you over here to eat in the cafeteria!" The next morning I sat myself down on the couch and said, "Okay, Beverly, this is what you wanted. You wanted to come over here so badly—in fact, you even prayed to come over here! Now, what are you going to do about it?" Was I going to ask for a plane ticket back home, as I was told many women did, or was I going to adjust?

I learned to spread the flour out in the sun so most of the bugs would crawl away and then sift it as a backup measure. Quickly, I realized what happened to at least some of the expired items from the States— they were sent to Saudi Arabia—and if we were going to eat, I'd better consider them perfectly fine. I will add that the camp commissary did get better around the time that shipments of food arrived and that when something came in, I'd better grab it, freeze it, or whatever, as it would quickly disappear from the shelves. I did purchase vegetables from the market in Hofuf, even though I tired of bargaining, as was expected, over the price. I learned to avoid the kangaroo rats and get my items to the counter before "time of pray." One thing I could never bring myself to do, however, and that was to buy the fly encrusted meat hanging in the meat markets.

Friday is the holy day of the week in Islam, so Thursday and Friday are the equivalent of our weekend of Saturday and Sunday. While men working directly for Aramco had both days off, men working for contractors such as Fluor, only had Fridays off. A bus went from the camp to Hofuf on Friday, but the ladies of the camp only used the midweek bus. Their husbands took them by car for shopping, an outing, etc. on Fridays. It was a risk to use the cars because they were supposed to be for business only, and, though everybody did it, Buddy would only occasionally break the rule. On the first Friday we were there, I was eager to take the children to show them Hofuf. To say it was a risk to be on the roads is an understatement. As the locals believed everything was determined by Allah, they didn't mind passing on a hill, etc. They genuinely believed that if it were their time to die, they would; if not, they wouldn't. The driver of a car always had to be prepared to leave the road if he were being met head-on. Buddy cautioned me to sit near the middle of the bus, as it was usually the people at the front or at the back that were killed in a wreck. It was with these admonitions that Tim, Linda and I boarded the bus for Hofuf on our first Friday in Saudi Arabia. The only other passengers were two young Arab men. When we arrived, I asked the driver what time the bus would be taking us back to 'Udhailiyah. His answer was, "Ma-fee go back." In my few days in Arabia, I had already learned that the oft-used "ma-fee" meant, "There is none," or "No." I turned to the children and said, "The bus isn't going back." We were on our own.

As I previously stated, Hofuf was a completely Arab town—not Westernized at all. To my knowledge, there were no Westerners living there, but I was not going to let a little thing like not having a way back home deter me from the excitement of sharing Hofuf with the children. Now, these were pre-cell phone days, so I couldn't just pick up a phone and call Buddy. I did go to a call-center and place a call to both the house and his office but did not reach him. So, for several hours Tim, Linda and I made our way through the "zouk" (market), absorbing the sights, sounds, and smells of its various sections where gold, cloth, food, spices, and other items were for sale. It was Tim who began to get a bit anxious and asked, "Mother, don't you think we should start looking for a way back home?"

Hofuf was a Friday tourist destination of sorts for the men who worked in the northern part of the province. Buses would bring them down from their camps for a day in Hofuf. I saw several people who were white, but it's amazing how many white people in the world do not speak English, and there were more than a few that day in Hofuf. Finally, I found an American man who had come down on a bus with others from Ras Tanura, about a hundred miles to the north. He was sympathetic to our plight, but I knew I should keep looking. To take us home, these people would have to ride for over an hour the forty miles south and then the forty miles back before continuing north to their camp. In the late afternoon, we finally found a man who had brought a few men from 'Uthmaniyah, a camp for single status men that was near ours. They were in an extended cab pickup, and he would ask three of the men to ride in the pickup bed and give us their seats. As we were making these arrangements, the American man from the Ras Tanura group came running up. He said, "I have talked with the people on our bus, and they have agreed that we will take you back to your camp. I have a wife and children back in the States, and I have been thinking all afternoon that if they were over here and stranded in an Arab town, how much I would want somebody to help them!" I was glad we didn't have to accept their gesture of kindness. Our first week in Arabia was thus burned into our memories!

The food item I missed most in Saudi Arabia was milk. I am a big milk drinker—I drink milk when other people drink coffee and soda pop. I never could get used to powdered milk or canned milk, and that was all we had. It has been a long time since I've eaten a bologna sandwich, but back then I liked them occasionally and missed having them. We could never get that soft, doughy, almost nutrition free bread that we grew up on in the States. And lettuce, all we had was a type of small leaf lettuce. It was not that longed-for crunchy and almost nutrition free iceberg lettuce that we thought so necessary on a sandwich. We could get frozen bologna occasionally but had to use dry mustard powder mixed with water. I remember well the day that some jars of genuine French's yellow mustard arrived in the commissary. I eagerly anticipated the next time some bologna would arrive. What a treat! An actual—well, almost anyway—honest to goodness bologna sandwich!

Speaking of iceberg lettuce, after we had been living in Saudi for over a year and had moved to Abqaiq, a larger camp closer to the more modern city of Dhahran, one day Buddy came in with a head of iceberg lettuce. I was ecstatic! I started jubilantly jumping up and down! I wanted to know where he had found it, and the next question was, "How much did you pay?" He said, "Eight dollars." I never even winced, I said, "Well, that's okay. It's worth it." I have often told others, "Buddy has never brought me flowers, but one day he did bring me a head of lettuce!"

Life in Saudi Arabia

What's it like? What's it like living in Saudi Arabia? I could show you pictures. I could use many descriptive words for many pages and still could not capture what it's like. Of all the places I've been in the world, I would say that one DOES have to experience Saudi Arabia. Words and pictures are not a sufficient substitute!

'Udhailiyah, as it was away from the cities where more comfortable amenities could be found, was considered a hardship area. Buddy was paid extra for working there. The experiences one could have away from more settled areas greatly compensated for any perceived hardship! Almost every time I passed through the guard gate as I left the camp, my camera was in tow. It never failed—if I had forgotten it, I was sorry. We might come upon a camel train with hundreds and hundreds of camels being led by Beduoin. A masked, not veiled, regal young woman might be riding on the lead camel. We might come upon a watering trough with a herd of camels, each trying to get its share. The everyday occurrence of a camel riding in the bed of a Toyota pickup (these were the small ones—not the larger ones Toyota now builds) always brought a smile. While stopped to let camels pass, a curious one might poke his head in our vehicle window.

Seeing the black goat hair tents that the Bedouin lived in and moved from place to place, as they herded their goats and camels, also occurred often, and I longed to take a peek inside. One day we were riding around in the desert, and my wish came true. Guess Buddy's job had been in that area for a few days, at any rate, one of the men recognized Buddy and invited all of us to their enclave of tents. The interiors were filled with beautiful hand-woven carpets, and as we were led from tent to tent, at each home we were served the traditional cardamon laced coffee and sweet mint tea (with no bathroom in sight). The masked women were in awe of Linda's and my white skin and would come up to rub their hands on our faces. One of the men, who spoke some broken English, made us understand that these women had never before seen a white woman. Oh, how I longed to take pictures, but that would have been not just a breach of etiquette; it would have been forbidden, as no photos of women, even masked or veiled, are permitted in Saudi. The warm welcome and friendliness that we felt is a mark of Bedouin hospitality. This is a memory we have to hold in our heart.

One of Buddy's Saudi co-workers in the office announced that he was getting married, and we were invited to the wedding. I eagerly anticipated the event! We rode on a bus, along with a few men from the office, to a village deep in the desert. Arab wedding celebrations last for several days. We only experienced one night of the celebration, but what a night it was! Soon after our arrival, Buddy and Tim were taken to a separate location where the men were celebrating, and Linda and I were taken to the quarters where the women's festivities were taking place. There was lively folk dancing going on, and Linda and I were invited to dance. All of the younger women were very friendly, but I remember that one older woman seemed very displeased about our presence—especially our attempts at dancing with the others. She did nothing overt, but with veils off, her displeasure registered on her face. Traditional foods with whole sheep, rice, fruits, etc. were brought out on platters. Again, as is traditional, we sat on the floor and ate with our right hands. The bride came out, all dressed in a gorgeous, bright red, floor-length dress. I was told this was the traditional color and style of an Arab wedding dress. Then, later in the night, she came back out dressed in a beautiful, white traditional Western wedding gown. At one point, Linda and I were escorted outside to join Buddy and Tim and the men in a procession through the village. I can still see and hear the Arab men, dressed in their long white thobes, with their swords flashing and crossing in the air, leading a dance through the streets, accompanied by musicians with their traditional Arab instruments. We did not see the actual wedding vows performed—that was going to be saved for another day. I was told it was not like our wedding ceremonies, but more of a prearranged agreement, with proof of virginity shown. Attending this wedding celebration was an experience that none of the other Western families in Arabia that I have known were privileged to have.

Aramco provided many perks for the fifty or so families in our camp—one of the advantages of being in a remote, hardship location. They tried to keep the women happy by doing something special for them at least once a month. One such event was an outing to a location where few people in the world have traveled. We flew on an Aramco plane into the heart of the Rub' Al Khali, known as "The Empty Quarter," the great desert with the highest sand dunes in the world. Looking out the plane window at this ocean of shifting sands is one sight I was able to capture on film. Could an artist do justice to this sight? No. Do the photos do it justice? No, they do not. It is another of those things in life that one experiences and has to hold on to the moment. We landed on a salt flat and got out of the plane into unimaginable heat, but scrambled up dunes long enough to get photos made of ourselves in this vast portion of the globe, the heart of which even the Bedouins don't roam. The plane ride back to our civilization reminded me of a mountain drive where reversing the trip provides scenes entirely different from those that one saw on the way out. As the winds shifted, so did the dunes and that lovely palette of hues.

Tim and Linda went to the International School in our camp. There were about twenty students for nine grades and kindergarten, so it was almost like one-on-one tutoring. As would be expected with all the oil money floating around, the latest textbooks and the finest equipment were provided. Field trips for the children included a weekend of camping in the Rub' al Khali. Linda has just come in and reminded me to put in that Tim climbed up a sand dune on this trip and found a wildflower growing. It is not completely an empty quarter, as lizards and other small animals can be found. When we moved to Abqaiq, which had a larger school, I taught part-time, classes in reading, to multinational students. It was a nice experience to teach these polite students from various countries. This was, unfortunately, a far cry from my experience teaching students in an American school a few years later.

The children studied Arabic, and Tim, who has a gift for languages, became proficient enough that he could read a newspaper in Arabic. This ability for the language prompted an invitation from one of Buddy's Arab friends, Mohammed, to take Tim across the country to the western province of Asir, his homeland. He kept emphasizing that Tim would REALLY be proficient in the language by the time he got back. We were getting ready to come to the States on leave, and no way was I going to agree to leave Tim behind. Mohammed offered to take our family on such a trek, and we fondly thought how neat that would be; however, it is one of the events that did not materialize. We could never get our schedules to coincide.

Aramco provided a plane that seated fifty or so people to fly into Dhahran on a weekly basis to shop for items that we couldn't get locally. I seldom signed up for it, as the flights could be a bit harrowing. I have a tendency toward motion sickness, and often this plane would bounce around in the shamals (dust storms) beyond my comfort zone. The pilot frequently had trouble getting the landing gear down, and his attempts to correct the problem often resulted in maneuvers that were quite scary. Many times I swore off ever getting on that plane again! While it may seem exotic to ride a plane to go shopping, it wasn't considered as such. Once, a young Arab was sitting by me, and he very disdainfully said, "I wouldn't be on this plane, but my car had an accident." You read that right, his car had the accident—he didn't.

Usually, when there was a car accident or even a bus accident in Arabia, there were no survivors. With huge oil field trucks, head-on collisions from passing on the wrong side, etc., the remains were just scraped up off the pavement. When asked how many got killed, often the reply was, "Oh, four or five people (or whatever the number) and some women." While we were living in Abqaiq, about forty or so miles from Dhahran, I developed pain in my neck area and was sent for a while on a daily basis into a doctor in Dhahran for therapy. I was provided a car and driver. If we approached a hill, he invariably started to pass. I would start screaming for him to get back in line. His reply, "Inshallah," meaning "God willing," that if it were his time to die, he would, and if it weren't, he would not, did not satisfy me. I would reply, "Maybe you and I are not scheduled to die at the same time." Now, all of my life, I had heard people talk about "if it were their time to die, they would" (even my beloved grandpa said this about tornadoes), but this was the first time I had ever been around people who TRULY believed it! Actions DO speak louder than words!

One of the Aramco ladies in the main camp in Dhahran organized small, personalized trips to Egypt. Though I'm not a tour-group person, this is one trip—not a standard tour, for sure—that I'm so glad we took. The children and I joined a group of about a dozen others for an unforgettable Christmas and New Year, with their adjoining days, touring by land, river, and air, that ancient land. We approached the pyramids by camel, and as we first glimpsed them on the horizon, it was as though we were on a journey from the past. We toured the antiquities of the Nile Valley by excursions from our riverboat. We flew to Aswan to see the dam and to Abu Simbel. We stayed in a hotel there that was taken over the following week for the Shah escaping Iran.

After the other members of our tour returned to Saudi, the children and I continued to the States via Rome and Venice, Italy. As we stood inside the Roman Colosseum, Tim observed, "It's hard to get excited about the engineering of the Romans two thousand years ago, when we have just come from seeing what the Egyptians built over four thousand years ago." Were we jaded travelers, or what?

It was on our return from this trip to the States that we stopped for a few days in Athens, Greece. The children—and anyone else, for that matter—know to expect the unexpected when traveling with me. I will go where angels fear to tread, and this is intensified if I'm traveling with Frommer and a "ten dollar a day" guide. Such a remembered experience happened in Greece. We had walked up the hill at sundown to see the Sound and Light Show at the Parthenon. I felt the prices the taxi drivers wanted to charge at the end of the show to take people back into the city were exorbitant. We were staying, on a recommendation from Frommer, at a tiny little B & B on an out-of-the-way side street in Athens. Now, this one REALLY ended up being out-of-the-way. When we got back to the city proper, I wanted to take a taxi back to our lodging. The taxi driver did not know the name of the street. I spoke no Greek, and trying to show him on the map did not seem to work. We rode and rode and rode around the city. I would get excited when I recognized a street name. I had begun to get worried that this driver was really doing this just to collect a large taxi fare. He gave up, stopped the car, and motioned for us to get out. He refused to take any money at all, so he certainly wasn't doing all of this driving deliberately. From looking at the map, I realized we were completely on the opposite side of the city from our B & B. By this time, it was well past midnight. There were not many street lights, few cars, and certainly no taxis. There was nothing to do but start walking. We walked and walked and walked, fearful out there in that darkened city. With all my childhood traveling, fortunately, I was reading maps before I started to school, and sometime around three o'clock in the morning, the children and I arrived at our B & B and fell into our beds exhausted. It was the next day or so that we were in a large department store with a huge marble staircase. The soles of Linda's tennis shoes were worn so slick that she stumbled on the top stair, and before she could prevent it, had slid all the way to the bottom!

Now that I'm a bit older, I reflect on some of the things I've done;

and it DOES unnerve me! My guardian angel surely must work overtime! It was on this same trip to Greece that I did something else I would not do at all at this stage of my life. I didn't want either child, because of our nomadic lifestyle, to be deprived of developing musical opportunities. While I was in the States, I bought an electronic piano keyboard to take back to Saudi, so that I could give the children music lessons. When we arrived in Greece, the customs authorities would not let me take the instrument through without paying huge customs fees. No amount of explaining that I would be taking it on to Arabia in a few days availed. I was told I would have to leave it and pick it up before we continued our journey. There were two airports in Athens, one for flights coming in from America and some European countries and another one across town for departures to points such as the Middle East. So, the keyboard was at one airport, and we would be flying out of the other. We took our luggage to the airport of departure, and I was told I would have to have a police escort to pick up the keyboard and return to my point of departure. I left the children standing at the curb with our luggage while I got in a car with officials to go get the keyboard. It was with a sigh of relief, as we returned to our departure airport that I saw Tim and Linda there waiting for me. At this point, time was of the essence, and I placed a call to Buddy in Saudi to let him know I was under police escort, and, under their watch, checking the keyboard, but that we might not make the flight. As Buddy picks up the story, he and a co-worker were working on their office telephone at the exact moment I called. They held two wires together while Buddy talked. Midway in the call, we got disconnected. Buddy turned to the other man and said, "Beverly said she is under police escort and may not make the flight." The man, said, "What are you going to do?" Buddy answered, "Nothing. I'm not worried about it. Whatever has happened, she'll get out of it. She always does!"

Buddy has a very open personality and gets along well with all nationalities. He invited many people into our home for a meal. Since

I love to cook, many got a taste of my version of American Southern cooking. If the guests were Muslims, I knew not to fix pork, since eating pork is forbidden in their religion. It is with humor that we recall a couple of men who told me if they ate pork, they would have to be vaccinated. Only one time did we have an Arab woman and children as guests in our home. This was the wife of a co-worker of Buddy's, a younger Arab man who let his wife come in and take off her veil in front of Buddy—unusual for sure. What an enlightening evening! They had two children of early school age—a boy and a girl. The mother and children had never eaten with a knife and fork. Soon after arriving in Saudi, I had started taking Arabic classes, so in my broken Arabic, I could communicate after a fashion. The lady wanted to go through the house and touch many things, including my clothes. She wanted me to try on my bathing suit. Then she was curious about the swimming pool and asked me to take her out to see it. I had seen Arab women in full abaya and veil carefully lifting the bottom of their clothing to wade in the Arabian Gulf, and I could see the spark of this new found knowledge whirling in her brain. She wanted to know if she, too, could come and swim in the pool. Uh oh! "How is one going to be kept on the farm after they have seen Paree?" The evening conversation took an interesting turn as we discussed the rising cost of things— food, clothing, etc. As brides are purchased in Saudi Arabia, without missing a beat, the Arab man, in the same sentence that he discussed the rising cost of watermelons, said, "And the cost of women—a woman like her used to cost (x amount of riyals)—now she would cost 3x."

Once, when we went to Hofuf shopping, there was a large white banner maybe three feet high and ten feet long at the little park with the chopping block that was in the center of town. There were large black letters in Arabic on this banner. Though I could speak a little Arabic, I could not read any. Little did I know the event that these words were advertising. Within a week or so, we found out. As the children and I got off the bus for a shopping excursion in Hofuf, the air was charged with electricity. Throngs of people were frantically pushing and shoving and making their way in one direction—toward the center of town. The intensity of the noise of the crowd was heightened all out of proportion to any semblance of normalcy. As some of the ladies from our camp and we were pushed along, suddenly, an American man appeared and instructed us to get into a nearby building. He explained that a stoning was taking place. A woman who had been accused of adultery was being stoned to death. We had been told that if foreigners were present at a stoning or beheading, the locals wanted to push them to the front, so they could see how seriously forbidden acts were taken. We had heard rumors of Americans who had thought they wanted to see such, but then just started throwing up when they got their wish. As we sat there in that building and listened to the agitated crowd, it seemed like hours and hours, though it probably was no more than two hours at the most. Finally, the den of agitated shouting and screaming ceased, and the noise level returned to normal. It was with a bit of a sick feeling in our stomachs that we ventured out for just a bit of shopping before we returned to the bus to go home.

Several times we were invited to Arab homes. Linda and I were usually permitted to sit with the men not only while we ate, but throughout the evening. We would be taken to the back quarters to be introduced to the wives—often multiple—and children, and we could sense that touch of envy as we would be allowed to go back in with the men. As always, we sat on beautiful carpets while platters of whole roasted lamb or goat, with eyes and tongue intact, surrounded with mounds of rice pilaf, would appear. The eyes of a sheep or goat were reserved for guests, but the men were the lucky recipients. Buddy said they were very good. The tongue is also considered a delicacy for guests, and Linda and I got to sample a portion of it. I can tell you that I easily see why it is an honor to be served the tongue, as it is quite good.

Sometimes we were invited for picnics and would be taken to an oasis. On one such occasion, Buddy teased me about why I wouldn't go with Faisal, an Arab co-worker, to the meat market in Hofuf while he chose chickens for the cook-out. No, thank you, I just sat in his air-conditioned Mercedes and waited until he returned with the ingredients for our meal. Well, at least I wasn't too squeamish to eat the finished product!

Every two or three weeks or so, we would have a lot of the Western guys who were in Arabia on single status in our home for a meal. I would start preparing the food two or three days in advance. Once we were all sitting around enjoying the last morsels of our meal when I realized I had twenty-six baked potatoes warming in the oven. With me not willing to waste food, Linda still comments that we ate mashed potatoes, hash browns, potato cakes, potato bread, etc. until we had used up all twenty-six potatoes! This was a great opportunity to experience people from European countries such as England, Scotland, Ireland, Belgium, the Netherlands, and Germany, as well as those from various parts of the United States.

When one entertains a lot of people, there will always be one or two that will become special and be added to our friends for life. Out of this group, Jackie Corbett, from Ireland, became this special friend. We had outings together, such as hunting desert roses (rock formations) in the desert and camping on the Arabian Gulf. On several occasions, we joined him in Ireland for escorted trips around that beautiful island, once even to Northern Ireland. We became friends with his brother, Tommy, and wife, Turi. They visited us in Tennessee when we lived there. It was fun staying in their home just outside Dublin. From his sister, Helen, and Turi, I learned many tips about Irish cooking. Tommy and Turi would take us to music clubs in Dublin for real Irish music and patiently wait for me, as I sat mesmerized with the music and dancing, long after they wanted to be home and in bed for the night. Helen has come to our homes, both in Tennessee and South Carolina, several times for extended visits, even after Jackie's death in 1999. She has traveled with us in our various motorhomes to New Orleans, Oklahoma, Arizona and the Grand Canyon, and Colorado, among other places. We still speak to her several times a year and consider her among our dearest friends.

To show their appreciation for our hospitality, some of the men, Arabs, Pakistanis, East Indians, Europeans, and Americans brought me gifts—an item native to their country, a piece of cloth for a dress, a table linen, or a piece of jewelry. Once, I answered the door, and a man was standing there with a brown paper sack. He, of course, did not come in, as it was the middle of the day, and I was home alone, but he wanted to give me something if I would promise to use it for myself and not give it to Buddy. I agreed. He handed me the sack and left. When I opened the sack, I immediately sat down. In it was one thousand riyals, the equivalent of $3,500 U.S. dollars. Diamonds had never been on my wish list, but the next time we were in the States, Buddy and I were shopping, and a salesman mentioned that diamonds were a controlled market and that they were soon going to escalate in price. Buddy turned to me and said, "Why don't you use the money given to you and buy yourself a nice diamond?" Buying the beautiful two-carat diamond that I wore every day for the next twenty-five years was truly purchased in that spur of the moment. It turned out that the price increase truly was not a sales pitch, as the diamond became very valuable. I later gave it away, with the money from its sale used to build an addition to a school in Uganda.

Another gift remains indelibly in my memory as a definite tale from Arabian Nights. Buddy, the children, and I were at the curb of the airport unloading our luggage for a trip back to the States, when, suddenly, a black Mercedes appeared, and it was Faisal Q. He said, "I just heard you were leaving, and I wanted to come say, 'Good-bye.'" He asked me to get in the car. He took my hand and said, "When I heard you were leaving, I wanted to get you something, and I got this small token." He apologized for getting this in a hurry. This small token was a heavy, gorgeous European style 18k gold bracelet which he placed in my hand. I definitely save it to wear for only the most special occasions and always fondly remember the night. But oh, the best part for Tim, Linda, and Buddy, anyway, was that Faisal summoned people to take our luggage and escorted us in front of the crowd for immediate check-in. We were treated like royalty and whisked away, much to the consternation of the hundreds waiting to board this aircraft.

Often I got letters from people asking me if I ever got bored. Sometimes swarms of flies came in with the dust storms. On one such occasion, I wrote back that I didn't see how anyone could have time to get bored if they were swatting flies all day. Was I ever ready to give up and ask for a ticket home, as some women did? One day using a tea towel to swat flies was just not very effective. I went down to the commissary in hopes they would have a fly swatter to replace the one I'd worn out. I was told the proverbial, "Inshallah," if it were God's will, they would get some in soon. Furious, I came home and called Buddy at his office, explaining the situation like this, "I have just come from the commissary after hearing that if it's God's will, they will get some fly swatters. I don't know if it's God's will or not that I get a fly swatter, but I will tell you this: I EITHER WANT A FLY SWATTER OR A PLANE TICKET, AND I REALLY DON'T CARE WHICH!" In a few moments a car pulled up in front of the house, and Buddy got out with a fly swatter.

It was in Saudi Arabia that I had one of the most profound experiences of my life. In those days before cell phones, calls to the United States from Saudi Arabia had to be booked through a call center. It then usually took two or three days to be able to place a call. When it came to your slot for the call to be put through, you would be called at any hour of the night or day. Calls were very expensive, costing around $3 a minute. Though some people allotted some time each week or so to call home, we just never did that. My granny had had a stroke in December 1978 and was quite affected by this. In January, my cousin

Bonnie, who is a nurse and lives in Idaho, had come down to help care for her. It took from ten days to two weeks to get a letter from the U.S. to Saudi Arabia, so I was always way behind on information regarding Granny's condition. One day in mid-April of 1979, I had a feeling that I should call home. I mentioned this to Buddy, and he said to go ahead and book a call if I felt I should do this. About three days later, the operator called to say it was time for my call to be placed. I gave the operator my parent's number in Tennessee. The phone rang and rang, but there was no answer. Before the operator hung up, I quickly asked if, while she was on the line, she would place one more call for me. I asked her if she would call Oklahoma, and I gave her my granny's number. Again, the phone rang and rang with nobody answering. I was just about to hang up when someone picked up the phone. It was my cousin, Bonnie. She said, "Beverly, everybody is walking to the church for Granny's funeral. I was already out of the yard on the street when I heard the phone ring and decided to come back and answer it." She added, "Everybody is here, Beverly, everybody but you." Over 7,500 miles and eight time zones away, at that very instant in time, I was allowed to be there, too.

Abu Dhabi and More

Buddy developed some health problems that required surgery, and we came back to the States for this. One shouldn't make major decisions while other traumatic events are occurring in one's life, but we did, and paid for it, too. We had been fairly careful with money and had enough saved to buy a house, with money left over. We intended to go back overseas but thought it would be nice to acquire a home to live in when we were in the States. We had not looked at any houses yet but were driving to Gallatin (TN) and saw a "For Sale by Owner" sign in a yard. It was the corner one-acre lot of a subdivision. This lot bordered the highway on one side and on the other side, Corp of Engineer property leading down to the Cumberland River. Buddy liked the idea that it was near a river, as he loves to fish. We stopped and went in to look at the house. It seemed to be something we would like, so I told Buddy I would go get the kids to come look at it to see what they thought. Buddy wanted to stay with the owners and visit while I drove the ten or so miles back to our trailer. When I arrived back with the children, Buddy said, "I have already bought the house." Now, he didn't ask the people if they would take less than the asking price; he just bought it a few minutes after we looked at it. He had asked the owners if there were any restrictions on the property, as he likes to do mechanical work on vehicles and tractors, and they told us there were no restrictions. As we had cash money, we set up the appointment with a lawyer to finalize the deal in a matter of days. At the closing, the lawyer mentioned the covenants associated with the house. The owners were sitting there but were very quiet. Buddy brought up that they had told us there were no restrictions. The lawyer said, "Do you want to see the covenant?" We, of course, said, "Yes." This was brought and read. There were the usual things associated with most subdivisions—no mechanical work on cars, etc. Obviously, because of the owners not telling the truth, we could have canceled the deal and received our earnest money back. This is what I suggested we do. Buddy then said, "Well, I have given my word that we will buy it, so we will." I couldn't believe this! It was totally irrational.

At this point, I want to say that in our marriage, I had been extremely passive, never putting forth my opinion about much. It was when we went to Saudi that I began to come out of my shell and start exerting some independence. I wouldn't have thought my change was noticeable to others, but, indeed it was. On one of our vacations home, we were in Athens at a gathering at the home of a friend. Several professors from Athens University were there. Buddy and I both had had a history class under Dr. Pabst, and she commented to me in the presence of the group, "Saudi surely has been good for you!" I had never been to a social gathering before with her; she only knew me from the class. So the very fact that I contributed to the conversation elicited the remark. When one is trying to change, one just takes baby steps. So, in answer to Buddy's comment that we would still buy the house, I said no more. Would I be this passive today? No way!

The house was filthy—absolutely filthy! How a one-year-old house could get this bad is beyond me. All of the used trailers, cars, etc. that we had ever bought were well cared for and immaculately clean. Buddy and I started working. If the bathrooms had ever been cleaned, it had been months. At times, we even got down with a toothbrush to clean. We repainted the interior of the whole house. For one whole week, we worked long, long hours. Late one afternoon, we were finally finished. We laid our brushes down the final time, and Buddy said, "I don't want this house. I want to sell it. I don't want to move in." I was mortified! I did something no one should ever do. I had bottled up sixteen years of perceived hurts in a marriage where I had been told repeatedly that, "You don't ever have an original thought!" I had swallowed that lie and believed that I had nothing of value to say. That day thoughts came gushing out of me—they may not have been original, but they were thoughts none-the-less. I DIDN'T EVEN RAISE MY VOICE, but what I did was sit down and put my back against the living room wall (there was no furniture). I asked Buddy to do the same. I started talking. I started with the earliest thing I could remember concerning Buddy. I talked in a normal tone of voice. I was slow. I was methodical. I gave details. You may think I remember a lot of details that I have recorded in the previous pages I've written during this past year. They are nothing compared to what I said that summer day in 1979. I quoted whole conversations—many of them— what I had said, and what Buddy had said. I talked ALL night long! I never stopped. I used to say I talked sixteen hours, one for each year of my marriage, but I'm not sure about that. I DO KNOW this. It was daylight the next morning when I stopped talking. Buddy sat in deafening silence. When I finished, I stopped. Buddy looked at me and carefully said, "Beverly, I have no doubt that everything you have said is true. The conversations you quoted sound like you, and they sound like what I would say. What I can't get over, though, is the mind that could contain all of this. I am just amazed, that's all I can say. I am amazed." In a later year in our marriage one time Buddy commented, "Beverly, do you have any idea what it's like to be married to somebody who can quote whole conversations that took place years ago, and I can't even remember what I said fifteen minutes ago?"

We contacted a realtor and put the house up for sale, with the asking price $55,000, the price we had paid for it. Interest rates had skyrocketed, and several months later it still had not sold. We were in Abu Dhabi by then, and Buddy said, "Drop the price $10,000." I came back to the States to close a deal where we got $45,000 and a few hundred, with the realtor taking a reduced commission.

On November 4, 1979, we were aboard an aircraft to Abu Dhabi, United Arab Emirates, and while we were still in the air, rumors circulated throughout the plane that American hostages had been taken in Iran. We didn't know what to expect when we landed at the Abu Dhabi airport to begin our next adventure. Soon, from our apartment window, we could see the guns that were placed on the beach. Linda and I only got to stay about a month when a note from Fluor was slid under our door asking us not to leave the apartment, but to prepare to evacuate. As we readied for our journey back to America, Buddy flew in for a quick good-bye. I stayed in Tennessee for a few weeks until things settled down, then returned to Abu Dhabi, leaving Linda with my parents to finish the school year. I then came and brought her back to Abu Dhabi.

Abu Dhabi is one of seven sheikdoms (absolute monarchies ruled by a sheik) that comprise the United Arab Emirates. It is on the Arabian Peninsula and is on the Arabian Gulf. Even though we were in a conservative Muslim country, life was very different from our stay in Saudi Arabia. Buddy's job site was out in the desert with only dirt oil field roads connecting it to the main highway. He lived in a construction camp there and flew in and out for work. Those who had family status were housed in high rise apartments in the city. The men would fly in after work on Thursday and leave early Saturday morning to be back at work for the week. So, the women and children were living on their own in a city, at that time, of about one-half million people. Linda went to the American School across town. She rode each day by taxi. Middle Eastern countries did not provide for high schools for Western children, so after the ninth grade, students had to go to European or other boarding schools or live with relatives in the States. Tim chose to go to Hawaii Preparatory Academy, at company expense, on the big island of Hawaii, so that he could learn to scuba dive. He traveled alone to visit us on holidays and school breaks.

Living in a big city insulated us from the kinds of local experiences that we had enjoyed in Saudi Arabia. We lived on the thirteenth floor of our high rise and sat on our balcony to see the motorcade the day President Jimmy Carter came to Abu Dhabi. Since we were in the heart of the city, if the weather was cool enough, we could walk to whatever shopping we wished to do. At other times, we took taxis, which were plentiful. As we women were on our own for six days out of seven, we formed close bonds with each other. We still had to make our own entertainment, so we had a lot of teas. I brought my accordion over, and those who were inclined would congregate at my flat and sing. Sometimes this would be just women, but other times it would include the men for a Thursday night sing. My close ties with Maureen and Ian Cook and girls of Scotland came out of our mutual love for music. When Maureen went home on leave, she brought me back music books of her beloved native songs. We maintain our friendship with postcards of our trips, letters, and phone calls. She and Ian have not been privileged to visit me in America, but I spent a lovely week in their home in Scotland, with Maureen taking me to the best shops to buy tweeds.

We still needed to dress conservatively, but women were allowed to drive cars in the Emirates. In fact, I got my driver's license, with photo, to have for a souvenir. The company leased a few houses on the beach at Sharjah (an emirate close to Dubai) for employees to have for relaxation on our weekend. We could sign up for cars and for a house. Once, I drove a car to Sharjah, with Buddy along, of course, just for the thrill of doing it.

The architecture was stunning in all of the Emirates. The huge mall in Sharjah was one of my favorites. The airports, the mosques, office buildings, and shops were like a fantasyland, especially when they were lit up at night. Dubai even had a museum of the history and culture of the city—a good one, too, I might add. The food was outstanding— truly some of the best restaurants in the world are there. Linda says her favorite restaurant in the whole world was "The Golden Falcon," located in the next building from our apartment. We could just call on the phone, and in due time, our meal would be delivered to our door.

Speaking of food, I love to cook as well as I like to eat. I don't remember the circumstances of our meeting, but I met a lady from India who agreed to teach Indian cooking. I contacted other ladies in our group, and we enjoyed taking cooking classes from her. Most of all we looked forward to the finished product. I remember the day she said she would do a curry the following week. I mentioned that I really didn't care all that much for curry powder. She said, "Curry powder, what's that?" So, I learned curry powder is a shortcut, and not authentic at all. Then we had a lady from France teach us French cooking. These were among the diversions we enjoyed as we tried to fill our time.

It was in Abu Dhabi that I did another thing for which I'm not qualified--I taught kindergarten for a semester. Maybe that is the most tiring thing I have ever done. Those kindergarten teachers really earn their money, as far as I'm concerned. I had about twelve students and an aide. Our class was for half a day, and yet I arrived home every day ready to fall into bed for a rest.

There was a Dairy Queen in Abu Dhabi, down on the Corniche (seaside avenue). About once a week or so, I would go down for a burger and fries. One day when I finished and was waiting for a taxi, I looked up and there stood a young Arab man beside me who had been in the restaurant. He was extremely good-looking, a real live Omar Sharif, that's for sure! He invited me to his villa. I nervously said, "No." He didn't take "No" for an answer. He offered me money. I said, "No." He specified an amount of time. Again, I said, "No." He reduced the time and increased the monetary offer. The dialog continued, and by this time, I was really getting nervous. It seemed unreal that no taxi had come along when normally they were right behind each other any time one walked to the curb. Finally, with the monetary offer up to about $300, with me still saying, "No," a taxi pulled up, and I jumped in. Low and behold, a taxi pulled up right behind us, and he jumped in and started following us. I frantically struggled with my

Arabic, explaining to the taxi driver to turn left, right, etc., so that we could lose him. I was an absolute wreck by the time we arrived safely at the apartment building. Then I was scared to ever go back to the Dairy Queen, so that ended my lousy hamburger treats in Abu Dhabi. Several months later, I was walking down the main street of the city, when I saw him on my side of the sidewalk. We were very close before I recognized what had happened. We made eye contact; he recognized me, and I recognized him. His face sought to remain expressionless, though a touch of disdain slightly appeared. He just kept walking. A small smile comes to my face as I remember how seriously disturbed I was over this neat little incident.

There was one incident that might not have ended so well. One day I decided to go down to the main mosque and watch the worshippers perform their prayers. I, of course, was on the outside looking in. Truth be known, I probably should not have gone down there, but, being ever curious, I did. After prayers were over, as I was walking back toward the heart of the city, I distinctly had the feeling that someone was following me. The feeling became more intense, and I turned to see a very sinister looking man following me. I was near a carpet store and quickly dashed in. I explained, in my broken Arabic, what was happening. The owner acknowledged that I could stay as long as needed. This man stayed near the store for considerably over an hour. While there, I thought, "Well, I'm in a carpet store, so I might as well shop for carpets," so I did just that. Finally, I had the all clear and got a taxi back to my abode.

It was in Abu Dhabi that I first tasted horse meat. In the feasting at the end of the Muslim holy period of Ramadan, because of all the festivities, food got scarce. I wanted to buy some hamburger and was pleased to find it when I thought there was none available. My meatloaf tasted especially strong. We women were comparing notes and soon found out that our new supply of hamburger meat was ground horse.

Yuk! No, I didn't try to use it all up like I did with the twenty-six baked potatoes!

As I close out this chapter about my years in the Middle East, I want to say, in all sincerity, that I, overwhelmingly, was treated with the utmost respect in both Saudi Arabia and the United Arab Emirates. I think about drinking cardamon laced coffee in tiny cups that were swished out in the water of a kid's plastic sand pail, with the men in the Beduoin zouk in Hofuf. They helped collect for me, week by week, as they became available, my collection of antique brass Arab coffee pots. I think of the kind man in Abu Dhabi who owned the silk fabric shop. He had lots of beautiful French silk material, but when I explained I was looking for the less expensive Thai silk, he didn't just tell me where to go; he walked out of his shop and up the street to show me where I could purchase it. When I tried to thank him for his kindness, he said, "No, I do not deserve thanks. You are a guest in my country. This is what I should do."

What a wonderful opportunity to experience the Middle East in the late '70s and 1980. Perhaps now, I often muse, there is a generation arisen "who knew not Joseph."

The Half-Way Point

The job in Abu Dhabi drew to a close in December 1980 and Buddy, Linda, and I flew to Greece to wait until after the New Year to fly home. For income tax purposes it was better to wait until after January 1 to come into the States. A lot of our travels as a family were arranged around the tax benefits, as Buddy does not care much for travel for travel's sake.

We rented a car and spent a wonderful three weeks driving all around Greece, as far north as Macedonia and Thessaloniki, near the Bulgarian border. We spent Christmas Eve in a small bed and breakfast without any heat, and it was frosty, to say the least. On Christmas day, we found a tiny restaurant open, and, speaking no Greek, were invited into the kitchen to point out what we'd like to eat. I always plan trips well ahead, so our itinerary was full. I research and then fit in as much as possible, as I don't want to get home and discover something that I hadn't known about that I wished I had seen. As we flew out of Greece toward home and looked out the window for our last view of the Parthenon, Buddy announced, "Well, now I have seen every major rock pile in Greece. Thank God that's over!" Everyone on the plane within hearing distance gave a hearty laugh.

So that pretty well sums it up. I would describe a trip as wonderful, and Buddy was just glad "that's over." I am well aware that is the way writing is—it's told from one's personal perspective. In the type of writing I am doing, the burden is on the author to be as authentic as possible, yet bias creeps in. One should be thorough, but one is often selective, too. The following is an example. When I wrote about our family attending the Arab wedding, I didn't tell the whole story. It was a wonderful opportunity, and I wanted to keep a positive note throughout my retelling of the event. Now, as is often said, "for the rest of the story." Buddy actually didn't want to go. Even that very night, he said he was really tired, and tired of working with Arabs all day, and he just wanted to rest. I was REALLY upset. NO WAY did I want to miss such an experience! Words got heated. Yes, I raised my voice! I said I was going to get on that bus and go anyway, whether he came or not, or whether he liked it or not. I wasn't about to miss that opportunity for the children or myself. There were a few guys from the office that were going to be on the bus, but Linda and I were the only females, and I can tell you for sure, just the children and I going without Buddy would not have been acceptable! Well, Buddy relented and went and actually seemed to enjoy himself, after all.

Completing my writing of the final days of my stay in the Middle East represents half of my chronological life thus far. At this mid-point of my writing, I feel it's time to take stock of what I've written. Definitely, there will be a shift of tone just as there was between my life until marriage and then another shift with the Athens years. Perhaps I should review what I've written thus far and review the letters and writings from years past that I wish to include.

When writing about oneself, it's hard to keep from using "I" a lot. By the very nature of this writing, "I" is used often. When I started this project, I said, sincerely, that my first priority was to write for my family, both immediate and extended. I felt it would help them understand me, our family life, the reasons I did many of the things I did. I felt it would be beneficial, for the same reasons, for Sue's and John's children. Even though some months ago I realized this writing was probably more for my own benefit than for others, even those close to me, I now know it more than ever. But the writing does continue to weave its magic for me for my continued growth.

As I begin writing about the second half of my life, I know there will be a lot more introspection, maybe one should say, a lot more opinion, and I DO want to be fair. It is not my desire in any way to be vindictive—that would not produce the desired result in my continued healing. In this first half, I have not used notes nor an outline. I do not expect to write any differently in the second half. I write as the words flow. I try to remember to say a little one-sentence prayer each time I sit to write. I ask for guidance for the words to come that should. So far, I'm satisfied that they have.

Back Home

Back Home, 1981-1985

One of my favorite pastimes is looking at house plans. Whether I'm troubled about something or just relaxing, I can get immersed in planning houses. While we were in Abu Dhabi, I did not have any house plan books to look at, but I drew in detail my ideal house and brought the plan home with me. It was about 1600 square feet, three bedrooms, and two baths. My dad had bought an acre in Trousdale Co., Tennessee, and placed three mobile homes on it for rentals. Nearby was a house and three and a half acres on a deep water creek, a tributary of the Cumberland River. It had a boat dock and was ideal for a fisherman. It had been built in 1976, but the owner decided country living wasn't for her and wanted to sell it in 1977. At that time, I inquired about the price but did not look inside, as Buddy thought the price was too high. This house on the creek would have been much more ideal for us than the one we bought in 1979, and I regretted that we hadn't bought it previously. When we came back in January 1981, it was available again. When we looked at the house, it was UNCANNY! The plan was almost exactly like the one I drew while in Abu Dhabi. It was unbelievable how the layout and room sizes were almost identical. As this place was not part of a subdivision, it had no covenant restrictions—again, ideal for us. What a beautiful, one of a kind setting! The property backed up to Corp of Engineer land behind the house, and hundreds of acres across the creek were Corp property.

Buddy's next job assignment was in Venezuela. He did not like the situation at all and only stayed a week. He was told that if he quit, he would be quitting Fluor. Never-the-less, he made the decision to leave. Linda did not want to go to boarding school, so we decided for me not to consider going back overseas. I would stay home and let her go to the local school. Tim had enough credits from Hawaii Preparatory Academy to allow him to finish high school in three years, so he graduated from Trousdale Co. High School. Buddy applied to other companies and was soon working back in Saudi Arabia on single status. We moved our Vindale mobile home down to our property and let Mother and Dad move in it.

With our move to the Trousdale County area, another interesting adventure in my life began. Mr. and Mrs. Lewis Crook lived about a mile from our new place. Lewis was part of "The Crook Brothers" band. They were the oldest band playing on The Grand Ole Opry, having joined soon after the Opry was founded. Lewis was in his mid-eighties and had recently had heart surgery. He did not drive at night but wanted to continue playing for the square dancers in his Saturday night slot at the Opry. He and Dad became acquainted, and when this need was mentioned, I volunteered to drive Lewis each week to the Opry. We, of course, were not part of the audience. We spent the evening backstage in the dressing rooms and lounge area. I knew nothing at all about country music. When I was at my grandparents' home, Grandpa looked forward to the Lawrence Welk show on Saturday nights—there was no such thing as listening to the Grand Ole Opry. When I first started taking Mr. Crook to the Opry, I didn't want to appear so ignorant of the music, so I quickly ordered the Smithsonian Collection of Country Music. I thought I could become knowledgeable in this genre of music fast. This collection gave me a good foundation of the roots of country music, but it wasn't much like most of the music that was currently playing at the Opry. I never grew to like much of the music I heard on stage, but what I did enjoy was the jam sessions backstage. That's where the real country music was played.

Certainly, one of the most exciting things about being backstage at the Opry was meeting all of the stars, and during the over three years that I took Mr. Crook, I met many big names. I have always liked to study people, and I got to do a lot of that on those Saturday nights backstage. Most of the stars were very accessible, though a few had security guards who, necessarily so, kept them protected. I want to share my observations of some of my favorites. Loretta Lynn was one who usually came in for just her performances and was heavily guarded, but there was one time I found myself seated next to her while she awaited her turn to go on stage. The movie about her life, *A Coal Miner's Daughter*, had recently been released. As we struck up a conversation, I told her that my mother was a coal miner's daughter, and that when I took Mother to see the movie, she cried. Loretta said, "When I saw it, I cried, too."

Of all the big names I met, Dolly Parton is one I really admire. She probably came only two or three times while I was going, but one could quickly observe that she had not forgotten her roots. She was not only gracious to Roy Acuff and his band members in dressing room #1, but equally so to Lewis and Herman Crook and their band in dressing room #2. When Dolly was scheduled, Lewis would say to me, "Dolly's here. Let's go out to her bus and visit." I'm sure she wouldn't remember me, but on those short visits, I so appreciated her kindness. Though she probably would rather have not been bothered, she was always so courteous and respectful. I just have to say this. She is so very, very pretty. I wish I could have said to her, "Dolly, I'm sorry you have to be so 'made-up.'" She is so beautiful without her wig and stage make-up on, much more so than with it—at least in my opinion.

Charlie Pride came once. He and his wife sat back-stage, and I got to visit with them. I found them both delightful. Of all the people I met, Charlie Pride definitely remains one of my all-time favorites. We really hit it off well.

I didn't go out to the stage area much. I preferred the music backstage and the visiting. Saturday night was like a weekly visit with the people who make up the bulk of the Opry, the regulars. When I had the mental breakdown in December 1986, Mr. Crook had to replace me with someone else to drive, so my weekly associations ended. From that era of my life, though, I gained another friend for life, Euneta Kirby, Bashful Brother Oswald's wife (he played banjo in Roy Acuff's band). I enjoyed visits in their home, and though Oz passed years ago, Euneta and I have remained friends. She and I talk regularly by phone, and I stayed overnight with her when I went to Nashville last year. In fact, we went backstage at the Opry and reminisced about our many Saturday night visits there in the '80s.

It was soon after we moved into our house that I reconnected with Dr. Slate. I was such a troubled person, and I knew that I needed help desperately. I wanted to go for psychological counseling. When I got the minor in psychology, it was mainly in order to try to help myself, but that wasn't enough. I read quite a few psychology books written for the layman—self-help books of the pop psychology genre. All of this helped, that's for sure, but it wasn't enough, and I knew it. I remember well the day I first called Dr. Slate. I can see myself standing in the kitchen, facing north looking out the living room window—and calling. I started trying to explain who I was. I vividly remember his answer. He said, "Beverly, you need no introduction. I remember well who you are. I would never forget you." I asked him if he knew any psychologists in our area and explained that I wanted to go to one. We finally had the money for me to try to get the help I needed, and for me, the lack of money had been the reason I hadn't sought help sooner. What I hadn't counted on was Buddy's reaction. He said, "No. Solve your own problems. You are the strongest person I ever knew." How much I now realize it's the wise person who asks for help. There's no shame in admitting you need help and asking for it. It's not a sign of weakness. Buddy said, "No," and I'm sorry to say that I thought that was the end of the story. Just as when I was a teenager and asked permission to go to a party or event, and my dad said, "No," I not only didn't talk back, it didn't even cross my mind to question the answer.

Down through the years, I had continued to hang on to and rehash details in my mind of horrible events I had experienced as a child. As I said earlier, this was especially pronounced if I experienced a perceived current hurt. I knew this was abnormal. There were positive steps I took to overcome frightening events. Tim loved to target practice. He never cared at all for hunting. He just loved to shoot and was exceptionally good at it. With our house bordering Corp lakefront property, it was an ideal place for this sport. When he and a friend would spend time shooting, it was an extremely traumatic event for me. I have never related this to him, but when he would be target practicing, I used to go to bed and get under the covers. Every time the gun would go off, I would jerk really hard. I knew it was up to me to try to deal with this behavior, and I did this time after time until gradually I became less frightened and began to jerk less and less at the sound of the gun. Guess one could say that I desensitized my reaction to the sound of a gun going off. While the fear never left completely, it did eventually get bearable enough that I didn't need to go to bed every time he wanted to target practice.

There were times during this period that Buddy was unemployed. Life was not pleasant. He had started drinking alcohol while we were overseas, and Buddy has that addictive personality that cannot seem to exercise moderation in many areas, whether it's eating, drinking, working, or playing. Buddy was not a happy drunk. It didn't take more than a couple drinks before the anger boiled out of him, and Buddy didn't stop at a couple drinks.

The Trousdale County School system needed an English teacher for the second semester for the Junior High students, and I was contacted. We needed the money, so I eagerly accepted the position. It was quite a challenge to go in behind another teacher during the midterm and try to implement my style of teaching, which was stricter than the previous teacher's had been. The school principal expressed commendation on my handling of the situation, but it was clear that disciplining kids was very tiring for me. I arrived home at the end of the day exhausted. All teachers know that the best way to learn a subject well is to teach it. It is a minor regret to me that I didn't teach long enough to really learn the subject well. Perhaps the whole year would have been enough, but half a year was all I taught English.

At the beginning of the following year, a position for an English teacher became available at a nearby town, and the Trousdale Co. principal notified me of the opening. With my credentials in hand, including the requested college transcript, I eagerly went for the interview. Fairly soon into the interview, that principal opened my transcript with its dates, all A's, majors, etc. and just folded it up. He gave me a straight look and said, "Can you even relate to children?" I offered a feeble, "Yes." As I walked out of his office, I knew I'd better get some qualifications for a subject where teachers were really needed if I wanted to count on getting a job.

So, it was in 1983 that I enrolled in Cumberland University in Lebanon, Tennessee, to seek certification to teach high school mathematics. As most math courses build on each other, I knew it would take me a couple years to complete the requirements, so I decided to pick up enough business courses to get a business degree, also. In 1985 I graduated from Cumberland, ten years after graduating from Athens.

It was while I was taking a computer programing course at Cumberland that I had one of the most profound dreams that I've ever had. To recount it, I was taking a computer programing course called Cobol. With rapid technological advances, the course was probably obsolete by the time we finished it, but it did involve a lot of complex thinking; so, for that reason alone, our time certainly wasn't wasted. Problems to be programmed in this computer language were often many pages long—thirty or more were not unusual. Each student was given a complex problem for which to write the program. This involved weeks of work. Our semester grade was primarily based on this task. As luck would have it, page after page of my program worked, but there was still a glitch. I could not get it to run completely correctly. Even the professor decided to weigh in on it, and even HE could not get the problem solved. Every professor who has ever had me for a student knew that not only was I interested in learning but that "A's" were very important to me. He finally gave up, but said, "Beverly, don't worry. Just go ahead and turn it in. You are going to get an "A" for this course." While it's true that I DID want an "A," I also sincerely wanted to solve the glitch and get this program to run properly. This was a night class, and the last night of the class before we were to turn our work in, I went home a bit despondent. In the wee morning hours I had a dream, and in this dream, the problem was solved—I was given the details of how to complete the program. When I awakened, I immediately grabbed paper and pencil and started writing down what I had dreamed, lest I forget some of the descriptive details. At the time, I did not have a computer at home; I used the college computer lab. I wasted no time putting on make-up. I just threw on my clothes and rushed to the computer lab. It only took one try. I put everything I had dreamed into the computer, and this program worked like a charm! Was the professor ever surprised! He was nowhere nearly as elated as I!

The Year I Turned Forty

Getting qualified to teach Math was definitely the ticket to job security. Soon after receiving my credentials, the principal at Trousdale County High School offered me the opportunity to teach high school Algebra I and Algebra II. Discipline among these students was a real challenge when compared to the sheltered experience in my practice teaching at Athens High School ten years earlier. At the end of the day, I arrived exhausted to a home life that was not good. Buddy did not have work again and was drinking heavily. As I mentioned in the previous chapter, Buddy was not a happy drunk. His language was very abusive toward me, and I did not have the skills to cope. Not only did he call me many terrible names, but almost daily would scream, "We just need to get a divorce. We have nothing in common and can't get along." Those words were all it took for me to succumb. After all, with all the separations and filing for divorces that took place in my childhood between my own parents, the last thing on earth that I wanted was to put my own children through this. I do not need to put words on paper of a "he said," "I said," nature. For those who have lived with an alcoholic, they know what it's like. For those who have not, no words can convey the pain of being torn down on a daily basis.

In the previous chapter, I mentioned the principal in the job interview asking me if I could even relate to children. In my short teaching career, one little boy stands out. He was in my sixth period Algebra I class. This end-of-day class was filled with tired ninth graders, most of whom were only taking the class to get their math requirements for high school graduation. I was given some background on the boy in question. He was now being cared for in a foster home and had moved down to Tennessee from New York. While living in New York City, he had come home to find his older sister dead, her body having been cut in pieces. It was too horrible to comprehend, and this child needed special handling for sure. Though I tried my best to make the subject material understood as plainly as possible, grasping Algebraic principles was extremely difficult for him. Though kids can be cruel to each other, they can also be very encouraging, and I got to see this kind of treatment toward him. Guess most everyone knew some of his previous life, and when I'd call on him for an answer, those kids would rally around him. His face would beam as he struggled and began to answer successfully. He was actually doing well enough to start passing the tests. Then the bombshell came. The principal called me to his office and explained that the boy's test results had come back, and they showed that there was no way his IQ was high enough to pass Algebra. He was going to be removed from the class. I explained to the principal his progress and how the kids helped him and gave my opinion that I thought he could pass the class—yes, maybe with a D— but, none-the-less, with a passing grade. I asked if he could stay in the class for a few more weeks. My words fell on deaf ears, and he was removed. The day after his removal from my class, I saw him in the hall, and I said to him, "I know you have gone through hard things— things I can't even imagine. I want you to know I have experienced hard things, too, though nothing like yours. I know you have been told that your test scores indicate you can't pass Algebra, but test scores don't tell everything. I don't care what the scores said, you and I both know you could have passed my algebra class." He looked at me, and his face just beamed. I heard later that his parents came to the school and begged the principal to reinstate him in my class. but it was to no avail. I never knew what happened to him, but I was told that because they couldn't get resolution on the issue, they moved. Perhaps my words were out-of-order, but I would like to think that he never forgot my words and that they made a difference in his life. What admiration I have for the people who truly care about and will take troubled children into their homes!

One would think, or at least I did, that the smarter kids who took Algebra II, would be eager to learn and be among the best-behaved students. That is certainly not the case. Though some in my Algebra II class fit in that category, others did not. As the semester drew to a close, one such boy that I'd had considerable trouble with came into the classroom with a real attitude that day. He had his jacket on. As we exchanged a few heated words, he reached into his jacket pocket as if going for a gun, and said, "I'm going to kill you." Now, there had been a school shooting with fatalities that week in another area of the United States, so this was in the news and on everyone's mind. I was genuinely frightened and immediately walked across the hall with him to the principal's office. As the day wore on, I slowly became more distressed. This was on Thursday, and on Friday I came to school knowing that I was not dealing very well with this incident. Perhaps someone who had not had a childhood such as mine, where guns had figured in such a dramatic way, would have dealt with this much better. The school officials took the incident very seriously, as well they should, and I guess the next event that occurred was meant as a test for me to see how seriously I really viewed things. I never asked, but I assumed this was the case. The boy had been suspended from school, and I had been told that. On Friday afternoon, over the intercom, the principal called me to his office. As I stepped out into the hall, no one was in sight except this boy, and he was wearing a backpack. He was just slowly walking. I knew he was NOT supposed to be on the school premises, so I was genuinely afraid he had come back to kill me. As I rushed into the principal's office, my voice and countenance expressed fear, and I demanded to know why the boy was there. After being given assurances that he would be taken care of (he was expelled from school), I went back across the hall to the classroom. Something was triggered in me, though, and I knew I was losing control. After an hour or so, I went back to the principal's office and asked that he bring another teacher to finish the hour or so left in the day. I explained that I was coming completely unwound and needed to go home. He complied with my request.

Once I got home, things went from bad to worse. I was truly losing my mind—my very sanity. As the night progressed, I was walking the floor and believing people were out to kill me. I was supposed to be going that weekend to Dallas with my dad for an oil company meeting with Amoco officials and Billy Graham Association lawyers. I began to believe that Amoco officials were planning to kill me—that they would seek me out to shoot me, and would come to get me. There was nowhere I could hide from them. I began to talk about people I had met at the Opry, and I thought people were coming to kill them— that I needed to get word to them that people were going to shoot them. It seemed that I was seeing a blinding light and walking through fire. By morning, Buddy and Linda took me to the emergency room at Vanderbilt Hospital in Nashville. I was immediately transferred to the psychiatric ward of the hospital for examination.

There are, in my opinion, no tests devised that can truly test for the mental state I was in. For sure, I was out of touch with reality, though, for that episode, I did not believe that I was. I could certainly answer all the "what day is it, who is the current president" questions. The examiner, reading my chart, saw that I was a math teacher and rather condescendingly, I thought, said, "You are good at math. Count from 100 backward by seven." I rattled those numbers off as fast as I could talk—no thinking needed—and being annoyed, then said to him rather abruptly, "Being able to count backward by seven has nothing to do with being good at math, and you know that." Being able to add and subtract quickly are good skills to have, but they are arithmetic skills, NOT math skills, and I was quite put out by the test in general. I passed this test with 100%. As I've had other similar tests down through the years, I don't believe the testing, for at least some types of mental illnesses, has improved.

I told the examiner that I needed to get out of there quickly, as I was to go to Dallas to meet with executives of an oil company and lawyers from the Billy Graham Evangelistic Association. The claims, of course, sounded off-the-wall, so the examiner went out to verify this with Buddy and Linda. It was true, of course, and he told Buddy that, obviously, I was in no shape to sign anything. Dad and I were to leave that weekend for Dallas, and Dad did not let my mental condition get in the way of his going. He left that Saturday morning while I was at the hospital. I had thought it was very important I be at this meeting, but, for sure, I was not indispensable. The meeting took place on Monday and did not miss a beat due to my not being present.

The consensus among the doctor and the assistant who examined me was that I needed to be placed in a psychiatric hospital. This was going to cost $30,000 per month. As I've previously said, Buddy was not working. We had our house paid for, and $30,000 in the bank. One month, and that would be gone. Buddy asked—maybe it's okay to say "begged"—them to let me come home. Finally, it was agreed that I could be dismissed to come home with the stipulation that I was to be placed under psychiatric care immediately. When I was told that I could go home, I was adamant that Buddy not be allowed to come into my room. I genuinely felt his verbal treatment of me was part of the problem and recognized that I couldn't deal with it. That request was granted and made a requirement to be observed if I were allowed to go home. I was given a powerful shot that knocked me out almost immediately and given enough medicine for the weekend.

For the next month, because of being so heavily medicated, there is very little that I remember. On Monday evening I was taken to the mental health center in Lebanon, TN, and I can remember sitting in a psychiatrist's office. She smoked the whole time and never asked me if this was okay. Smoking bothers me greatly, and I walked out of there to the waiting room, stating loudly that I certainly wasn't going back to her! I had to be under the care of a psychiatrist since I needed medication. Whether I saw her again, or somebody else, I don't remember. I can remember getting some flowers from my sister Sue and they had been sent through a Megee Florist Shop. As Buddy's mother's maiden name was Megee, I remember voicing some wild connection about them coming from Buddy's mother, who was deceased. I can remember Linda coming into my room once and saying, "Mother, you need a bath." I can remember asking, "Do I need a bath?" and her replying, "Yes, Mother you smell bad." I can remember her leading me to the tub and bathing me. For that month of my life, these are pretty much the only things I remember.

Buddy kept the promise about not coming into my room, and I did not want to see him. It was a very long month for my family, as I just did not seem very responsive. Finally, Buddy did intervene—I can remember him standing at the door—saying he thought part of the problem was that I was just too heavily medicated. That proved to be right. It was decided to cut back on my medication gradually, and I did become more alert. As I came out of this stupor, I was also okay mentally. Linda later told me that Mother had sat in the trailer often crying, "It's my fault. I should have gotten her away from him," referring to Dad and my childhood.

So many people were so very good to me. I got books, magazine subscriptions, and many other items from friends and relatives. I never knew how many friends I had until this happened. Buddy had always been the life of the party type. He was always telling jokes at any gathering and keeping everybody in stitches. I usually said very little and definitely felt the wallflower role. I even felt that most of our mutual friends didn't care much about me, that it was Buddy they liked. After my breakdown, Buddy said to me, "Beverly, it has really been you, after all, that they really care about."

When I was able to start my regular therapy sessions at the mental health center, I was so eager to go that I looked forward to every week. For sure, I had begged to go for therapy in recent years, and guess one could say that I finally got my wish! I was assigned to a psychologist who had finished his coursework for his doctorate but was still working on his dissertation. I still called him "doctor," though he did correct me. Though I would have classed myself as being a very passive person, I did hold my own with him. I remember the time early in my therapy that he would not recognize the validity of me saying I felt I was receiving messages from external sources. From reading my hospital records, he even stated that I said I heard voices. I corrected him on that one and emphasized that I never said I heard anything audibly. He put his hand down hard on the desk and said, "Beverly, there are only five senses—sight, hearing, smell, touch, and taste. There is no such thing as a sixth sense." I had been trying to tell him that I believed I had a sixth sense at times. I was so disturbed that I went down to Alabama to talk to Dr. Slate about this. I was even thinking of changing therapists. So well I remember Dr. Slate's words of wisdom and the calm manner in which he spoke. He said, "Some people believe in a sixth sense. Other people don't. That's okay." His manner and words were so non-judgmental. He went on to say that I could change to a different psychologist, or perhaps I could find this one helpful even if we didn't agree on everything. It was my choice. I remember going back, and in the very next session, I let it slip—it was as though I couldn't help myself—that I had gone to see my college professor to talk about the sixth sense business. Dr. C. reacted to my lack of confidence in him in such a confident way that I decided to stay with him. Am I ever glad I did! I would love to be able to write and tell him how much I appreciate him but I have lost contact.

Soon after starting counseling, I asked Dr. C how long he thought I would need to be in therapy. He didn't want to answer, but I pressured. He finally said, "Well, based on what you've told so far, I think at least three years." I answered, "Well, it won't take me that long. I learn quickly!" And I hadn't told him a drop in the bucket—that's for sure. In fact, there were some serious issues that I never got around to discussing with him—they were discussed with others. For the first six months, I had sessions every week. Then we decided for me to come every two weeks, and I did that for three months. For the last three months, I went only once a month; and we mutually decided it was a good stopping point. He did correctly advise me that, while he was comfortable with this decision, there might be times in my life that I would find it beneficial to go for more counseling. So, I had a total of around 40 or so sessions with Dr. C. Within the first few weeks, I was really trying to impress him with how well I was doing and how fast I would be out of there. One day he stopped me with these words, "Beverly, you are telling me what you think I want to hear. It has taken me three weeks to catch on to what you are doing. If you don't stop this, you are never going to get well!" I will admit that I thought I was smarter than he was and also had said some arrogant things to let him know that. He had mentioned something about most people who came for therapy having such a hard time truly making lasting changes (in fact, he said that only about ten percent TRULY did so), and I pinned him down on this one, too. I asked him if he thought I could be among the ten percent, and he said that he knew that I could be from the first night I was brought in there. He said some very wise words that I have never forgotten: "Beverly, the first night you were brought in here, I knew you were a lot more intelligent than I. That doesn't bother me. I am very comfortable with that. I've had a lot of training that you haven't had and can be of help to you if you will let me." I'm glad I settled down and let him.

It wasn't long until I felt that not just my own family, but everybody I knew could benefit from counseling. (Actually, I STILL feel this way.) I wanted Buddy to come for counseling and asked him to do so. His answer was chilling. He said, "I'd die and go to hell before I'd let some shrink probe into my demons!" And he believed, and still does, in a literal hell as a lake of fire! A couple weeks or so later Dr. C. asked me if I would ask Buddy to come in. I told him that I already had. He correctly observed, "So, the answer wasn't 'NO,' but 'Hell no.'" I told him, "You got it about right."

As I knew it shouldn't be long until I had my own money coming in, I offered both Tim and Linda the opportunity to go for counseling. I told them that in growing up with a mother like me, while I did the best I could as I went along, I knew there were a lot of things I'd done wrong in their childhood, along with a whole lot of things that I didn't know about. I offered each of them counseling as my gift to them. Neither one accepted my offer, much to my dismay. To this day I think they both made a mistake in not accepting this gift.

Many times I've mentioned that in doing this writing I've cried rivers of tears. When I was in counseling, it was a source of pride for me to have a stiff upper lip. I prided myself on not ever breaking down. The crucial breakthrough in therapy for me was the day I formed words of admittance that my mother, my saintly mother, had really not been able to offer the kind of support that I needed. As I hesitantly formed those words in a near-tearful fashion, Dr. C. reached for the Kleenex box and offered it to me. In an instant, the moment was lost as far as tears were concerned. I immediately bristled and said, "I know what you are trying to get me to do. That's what you've been trained to do. It may work for others, but it doesn't work for me!" While I quickly gained emotional control and never shed a tear, he and I both knew that we had reached a breakthrough. It was important that I recognize certain things. Place blame—no way. Just acknowledge and accept.

There is one other incident in my therapy that I want to relate. It has to do with coming to the recognition and admitting that life is about choices—choices we make. This can be a very awkward and painful kind of admittance on the part of oneself. Sometimes words are not well chosen by professionals in trying to convey the necessity of seeing choices that, as individuals, we make. Dr. C. had stated something to the effect that when confronted with the boy threatening to shoot me, I had chosen to have a breakdown rather than face issues that I needed to address. Boy, DID I COME UNWOUND! I let him know that in no uncertain terms did I WANT or CHOOSE to be sitting there in the circumstances in which I found myself. I certainly hadn't chosen it. I quickly reminded him that the gun situation in my childhood certainly wasn't my fault, and I had no control over my reaction to the recent incident. I better realize now the suppressed roll the incidents played and probably that the unconscious gets involved, but I vehemently told him, "You had better not ever say such a thing to me again!" This came from the little meek me. He sat there in silence for an eternal few seconds. He then said, "You are right. You didn't choose this. I am not ever going to say this again, to you or to anybody else."

Letter to Dr. Slate

In 1990 I wrote the following letter to Dr. Slate to tell him about my experience in buying back the royalty my dad had given to the Billy Graham Evangelistic Association. It was also a letter to help me cope in dealing with the worsening problems with Mother's Alzheimer's disease and Dad's refusal to get help for her.

April 29, 1990

Dear Dr. Slate,

For about a month I have been thinking about writing to you, but things have been unbelievably hectic. By the end of the day, I am just too tired to think even well enough to write a letter.

The primary reason I am writing is to tell you about a very strong and VERY IMPORTANT experience I had in February. To give some background, you may remember me telling you that when my father divided his estate four years ago, he gave ten percent off the top to the Billy Graham Evangelistic Association. Some of Dad's mineral properties only involve royalty interest, but quite a few also involved the working interest. This means the total 8/8ths. You have the option of paying your part of drilling costs in a well and receiving your total portion of revenues. Soon after acquiring this, the Billy Graham people indicated they may have to divest the working interest portion. As a non-profit organization, they could not be in the oil and gas business. I told them that if they got ready to sell, I would appreciate the opportunity to buy. They agreed to let me know.

The night of February 26, I had a very strong urge, feeling, etc.— something telling me, "You need to call the Billy Graham people immediately!" I pushed it back with, "Oh, this is really not a good time for me. If Buddy were working in Saudi, I'd call." The next morning the words were very clear (not audible, of course—I don't mean that), "Beverly, if you don't call the Billy Graham people now, it will be the last chance you will ever have to acquire that interest." This was too strong! Immediately I went to the phone and called. What a bombshell did I receive! The lawyer said, "Oh, Beverly, I actually have all the paperwork of the interest your Dad gave on my desk. We are figuring up the 1989 total revenues and are sending it out in a few days, along with other properties we have been given, to some oil companies and investment groups who have requested it. We not only want to sell the working interest but the royalty interest, also. We want to sell the whole package." What a shock! I never expected the opportunity to ever buy the royalty interest, too, and that was really going to make the price high. I did some instant thinking and quickly said, "Would you be willing to pull my dad's property out and let me make an offer before you send it out for bid?" They said, "Yes." I spent the next two days doing some frantic figuring. I knew I had to be high enough that they would accept, yet I wanted to be able to afford it. After some negotiations, we reached an agreement that I would pay five and a half times the 1989 revenues.

At this time I called my half-brother and half-sister and offered them the opportunity to buy a third each. They were doing other things with the money they had coming in and declined. So, after going to Minneapolis and closing the deal, I thought, "Am I ever glad I listened to my feeling. Even if natural gas prices stay at the 1989 level, I've increased my income almost half again—I already owned twenty-two and a half percent of the estate and was buying another ten percent. It's supposed to be a 300-year gas field. How many people EVER have this kind of investment opportunity. Even if things stayed the same, I had increased my standard of living from comfortable to very comfortable.

Now for the next bombshell! After leaving Minnesota, I went to

Oklahoma to record my deeds and go to the oil companies turning in my new ownership records. Arriving at my aunt and uncle's house, I told them what I was doing there. Uncle Charles said, "Take a look at the newspaper. Royalty is out of sight here, Beverly. They are offering ten times the '89 totals. You were very wise to get it bought before the Billy Graham people let it out for bid. Things have gone wild here." All of this was totally unknown to me even by the time of our completed transaction on March 16, and when I had the urges to call on February 26 and 27, this information had not been published in the local newspaper.

I'm going to close out this letter very shortly. I am under a tremendous amount of stress right now, and I may write another letter in a day or so just for therapy. To be brief, the first part of February, my father blacked out and fell and fractured his skull. They put a pacemaker in his heart. Dad was delirious and trying to climb out windows of the hospital. The nurses requested a family member to be there 24/7, but there was no way I could do this alone and take care of Mother. John and Sue had other obligations. John said, "Tell them to restrain him when you can't be there." In spite of all this, Dad will be put back in jail next week. The judge said he didn't care if he (Dad) died there. He had lost patience.

In the meantime, Mother's Alzheimer's disease is escalating rapidly. She is so confused at times that she can't remember where the bathroom is, and she goes in the floor. She has begun to wander, hunting Dad when he's gone even thirty minutes, or even when he's in the back room sleeping. Dad is giving me pure HELL! I had a woman help me two hours a day this week clean the kitchen—molded food that I had brought up was found in the dishwasher, bologna in Kleenex boxes in the pantry, melted ice cream in the cabinets, etc. The roaches were falling in my hair as I tried to spray and clean. And my dad SCREAMS at me, "It's your fault she's so confused by bringing this woman in," and he's "going to blow his brains out," etc. No, it won't be better for me for him to be in jail. Mother will be CONSTANTLY hysterical. And yes, I have seen a lawyer—two of them. I can't be declared her guardian while he's still considered competent, and he can still answer of the standard "what day is it, what season is it, who is the president" questions—probably a lot better than I could at the moment, so it would be hard to get him declared incompetent. He still sends away thousands every month to the TV evangelists. Last week I saw a receipt from Falwell where Dad had gotten mixed up and sent him two $1,000 checks in one day. Now if he'd wanted to send him $2,000, he'd have written one check. The State is going to put him in jail this time, so I'm told. I'm getting pretty fed up. If "they" are going to put him in jail, why won't "they" do something to give me some kind of relief?

Well now, I'm very much aware that I'm under a tremendous amount of stress. Night before last I went to sleep at 5:30 a.m. Slept till 8:30 a.m. Last night I went to sleep at 7:30 p.m. Awakened at 9:30 p.m. and went back to sleep after 3:30 a.m. Slept till 6 a.m. I know I'm stressed when I go to the cabinet and have to think, "Now what did I get this bowl for? Oh yes, it was to get some cereal." And I have eight important documents that await my signature in the morning.

Sincerely,

Beverly

The Hardest Decade

The Hardest Decade – The Beginning

The years that involved dealing with my mother, who had Alzheimer's disease, and my father, who had impaired judgment and some dementia, were the hardest of my life. I wrote profusely during that period. Some writings involved material presented to doctors and lawyers, and other writings became public record in court proceedings. There were also letters sent to Dr. Slate as a coping mechanism for me.

For these years, I want to use the primary source material—writing that took place as it happened. It is far more detailed and graphic than anything I could possibly write from the now twenty-five plus years since the events occurred. Making a few comments here and there may be the only writing I will have to do to present this story. The documents speak for themselves.

There is much material, and I hope I will choose wisely. As it did comprise over ten years of my life, it will be lengthy. This is for two main reasons. The first, of course, is to review that segment of my life and achieve further healing. I want to gain further understanding of myself and the person I am. In addition, this particular segment, maybe more than any of the others in the story of my life, may be of help to those millions who are presently dealing with many of these very issues.

In July 1990 we began the process of my becoming conservator to handle the affairs of Mother and Dad. I wrote two documents for doctors, lawyers, and the courts as we continued the necessary legal steps. They outline problems of Mother and Dad, respectively. The final entry is a ten-page letter from Sue to Dad, written on January 9, 1991. These documents cover one year of this horrendous decade. As we move along, I will present other segments for subsequent events.

Problems of Edith Rider

Present condition:

1. Has not been able to cook or wash clothes for over a year.

2. Cannot dress properly nor take baths. One may find her with a half slip on and an old dirty shirt of Dad's—or a half slip and five or six blouses, some of which will be inside out and on backward.

3. For the past year, she has not recognized me nor known my name most of the time.

4. For several months she has not been able to find the bathroom in the trailer and goes outside in the woods. She has gone in the floor, in freshly washed and dried baskets of clothes, in garbage cans, etc. and has wet herself. This month she has even gone outside in broad daylight in the yard without having mind enough to hide in the trees. Dad has stood by and let her—not having the presence of mind himself to take her to the bathroom.

5. She has been disoriented as to where she is for a year and a half.

6. Dad screams at her for hiding things. Then she really gets disoriented. He loses his temper and acts like he's going to hit her, which terrifies her. She has come to my house at 11 o'clock at night in such a state, though she is scared of the dark and many times cannot find the way between the trailer and my house. Dad forces her to eat food such as donuts and cakes, even when she is telling him she doesn't want it. He'll scream, "I said eat that!" and she will start forcing it down.

7. She throws garbage out the back door.

8. She wanders a lot and has to be watched constantly. She used to wander only when Dad was gone and she was trying to find him but now wanders regardless of whether or not Dad's home. When he's home, he's either looking at TV evangelists for hours at a time (which scares her—she thinks it's people in the trailer hollering) or stays in the

bedroom reading the Bible. He does not watch her nor help with any dressing, baths, etc. (He does not even bathe himself.)

9. She has set plastic containers on the stove trying to warm up tea, coffee, etc. Once, she had been at my house for about thirty minutes. I led her home to find the stove on and two smoking hot iron skillets and two pots with nothing in them on the burners. She started to grab an iron skillet with her bare hands. I screamed, and she didn't.

I have pleaded with Dad on numerous occasions to get some help for me, but he screams, "I'm not going to throw away $40 a week for anyone to take care of her. I can take care of her myself." Of course, he does not even attend to his own needs, let alone hers, so the responsibility rests entirely on my shoulders.

Beverly Biggs
August 31, 1990

Problems of Frank Rider

<u>Medical</u>

1. Blacked out Jan. 31, 1990, and fell and fractured his skull. Had a pacemaker installed in his heart at this time.

2. Is supposed to be on heart medication, but refuses to take it, saying he doesn't need it and told his doctor so.

3. Was very confused in hospital in February as to where he was and what was wrong with him. Doctors asked me to sign for him to have the pacemaker put in, as they did not feel he was capable of making decisions. Doctors said confusion would grow worse. He has taken a nap and gets up thinking it is morning. A couple weeks ago he went to Murphreesboro to pick up a car part and was to come straight back. He did not return for six hours, saying he couldn't find his way home and couldn't find anyone who could give directions well enough to tell him how to get home.

4. Diet consists almost entirely of sweets—donuts, pies, ice cream,

cakes, and cookies.   A doctor's checkup in June showed sugar in both the blood and urine.

5. On last visit to the doctor about two weeks ago, he told the doctor they nearly killed him in the hospital, that he hadn't felt well a day since. Said someone gave him a shot while he was on the stretcher and knocked him out for four days. The doctor said he got irate with the nurse and ran out of the office.

<u>Personal Affairs</u>

1. Gives away large sums of money to TV evangelists. In 1989 he had a taxable income of approximately $27,000, and gave away $29,000. Half of this money is supposed to be Mother's, but he refuses to pay even $40 a week for anyone to help take care of her. He even takes her Social Security checks (has them deposited directly to the bank). His royalty checks have dropped dramatically this year, but he is still giving away thousands of dollars—far more than he is taking in at the present time. He says the Lord tells him to do this. (I want to insert here that when the Billy Graham Evangelistic Association was made aware of the circumstances, they offered to give back all monies Dad had donated for that year and the previous year. It took stern letters from our lawyer to get any of the other evangelistic associations to quit contacting Dad with their urgent appeals by phone and express mail.)

This May he gave away five lots and a trailer to a so-called church that nobody attends but the preacher and his wife, Mother, Dad, and one of Dad's renters. He must be paying the preacher with cash, as I have seen very few checks to this church. He says he is giving all of his money to God—that he will not spend any on someone to help take care of Mother.

2. Had his driver's license revoked last September due to having a wreck with no insurance and refusing to pay the $900+ in damages.

3. August 12, ran into a car parked 150' from where he was turning around. Left the scene. When later questioned about it, he said, yes, he

ran into it, but he wasn't paying for it. It was in his way.

4. Went to jail in November 1989 over refusing to move a rental trailer parked too close to property line. There is presently a case pending against him by the State over sewage problems on two trailers parked on two small lots.

5. Won't pay medical bills or even sign forms to have Medicare and insurance make payments. Says the county should have to pay because he blacked out (January 31) from cigarette smoke breathed while he was in jail in November.

6. Is constantly behind on credit cards, telephone, and other bills.

7. Carries large sums of cash at all times—approximately $500. Wants a gun to protect himself because he carries large sums of cash. (I have seen him give away large bills to people who just listened to him talk for awhile.) Is careless with guns. Mother has come out of a room with a loaded gun in her hands. This is especially frightening considering her condition. Dad has a history of making threats with guns, both to himself and to others, and has threatened himself several times this year.

8. Makes copies of gas royalty checks he receives, as well as those checks he writes to TV evangelists and shows them to many people—including strangers.

9. Has a history of sexual problems. I hired a woman for two hours a day to help with Mother and fix a lunch. He made sexual advances toward her. She refused him and told me about his advances. He refused to let her come back. One of his renters came to me and said he put his hands on her daughter's breasts. I told her I couldn't do anything with him—she'd have to call the law. One man called on the phone to Dad's. My son answered the phone. The man was livid and cursing him out for putting his hands on his wife. My son told him he was talking to the wrong person. They moved out immediately.

10. He is easily conned. Last year he was approached by a man in a parking lot at K-Mart in Lebanon. The man showed him a large roll

of bills and told him he had just inherited it but was afraid to put it in the bank. Wanted Dad to drive him to UMC to meet a friend. Dad did. The other man came out and got in the car. They started playing a gambling game, as they called it, with Dad. He was to take off his watch, a diamond Masonic ring, his billfold with several hundred dollars in it, an expensive camera, etc. and put them in a sack. He did so. Then he thought the game was over and asked for them back. They wouldn't return them. Then they asked him to take them to his bank and draw money from his account. He took them to the bank but said he wouldn't get out and get the money. They told him, okay, to wait there, and they would go in and make a phone call and come back. He waited about thirty minutes for them and decided to go to the bank and tell what had happened. The police were called, but they said it was too late to do anything, that this sort of thing happened frequently.

11. Until recent months he made several trips a year to Oklahoma and other states. He will not stay in motels but sleeps in his van. About two years ago, he stopped at a service station in a rough section of Memphis at three o'clock in the morning and went to sleep. A man mugged him. He managed to get the van started but arrived home black and blue.

12. He has an old violin which he claims was made by a famous Italian violin maker and is worth hundreds of thousands of dollars. He says it was brought over on the Mayflower by the family of the man he bought it from. It does no good to point out that the Italian he claims made it was born sixty-seven years after the Mayflower sailed. He has spent thousands of dollars taking it to Chicago, Minneapolis, the Smithsonian in Washington, D.C., New York, San Francisco, all to be told basically the same thing—that it's about 100 years old and was worth between $1,000 and $1,500 until he cracked it. Now the estimates are running between $100 and $300. Yet, he will not give up.

Beverly Biggs,

August 31, 1990

Letter from Sue to Dad

Sue wrote the following letter to Dad to try to explain our position in trying to care for him:

January 9, 1991

Dear Dad:

I have received your letters and after trying to talk to you on the phone last night, I have decided the only way to be heard is to write to you. It is time for me to speak up. I'm tired of Beverly taking all the blame for your being in the rest home.

I am going to try to make you understand what has happened to you and why it has happened. Also, I am going to try to explain to you how I feel about things. By the time you finish reading this letter, you are going to know my feelings on this matter.

I am not writing this letter to be mean or disrespectful, vengeful. I am writing to you because I truly believe that you need to get some things straight. I pray you will understand me.

To begin—you have always lived in a fantasy, make-believe world. No matter what the facts are in any given situation, or what someone says, you take things out of context and twist things around to have the person say what you want them to have said—not what they really say.

You are a great rationalizer, and you always blame all your problems, sins and transgressions on someone else. You always end up the 'good guy'—the innocent victim, and the other person is always the 'bad guy.' The situation you are in right now is a good example. You see yourself and want everybody to believe that you are the 'good guy' and that

Beverly is the 'bad guy.' Your mind is twisted and mixed up so you are able to believe only what you want to believe. You have no regard for the opinion of experts, facts, the law, or the opinions of your family members.

The old violin story is a prime example. You have been told by violin experts from all over the country that your old violin is worth a couple hundred dollars. Nevertheless, you insist that its value is $200,000 or more. No one in the world can convince you that you are wrong, because you want to believe that old violin is worth $200,000.

Once you get our mind set on something, no one can reason with you and nothing can ever convince you any differently. Nevertheless, I am going to try to explain the present situation to you and what I believe to be the facts of the matter at hand. The reason I am spending so much time on this letter is that I pray that by some miracle (all things are possible) you will believe me.

COMPETENCY HEARING (TRIAL)

For some time I have known about the problem of you and Edith. Beverly and I have had many phone conversations about this over the past several years. I have known for a long time that the day was coming when something would have to be done.

When you visited me in California last year, I tried to talk to you about this problem of Edith's care and tried my darndest to convince you that you needed to cooperate with Beverly and get some help with Edith. I thought when you left that you were going to cooperate, but when you got home, you refused.

Because of this and your own mental deterioration, plus the fact that you were squandering thousands of dollars on those TV evangelists, something had to be done. You were spending money that we knew was going to be needed for your care and Edith's care. We did not have any thoughts of getting our hands on your money!

Your doctors and the local authorities first suggested to us that you needed a guardian about two years ago. When matters continued to get worse and worse, and Beverly was at the end of her rope, we finally decided to do something. Beverly contacted John and me, and we asked her to find an attorney to take the case. We got a date set up for the hearing. This process took several months. Last September, we petitioned the court concerning your competency to manage your affairs. John and I were contacted and made arrangements to be at the hearing. We are both in full agreement with what was done and how it was done. We both stated that before the court.

The court appointed you and Edith an attorney to serve as the guardian ad Litem. His job was to represent your and Edith's best interests. Unfortunately, you refused to meet with him or to talk to him when he tried numerous times to meet with you in person and/or to reach you by telephone. It is too bad that you didn't cooperate with him. He was your best hope of remaining on your own.

Before we had the hearing Beverly asked me to be your guardian, and I refused. Then she asked John, and he refused. That only left her. As it turned out, she was the only one that could be your guardian. The law in Tennessee is that because you are a resident of Tennessee, your guardian also has to be a resident of Tennessee.

The judge was very patient with you, and you did get a fair trial. You argued that you were capable of managing your own affairs. The judge and you agreed that you would go for a complete evaluation for the experts to decide the issue. The judge ordered you to a hospital for a complete evaluation by experts in psychiatry and medical fields to determine your ability to manage your affairs. It was the judge that ordered you to the hospital. No one tricked you. You and the judge agreed! You asked me if you got a fair trial? My answer is YES, you did get a fair trial.

MEDICAL EVALUATION

John, Beverly, and I took you that same day to Madison, Tennessee, where you were admitted to the Tennessee Christian Medical Center.

You say in your letter that Beverly has tricked you into this. John and I were there and were both in full agreement. You were evaluated for two or three weeks by a number of psychiatrists who were experts in their field. But, contrary to them telling you that "you have one of the most brilliant minds for a man of your age," they did not say that you are brilliant, or that you are capable of managing your business or personal affairs. This report went back to the court, and the judge appointed Beverly as a guardian for you. I want you to understand this. Beverly gets no money, zero, for taking care of your affairs. She is really doing all of us, you included, a favor, looking after things. It takes a lot of her time, and she doesn't get any pay.

Also, just remember that all three of your children initiated the action to have you declared incompetent. None of the three of us thought you could manage your affairs. Further, we all three believe that what we did was done in your best interest.

Beverly didn't trick you into the rest home as you like to believe. We all three are equally responsible for having the competency hearing, and for you now being in the rest home. She doesn't get a dime for being your guardian. She is required by the judge to make a full accounting of the money that is spent from your accounts. There is no way she could take a penny. Neither do John and I, we also don't get a dime from any of your accounts. So, none of us had any intention of profiting financially by putting you in a rest home.

Now I hope that this clears up the notion you have that your kids put you in a rest home in order to steal your money. The facts are that your kids will be lucky if they don't end up having to pay for your care when the money runs out. With the royalty checks as low as they are, there is barely enough to pay for your care and Edith's care. It's too bad you didn't think of that when you were writing checks for thousands to the TV preachers. Who did you think was going to pay for your care when all the money was gone?

REST HOME & YOUR CARE IN GENERAL

Now about the rest home. You told me on the phone that you were unhappy at the rest home—that everyone was nuts but you. I called the rest home to check out the stories you told me on the phone the last time I had talked to you in December.

(1) You said that Beverly has to approve all your visitors.

The administrator at the nursing home told me that Beverly does NOT have to approve your visitors. Anyone who wants to visit you can come to see you. I wonder who is wanting to visit you that can't get in to see you???

(2) You said that you were not able to receive any phone calls.

The nursing home told me that you can have phone calls. If the person calls the rest home, they will get you to the phone. The rest home will NOT give you money to make calls or let you make collect calls to the FBI or the IRS on their phone. Why in the world would you be calling the FBI or the IRS?

(3) You said that you couldn't go outside for a walk.

Well, that is true. The nursing home administrator told me that you can't go outside because they are afraid you'll run off.

It seems to me that you are in a really good nursing home and that you are getting good care. No one is mean to you, and you can be thankful that you are better off than a lot of old people. Luckily we got you in there before you spent all of the money on TV evangelists. From what you told the psychiatrists at Tennessee Christian Hospital, you had plans to give all the money away. At the rate you were sending the money to the TV evangelists, you'd have been broke by now, and you'd be in a state or county old folks home.

MONEY

You have often stated that "IT'S YOUR MONEY AND YOU SHOULD BE ABLE TO DO WITH IT WHAT YOU WANT." That's true, but only to a point. Also, it is true that charity begins at home.

Before you can do with your money what you want, you must first pay for the responsibilities and obligations you have taken on—a wife, household expenses, medical expenses, your bills, etc. It IS NOT true that everyone can do just what they please with their money. Don't worry about trying to even things up between your children as far as money is concerned. You won't have enough left to quibble about. I have every confidence in Beverly's honesty and know that if there is anything left to divide, she will be fair.

BEVERLY, TIM & LINDA BIGGS

Dad, you have made some pretty terrible accusations about Beverly, Tim, and Linda that just are not true. Because of the way you treat them and mainly because of the way you have treated Edith, you have provoked them to do and say some things that they might not have otherwise said or done.

Ephesians 6:4 "And, ye fathers, provoke not your children to wrath; but bring them up in the nurture and admonition of the Lord."

Over the past years, Beverly and I have become very close. I love her very much and consider her to be one of my best friends as well as my sister. I trust Beverly totally and completely. I have never caught her in a lie, and she has never given me any reason to doubt her. I have placed my trust in her and believe she will manage your finances in a fair and equitable way.

How can you even hope or expect that Tim or Linda will come to see you when you say such terrible things about them and treat them the way you do? Also, if you really believe they are so bad, so evil, well then forgive them, and pray for them. For heaven's sake, don't keep telling everyone how badly you have been treated. Your grandchildren, Timothy Biggs and Linda Biggs, are fine young people from all I have seen. They are kind and courteous, and I'm very proud of them. I was impressed with the exceptional love and compassion I saw them exhibit toward their grandmother, Edith Rider, your wife. They are not wicked bad people as you would have me and others believe. You should be very proud of them. Again, by the lies you have told about them, you have done them a grave injustice.

The latest is you are now claiming that Edith isn't really even your wife. Well, I called the County Clerk's office in Latimer County, Oklahoma, to check. They sent me copies of the two divorce actions that were filed in Latimer County in 1971 and in 1972. The final decree was set aside. The decree was set aside while you lived in Alabama. As it turns out, you are indeed married to Edith. I can make copies for you if you want to see this in writing. Now you are saying that I told Beverly that you said Edith wasn't you wife, when in fact, Beverly told me that story before you ever wrote it. You first told that story to Edith's brother when he visited you at the rest home. Beverly told me about you telling him that story before you ever wrote about it to me.

I don't understand why you would tell something like that. And, even if it were true, how could such a good Christian as you profess to be, live for twenty years as husband and wife with a woman he wasn't married to? This doesn't set a very good example for your grandchildren, does it?

LAW ABIDING CITIZEN

You say that you have always been a law-abiding citizen. Last year you spend a week in jail for contempt of court. Years ago you were married to Mother and Edith at the same time. That's bigamy and against the law. In the past year, you have driven with an invalid driver's license, and that's illegal. You hit a car and didn't report it to the law, that's illegal. This is not what I'd call being law-abiding.

SUICIDE THREATS

You deny ever making suicide threats, but all three of us, John, Beverly, and I, all know that you have threatened to commit suicide for years. I think it is even in the reports from your evaluation that you had thoughts of suicide.

CURRENT SITUATION

Before you called last night, I had a call from Beverly. She was very upset and had been having a terrible week. She told me about the way you had acted and about you drawing back your fist to hit her. She told me about the way you had shown out at the doctor's office and about the lies you were telling about buying them the brick house. Because of the way you treat her, and the horrible things you write about her and her family, my advice to Beverly is to not go around you until you can act right, or even civil to her. She is trying her best to have some pleasant contact with you, but when you act like that, it just keeps her upset. I wouldn't put up with your treating me that way and don't think she should. Like I said earlier, she is really doing you a favor coming to see you and taking you for doctor's visits, etc. What you are doing is like the old story of "biting the hand that feeds you." It doesn't make any sense to me that you would act like that. All that kind of behavior is going to get you is that NO ONE, not even Beverly, will come to see you. She can get the nursing home to hire someone to take you to the doctors and dentists, and that will cost you money!

You should remember that Beverly has a very busy life and that she is doing her very best. She is taking care of Edith, your financial affairs, and her own business, and she also has a husband and children. You at least could show her some consideration and kindness.

The last thing I want to say is: I am not proud of you sending your money to TV evangelists. I feel about them just about the way you feel about doctors and lawyers—in other words, I don't have much respect or use for them. I can't be proud that you'd send thousands of dollars to strangers and not even look after your own—like your own sister needing money for glasses and teeth, or your own children or grandchildren having needs. No, I think that kind of giving is sick. Like I said earlier, I think charity begins at home.

You'll probably not be writing to me anymore, but at least I thought I'd better let you know how I feel about things.

Sue

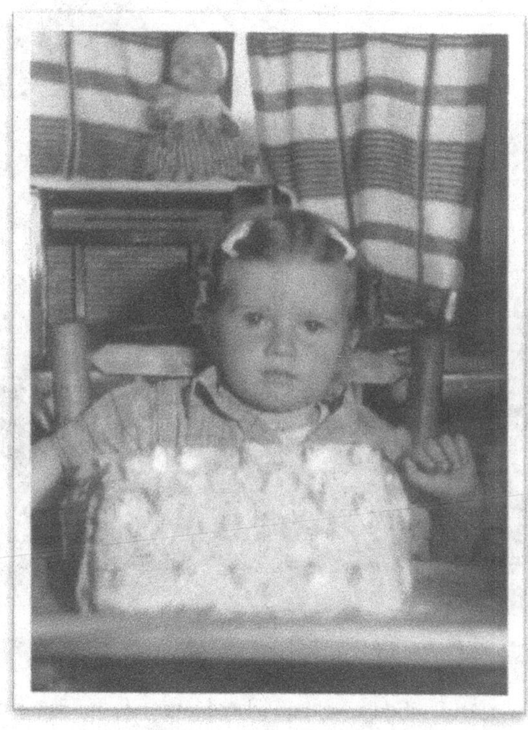

My second birthday. Sally Jane, the doll Dad made me give away is on the shelf. In my Baby Book, Mother wrote that Sally Jane was my favorite toy at 18 months. I do not have a picture of Cynthia Sue, the other doll Dad made me give away.

Frank Rider, in 1951, has just finished a weld on a large piece of pipe. The picture shows my dad with a welding hood on, and rod in hand as he was welding on a large pipe.

Mother holding me in her arms. I was 23 months old.

Me at age 2 years

Me in Granny and Grandpa's yard with their dog.

My home from the age of 5 months to 4 years

Me at age 3 yrs., in yet another trailer park, wearing Daddy's boots.

Our Spartan, acquired when I was 4 yrs. We lived in it until I was 9 yrs. old. Mother is standing in the door. It was 27' long, including the hitch. Still no bathroom. This is the one where I slept on the green wooden folding chairs.

Me at age 2 years

Some times our trailers were parked really close together. Mother does not look too pleased in this photo. We did not have nice campgrounds like those now. Our parks, which we called trailer camps, were often built in haste, with few amenities. As most trailers did not have bathrooms, we shared a building with common facilities.

Me at almost 3 yrs., wearing the coat Granny had made for me. She either made my clothes, or Mother bought them at rummage sales or the Salvation Army. When I was 5 yrs. Dad bought Mother a sewing machine, and she then started making my clothes.

Me with Sue and her children, Mike and Terrie.
They visited us in Palmdale, California, in 1956.

Our last trailer was bought when I was 9, and we were in Colorado. It was 35' long, including hitch. It had a small bathroom with a little tin shower and a bed along a wall near the middle of the trailer. At last I had a bed of my own. We lived in it until 1960, when Dad built a small house in Red Oak. Buddy and I lived in this trailer for the first three years of our marriage.

This was taken when I was eight years old, a few weeks before my "TV debut" in Grand Junction, Colorado, Sept. 14, 1955.

Granny and Beverly. How much I loved my Granny!

Aunt Eunice and Uncle Charles Gallagher. Aunt Eunice was a big presence in my life. I grew closer to Uncle Charles during my adult years.

Mother in 1942.

John, Dad, and Sue, with Beverly standing in back. It was December 27, 1958, the occasion of John's 21st birthday.

Dad, in 1949, with his airplane.

Three generations: Grandpa, Dad, and Johnny

This was the picture Dad took on my 8th grade graduation, May 1959.

Our wedding day, with the cake brought down from
McAlester on the bread truck.

Our wedding party: My good friend, Linda Brewer; Duchess Thompson, my
childhood friend from pipeline days; Buddy and I, his brother, Floyd G. Biggs, Jr.,
and Buddy's friend, Tony Joe Daniel

Granny and Grandpa on their 50th Wedding Anniversary with the cake brought down from McAlester on the bread truck. Granny had looked forward to this celebration for quite some time. It was August 15, 1960. Grandpa died in November.

Letter to Buddy

As I stated in the letter I wrote to Dr. Slate in October 1991 describing events in July of that year, Buddy's leave of two months home from Saudi was no vacation for me. When he got ready to return to Saudi the first week in June, Buddy informed me that he wanted "to make other arrangements with his life." I believe I had felt for years that if someone didn't want me and didn't appreciate the qualities I had to offer in a marriage, I would not hang on. Let him go for it—let him make the choices he wished to make. I know for sure I felt this that week in 1991. Arguing nor begging is not who I am. I also thought that while I would be (and was) devastated, I wouldn't bury my head, but would deal with the pain deeply and move on quickly. After all, with my upbringing, life had been full of changes, and with this oft change, there was not much time spent being stuck in the moment.

Screaming and hollering and venting, whether that's for better or for worse for one's psychological health, are also not who I am. What I do is carefully weigh the situation, go over the alternatives, and evaluate the solutions. Just as I recently did regarding the hurt of having my breakdown thrown up to me one more time, I don't necessarily answer at the moment or the day or maybe even the week. For sure, I make sure I don't say something that I may regret, or make a decision that I'm not willing to keep. This was no exception. As Buddy left for Saudi, I did not give an answer. I went to a lawyer and found out how I stood on things. So, it was on July 7 that I wrote my answer. I've already covered some things surrounding this letter, and I'm not going to repeat them here. As I broke down and sobbed on the way to Athens to see Dr. Slate, for sure I knew it was the hardest day yet of my life. This was the night of the healing dream. I felt then, and still do, that my ancestors came and rescued me.

This is the letter:

July 7, 1991

Dear Buddy,

On May 31, 1991, we had a conversation. At that time you expressed that you were thinking of "making other arrangements, and getting on with your life." You asked me for an answer. At that time, as you have so many others, you said I was "just like my old dad," and that I would give up my children before I would give up my g. d. royalty. You said that you would give me the royalty and everything else we had because you could make plenty of money. You said that there were plenty of women out there that would be glad to have a man like you. I noted that at no time did you suggest there existed the same possibility for me.

After much thought and due consideration, I have arrived at my answer. Tennessee law provides that in case of divorce, each spouse is entitled to his or her inheritance. All other property acquired after the marriage is divided equally, regardless of whose name it is in. The only things that are of value to me are in my name only. These include the royalty purchased from the Billy Graham Association and the antiques. I will give you one half of the royalty. I assume you would want to give Linda your half of the antiques anyway. In addition, I want one half of the Bell Heirs royalty. As for my inheritance, I would fight you 'til the last drop of blood drained from my body.

If you wish to make "other arrangements" and get on with your life, you are free to do so.

Sincerely,
Beverly Ann Rider Biggs

The Healing Dream

In dealing with events in June and July 1991, I was on the brink of a full blown episode of mania. I went to Alabama to talk with Dr. Slate. The night before our meeting, I had the most profound dream I have ever had in my life. Ever since then I have referred to it as "My Healing Dream." I was having to meet with lawyers and scared beyond description that my mental state would be apparent and be used against me in court. It remains my firm conviction that without this dream, I would have become completely unwound and gone into a profound psychotic state. In this letter I describe the dream in detail and the events that led to it:

October 13, 1991

Dear Dr. Slate,

At long last, I am writing. For two weeks I have intended to write and tell you about the healing dream that I had, as I said I would, but I just couldn't get in the mood. I am still not in the mood to write to anyone, but I'm just going to do so today. For the past two weeks, I have been experiencing a low-level depression. I cannot seem to shake it. I guess it is a result of all that is going on right now. Without further ado, I want to describe the events leading up to the dream and the dream itself.

Dr. Slate, I can tell that words are not flowing as they should. This is a struggle, but maybe I can get the important things down.

For my own records, and because it is so important for the significance of the dream to me, I am going to summarize some of the stresses leading up to the dream. The past two and a half years have been very difficult for me. My mother started showing signs of Alzheimer's disease. As she progressively got worse, my concerns for her well-being and safety grew. Dad was verbally, mentally, and sexually abusing her. She would wander away daily. Dad refused to pay for help and refused to let me get help. He went to jail rather than obey the law, saying he wanted to be like Paul, Jesus, and John the Baptist. He sent to TV evangelists far more than his income. He fell and fractured his skull, and at that time the doctors told me that his tests showed early dementia/Alzheimer's, also. Finally, last September I went to court and was appointed as conservator for both of them. Dad was placed in a nursing home, where he continually caused problems—the worst being his inappropriate sexual behavior. I kept Mother in her familiar surroundings. I started hiring sitters to help out, gradually adding more help until I stayed with her sixty hours a week, hiring sitters for the rest of the time. Even this had its problems. I had a sitter who stole Mother's sleeping pills, large quantities of food, etc. The next one took her own sleeping medication (though she was staying nights) and did not wake up when Mother did. Finally, I hired two people who seemed to work out well. I continued to stay sixty hours with Mother and take care of Dad's needs as well. In addition, there were weeks I had to work ten to fifteen hours on business.

My husband was in Saudi during this time, and for months there was the added stress of the Gulf Crisis, and finally the all-out war. My husband lived only one-quarter mile from the barracks where the scud missile landed and killed twenty-six people. As soon as the war was over, he went into Kuwait to oversee the setting up of a camp for workers to get electricity on in Kuwait City. With landmines and sporadic fighting, the dangers were greater there than they had been back in Saudi during the war. Also during this time, my son was making plans to go over to work. His dad was encouraging this and was hoping to get him over before the war actually broke out. Due to paperwork problems, this was not accomplished, and civilian flights were canceled (there was even talk of him going over on a military cargo flight).

In April, my husband came home for two months. This was not a pleasant time. He drank for most of every day, never hesitating to drive. Although he started drinking moderately about fourteen years ago, during the past six years he has felt on four separate occasions that things were bad enough that he voluntarily quit for a few months at a time. Each time he started back drinking, he got worse quicker. During April and May, I was quietly coming to the conclusion that I was unwilling to tolerate his behavior and the chances he was taking driving and drinking. I was not unhappy to see him go back to Saudi in June. In fact, if he had stayed home another month, I think I would have gone into a state of collapse.

Dad's sexual behavior escalated. June 14 he was placed in a hospital psychiatric unit for twenty-five days. The nursing home that he was in recommended that upon release he be placed somewhere else. This begins the exceedingly stressful week in which I had the dream. On July 5 I met with Dad, his doctor and health care workers in a stressful (for me) confrontation concerning Dad's sexual behavior. On July 6 I met with Dad's psychiatrist for two hours. At this time he took me into regression, and I saw the repeated sexual behavior of my father toward me during infancy and early childhood. That afternoon, my mother had a light stroke but was not kept in the hospital. On July 9 Dad was discharged from the hospital. He arrived at the nursing home very disoriented. At 5:30 p.m., he ran away. I received an anonymous call that he was at the home of a man who has a bad reputation. The county officials refused to investigate. I was terrified that Dad may come with a gun, as he has a history of this behavior. At midnight the man took Dad back to the nursing home (I was told that Dad's behavior began to frighten the man). The next day, July 10, I was given a letter that Dad was being discharged from this nursing home, effectively immediately—that I would have to hire sitters if he were even allowed to spend the night.

For more than a week, I had slept hardly two hours per night. In this highly stressed condition—almost hyper or manic—I seemed to be almost living on another plane or in another dimension. To recount, Dad was discharged from the hospital and ran away from the nursing home on July 9. On Wednesday, July 10, I decided to come to Athens and made arrangements to meet with you on Thursday morning, July 11. It was obvious to those around me that I was nearing a breaking point. I made arrangements for sitters for Mother, and Linda and I started to Athens. The previous week I had written Buddy a letter as to my decision about how I felt about our situation. I had told him I had written my answer and would mail it as soon as he called and gave me his address, but he never got me the address. I decided to read him the letter over the phone and had done so that day. About midway through the letter, he said, "Beverly, you are just being dramatic." That statement cut me like a knife. I continued reading, and he got very quiet. At the end of the letter, he was promising me all kinds of things, but that didn't matter. The damage had been done. He knows me well. He knows that I sometimes will take weeks to ponder a situation, but that I never make a threat or a statement that I'm not willing to carry out (my children know that I was this consistent throughout their rearing, too). So, his statement hurt me greatly. About midway to Athens (Linda was driving), I started sobbing. I am not really a cryer, and it is rare that I do this. I do not ever remember having felt so devastated. It is the first time in the twenty-eight years that I have been married, that I felt as though I didn't care if I ever saw Buddy again. I felt even further that I did not want to see him. I really felt alone and that I would have to solve all of my problems alone. I was so numb that I could hardly talk. It was in this condition that we arrived in Athens. It had been many nights since I had slept well, and I knew that most of all, sleep is what I needed. We rented a motel room, and I did fall, exhausted, into a sound sleep.

During the night, I started dreaming. It was the kind of dream where I was actually there experiencing things—I did not feel that I was dreaming. In this dream, I was an Indian woman. I suffered many hardships, some for my existence, and others at the hand of "the white man" (meaning is plural). Then I was on the Trail of Tears. Many nights I was cold and hungry. There were rivers to cross and mistreatments to bear. This dream seemed to take a long time, and I lived through so many trials. Many times I felt as though my spirit was broken, but some inner strength would keep helping me bear these burdens. An inner voice would keep prodding and telling me that I was Indian, and that "the white man" could never keep me down. I would survive. This reassurance reoccurred periodically throughout the dream. At the end of this period of the dream, I saw the famous statue of the slumped over Indian usually called *The End of the Trail*. It is also known as *The Last Warrior* and *The Fallen Warrior*. I had always thought that this statue represented a fallen Indian, one who had been killed in battle. During the dream, it was like I went into this statue. I suffered humiliation and defeat as well. It was though I empathized. I, for the first time, really understood and could truly appreciate what this statue represented. It seemed that I came out of the statue, and when I did, I had a different interpretation. I knew that it was wrong to call him the last warrior or a fallen warrior. This Indian was definitely not dead. Outwardly, his spirit may have appeared to be broken, but this was only for appearance. He would go on. He would make it. Inwardly, his spirit was strong. I left the statue. As I neared the end of this dream, I was overlooking a vast prairie. As far as the eye could see, there was vast sky meeting the vast ground—a marvelous horizon. At this point, white smoke started slowly coming up from the interior of the earth. It started rising slowly, ever so slowly, until it filled the earth and then the whole sky. As this smoke was rising, it seemed that a warmth— a warm energy, started coming up from the deepest part of my being. It was like some kind of dual existence. I was on this prairie watching the pure white smoke, and yet this healing energy and smoke were covering my body as I lay on the bed. It started at my toes, and as the smoke rose in my dream, simultaneously, this warm, healing energy slowly covered my body, little by little, until it reached the top of my head. At the same time, something was telling me, and the words remain so clear, "The white man can never get you down. You will always survive. Though your features are now white, your spirit is Indian. Though you may appear to be broken, the white man can never destroy you, because you have an Indian spirit."

At this point, I awoke. I felt refreshed. Though I do not eat well in times of stress, I was hungry. It was at least an hour or so until daylight. I did not try to go back to sleep. I wondered very seriously about reincarnation. I have had fleeting feelings about this before, but no experience so profound as the dream that I had just had. I did feel that this dream was very important and that I had something to hang on to—continuity. This dream, which I think was a healing experience from my deepest unconscious, was so significant. It certainly came at the night in all my life that I needed it most.

When Linda got up, we had a nice breakfast. She was shocked at the change in me. As we prepared to go meet you, she handed me the car keys, signifying her trust in my change. After we met you, she told me that she was embarrassed—that she had told you how bad off I was—and that I seemed so well. She was afraid you would think that she had exaggerated. As you know, I was by no means well, but I was surviving.

As you know, also, the week got tougher. It was that afternoon that Dad's scummy lawyer made all of his treats, and I hadn't thought I could survive any more stress that week. I came to see you a second time—this time with Tim.

To bring you up-to-date about my life currently, the lawsuit hearing is set for October 29, at 8 a.m. There had been some errors in the first hearing last year. The notarized letter from one of Dad's doctors stating his medical opinion had been presented to the judge but had not been filed. My lawyer had forgotten about it, and it was found in her files. It has now been filed—one day before this current lawsuit was filed. The other error was also important. The judge based his decision on the psychiatrist's report from the first hospital. He did not ask him to sign a similar notarized affidavit, and according to the law, there are supposed to be two signed affidavits regarding competency, even though the opinion is clearly stated in the signed medical report. My current lawyer contacted the psychiatrist from last year's hospitalization, and he signed the statement. It has now been filed. My half-sister is being very supportive of me and plans to come to the hearing to testify on my behalf. She has written some very complimentary letters to the lawyer in support of the way I have handled everything. So the saga, drama, soap, or whatever it is, continues. I won't bore you with the pages of stuff that I could write about that has happened since July.

As for me, I feel that I am holding up well. As I stated earlier, I have had a low-level depression for about two weeks—the main reason that I did not write sooner. But I am aware of it and am working on it. Please send some positive thoughts my way on the twenty-ninth.

Sincerely,

Beverly

More Experiences of Growth

Before I continue with the second year of the decade of carrying for my parents, I need to again pause to reflect on some growth experiences. The first involves my reaction upon rereading the documents I had written twenty-five years ago. I was appalled as I relived the horrible things my dad did to Mother. I felt an anger toward him that I don't believe I ever felt before. I didn't dwell on this but a couple days, but I believe it was a necessary and realistic part of healing that I had never done. It was hard to believe I wrote Dad such a kind, loving letter for his 85th birthday just two years after the court cases were finally over. Certainly, I do believe the power of forgiveness is great and promotes healing of the body and soul, but one should not gloss over the injustice. As I read Sue's letter to Dad in 1991 and her profile of him which she sent to the lawyer, I knew I had further healing work to do. At this time, I feel I have sufficiently addressed the anger and released it.

There are two areas that I addressed with my husband that were much needed. I found I could do this after having worked through my emotional/mental breakdown in writing. Again, I was not aware of how helpful this therapy would be, but it has caused me to release tension that I did not know I was holding.

Buddy likes tractors, and in the last twenty years has had four new ones and one that was almost new. These are for his enjoyment riding around on them, as he does no actual farming. They are expensive toys—costing from $30,000 to $35,000 each. Well, one day almost two years ago, I was looking out the window of our house and thought, "That looks like a new tractor out there." Now, it was orange, like the other Kubotas had been, but it definitely looked new. When I inquired about it, yes, Buddy had had it about four days. I was aware of the other purchases, and we had paid cash, but unknown to me, he had bought this one on credit. It cost $30,000. To say I was unhappy puts it mildly. Buddy recently sold this tractor for $17,500 and is now trying to buy one just like the one he traded in. He received $13,500 as trade-in value, but is now finding this model is so desirable that it's hard to find one, and a good used one even fifteen or so years old is running $15,000 and up. He told someone on the phone that he lost about six or seven thousand dollars when he sold this tractor. After he hung up, I said that it took some tricky accounting to conclude he lost only six or seven thousand dollars. He, of course, got mad. When I criticize Buddy's business deals, he immediately starts hollering that I am "so selfish, that I was an only child and born with a silver spoon in my mouth and had everything handed to me on a silver platter." He has done this for our entire married life, but after my breakdown, he always adds, "And you couldn't hold a job in the REAL world; you can't take it, and you KNOW what I mean." He, of course, is referring to the fact that I was several months recovering from the major breakdown I had when I was forty. These incidents happen on a regular basis, probably more than once a month on average.

For the first putdown, I have always felt he must be right—after all, I am essentially an only child. So, I've always worked extra hard to try to please and to try to make sure I am not being selfish—that is until this past year when I read in Dr. Kevin Leman's book, *The Pleasers*, that being selfish is usually not a character trait of an only child at all. The only child is usually studious, eager to please, conscientious, eager to obey the letter of the law, etc. When he talked about the lies we believe about ourselves when we are put down, it was a revelation to me. I decided that no more would I accept this putdown. I said nothing immediately after this current incident. Buddy went outside, and I gathered my thoughts. After about ten minutes he came back in, and I quietly stated my position—that I would not accept this assessment any longer. In fact, buying this tractor on credit without telling me was a VERY selfish act. I talked about the fact that often it's the baby of the family that's selfish—he is the youngest of seven—the older children cater to the baby, and the parents usually are not as hard on the baby either. I talked about that listening to a person tell of their early memories says a lot about them. The babies of the family usually talk about being in a play or other activity that calls attention to themselves. They like to be the life of the party and the clown. I pointed out how true this is was of him—that I have often heard him tell of being in a Christmas play holding a sign with "S" on it for "S is his sleigh," and the crowd burst into laughter. He tells that they were laughing because he was barefooted. Well, I finished what I had to say and came into the office and sat down at the computer. In a few minutes, Buddy came in and said, "I know that I lash out at times." I said, "Yes, and I believe you are going to do that for the rest of your life." He stated, as he often does, "Well, we've made it over fifty-two years." I said, "Yes, and I believe I know the reason why. After doing the writing I've done so far, I believe we have made it because I went through such pain as a child with my parents so often divorcing, filing for divorce and separating, that the last thing in the world I would ever want to do is to put my own children through such pain. That is the reason I believe I've stayed with you. I believe it was the right choice, and I still do." He didn't have anything else to say.

At this time I only addressed the putdown about being selfish. I did not address the "can't live in the real world issue," though that is the one that always hurt me the most. Perhaps it is because, as I related earlier in my writing, I stated to the psychologist that I didn't consider the breakdown my fault. Perhaps I really wasn't that sure of myself on this point. I do know that somehow "on the surface" I would think Buddy's statement wasn't true, but then "deep down" I wondered. On the other hand, was it "deep down" that I didn't accept it as truth, but "on the surface" I did? I knew that last week I had endured this pain long enough. A couple mornings after the incident, Buddy was up before daylight sitting by the wood stove. I got up and went in and started talking about this. I brought it up and pointed out that when I was teaching in college, I was called into the administration after that first year and offered a full-time position if I would agree to begin a graduate program. Though I declined the offer, I pointed out to Buddy that I HAD held the job. Then I pointed out that I had taught English for a semester, and that the principal told me I had done such a good job dealing with some adverse circumstances surrounding the classes, that is why he wanted to hire me for the math position. I pointed out that the summer after my breakdown, I was asked if I would come back and teach the whole year of Algebra in the summer for those who had failed the regular session. I did this. What I didn't point out to Buddy was that the following year, I was offered a full-time position in the math department at the same school. I declined it because I was receiving money from my inheritance and wished to devote my time to managing this mineral interest. But I DID point out to Buddy that what he had said to me over the years had been very hurtful, and that it was CRUEL to do what he'd done for years! Buddy was very respectful. He did not interrupt me. He just sat there in silence. I sat in silence, too, for about five or ten minutes and then got up and went into another room to read. In a few minutes, Buddy came and asked me to come listen to him. I did this and showed him the same respect. At first, he seemed contrite and somewhat apologetic but then started talking about religion and the Bible in defense of himself. In recent months he sometimes does not seem to comprehend things adequately, and it seemed this was one of those times. In fact, in recent days, he has brought up what I said and does not appear to accept my words about the subject at all. Whether or not he is truly processing what I said, I do know that I needed to address this subject and let my feelings be known. I feel cleansed and that I got something out of my system that I should have been able to address years ago. It is indeed because of my writing and recently finishing the chapter about the breakdown that I was able to express myself verbally. For this I am grateful.

The Second Year and Beyond

Yesterday, I finished reading the court transcripts for the various trials, hearings, and court proceedings that took place between 1990 and 1994. There were six. This does not include the case before the Tennessee State Supreme Court in 1994. Some are over one-hundred pages long. They represent five long agonizing years where I was physically caring for my mother as she advanced deep into the world of memory loss. While I have said that 1991 was the hardest year of my life, for sure, these five years were the hardest five years of my life. I look back and wonder how I cared for Mother, constantly dealt with the fear of the court cases, (and, believe me, there were many times when fear was the most prominent emotion I felt), kept a detailed accounting of every expenditure for my mother and dad down to the penny, with canceled checks backed up by the receipts (my lawyer said that in all of his years in practice, he had never handled such an accounting), took care of the business interests of Dad and Mother, as well as my own and those acquired with my husband. It's a good thing I was in my forties—no way could I do it now!

Dad was put in a nursing home in Gallatin, Tennessee, about fifteen miles from our home in the country. In the letter that Sue wrote to Dad, there are some humorous incidents (for sure, at that time, I couldn't see enough humor from my side of things) that occurred there. Dad was given an allowance, and he often used the money to make calls to the FBI and IRS asking those answering the phone in those agencies to investigate me. On one such occasion, Dad dialed 911. In a manner of minutes, fire trucks, ambulances, etc. descended on the nursing home. When it was determined who had made the call, it was explained to him that one should ONLY dial 911 in case of emergency. Dad said, "It says to 'dial 911 in case of emergency.'" When the person tried to further explain, he replied, "It WAS an emergency! I   lost my quarter."

Dad did not like to bathe, and I have numerous pages where Dad, on a daily basis, would sign a form refusing a bath, and write, "I am allergic to water." His inappropriate sexual behavior escalated there to the point families were threatening to sue the nursing home. He refused all medication, which, even though he had been declared incompetent, he had a legal right to do. After many patient months dealing with Dad, I was told he would be discharged or I could have him sent for evaluation. It was at this time that he was sent to St. Thomas Hospital and placed in the psychiatric ward for a month. His reports from there emphasized, even more strongly than the initial reports, that he needed to be confined. It was while he was in the locked psychiatric ward that he had a visit from a lawyer who promised Dad that he would get him free. This is where the multiple lawsuits began.

The lawyer was one who quickly tried to intimidate and he succeeded with me for a week or so until Sue arrived to help me see the balance of things. Her head was definitely more level than mine at the time. This lawyer called me and immediately told me the schools he had graduated from—saying, "I am no dummy; I have connections; I can get things done!" The lawyer was threatening to go back for years and say that the royalty division that Dad and Mother had done in the mid-'80s would also be declared invalid and that each of us children would have to pay back everything we had received to that point. He also threatened me with the charge that I should have sued all the TV evangelists for the money Dad had sent them, and I would be responsible for that, too. Yes, I got accused of letting Dad have "that valuable violin" in the nursing home. He said I would have to pay back out of my pocket everything that had been spent on Mother and Dad. He even came to my house, got out of his car and walked around the place like he was stalking it. Mail in my mailbox was opened and put back in the box. He wrote me threatening letters—my lawyer said he hated to take someone before the bar, but for me to not open any more letters—just send them to him; he would expose him if he had to. Dr. Slate, these things all happened the week after I got home from visiting you when I told you about the healing dream. And I thought that week had been a bad week! I called Sue and John, and they both came as soon as they could. Sue was never intimidated. John and I were. With Sue's rational analyzing, I quickly saw that she was right, and we shouldn't have anything to do with Dad's new lawyer. It was at this time that I, with Sue accompanying me, met with a lawyer, and hired him for this next round of cases.

This gives some background, and I am now going to rely on documents written at the time to tell more of the story. The first is a paragraph from a letter Sue wrote from California on Sept. 15, 1991, to the new lawyer. She states:

"My opinion of Beverly has not changed. If anything, my respect for her and her ability to deal with adverse family situations has increased. I don't know how she manages to deal with so much. This letter, therefore, will reaffirm my trust and confidence in her. She deserves a medal! I will do all within my power to help see that she remains as Dad's conservator."

Profile of Franklin Edward Rider

Sue wrote this document Sept. 30, 1991, and sent it to the lawyer to be used in court for the upcoming hearing of Dad petitioning for his competency to be legally restored. It is a good biographical sketch of Dad, from Sue's perspective.

Profile of Franklin Edward Rider

Franklin Edward Rider was born July 28, 1911, in Pomona, Howell Co., Missouri. He was the oldest child of John Quincy Rider and Myrtle Laura Phillips. He has two sisters, Alice Amelia Rider Hunt Stanley and Eunice Augusta Rider Gallagher.

In 1917 the family moved to Latimer County, Oklahoma, and settled in Lodi, a rural farming community.

The Rider Family:

My Rider grandparents were wonderful people, and we loved to go to their farm and visit. John Q. Rider was a rather serious man, calm and soft-spoken. I don't remember ever seeing Grandpa Rider smile. He was a hard-working farmer, deeply loved and respected by his family and the community.

Myrtle was quite the opposite of her husband in stature as well as temperament. She was fun to be around and always had a lot going on.

The family were Baptists and faithfully attended church regularly. The Rider children grew up with a good religious foundation. John and Myrtle put their religious beliefs into practice and were good Christians and excellent neighbors. They were well known for the caskets they made for the poorer families. Granny tended the sick and acted as a midwife and delivered many babies.

I don't understand how their child could turn out like my Dad. I don't think that they could ever control Dad. He didn't like to help on the farm but had a talent for mechanics and liked to tinker with cars. He would do mechanical work in exchange for farm work.

Dad likes to quote the Bible, "Children, obey your parents," and "Honor thy father and thy mother," but he didn't practice this where his own parents were concerned. Dad quit school sometime during his eleventh year, and that was the end of his formal education.

I know nothing else about his childhood except that he was devoted to his grandfather, Charles Judson Rider. He still tells in great detail about his grandfather's illness and subsequent death. He shared visions of his grandfather's journey to heaven and his description of what heaven is like during his grandfather's final hours on earth.

History of Frank Rider's Marriages and Divorces:

Marriages:

Jul. 29, 1933   Frank Rider marries Eunice Agnes Whitmore, Poteau, LeFlore Co., OK

Aug. 7, 1942   Frank Rider marries Edith Alamo Andrews, Reno, Washoe Co., NV

Sept. 9, 1944   Frank Rider marries Myrtle Stubbs Thomas, Winnemucca, Humboldt Co., NV

Divorces:

Aug. 14, 1944   from Eunice Rider, Carson City, Ormesby Co., NV

Sept. 8, 1944   from Edith, Virginia City, Storey Co., NV

Jul. 6, 1945   from Myrtle, Wilburton, Latimer Co., OK

Note: From August 7, 1942, until August 14, 1944, Frank Rider was married to two women at the same time. In August 1944, he filed for two divorces, one from Eunice and one from Edith. His grounds in both cases were "extreme cruelty." His testimony relates how both wives treated him so badly that his health was adversely affected. These two divorces are examples of how he will say anything to get what he wants. Also, being married to two women at once clearly shows his disregard for the law. The day after his divorce from Edith, he married Myrtle Thomas.

Eunice Rider and My Childhood Recollections:

Dad married my mother in 1933. He bought his own garage in Wilburton, Latimer Co., Oklahoma. Both John and I were born in Wilburton; I was born in April 1936, and John was born in December 1937.

I never felt that my Dad loved me. I have serious doubts that he ever loved anyone. He never had any patience with children. I was a mama's girl, and I can never remember when I wasn't afraid of my Dad. I didn't like to ask him for money because it wasn't worth the lecture.

During World War II, my parents' marriage started to fall apart. In March 1942, we first came to California. We lived in the Bay Area, and my parents both worked in the shipyards. One of Mother's sisters took John and me back to Oklahoma in August 1942. We stayed with another of mother's sisters and her husband, and I started first grade at Red Oak.

During 1943, Mother taught school in a one-room schoolhouse in Lodi, Oklahoma. We lived in the old schoolhouse across from the newer school. I was in second grade. We attended the same Baptist church our grandparents attended. We walked to church because Dad took the car to town. I can remember begging him to go to church with us. He was too busy; he had begun to court Edith by this time.

There were fights and arguments between my parents. He broke Mother's nose during this period. He wasn't there much, but one night Dad came home while Mother was bathing John and me in a galvanized tub. We had no electricity or indoor plumbing. Another argument started, and he became quite upset and began to make threats that he would just shoot us all. While he went for the gun, Mother grabbed John and me, and we made a run for it. After almost fifty years, I can still remember that night. I was scared to death! I was naked and didn't want the neighbor boys to see me with no clothes on, but I didn't want to get shot either. What a horrible experience. I think Dad's sister came along in her car and rescued us.

The order of events between 1942 and 1944 are confused in my mind. At some point, probably in 1944, Mother returned to California to work in the shipyards to support us. Dad had completely deserted us and was not paying any support.

In 1944, Dad wanted to marry Myrtle Thomas and evidently, Mother didn't want to divorce him. In order to get her to agree to a divorce, Dad knocked her around, and she finally agreed. Also, in 1944, Dad threatened our lives again. Mother was working in California, and John and I were living with our paternal grandparents. Dad called Mother long distance and made threats to kill John and me and himself if she didn't come back to Oklahoma. Granny wouldn't let John and me go anywhere with Dad in the car. He was very crazy at that time, and everyone was afraid of him.

After he sued our mother for a divorce in August 1944, the judge gave child custody to Mother. Dad was ordered to pay her $15.00 a month for each of us as child support. Dad never paid one cent. Mother married Frank Adam Phillips on September 12, 1944, in Reno. She came directly from Reno to Oklahoma. In November, we returned with her to California and started a new life there. I was very happy to be living with my mother again. Our stepfather and Mother supported and raised us until we reached adulthood.

While I was in high school I started smoking. I received a letter from Dad that I'll never forget. He wrote me that he had a vision from God in which he saw my mother dead, lying on a cot at the judgment seat. God was condemning her to hell for the way she had raised her children. Dad continued by saying that he regretted that he hadn't been around to see to our religious upbringing. He said nothing about not being around to see that we had food, clothing, or shelter. This letter really upset me, because Mother was a wonderful person as well as a model parent.

My contacts with my dad during my childhood were rare. I visited him in Wyoming when I was twelve, and in North Carolina, when I was fourteen. A typical Christmas gift would be a short letter from Edith and a check she signed. I never received other gifts during the year. Dad was never in attendance at any significant events of my life like birthdays, graduations, baptism, or marriages. I've received a dozen or so letters from him during my entire life. During the past year, I've received about 25 letters. Normally, he would call me about twice a year. I have had two major surgeries but never received even a get well card.

Edith Rider

On August 7, 1942, Dad married Edith for the first time (while he was still married to my mother). Their son, James Edward, was born in October 1943, lived two days and died due to lack of medical attention. Edith never got over the loss of her baby boy. I think that by the time this baby was born Dad had dumped Edith with his parents and was chasing after Myrtle Thomas.

On July 28, 1945, Dad remarried Edith in Reno. Dad has been abusive to her throughout their married life. Most black slaves were treated with more dignity and respect than he ever showed her. He always placed the full blame on Edith for causing him to divorce my mother and desert his children. John and I have often remarked that she sure did us a favor "taking Dad away from us." Edith is a wonderful person. Regretfully, she lacked the gumption or the courage to stand up to his abusive treatment of herself and Beverly.

I always enjoyed my visits with Edith and Beverly. Edith treated me like a princess. She is one of the sweetest persons I have ever met. The purity of this woman's soul is evident even now, even though she has advanced Alzheimer's disease.

Several times during the course of their marriage Edith and Dad have been in divorce courts. Usually, they would reconcile, resolve their differences, and the action would be dropped. The causes of this were Dad's extra-marital activities, his mistreatment of them, and his lack of financial support to this family. He thinks he has been a good husband and a good father and always denied this.

On June 5, 1972, Edith sued Dad for a divorce in Latimer Co., Oklahoma, on grounds of extreme cruelty. She was awarded a final decree on March 27, 1973. On August 8, 1973, they jointly filed an "Order Setting Aside Decree" in Latimer County. He contends that the cause of this divorce was that Edith would not agree to divide the gas royalty evenly among us three children. In July 1991 he was claiming that Edith wasn't his wife and denies that he participated in any action to set the divorce aside.

Beverly Ann Rider Biggs

Beverly was born May 28, 1946. Dad and Edith raised her. Beverly never had a normal childhood. Dad worked as a welder, and they moved all over the country. As a little child, Beverly had a nervous tic in her eyes which indicated to me that she was under a lot of strain. She witnessed many incidents similar to the ones I described earlier involving Dad and his threats with guns. Dad frequently threatened suicide, and more than once, sat with a gun in his mouth threatening to pull the trigger. Beverly would cry and beg him not to kill himself.

The Old Violin

Dad has owned this old violin for many years. There are many stories, mainly contrived, concerning the old violin. Dad believes it is a Guarnerius and about 500 years old. Dad has been told by violin appraisers all over the country that the violin is a reproduction of a Guarnerius and is worth several hundred dollars. I personally heard appraisers in the greater San Francisco Bay area give verbal appraisals of approximately $200. Dad believes it is worth about $400,000, and, evidently, so does John. The old violin was first given to me in 1945 when I was nine years old and taking violin lessons. As with other gifts Dad has given, it was taken back, but I don't remember when or where.

Conclusion

I have tried to love my Dad, to honor and respect him. That is the way my mother brought me up. But it has not been easy considering the kind of person my Dad is. With God's help, I keep trying. I respect the role of father, but can't respect my father as a person. Every time I have counted on Dad, he has let me down. When I have thought he was on my side, he has betrayed me. He has never accomplished anything that I could be proud of. I have been unsuccessful in my attempts to establish a good, loving relationship with my dad. Dad is almost like a stranger to me. My contact with him has consisted of a few letters and a few phone calls with a personal visit every five years or so. The only thing Dad ever had to give was money. He had nothing else to give.

Frank Rider was eighty years old July 18, 1991. For the past eighty years, he has lived solely for himself without regard for anyone else, especially his family. He managed to get everything he wanted in life. He has had fancy cars, an airplane, expensive hunting dogs, pedigreed cattle, photographic and movie equipment, and recording equipment. I personally don't know of anyone who has ever made a bigger mess out of his life than my father has. He has never been happy, but he has had all that money could buy and what he thought he wanted. He didn't seem to realize that in order to ever be happy, he needed to give and receive love. I never remember him showing any love or tenderness. My earliest memory and the most lingering one is being afraid of him. If I could use only one word to describe my Dad, it would be "evil."

I apologize for the length of this document. I have tried to recall events, state acts, and express my opinions and feelings on the subject of Frank Rider. Thank you for your patience.

Frankie Sue Rider Rogers,   September 30, 1991

The Saga Continues

February 22, 2016

On August 21, 1991, a sheriff's car pulled into my driveway. I was presented with a summons to appear in court. I was being charged with the numerous things that I mentioned in the previous letter. Was I scared? Yes, very scared. To be at the mercy of one person, a judge, who can alter one's life forever is a very scary thing. Dad was suing to get his competency restored. Would I, as the lawyer threatened, have to reimburse the estate for everything spent on Dad and Mother's care? Those were among the threats. So, I had to begin the process of defending myself, and in trying to do so, wrote much. Oh yes, my lawyer said I should just trust him. I replied, "I don't trust anybody." I prepared many folders of paperwork and took them to court. This case was heard on February 20, 1992. At this hearing, testimony was given that, if declared competent, Dad would leave the state and go to Oklahoma to be near John. Dad was declared competent to manage his affairs and did leave. Thank God, I would NO LONGER have to be responsible for him. He only lasted a few days in Oklahoma, though, as he and John just couldn't see eye to eye on much of anything. Dad then went to Idaho to live with his sister, Alice.

The day of that hearing, I was such a nervous wreck. Even though I was not found guilty of any wrongdoing in the charges, none of the threats materialized, and I didn't have to reimburse the estate any monies, I didn't even understand that technically I had lost. It was a call from my lawyer the next day that jolted me into this reality. I had been sued "personally" and as "conservator." I would be "personally" responsible for the nearly $10,000 in legal fees for this case!

It was near the conclusion of this case (after the judge had declared him competent to manage his affairs) that Dad testified he was not married to Mother. Sue has covered this, and Dad's error in thinking, in some of her writings. This did pose a problem. The judge, in all fairness, I believe, honestly wanted to help me. Dad was still adamantly refusing to consider that he needed to help pay for Mother's care. Since the judge couldn't FORCE Dad to pay, and he had, just moments before, declared him competent, he tried to find a way to legally get some monetary help for Mother. He suggested that maybe the legal way would be for Mother to obtain a legal separation from Dad, a Divorce from Bed and Board, as it is called in Tennessee. This just started another round of cases.

That Old Violin

The old violin has been mentioned previously. It was in this second case regarding Dad's competency that I was charged with mismanaging this violin. For something so humorous, it caused me a lot of grief.

Among other things, I was accused of letting Dad have his violin with him in the nursing home—an irresponsible act on my part, considering its value.

In a document Sue wrote in support of me for the upcoming court case, Sue says: "Dad believes it is worth approximately $400,000. He has been all over the United States, including to the Smithsonian, and to appraisers in New York City. All of them have told him almost the same thing, but he never gives up. He doesn't believe there is anyone in the United States qualified to appraise this instrument. One of his plans, after he gets his liberty back, is to take the old violin to London and get it appraised there. If that old violin is worth thousands of dollars it should stay with the estate. It may need to be sold to pay for attorneys' fees and court costs. "

I prepared a document for the court in my defense, also. The remainder of this chapter comes from this document. In it I wrote:

When Dad was a young single man, he purchased a violin from a neighbor named Jack Tidwell. When Sue was small, she says that she carried it to school for violin lessons and that Dad gave it to her. Perhaps the same applies to John. Although I never remember Dad giving it to me, it was in our home all during my childhood, most of the time up in the top of the closet, forgotten. From 1968 until 1981, it was left in an empty house in Red Oak, Oklahoma, as Mother and Dad were living away from their home—Dad working in various states. In 1981, when Mother and Dad decided to move all of their possessions out here to Tennessee, Dad took the violin out to John's house. In 1982 Dad suddenly decided the violin was a very rare and valuable instrument and went back and brought it to Tennessee.

Dad thinks that it is a very rare instrument made by a member of the Italian Guarneri family, second only in fame as violinmakers, to the Stradivari family. Dad decided, though I had never heard this during my growing-up years, that it was brought over on the Mayflower. I tried to show Dad from the encyclopedia, that even if it were made by the famous man that he claimed, the man was born sixty-seven years after the Mayflower sailed. Dad's reply was, "Old man Jack Tidwell said his family brought it over on the Mayflower, and 'old man Jack' wouldn't lie!"

From Dad, I have constantly had to listen to the way I was interfering with God's direction in helping get the violin appraised and sold. He was so worried about it and wanted me to let him have it so that he could be sure it was safe. After bringing written appraisals to the Pinnacle Care administrator, and having Dad sign a release of responsibility, I brought him the violin. After all, I was entrusting him with his false teeth, needed for his physical well-being, and they had cost a whole lot more than the violin was worth. I certainly saw no harm in bringing him something that was so important to his emotional well-being. As I have said earlier in these writings, when I could comply with a request from Dad that I felt was in his best interest and would make him less unhappy, I was always willing to do so.

The first written appraisal that I have on the violin was made in 1982 in Nashville; the value was placed at approximately $1200. Dad was not satisfied. The value of the violin went down from the earlier appraisals because Dad thought he would improve it by replacing a lot of the original parts such as carrying case, chin-rest, bridge, etc. with new ones. In addition, he poured a lot of glue in the sound post cracks, which had not really been a tone problem. He took it to Boone, North Carolina; the Smithsonian Institution in Washington, D.C. (he was especially mad when he came back from there--he said the man told him ". . . it was a piece of junk."); Chicago, Illinois; Milwaukee, Wisconsin; Minneapolis, Minnesota; New York City; and San Francisco—all to be told basically the same thing—that it was a reproduction made around the turn of this century in what is now Germany.   End of quote.

To end the violin story without further adieu, Dad gave the violin to John. What a relief to me to FINALLY not have to deal with that old violin!

More Lawsuits

If those who are reading this book are wondering, "Will these lawsuits ever end?" well, believe me, I was wondering the same thing! As I mentioned earlier, when Dad was declared competent after being declared incompetent, we were still left with the initial problem we had at the beginning of all of this—how to get Dad to be responsible for paying for care for Mother. As I related in an earlier chapter, at the end of that lawsuit, the judge had suggested that maybe we should file for a legal separation, a Divorce from Bed and Board, as it's called in Tennessee. I was so frazzled by that time that I didn't even understand that this would not work. Indeed, I, too late, came to understand that it would never work under the current laws of the state. As things ended, the lawyers wanted to make this a test case. When this eventually wound up in the State Supreme Court, with me begging just to be done with it all—to be left alone—that I wanted NO MORE COURT CASES, it was too late.

This was the problem. Mother was not capable of signing to file for this legal separation. With a lawyer's guidance, I was allowed, as her conservator, to sign her name. Not knowing the law or, at this point, understanding the plan, I agreed to file for this action.

In the meantime, that first lawyer that had come to the St. Thomas hospital ward to see Dad had not turned out to be very good at all. Before the competency case was heard, Dad hired another lawyer to help the first. How he got in the picture, I really don't know. At least, in my dealings with him, he was professional, as lawyer's go. In addition to being retained for the competency case, he was retained for the Divorce from Bed and Board case. On top of that, he filed a case against me which was called, Objection to Final Accounting. Now, my final accounting for Dad was filed for Dad within days of him being declared competent. It was approved by the judge. The charge NOW was that on months when the royalty checks were not sufficient enough to cover Mother and Dad's expenses, I had moved money over from their passbook savings account to cover the expenses. Conversely, the months where the royalty checks were greater than the expenses, I had taken the extra and put it in the passbook savings. I did this, of course, to draw the extra bit of interest on the money. Well, the charges were: I was dipping into the principle of the estate, and this was not supposed to have been done without going before the court for the judge's approval. My job was to prove that this passbook savings account was not principle—the income-producing mineral interest was the principle of this estate. It was decided for both of these cases to be heard on February 22, 1993. The Divorce from Bed and Board case was heard in the morning, and the Objection to Final Accounting was heard in the afternoon.

February 22, 1993, was another of one of the hardest days of my life. As I write this, it has been twenty-three years and two days since that excruciating day. It is another of the days that is indelibly stamped in my mind—a day that things happened of a supernatural nature. And no, I don't hesitate to use the word supernatural to describe two events—one that happened on the 22nd and one on the 23rd. For those two events, I am copying letters I wrote describing them to our Irish friend, Jackie Corbett, who had terminal cancer. It was a way for me to put these experiences on paper without wasting time. Somehow, I've always felt that just writing things down for writing's sake was somewhat of a waste of time. I always wanted any writing I did to serve a purpose outside of myself. Though I thoroughly realize now that this is not so, it always seemed a bit self-centered to me to just write for my own sake. The first letter gives an account of an experience that happened the morning of the 22nd as I was preparing for court. The other two letters could be considered as one, as the second is a continuation of the first.

I was periodically sending Jackie get-well cards and other cards, sometimes with letters, to cheer him in his situation. The card I chose for this letter had an artist's rendering of the famous *End of the Trail* statute that played such a prominent role in my healing dream to which I so often refer.   I am getting goosebumps. Until this moment, I had never made a connection between using this card with this particular painting to describe this experience, but I'm doing so now.

This letter was written four years after the event and starts off with Buddy and me flying from Calgary, Canada, to Dallas. He was in from Saudi on business in both cities, and I had joined him for those few days. Now, for the card and letter.

The card is inscribed with the following verse:

Indian Prayer for Peace

Oh, Great Spirit who dwells in the sky,
lead us to the path of peace and understanding,
let all of us live together as brothers and
sisters. Our lives are so short here, walking
upon Mother Earth's surface. Let our eyes be
opened to all the blessings you have given us.
Please hear our prayers, Oh, Great Spirit.

1 May 1997

Dear Jackie,

The evening we flew from Calgary to Dallas, on the way to the hotel from the airport, we witnessed the most beautiful sunset—as only those sunsets on the plains can be. Buddy said, upon my excited exclamations about it, "I guess this sunset was just for you, Beverly." I replied, "This sunset IS for me." I didn't say "JUST for me," but it was for me, and anyone else who wanted to claim it for their own.

As you know, the sun loomed large in the life and religion of the

Blackfoot Indians. They have a saying that can best be translated:
 "The sun rose the day I was born.
 The sun rests when I sleep.
 The final sunset is the day I die."

Tim and I have discussed this and its meaningfulness. The day before I was to go to court for the trial to answer for the charges against me, Tim called from Saudi. No matter where in the world he is, Tim always has this "sense" when I need help and calls and with very few words says what I need to hear. That day, when I answered the phone, Tim said, "Mother, how long has it been since you've seen the sun rise?" He did not have to say more. I knew what he meant. I replied, "It's been a long time, but tomorrow I need to watch the sun rise."

I got the newspaper out to see the time predicted for the sunrise, which was 6:26. I set my alarm clock early enough that I would be up and around and fully alert, so I could watch the time. Actually, I woke up much earlier, so I got up, took a bath, dressed, and was sitting at the make-up table putting on my make-up. In my preparations, I had forgotten that I intended to be staring at the clock. All of a sudden, my whole body jerked, and I turned toward the clock, and the digital reading said, "6:26." I tore into the living room to look toward the east, and just as I got to the window, the sun rose in all its splendor. It was only brilliant for an instant. It went behind the clouds, and the rest of the day was cloudy, windy, and cold, with even some mist occasionally.

But that day that was so emotionally and mentally critical in my life, I felt my ancestors had come for me. They had given me a sign so that I might have the confidence to make it through the day and to know, that regardless of the verdict, I would come through whole in mind, body, and spirit at the close of the day. As I left that morning, what a wonderful feeling it was!

Beverly

There are a few observations I want to make about that day in court, Monday, February 22, 1993. Earlier, Dad's lawyer had sent notice to the court and to my lawyer that he was subpoenaing Mother to court. Mother, of course, was scared to get in a car, as I've related earlier. Also, her mind had so deteriorated that she could not say her name, let alone mine. My lawyer said we would get her doctor's affidavit that Mother was in no condition to appear in court. This was done. Sunday night, the night before the case was to be heard, my lawyer called. He said, "Beverly, I have just come home from church. While there, I couldn't help thinking about this case, and I have changed my mind. I think we should physically have your mother in court tomorrow morning. I know this is late, but I want you to arrange for an ambulance to bring her." So, I got on the phone and got this arranged for the time he thought I should have her there. I would have to be in court early and had arranged for her sitter to be with Mother all day. Trousdale County, Tennessee, is a small rural county with an old-fashioned courthouse on a central square in town. It had only stairs—no elevator. As we sat in court in the mist of proceedings, Dad's lawyer is expounding, "I've subpoenaed Mrs. Rider to be in court, and she is not here!" At that point, my lawyer dramatically—it was like actors on a stage—arose and said, "She will be here." At that instant—I'm not kidding—at that very instant a siren sounded down below. The ambulance had arrived and had the siren on to clear the people who were gathered at the front of the courthouse. Mother, on a stretcher, was carried up the stairs and into the courtroom. I sat there with a detached feeling from all this—it was almost as if I were embodying the line from Shakespeare, "All the world is a stage, and we are its players." This exact line was exactly what I was thinking at that moment. Both lawyers had put on such an act. I thought, "What a movie this would make!" The lawyer's lines, the ambulance, the siren at just the right moment, the sounds as Mother was being brought up the stairs, the impact in the courtroom as the door was opened and Mother brought in on a stretcher—the timing of it all was oh so surreal.

Judgement was rendered in favor of Mother. Unbeknown to me, that only started the next round. Dad's lawyer appealed the case to the State Supreme Court. That case was heard in 1994. The law just did not cover a situation like this—forcing a competent to pay for the care of an incompetent. The case, therefore, was overturned, with a reprimand to the judge who had declared Dad incompetent and then competent. One judge said that the way to solve all this was to restore my conservatorship over Dad. Oh my, how little did those judges really know of the total problems! During this time, I did learn that twenty-six states already had laws already on the books to deal with a similar situation. Unfortunately, trying to make my case a test case did not work. Whether Tennessee lawmakers have covered this scenario since I do not know. This I do know. From beginning to end over $52,000 was paid to lawyers, and nothing was solved. Far better had this money been used for their care. I begged to not have to spend further monies taking it to the Supreme Court. I said, "I'd rather just pay for everything myself." But, I had no choice. I didn't really understand about appeals. To not go forward would have been viewed as an admission of guilt. I would have been held responsible for paying back everything I had been threatened within the suit.

In my own case that afternoon regarding the Objection to Final Accounting, the judge ruled that I was supposed to have come before the court asking approval to move the monies around as I had done. Since, however, every penny could be accounted for, and, prior to this, I had not been advised of the necessity of the court approval, I would not have to repay anything.

What a day! What an agonizing, grueling, intense day! What a comfort to have had the "sunrise experience" that morning and to be assured that I would make it through—whatever the outcome!

The day following I had an experience like no other that I have had in life. I believe it deserves a chapter all its own.

My Choctaw Commemorative Medal

The following two letters were written to Jackie Corbett to describe events involving my Choctaw commemorative coin, as I call it. Perhaps the word coin should be reserved for describing a government issue of a medium of exchange, but I've always used the word coin when I talk about this medal. February 23, 1993, the day after my grueling day in court on the defense of two cases, something happened that I've never before nor since experienced in life. I will let these two letters tell the story:

21 July 1997

Dear Jackie,

Today I want to write to you about experiences surrounding my Choctaw Nation commemorative coin.

First, I will tell you how I got this coin. When I was in college in Alabama, one of the required classes for me was an education class where you learned some teaching methods. The grade was mainly based on a 30 min. teaching session that each person had to do during the semester. Being the conscientious person that I am, and always wanting to make top grades, I knew the topic I chose would be very important. As History was one of my majors, I decided to teach the story of "The Trail of Tears" for my lesson topic. I got into it in a big way and prepared large charts. During our Spring break, I decided to go to Oklahoma and gather more information. My friend, Hazel Morgan, took me over to an old Indian who had been present at the last legal execution in Indian Territory, which had been at Red Oak. He told many stories of the old days, and I recorded them on tape.

We went to visit the Assistant Chief of the Choctaw Nation. After interviewing him, he said he wanted to give me a coin—a 99.9% silver commemorative coin with the Great Seal of the Choctaw Nation on one side, and a copy of a print of the Choctaws playing stickball on the other.   He said that he was presenting it to me because he knew I would always say good things on behalf of the Choctaws and teach others about them whenever I had the opportunity.

To continue the story I wrote the following letter:

9 Aug. 1997

Dear Jackie,

I chose this card to write the continuing story about my silver commemorative coin. I had received the coin in 1974 and had kept it in my china closet on display in front on the top shelf. I looked at it often. As I told you in earlier letters, the day of the court trial for me was very traumatic. I was really having trouble keeping my sanity.

The next day after the trial I was still in some sort of shock, I guess. I was almost in an altered state. The stress had been so great, but I felt it was all over at last. I was standing in the dining room of the house in Tennessee, when suddenly it seemed as though the room was filled with spirits, or much energy, if you will. I was being told (not audibly, of course) to go look at my coin. I kept hesitating, wondering why I needed to go look at it at that moment. This urging kept on a few moments, and it was as if I were pushed into the living room to the china cabinet. I looked at the coin. Then I was told to open the cabinet and hold the coin in my hand. I did so, and to my amazement, it had a golden colored ring around the edge on the side, and only on this side, of the Great Seal of the Choctaw Nation. I was shocked and also a bit scared. I was afraid I was hallucinating. But I was comforted by the presence of those who told me they were my ancestors—again—as in the powerful dream—they had come to help me and to take care of me and to see that I made it through this. I was assured that they were there for me, and that I could always call on them, and that the golden rim appearing on the coin was a sign that I could always count on them.

For a few days, I would go back and look at the coin—even fearful that it had turned back completely silver like it had been. When I got the courage and realized it seemed to be staying this way, I called my Choctaw cousin, Pat, to ask if her similar coin had ever turned. She said it had not, so I told her the story of what had happened. Then I called Hazel Morgan, who had been with me when I got the coin and knew it was silver and asked her if she would check around with those she knew who had a coin to see if any had turned. She checked and found none that had.

A few weeks later I took it and showed it to Dr. Slate, who told me he thought it was significant that the golden rim was on the side of the seal, which would have become sacred at the time of its adoption, and that it had not turned on the side of the picture of Choctaws playing stickball, which would have no sacred meaning.

Beverly Biggs

It is now 2016, and the coin still has its place of honor on display in my china cabinet. I held in my hand just yesterday. It still has that golden colored rim on the side of the seal and is still completely silver on the other side.

Divorce From Bed and Board

The following is a document I wrote and filed in court for this case:

IN THE CHANCERY COURT FOR
TROUSDALE COUNTY, TENNESSEE
RE: DIVORCE FROM BED AND BOARD

In my AMENDMENT TO THE AMENDED COMPLAINT AND SUPPLEMENTAL PETITION FOR DIVORCE FROM BED AND BOARD, under category II, items (1) and (2), I have made allegations of cruel and inhuman treatment and indignities to the wife's person. I would like to give the following as examples:

1) When Mother's mind started deteriorating, she would hide things, misplace them, or put them in inappropriate places. She would hide her purse and then think that someone had stolen it. I have spent hours looking through every drawer and closet, only to find it wrapped in towels, blankets, stuffed in pillowcases, etc. Dad thought that this was funny and would sometimes deliberately hide the purse. I would again spend hours hunting for it, only for him to bring it out of hiding and hold it up. She would plead for it, and he would say, "See Edith, I have your purse, but you can't have it. You will just lose it." She would start crying, begging for the purse. This example was repeated many times, as are most of the other examples that I will mention.

2) Dad would scream loudly at Mother for misplacing anything, and she would frantically try to find the missing item for him, only growing more confused as he continued to scream.

3) Mother would use the bathroom, including bowel movements, outside with neighbors watching. While I would be trying to clean it up, Dad would stand there and laugh at the situation.

4) Dad would scream at Mother that she wasn't worth burying—that when she died, he was going to throw her body in Carr's dumpster (the garbage dumpster up the road). She would sit and cry all day while I would try to comfort her and tell her that I would take care of her.

5) When his first wife, Eunice Phillips, died in 1988, Dad kept about a dozen copies of her obituary lying around on tables, near his bed, TV, etc. He would read them much of the time. If one was misplaced, he would scream at Mother, and she would frantically try to find it. He would scream at Mother that he never loved her, he only loved Eunie—that he only married her to teach Eunie a lesson.

6) When it was apparent that Mother could not prepare proper meals, I started taking up the meals to Mother and Dad. Mother would eat a lot better if someone sat with her. She would get up and wander without this supervision. Dad would ask me why I was sitting with her, and I would tell him. He would say, "Just let her starve. It would be God's will. She's ready to die and needs to die."

7) When Mother reached the stage where she wandered off, I often had to go through the woods hollering for her. I would sometimes find her at neighbors' homes, or before I missed her, someone would telephone me that she was at their place. We live bordering a creek, and I expressed fear that she might fall in and drown. Dad, again, would say, "Let her drown. That would be God's will." When I have gone into town for groceries and to do other errands, I would often come home to find her clinging to the stop sign on Highway #231, crying hysterically. When I expressed fear for her safety on such a busy highway, I would get the same answer, "Let her get run over. It would be God's will."

8) At this point in Mother's deterioration, I talked to Dad on several occasions about setting up a schedule with me for him to be responsible for watching her a couple hours per day. He would scream at me, "Nobody's going to tell me when to come and when to go. I will do as I please!" I would reply that I wasn't telling, that I was requesting, but

all my entreaties were to no avail. Even when he was home, I could not count on him watching her. He spent most of his time either watching TV evangelists or lying in the back bedroom reading his Bible. He was often oblivious as to whether she was in or out of the trailer.

9) When I asked him to hire some help, even for just two hours a day, he would scream, "I'm not going to throw away $4 an hour on someone to take care of her. I'm giving my money to God." In the summer of 1990, I hired a lady for two hours a day to come and fix lunch. Dad made sexual advances toward her, and when she refused him and told me about it, he would not let her come back.

10) Mother had grown terrified of riding in an automobile. Dad would make her get in a car or pickup, often non-air conditioned and in the heat of summer, and drive her around for hours. She would come back so disoriented and hysterical that she wouldn't know that she had been anywhere. For the rest of the day, she would be confused more than she was normally.

11) Dad refused to allow me to get proper medical treatment for her. It was always, "The Bible says, 'Woe be unto the doctors.'" If she became ill, and I felt it was serious enough to require medical attention, I would have to slip her to the doctor when he wasn't at home. Then he would often refuse to let me use the medication the doctor had prescribed, if I had to treat her at a time when he was at home.

12) Mother reached the stage where she would wander away from home in the night as well as during the day. At this point, she could find her way to my house, but had lost the sense of direction to return to the trailer. She would sometimes come to my house and get in bed with me. Often, after having been with me several hours, at maybe 2 a.m. or 3 a.m., Dad would call on the phone and say, "Is your mother down there?"

13) Mother and Dad's hours of getting up in the morning were so erratic that I abandoned fixing their breakfast, but tried to see that they had cereal. One morning, Dad ate the last of the cereal and forced

Mother to eat a bowl of sugar! She got sick to her stomach and was sick all day. He ate a lot of donuts, cake, and other sweets, and would often force Mother to eat some even when she pleading to him that she did not want it. Mother would eat nutritious meals if Dad did not force her to fill up on donuts and cookies before I could get up with the food.

14) Dad abused Mother sexually on a regular basis. I found blood on her underclothes on several occasions. She has come to my house crying hysterically, "He's mean to me. He told me to take my panties off. He's mean to me." On one such occasion, she added that he had hit her and that she had fallen and hurt her toe, which turned black the next day. Again, there was blood on her underwear. The following day I sought counsel from an attorney regarding becoming Mother's conservator.

15) After Dad received papers notifying him of my attempt to become his and Mother's conservator, I became especially fearful of his treatment of Mother. I tried to see that he did not take her in a vehicle. When I was a child, and he was exhibiting inappropriate behavior, he had often taken her away in a car with a gun, making various threats. I was determined that history was not going to be repeated.

These are a few of the examples of things that I KNOW PERSONALLY Mother had to endure. At the time I became conservator of Mother, she would try to tear the screens off the windows and would pull the heating vents up from the floor, with the longest nails I had not being enough to hold them. She would put a pillowcase on her feet and hop around the floor. These are a few examples of her almost animal-like behavior.

After getting conservatorship of Mother, I took her to the doctor to have a thorough examination to determine if there was anything that could be done about the deterioration of her mind. On her first visit, she was so uncontrollable that it was a challenge to keep her in the room. Medical personnel expressed amazement that I was trying to keep a person in her condition at home. The doctor cautioned me that

Alzheimer's disease does not get better. I was determined to give her a chance. After just a few weeks with me, she became peaceful, happy, easy to manage, and a real joy to be around. In commenting on this remarkable improvement in her behavior, her doctor said, "If I hadn't seen this with my own eyes, I would have never believed it!"

Beverly Biggs

Finally, It's Over

Just a few days after the two trials, I found out that Dad's lawyer was going to appeal the verdict in the Divorce from Bed and Board case and take it to the State Supreme Court. I have related this in a previous chapter and will not repeat it here. So, finally, in 1994 the lawsuits were over. Mother and Dad's bank accounts stood close to zero. In addition to the lawyer fees I had to pay, I had been contributing over $1,000 per month to Mother's care. The royalty checks were not large enough to cover the legal fees as well as the care for both Mother and Dad.

Sue had supported me with documents in the last two cases in February 1993 but did not come to Tennessee for the trials personally. How opportune that was. Dad was there, but Sue was not present in his face. Sue visited him in Idaho, and miracles of miracles, he signed for her to be his power of attorney. Thus, she was able to control the finances and take care of his mineral interest. The judge in Trousdale County had ruled that Dad was to pay Mother $700 a month for her care. Even though this judgment was overturned at the state level, and she didn't legally have to, Sue continued to send me a check from Dad's funds for $700 per month until Mother died.

In this final chapter regarding these trying times, I will talk about some of the ways I coped. After my recovery from my breakdown when I was forty, I had been stable mentally, but the stresses starting about a couple years later brought out symptoms that were problematic. During the week of the healing dream, I was dangerously close to another breakdown. I truly believe that experiencing this dream, to a large degree, helped prevent it. Meetings with Dad's psychiatrist at St. Thomas Hospital were stressful enough for me that I felt I needed further help. I remembered the words of Dr. C, the psychologist I saw at the time of the breakdown. He had told me, that though he was comfortable in ending our sessions, there would be times in my life that I would feel the need for help. I wasn't ashamed or afraid to ask for it. A wise person would do no less. I asked Dad's psychiatrist at St. Thomas if he saw patients privately. He said that he did. I asked him if he would see me, and he said, "No." He said, though, that he would recommend someone that he thought would be more helpful to me. I can tell you that his answer disappointed me. Dr. W. at St. Thomas was a clinical psychiatrist, cold, distant, and brilliant. I thought I wanted and needed someone just like that. I even envisioned that he was someone I could match wits with. I didn't feel superior to him intellectually as I had felt back when I started seeing Dr. C. I even felt he was my equal and that I wanted somebody who was cold and detached. For sure, I had no intention of becoming emotional and breaking down barriers with which I had surrounded myself. I did know that I needed help, so I accepted Dr. W.'s answer and made an appointment with his recommendation, Dr. R. I first saw him July 26, 1991, the month of the healing dream. What a wise choice for me. Dr. R. was brilliant, but his manner couldn't have been more of a polar opposite than that of Dr. W. Dr. R was warm and friendly, and I saw him once a week for six weeks. While I didn't go into a true mania, I did exhibit signs of hypomania and did take the medication that Dr. R prescribed.

With mutual agreement, we decided that six sessions were enough. For over fifteen months it was, but while in the throws of the events surrounding the 1993 lawsuits, I made an appointment on December 15, 1992, to see him again. I saw him ten times between then and May 3, 1993. Again, while I never went into a full-blown manic episode, I came dangerously close. While I wasn't comfortable with the label, I did accept that I met medical criteria for manic-depression or bipolar disorder, the current preferred term. Dr. R. wanted me to stay on medication permanently for this disorder. I refused, only staying on prescribed drugs long enough to not exhibit symptoms.

In March of 1994, I once again sought Dr. R.'s help, this time for only three sessions. He told me that he treated a lot of the musicians in Nashville, but that I was the only person under his care who had ever come to his office voluntarily. He said that it was remarkable that I could sense episodes developing and seek help. Most didn't believe there was anything wrong with them—it was everybody else who was messed up. Having said all of that, he said he felt the duty to again encourage me to remain on medication permanently. Medical evidence pointed to the necessity of that.

When Dad was eighty, there was more than one psychiatrist who felt Dad suffered from bipolar disorder. This is the first time the label had been placed on him, but I would agree. Later in this book, I will be talking further of my great-grandfather, Jack Phillips, Granny's dad, who died on the Crow Indian Reservation in Lodgegrass, Montana. From family stories, he seemed to exhibit the same symptoms. One of those stories related the time he allegedly shot himself in the head— most tell it that he was attempting suicide. A description of this incident, including an account of the conversation, is documented in a country doctor's journal that is in a museum in Newcastle, Wyoming. Granny has often told me, that as a young girl, she found him and ran barefoot in her nightgown in the snow seeking help. The doctor came, examined him, and turned to the wife, saying, "There's a ninety-nine percent chance he will die." At this point, Jack raised up in the bed and said, "One percent. That's all I need!"

Often in life, I've used this family story to help me in whatever I was experiencing. On the day of our last session, as I related the purchase of our house and farm in South Carolina, and my intended move there, Dr. R. made the statement, "There's a ninety-nine percent chance you will have to be on medication the rest of your life." As I stood at the door, in what were my farewell words, I said, "One percent. That's all I need!"

My Dream Home

My Dream Home

Of all the dreams I've had in my life, none have been more life-changing than the series I had in April and May 1994.

For most of the years when I was involved in the caregiving of my parents, Buddy was working in Saudi Arabia. He had three extended vacations a year. One was always at least six weeks in length. During this period he came home to Tennessee, as I was not able to travel foreign. Several times I arranged for sitters for Mother so that we could travel for a few days on short trips. Buddy would have been satisfied to retire where we lived, but I had had so much sadness there, and I didn't want to be constantly reminded of it. Buddy was agreeable to moving, but his one request was that he wanted ten or more acres of land, so that he could be a gentleman farmer. On our little breaks, we looked at states where we might want to move. After considering a few states, we decided to see what South Carolina had to offer. We went to a realty office and told them we were not ready to buy but wanted to see the types of properties that were available. We were handed a printed list of about a dozen properties and went off on our own to look at them. We became very discouraged. As Buddy said, "If it says 'gently rolling,' it means if you step off the front porch, you will 'roll' to the bottom of the hill!" As we climbed the mountain to look at the last property on the list, we thought, "Oh, another 'rolling' one." As we descended the mountain, the most wonderful little valley opened up. We found the twenty-one acre farm that was for sale, and the owner was out in the yard. Buddy did get out and feel the dirt of this farm and commented that the soil was good. The owner, a single man, asked me if I wanted to see inside the house, and Linda and I went in to have a look. Buddy was not interested enough to go inside. It was February. The thought crossed my mind, "If I like a place in the winter, I could really like it the rest of the year."

Buddy went back to Saudi. I continued my routine of caring for Mother for the next few months. Then one night toward the end of April, I had a dream about this farm that we had looked at in South Carolina. That wasn't so unusual, but after another night or so, I had another dream. I was decorating the room the owner used as a family room, but for me, it was a dining room. Another night or so went by, and I dreamed again about this farm. I was sitting in a gazebo by the creek that bordered the property and writing a book. Again, a few nights went by, and I had a few more dreams related to the farm and house. This was beginning to really disturb me. About ten nights and several dreams later, I decided to call Buddy. I told him that I knew the house needed some work, but that I wanted to come down and look at all the negatives and get this place out of my system. Maybe then I could have a good night's sleep and quit having these dreams!

Linda was attending East Tennessee State University in Johnson City, Tennessee. I called her and asked if she'd like to meet me to look at the farm in South Carolina that we'd looked at. When we pulled up, the place was ringed in dogwoods, and the azaleas were in full bloom. We got out of the car, and the first thing that popped out of my mouth to the owner was, "I could be buried here." He explained that actually one could be buried here—that it wasn't against the law. I have no idea why I blurted this out. When we left, Linda reprimanded me with, "Mother, you've gotten that man excited. He thinks we are going to buy that place, and you know we are not. You know why we came down here." Well, I went back to Tennessee with mixed emotions. I hadn't gotten it out of my system at all. When I called Buddy, he did not even say, "Hello." His first words were, "You want to buy that place, don't you, Beverly?" I said, "Yes." And that's how it all happened. I closed the deal on May 20, the week before my birthday. What a wonderful birthday gift it continues to be!

Linda graduated from the University that summer and moved down here. I didn't move down here permanently until June 1995 and will pick up more of the story from a letter I wrote to friends in November 1995.

Linda suggested we rename the farm. I protested that I'm not good at naming things, but since I'd had the dreams, and we bought it because of this, Linda wanted me to choose the name. You guessed it. In the wee morning hours, in that half-awake, half-asleep state, I had a dream that we should name it the Choctaw word for gift. I called a Choctaw friend in Oklahoma and asked her to find out for me the Choctaw word for gift. She discovered there were two words—one meant "like a bribe," and the other meant "a gift that keeps on giving and giving again." So, we chose *Habenna*, the gift that keeps on giving and giving again.

And so it has been. Pure, crystal clean water from springs deep in the ground for drinking, the creek that tumbles over the rocks, providing many calming moments to sit and watch a leaf cling precariously to a rock as I continued to cope with the years of caring for Mother, the deer that ate the peaches from our trees as we sat on the front porch and watched, the bear that poked his head up to our dining room window as we ate our supper, the mountains that surround with their spring green leaves and mountain laurel, redbuds, dogwoods, wildflowers— they are gifts all. These gentle Blue Ridge Mountains provide a soft mist that arises after a rainfall and give us an artist's palette of color in the fall. On some years a serene snow comes to envelop the land in a stillness all its own. These are just some of the gifts of this lovely land.

The house wasn't from a plan book. It was built in 1970 in the style of early nineteenth century Piedmont farmhouses in Upstate South Carolina. The late eighteenth and early nineteenth century antiques I had been collecting found a home that seemed to be made just for them. I renovated the kitchen with cherry cabinets built from wood from a virgin cherry tree that Linda had been given in Tennessee, and with antique pieces. Buddy and I drove to Pennsylvania to get other cabinets I'd had made by the Amish from the wood of butternut trees. I love the sense of permanence I feel when someone drives up and says, "What a lovely place! Has this been in your family a long time?"

Soon after coming down, I was visiting with elderly neighbors, sisters Helen and Sara. When I told them of the dreams of how we acquired this place and how the name came to be, Sara said to me, "And the best gift of all is your neighbors." Helen and Sara have long since passed on, but we still have their daughter Ann and her husband Terry for our good neighbors. In any given need, Ann will be first to bring a gift of food, as she has often done for us.

Habenna, what a lovely, accurate name. Some of those who occupy this little vale are on land passed down from their ancestors who received it in land grants not long after the Revolution. Two creeks converge at one corner of the property. Indians must have had many camps at this convergence, as we find beautiful arrowheads as a reminder of their time here, too.

Letter to Friends

After getting settled in my new home, I wrote this letter to friends and family. It contains a vivid description of some of the behavior of Alzheimer's victims:

September 4, 1995

Hello:

Greetings from the Carolinas. It is good to be alive and to be here in these lovely Blue Ridge Mountains.

It is 5:30 in the morning. I woke up at 3:15 (I haven't slept well the past three nights—stress, I guess) and after lying in bed for awhile, I decided if I were ever going to get a letter written to everybody, this would be the best time to do it. So far, I have twenty-seven letters to answer. So many of you have written after I sent my change of address notes. Several weeks ago I came to the conclusion that there was no way in the next few months I was going to get individual letters written to everybody, and that I would write a general letter instead. So, I hope you will excuse that this is a computer letter.

I will now take the time to fill everybody in on my year so far. January and February were rather uneventful—just the routine of taking care of Mother. During March, Mother seemed to go down rapidly, especially in her ability to walk or stand. For so many months, or even a year or so, we had had to hold her so she could walk across the room, but she got to where she could not do this. She would slump down and get on the floor. If someone extra wasn't there to help get her up, I would just make her comfortable on the floor until another sitter came. It was becoming apparent to me that I was going to have to make a change in her care. I had hoped that I would never have to put her in a nursing home and had said that I would rather she would die before I ever had to resort to this.

At this point, I am going to relate a bit about Alzheimer's disease. I know that it has been in the news a lot lately, with a lot of public education and awareness being accomplished, but there are still many who have not been touched by it and really do not know or understand the various stages and what this disease does. I know this from the questions I am asked and the surprised comments from relatives and friends. The following are some examples of behavior in various stages of Alzheimer's: Some of the first symptoms are forgetting and confusion. This will involve getting confused about where one is, getting lost, getting confused about the time of day, misplacing things and then later hiding things and not being able to find them. This latter usually involves thinking someone has stolen them. One of the things Mother did most often was hide her purse. She would put all sorts of things in it—wrap spoons in dish towels that she had torn up in tiny shreds, tying many knots in these strings, and putting other inappropriate things in, having the purse so full she could hardly carry it. She wanted it with her twenty-four hours a day. She would wrap towels around it and hide it, then come to the house and get me, telling me that someone had stolen it. I have spent hours and hours— sometimes all day hunting it. You would not think it would be possible to so completely hide something in a mobile home, but, take my word for it, it is! Sometimes I would be ready to conclude that maybe someone HAD stolen it. On top of this, Dad, who was having some problems himself, would sometimes hide the purse; and after I had searched for hours with Mother crying, he would retrieve it and dangle it in front of her, taunting her with, "Here it is Edith, but you can't have it. You'll just lose it."

Other examples of forgetfulness involve the inability to do routine things (Mother made Dad pancakes out of washing powders). This progresses to running away. The books on Alzheimer's call it wandering. When one turns one's back for a moment, answers the phone, and the person is gone, I hardly call it wandering. Mother has been gone in a flash so many times I could never begin to count them. She could get out of sight so rapidly. I have spent many agonizing moments in the woods screaming for her at the top of my lungs. As we lived by a creek, there was the fear of her falling in. Next comes not being able to recognize familiar people. It has been over six years since, if anyone had asked Mother who I was, she could have told my name. I remember one time I was trying to test her, and I kept saying, "Mother, who am I?" I thought saying "Mother" would spark her memory. I kept on asking, but she couldn't remember my name. Finally, she said, "I thought you knew who you were yourself."

One can no longer put their clothes on or do routine things like bathing. These things progress on to not being able to tell you when they have to go to the bathroom. Then comes not being able to remember how to lift a fork or spoon and put it in your mouth (I have been hand feeding Mother for five years now). Of course, all during this time, though one can still speak clearly, the words are inappropriate, but still actual words. Then, gradually the sentences become less coherent, with more and more words being replaced by unintelligible syllables. I remember one day about two years ago when all day long the only thing I understood Mother saying was "Mama." I said, "Yes, I am your mama now."

They progress on until they can no longer remember how to put one foot in front of the other and walk. That is the stage Mother is in now. The average span of Alzheimer's is seven years, but it can last fifteen or twenty years, depending on the health of the individual. Mother has had to have care for seven years but probably had the disease at least a year before when I didn't realize what the problem was. Many people who have Alzheimer's die of something else first, so they never progress through all of the stages. If they do live long enough to die of Alzheimer's, the last memory to go is the ability to swallow. They simply forget how to swallow and die of starvation. At this stage, many people put their loved one on tubal feeding, and the patient can live several more years on this. I do not wish to do this with Mother. Some nursing homes will refuse to accept a patient unless you agree to let them tube feed them. This should give you a little idea of what Alzheimer's is like.

It looked like the only thing sensible for Mother's best interest was to put her in a nursing home. I discussed this with the sitters, and they all told me they were ready to bring the subject up with me if I hadn't brought it up. They did not feel they could continue to care for her. I came down here and went to look at nursing homes. This same week we had a contract on our house—in fact, the man wanted both houses and the mobile home as a package deal. I was having trouble staying together mentally, but trying to get as much packed as I could. He wanted possession of the house the date of closing, April 18. I was trying to comply because we badly wanted to sell. I came on the 8th and selected a very nice nursing home, went back to Tennessee, brought Mother down on the 15th, and left her in this place three days. If ever the old adage "Beauty is only skin deep" could be applied, it was there. The place was new and lovely to behold—an ice cream parlor in the center for the patient's ice cream at 2 p.m., lovely reception rooms, meeting rooms, chapel, beautiful furnishings, and original works of art on the walls. I talked with people in the parking lot who had relatives in there and was told that it was the place with the best care, too.

The first night the nurse nearly gave Mother the medicine of Mrs. Riley, Mother's roommate. When I saw the name on the medicine tray, I quickly pointed out that Mother was Mrs. Rider, not Riley. At the point of near collapse, when I was ready to leave Mother at 11 p.m., Mother, who seldom ever says anything intelligible, was clinging to my arm and very distinctly saying, "Come with me! Come with me!"

I knew she was trying to say, "Stay with me." She was clearly aware that she was in strange surroundings. (At this stage, according to the books and Mother's home health nurses, they are not supposed to be aware of their surroundings. Mother's home health nurse in Tennessee said she had never seen anything like Mother's alertness for late stages and asked me on more than one occasion if I would get with Mother's doctor and write a book on caregiving. I told her I could write a book all right, but it wouldn't have a lot to do with caregiving. It would be about TV evangelists, the legal system, and a lot of other things.) I had thought that I had had some gut-wrenching moments in my life, but if leaving her with those pleadings and frightened look doesn't rank at the top, it is surely close. Usually, I can figure out why I go through various things, but I was having trouble wondering, after all I had been through, why I had to go through this, too. But, I quickly thought about the many thousands of people right now who have to take the same agonizing step about nursing home placement, and I knew that I could never truly empathize unless I had had the experience.

I had gone for weeks having not slept more than two and three hours a night and was on the verge of having some serious problems with my manic-depressive episodes, so I knew I had better come on home and try to get some rest. If I collapsed and couldn't take care of things, we'd both be in a mess. When I was contemplating moving Mother to the nursing home, Linda agreed to stay with her and feed her a couple meals a day five days a week, and I would try to do most of the rest. I knew not to expect any nursing home to provide someone to patiently take the time that it takes to feed her. It is very common for patients to have sitters if the family can afford it, especially if the patient has mental deterioration.

The next day Linda asked three times for an aide to help change Mother. It was two and a half hours before one appeared. That same day they forgot to bring her both lunch and supper! At 1:30 p.m., an aide came, for the first time that day, to the room and asked to pick up

Mrs. Rider's tray. Linda told her that, "Mrs. Rider has not yet had a tray." Fortunately, we had brought baby food for her. I quickly figured out that the corporation that owned the nursing home had made an initial investment in a beautiful facility for show, but that when it came to the day-to-day care—the kind of expenses that go on and on—they were spending minimal. And I was paying $3,000 per month, plus a fee for every diaper and each extra time they changed the sheets! The people there were not lazy. They simply had too many people to take care of to do even a mediocre job.   I brought Mother home.

Well now, I almost have my house straightened up. It's taken me longer than I'd anticipated, but it's presentable enough to have company. Come see me whenever you can. We'll sit in the swing on the front porch, listen to the creek falling over the rocks, and just gaze at the mountains. Just gazing at the mountains—what could be more tranquilizing. I have some nature CDs with water sounds, birds singing, etc. I was standing in my doorway the other day looking out and listening to the water and the songbirds and thinking that there was no reason I would ever need to play those CDs again.

Love,

Beverly

Birthday Letter to Dad

For Dad's 85th birthday on July 28, 1996, I send a card and wrote a letter. The cover of the card I chose said, " FOR YOU, DAD From Your Daughter With Love."
The words on the inside were:

"Your birthday seems the perfect time to tell you how much I appreciate everything you've done for me and how proud I am to be your daughter. . . . It seems the perfect time to say, 'Thanks, Dad, for everything. HAPPY BIRTHDAY."

I signed it, "Love, Beverly," and handwrote the following letter:

July 17, 1996

Dear Dad,

It will soon be the date of your 85th birthday, a milestone in any one's life. As this time approaches, I've been thinking and reflecting on your life—thinking of the many ways you have been blessed and of the qualities and traits in you that I respect and admire. I thought that this would be a nice time to tell you those things.

You have been blessed with a long, healthy life. Part of that is because your ancestors were long-lived, and part, I feel, is because you have taken charge of your health and avoided doctors except when absolutely necessary. I remember you often saying about doctors—that you knew more about how you felt and what was wrong with you than they did. You read about things and doctored yourself for the most part.

One of the things I admire about you has been your willingness to help others. If someone needed a job, you tried to help them get one. Even though we lived in what would now be considered crowded conditions, there was always room for someone to stay with us—whether relative or friend—while they worked and "got on their feet." You were never jealous of your job or afraid someone would take it or make more money than you did. In fact, I can never remember you being jealous of anyone nor envious of anything that they had.

In growing up, I can never remember anyone coming to our place around meal time, but what you didn't invite them to eat. It didn't matter whether you knew them or not. Your hospitality came naturally. Whatever you had, you wanted to share the best.

While you lived frugally in some ways, you were never tight with money when it came to helping others or causes that you believed in. You have always been generous in those areas.

You were never a sponge. If there were outings, you would be the first to get out your billfold and pay. You never went along on a free ride. You didn't sit back and let someone else do it. The Latimer Co. Royalty Owners Association is a case in point. I know that you got out and organized it and was the first president—giving generously of your time and money and knowledge trying to help others keep from being cheated by the oil companies. That is the reason I belong to the various royalty owner associations there today. Even though I can not attend personally, I can help pay my way for others that are working for my benefit, too.

You did not acquire what you have dishonestly. Though you could have, you never cheated anyone out of their royalty—to buy or to lease. You would counsel them not to sell and not to lease, but if they were determined to do so, to give you a chance to buy or lease.

Another thing I admire about you-you were never intimidated by what others thought. If you told about visions, and people laughed, that didn't bother you. People could call you crazy, but that did not phase you one bit. If you said the royalty was worth millions, and people made fun of you, you went right on. And forty years ago, I DO remember this happening a lot. I'm glad that you were able to live long enough to see all of this become a reality, but even if you hadn't, it would have never shaken your faith.

One of the things I most appreciate was your example of trying to find out all you could about something. If it were something you were interested in, you went out and bought a good selection of books on the subject and started studying. Again, the royalty is an example. You bought college level books on geology and started studying. I know that even in your late seventies you had complete maps of the Red Oak-Norris gas field in your mind and could sit and tell me where various anticlines, synclines and sands, etc. were.

In looking back on your life, when you set out to do something, you did it well. Your chosen career, welding and pipeline construction, is an example. I have heard Buddy tell many people that you were the best that he'd ever met. He has often said that in traveling and working halfway around the world, he had never met your equal. Even as recently as two weeks ago, he said he wouldn't be where he is and hold the job he has if "Frank hadn't been such a good teacher"—that he "learned from the best."

One of the things I have appreciated more and more quite recently is your skills as a photographer—again you didn't do things halfway. You went out and bought books and equipment to be the best that you could be. I have been doing a portrait wall up the stairway in our house. I am so glad to have many photographs and enlargements that you made over the years. I remember that Granny and I used to get aggravated because we wanted to be fixed up and posed, and you were always taking pictures sometimes with us off guard, saying they should be natural. It is only now that I realize those are the ones I like best. You, as you did with all things you pursued, developed your skills very well. If you had a goal, whether it be to fly an airplane or pursue a hobby, you made it happen and achieved what you set out to do.

In reflecting on your eighty-five years, you have done many things well. Your wisdom and beliefs and foresight have provided for us to have a very comfortable lifestyle. I appreciate the sacrifices, and there were those, that you made that provided for your old age, as well as a comfortable life for us. You worked long and hard and took what you earned and put it to the best possible use that you saw. And you have lived to see that you were right.

As I continue my life, I try to look at those things that I learned from you by example and incorporate them into my own life.

Happy 85th birthday!

Love from your daughter,

Beverly

Another Dream – My Mother's Death

Another Dream – My Mother's Death

One day in May 1998 as I was driving down from Hendersonville, NC, gazing at the seven layers of mountains before my turn on the road to home, having gone to get Mother's food and supplies for the week, I was feeling very, very weary. For most of my life, I have always felt I had a gift. Often people look back on their lives and say they can see why something happened, the good that came out of it, and how it helped them. I normally feel I don't have to wait until later. I understand why it's happening at the time it happens. My thoughts this day took the form of a discouraged prayer as I said, "I don't understand why Mother is still living. For most of these ten years, I have been able to easily see what I am supposed to learn, how it has helped me, how I can empathize and help others, but I don't see what I am learning now."

For years it had taken over an hour per meal to feed Mother. Now, as she could no longer remember how to swallow, it took even longer. We were pureeing her food and putting it in a syringe. After putting some in her mouth, we would gently rub her throat awaiting reflexes to carry the food on down. Many times I had read of the various stages of Alzheimer's and silently hoped Mother would never live to experience whatever the next stage would be. But Mother lived through them all.

The next night after I formed those discouraging words in my mind, I had a dream. I dreamed that Mother was going to die in about two weeks. When I have a vivid dream like this one, it usually comes true. I had a big decision to make.

Since I had been caring for Mother, except for the short trip to Canada, I had not traveled foreign. On occasion, Buddy would be on business in a foreign country (I would have especially liked to have joined him on a trip to India when he was there recruiting workers for Saudi) and would ask me if I would like to join him. Regretfully, I wouldn't have sitters that could cover for me, and couldn't. For the last six months of Mother's life, I had no sitters. Linda and I cared for Mother alone. Buddy was going to Austria on business and asked me if I would like to join him. This time, Tim was home between jobs, and Linda said she and Tim could manage Mother. She encouraged me to go.

The night of the dream of Mother's death, I had already purchased tickets to Vienna and was to leave in a few days. I was to be gone for two weeks. I took this dream seriously enough that if it hadn't been for Linda's reassurance that she and Tim could handle things, I would have canceled.

When I'm asked to name my favorite city in the whole world, without hesitation, I say, "Vienna." What a marvelous time we had in Austria. Buddy was in the country to purchase materials for the company he worked for in Saudi, and it was in the interest of the manufacturer of these items to see that we were treated royally. We were met in Vienna and taken to southern Austria where the factory was located. We had personal attention on excursions, restaurants, etc. throughout. After coming back to Vienna, we were treated to a river cruise on the Danube in the Wachau Valley, visited Melk Abbey and lovely towns along the river. We heard the music of Mozart in the Schonbrunn Palace and attended a performance of the famed Lippizaner horses. And, yes, I had days to shop and explore the sights I didn't want to miss. We attended a trade show for job-related implements that was held in the Vienna Woods. What an opportunity to be (and how inept I felt) in the company of men and women from Poland and other Eastern European countries who conversed in English and were so knowledgeable about world events. That night, with its food, the traditional music, and the people I met, ranks near the top in my memories of Austria.

All was well when I arrived home for a night of restful sleep in my own bed in my valley. It was during the wee hours of the morning during the following night that Mother had her stroke. Mother was seventeen days dying, but, essentially, the dream had come true.

I wrote the following letter to friends:

July 19, 1998

Dear Friends,

Sometime during the night of June 2 or the early morning hours of June 3, Mother had a massive stroke. When I went into her room about 7 a.m., I found her paralyzed on the left side. She had a couple more strokes later that morning.

It was never my desire to take her to a hospital and have her hooked to machines, poked with needles, feeding tubes put down her, etc. I had taken care of her at home for almost ten years. Linda helped care for her the final three years. When something happened to her during her last days, I wanted to give her comfort care and have the hands that touched her be only those that loved her.

The doctor came to the house in the evening. He said that he didn't expect her to live over two or three days—maximum five or six. He said usually someone in her condition developed pneumonia or septicemia and went quickly. Mother lived seventeen days on her reserves; she could not swallow food.

I have a friend who worked as a hospital aide, and she said that if we could get enough liquid down her, we might be able to prevent her dying a painful death from dehydration. Tim, Linda, and I took turns night and day giving her water and a sports drink with a medicine dropper. Sometimes we got as much as two to two and a half cups down her during a twenty-four hour period. The last three days, though, she couldn't swallow at all, so we moistened her mouth with a sponge tip. She seemed peaceful throughout the seventeen days, sometimes opening her eyes or squeezing a hand. She never made any sounds or facial grimaces to indicate she was in pain, as I was told that she would if this were so. She died very peacefully at 5:35 a.m.

Beverly

Mother's Funeral and Some Spiritual Things

In the deaths I have witnessed, it has seemed as though the air is filled with things spiritual. I feel compelled to write a bit more on the subject of death for those who may read this and be called upon to make decisions that I had to make. I was told by more than one person that it was sometimes necessary to ask a dying person to go on, to stop clinging to life. This is something I thought I would never be able to do—to ask a loved one to die.

A few days after Mother's stroke, I wrenched my back trying to lift her, so Linda and Tim had to do the care for her in anything that called for physical exertion. In the seventeen days Mother lived without food and with very little liquid, her body became so very, very frail. The breathing became so labored that for the last few days the sound of death permeated the whole house. On her last day of life, as Tim held her up while we changed her bedding, it was heartbreaking to see her little skeleton. Afterward, Tim spoke to me and said, "Mother, this cannot go on. Something has to be done." I knew what I had to do. As I sat with her that last night, in the wee hours of the morning, I knelt by her bed, took her hand and said, "Mother, please go on and join the ancestors in the spirit world." I calmly pleaded one more time, "Please, Mother . . ." I walked across the hall to my bed and lay down for a few moments. I heard her labored breathing soften and got up to go to her side to be with her for those last breaths.

All day that day I had kept music softly playing in her room—music representative of her mixed ancestry—the music that was played at the visitation the day of her funeral. For those of you who may not know, for the dying, hearing is said to be the last sense to go. No matter what you think their mental capacities are, please be careful in your speech.

As is required when a death occurs at home, we had to wait for the coroner to arrive and check her to verify that she had died a natural death. When the undertaker arrived, he asked if I wanted to leave the room while she was wheeled out to the hearse. I said, "No." Just as Daddy had told me to do way back when my grandpa died, I never shed a tear as I watched them take her out. Tim and I went out in the yard and stood together as the hearse pulled away. Tim asked me, "Mother, what are you thinking?" I replied, "I'm thinking of the lines in the ole gospel song, 'Will the Circle Be Unbroken' that say,

I was standing by the window . . .
When I saw that hearse come rolling
For to carry my mother away.
I said to the undertaker,
Undertaker, please drive slow
For this lady you are carrying Lord,
I hate to see her go."

It was probably close to ten o'clock in the morning by now. Linda had made the flowers for Mother's casket from dried wildflowers picked here on the farm. She and Tim readied themselves to drive to Oklahoma and carry these and other items we wanted for the funeral. Mother had lived seventeen days, long enough for my back to get well enough to fly in an airplane for the trip back, but not long enough for me to be able to ride that distance in a vehicle. Tim and Linda pulled away, and I sat down at the piano and began to play another song from my childhood, "Farther Along," with the words, "When death has come and taken our loved ones, It leaves our home so lonely and drear," words I truly felt for the first time.

It was Friday. When I spoke with the funeral director, I told him I would like to have Mother's funeral in Oklahoma on Sunday. When he thought he could not make that possible, I explained that to come to her funeral, many of mother's relatives would have to lose a day's work and with that a day's pay. It would cause a hardship on them that Mother would not want. In a few hours, he called me and said, "I haven't had anybody else come in that I needed to take care of. I have her ready and can have her on a plane this afternoon. Would you like to come down and see her?" I said, "Yes." As he and I went in to see her, I touched her cold body, looked at him dry-eyed and said, "Her spirit is not here." As he gave affirmation, he seemed at a loss as to how to proceed with someone such as I, but I briefly told him my story. He said, "As I prepared her body, I knew she had been well cared for. Her skin is without blemish. I never have anyone from a nursing home or hospital or anywhere brought in with skin like this."

Just a few days after Mother had her stroke, my cousin Charlene said, "Beverly, I believe Aunt Edith will die on my birthday." And so, a couple weeks later, she did. I made plane reservations for early Saturday morning and was going to have to get up at four a.m. That night Charlene and I discussed my exhaustion, and I assured her my alarm clock was set. A few minutes before four, just before the alarm went off, I awakened, and in no more than a minute, my phone rang. It was Charlene making sure I was okay and getting up for the flight. I said, "I told you that you didn't need to set your alarm (it was three a.m. central time)—that I would be fine." She replied, "I didn't set my alarm; I just woke up."

When I got off the plane in Ft. Smith, Arkansas, the town with the nearest airport to our home in Oklahoma, a burst of heat and humidity hit me not unlike what I experienced getting off planes on the shores of the Arabian Gulf in Saudi and Abu Dhabi. Aunt Eunice and Charlene had been telling me it was an unusually hot beginning for summer in Oklahoma, with recent days over 100 degrees, but the reality nearly overwhelmed me. I had wanted to have a graveside service for Mother. While relatives were gentle with my wishes, they did encourage me to be practical. Aunt Eunice said the elderly relatives might have to sit in cars in the cemetery and not be able to sit in the open for the service.

Still, I wanted to try. Charlene drove me out to the cemetery. I had not been there since I was a little girl of nine at my grandmother's funeral, but I had a sense of the area where the family graves were. We rode over there. With my back hurting and the extreme heat, I couldn't bring myself to get out of the car and check tombstones. Nearby was a large lovely elm tree offering shade, and I commented that it would be so nice if the graves were there, but still, I didn't feel like facing the walk and the heat to check the site. The next afternoon, as the funeral procession made its way through the cemetery, I looked up and there was the freshly dug grave, immediately under that elm tree.

Somehow, I knew the right people would be at Mother's funeral, so I didn't make a list of people to notify. Over fifty came. Of those who lived in Oklahoma, all of Mother's relatives, including nieces and nephews and spouses of those who had died, were there. For me, friends and relatives who were meant to be there found the right cemetery of the two in town. My brother John was not well at this time, and I had not contacted him. John and I had never had a cross word, but I had some ill feelings toward him. I looked up, and there was John, whose presence had required great effort. He took my hand and said, "Beverly, I know how you feel, for I have lost a mother myself." Any ill feelings I had melted away instantly. Most people didn't know how to express their sympathy—after all, I had cared for Mother for ten years, and they didn't know what to say. John said it best.

As all the relatives and friends, young and old, gathered under that beautiful elm tree, a most remarkable thing happened. In the midst of that almost unbearable heat and humidity, as the service began, a gentle wind started blowing. For the twenty or so minutes of the service, this breeze cooled all present. Immediately after the casket was lowered, the breeze suddenly stopped. It was so pronounced that those present started murmuring and talking about it as though it were phenomenal, as indeed it was. There was even an element of fear present in the crowd as some said, "This is of God." While I would not be presumptuous enough to say that God caused a breeze to come up for my mother's funeral, there are supernatural things that often happen in life and at death for which I have no explanation. Often I think of that event and the people from the dawn of time who are a bit fearful trying to put into words extraordinary events. They are not unlike the people in Wilburton, who two and three weeks later were still coming into the city office to pay their water bills to my cousin Reva with the inquiry, "Aren't you related to that woman that the breeze came up during her funeral?" When she replied in the affirmative, they would say, "She must have been a remarkable woman for God to send a breeze for her funeral." And indeed, she was a remarkable woman.

Mother's Obituary

IN REMEMBRANCE OF EDITH ANDREWS RIDER

As a gentle breeze cooled the nieces, nephews, sister-in-law, brothers-in-law, daughter, grandchildren, and friends, they gathered at 2 p.m., June 21, 1998, under a grove of trees in Old Section, City Cemetery, Wilburton, Oklahoma, to pay their last respects and honor the life of Edith Alamo Andrews Rider.

She entered this life July 13, 1908, seven months after statehood, at the Choctaw Indian Reservation near Wilburton, Oklahoma. Her spirit departed peacefully, June 19, 1998, at her daughter's home in the River Falls community, Greenville County, South Carolina, where she had lived many years. Edith was surrounded by her family: Daughter, Beverly Ann Biggs, grandson, Timothy Kevin Biggs, and granddaughter, Linda Rochelle Biggs.

Edith's husband, Frank Rider, resides in a nursing home in Auburn, California.

Remembering her mixed ancestry, Irish music and traditional songs in the Welsh language were played during the morning visitation at Waldrop Funeral Home. Edith was clothed in a white antique gown, intricately hand embroidered at the turn-of-the-century. Her head rested on a hand embroidered pillow that was also made about the time of her birth. The floral arrangement on the coffin was made by her granddaughter, Linda, from dried roses, and from dried wildflowers that were gathered on the family farm in the Blue Ridge Mountains at the North and South Carolina border.

The service was conducted by the Rev. John Coley of Red Oak, a school classmate of Edith's daughter. He and his wife, Jo Ann, sang "In the Sweet By and By" in the Choctaw language. The Rev. Norman Frye, of Kiowa, read the 23rd Psalm and the "Lord's Prayer" in the Choctaw language. In English, Rev. Coley read the verses from Proverbs, Chapter 31, describing a virtuous woman, made appropriate comments, and offered a prayer. He then sang "Amazing Grace" in the Choctaw Language. Immediately following, Mr. George Bishop, of Hartshorne, played "Amazing Grace" on a hand carved traditional Choctaw Indian flute, which he had started making for this memorial service as soon as he had news of Edith's expected death. He presented the flute to daughter, Beverly. When Mr. Bishop was a young boy, a school teacher had taught him to play an Irish lullaby, and he played this on an Indian flute as a final tribute.

Edith's remains were laid to rest with those of her parents, grandparents, uncle, brother, and her baby son.

The Next Three Years

There are six friends and family members who are reading this book as I get segments written. Their comments and feedback are quite helpful. After writing about Mother's funeral, one friend asked, "Where was Buddy's support in all of this? You don't mention him." Until this question was raised, I had not intended to mention Buddy in this segment. Buddy was back in Saudi after our Austrian trip. As I related earlier, Mother started her dying days within two days of my return home. Buddy did ask me if I would like for him to return home, but I asked him not to come. Buddy does not handle stress in a way that is supportive for me. His method seems to be to just get upset quickly and start hollering. I did not feel I had the strength to deal with that at this time. There was another reason that I asked him not to come. There had been an incident the previous year that I held against Buddy. When Buddy came in on leave, I always had arranged for sitters to cover all daylight hours, so that I would be free to spend the time with him and go on outings if he so wished. One particular day, we wanted to go out, and the sitter did not show up. Buddy got very angry and screamed, "When is that woman ever going to die?" I was very hurt! Buddy drank heavily at that time, and though it was morning, he probably had alcohol still in his system. Since he started drinking hard liquor around 10 a.m. in the morning and drank some all day most days, he probably always had alcohol in this system. I am not stating this to excuse his verbal behavior nor to imply it was the drink talking. It's just that this was the way it was. Mother was in bed in the next room, which shared a wall with the library where we were. It is true that Mother could not speak coherently and quite likely did not understand, but I never treated her like this was the case. One of my reasons for relating this incident is to ask those who may be caring for an impaired person to always assume the person may be able to understand more than he or she can communicate. Because of this outburst, I did not want Buddy to come.

Buddy loved Mother, and Mother loved Buddy. He, for the most part, did not show any resentment for me caring for her and was supportive of me. During the period when my parents started deteriorating, Buddy had left Fluor, and for several years he was on single status in Saudi Arabia, meaning there was no choice about my being with him anyway. Later, he went to work for an Arab company, and I could have gone over to Saudi and lived. We discussed the situation. I was managing the mineral interest I had inherited from my parents as well as some we had purchased. This required hands-on paperwork as well as decision making. While one can hire mineral managers, who usually work for a percentage of income, we felt that nobody would manage things as well as I. So, I probably wouldn't have gone back to Saudi even if my parents had been in good health.

After Mother's death in June, Buddy came in on leave in August. We flew to Alaska for a wonderful month. Our friend, Jackie Corbett, joined us from England. It was his last trip with us, as he died a few months later. One of Buddy's childhood friends, Jerry, had gone to Alaska in the '60s to work on the Alaskan pipeline and in the oil industry there. He married an Aleut Indian and made his home there, retiring in Seward. We spent about ten days in their motor home parked in the yard. He and Buddy spent the days salmon fishing, much to Buddy's delight. What feasting we had! Yes, we had salmon flown home to enjoy throughout the winter. We declined Jerry's offer to let us use their motor home and rented one for us to spend the remainder of our time touring Alaska. What fun we had! At Homer, Buddy fished for halibut and caught the largest halibut of the season that year in Homer—209 pounds were flown home to our freezer. What an incredibly beautiful state Alaska is! We've been to the fiords of New Zealand and Norway, and indeed they are magnificent, but those of

Alaska can hold their place among the best! We went to Fairbanks and North Pole, Alaska. We were there for the State Fair to see the huge vegetables that can be grown when it's daylight for most of the growing season. The fair reminded me of those in my childhood where the ladies' exquisite crafts--quilts and other handiwork--took center stage. We camped at the feet of towering mountains and by glacial rivers with moose joining us nearby. As a fitting end to that marvelous trip, as we flew home in late September, the airline captain came on the speaker to let us know we could look out the windows to an ethereal display of the aurora borealis.

It had been almost twenty years since I had been involved with church attendance. After Mother's death, I felt the spiritual need to seek out something more formal and participate on a regular basis. In spite of all the chaos in my life, I had a religious upbringing in Baptist and other conservative churches. At this point in life, I did not feel they would meet my needs. I attended several mainline and liberal denominations at least one Sunday each. Among the churches I attended was the Catholic Church. My mother had been baptized Catholic and attended Catholic school through the eighth grade. As an adult, she did not remain Catholic. She and I never discussed the reasons why, but I know that for a few months when she was in her twenties, she was married to a man who got drunk and came home and beat her badly. She left him and divorced him, which would have been frowned on by the church. However, I don't think she was part of the church at that time. Her own mother became a Methodist. Mother did not criticize any church, including the Catholic. She truly did not interfere with another person's belief. My father expressed venom against Catholics and believed they were not Christian. Mother did join the Baptist Church my father and his family attended, and I can remember her baptism in that church when I was four years old. Once when I was about five years old, she and I went to the church nearest the trailer court where we were living. It was a Christian Church, by denomination. I remember Mother saying that she liked that church. It was very quiet; it reminded her of the Catholic Church. I, too, was drawn by the quietness of the Catholic Church. When I am asked what drew me to the Catholic Church, the quietness is usually the first thing I mention. I loved the beauty of the art, the stained glass, the music, and the ritual which seemed so comforting, but most of all I loved going to the chapel at any time of the day and being able to sit in quiet contemplation knowing that nobody would come to me and say anything. I would be left in peace. It was during this time that Buddy retired and came home to live permanently. The first four years were horrible with his drinking and verbal abuse, and I had a lot of trouble with manic-depressive episodes. Being able to escape to the chapel played a crucial role in my coping and being able to withstand this sad period in my life. My friends and relatives were very surprised that I would choose this church, but they offered support by allowing me the privilege of making my own choices.

There were some of the teachings that I could never embrace, and ultimately I did leave the church. I learned so much—mainly that there are very good people, people who fit the definition of the label Christian, in this church. I gained two of my best friends in the Carolinas, Harriet and Frank, from my stay in the Catholic Church. Harriet was the person it was hardest for me to tell that I was leaving. I was afraid our friendship was mainly based on mutually being Catholic, but she was very understanding and remains my dearest friend here. I got to see first-hand some very good priests, those who dedicate themselves day in and day out to helping people in their many struggles of life. This period in my life prompted me to do a lot of reading, and I read over 350 books dealing with religious topics.

Buddy came home in December 1999, but officially retired January 1, 2000. Though we had done a lot of traveling, most of it was to places that I wanted to go. Because I wanted to travel, we bought our first motorhome. Buddy had said for years that there were two places he would like to go when he retired. One was to the Grand Canyon, and the other was to Australia. Some of the people we had known talked about what they wanted to do and did not follow through. Often, it became too late. I insisted we not fall into that category. In the summer of 2000 our friend, Helen Corrigan, from Ireland, the sister of our friend Jackie Corbett, came over and the three of us went in our motorhome to the Grand Canyon, Sedona, Arizona, Mesa Verde National Park in Colorado, and other points of interest.

In September 2001 we used Buddy's frequent flyer miles for what was supposed to be a six week trip to Australia and New Zealand. We were in Sydney when the Twin Towers fell. The church bells tolled all over the city, and we attended a memorial service. We attended a concert at the Sydney Opera House, that lovely structure where the acoustics are so good you can hear a pin drop. Australia was wonderful. We traveled by plane and by rented car to the outback. At Ayers Rock, we attended a Sounds of Silence event which was to look at stars and experience the silence when all lights were turned off. While most people were in awe, we talked of how we would have never had to leave home to experience the same thing. We took a five-day cruise on the Great Barrier Reef. I had planned the tour booking most of our accommodations at bed and breakfasts before we left. We met lovely people, stayed in oceanfront boutique accommodations going to sleep to the sounds of the waves lapping the shore. We loved Australia, but when we got to New Zealand, we loved it even more. We traveled by train (missed one connection and raced to the airport to catch a plane, so we could arrive at our night's accommodation on time). We traveled by public bus and then rented a car and changed our airline tickets so we could have an extra two weeks to tour both the North and South Islands thoroughly. No pre-booked accommodations this time. We traveled as we really like to travel—just taking our chances. We stayed at a bed and breakfast on a sheep farm in Rotorua and still correspond every year with our hosts, Norm and Judy. It was nearby that Buddy caught a huge trout. This was something most tourists could not master, and the locals definitely showed their respect to Buddy for his ability in the fishing department. Needless to say, Buddy LOVED New Zealand. He always remembers fondly the trips we have taken where he caught fish! One of our fondest memories of both Australia and New Zealand is the food. All of the food was prepared with fresh ingredients when you placed your order and was served on real plates every time—no paper plates there. New Zealand reminded us of America in the '50s, a gentler, slower time. Part of that may be because there are more sheep in New Zealand than there are people. Perhaps one just slows down a bit when you gaze at the animals.

Daddy's Death

Eighteen years ago today we buried Mother. On Sunday, June 19, when I called Charlene to wish her a happy birthday, she commented on how hot it already is in Oklahoma this year. I mentioned the heat we experienced at the time of Mother's death, and her immediate comment was, "But remember the soft wind that came up during her funeral." This paranormal experience remains cemented in the minds of many who were there.

In May 2001 I got a call saying Dad was very bad and not expected to live. Linda and I went back to Oklahoma. To everyone's surprise, he rallied and became well enough for Linda and me to take some delightful trips to attractions in the area while we were there visiting with him. Linda loves nature and was enamored with all the wildflowers. Whole fields of them were in bloom during our stay. In July I went back to help Dad celebrate his 90th birthday.

The first week in January 2002 I got another call saying Dad wasn't expected to live. My husband and children were VERY OPPOSED to my going back. I don't recall this anger presenting itself the previous year, but this time they all said some very harsh things in their opinion of him—things that should not be put in writing. As I stated in the chapter, "Hard Things," I stood my ground and said, "He's my daddy, and I'm going!" This was the time I wrestled so painfully with the determination to touch his hand and am forever grateful that he lived those extra months which gave me the opportunity to do something that helped a great deal in my healing. I left home on the path to becoming an emotional wreck, that's for sure. Daddy did not die quickly. He lingered on for several days.   I wrote of his death previously, so I'm not going to be redundant. My calls to and from home were terrible. Buddy, drinking heavily, would call me and ask where I was. When

I'd answer that I was at the nursing home, he would yell, "Why are you still there? Ain't he dead yet?" I would get so nervous because I thought the workers coming in and out of the room could hear. Buddy and Tim and Linda were not planning to come back for the funeral. This was known among my relatives and friends. It was during this week that an older brother of Buddy's was hospitalized. It was discovered that he had lung cancer, but he was told that with radiation he would probably live about five years. On January 8, when the nurses came to take him for his first radiation treatment, as they were helping him into the wheelchair, he slumped over dead with a heart attack. My dad died January 9. This really changed things! Buddy wanted to come to his brother's funeral and knew it would appear terrible not to come to my dad's, which was to be held the following day. Buddy, Tim, and Linda all got tickets to come to Oklahoma. A few days later, Buddy, in fear, asked me, "Do you think God caused Dale to die so that I would come back for your dad's funeral?" I answered, "I have no idea about that and wouldn't dare speculate, but one thing I know—my children needed to be at their grandfather's funeral, and it was because of Dale's death that they were."

Funerals in Red Oak were very traditional. It wasn't customary at that time for members or friends of the family to speak. There was normally live music with singing, a scripture reading, the reading of the obituary, a sermon and then viewing of the body. Afterward, people lined up outside the door of the church as the casket was brought out to the hearse to be taken for burial. In California, relatives and friends often spoke at funerals, and Sue asked me if we would like to speak ourselves and give others the opportunity to speak at Dad's. I was hesitant myself but willing to honor her wishes. I told her I didn't plan to speak, but about thirty minutes before the service I changed my mind. The stresses from all sources from the previous week had begun to take their toll on me. I wasn't eating right; I wasn't getting enough sleep; Buddy and the children's attitude was hurtful; and the extreme stress of dealing with my relationship with Dad was beginning to overload my brain. As our family and friends were in the social hall of the church before the service eating the wonderful meal prepared by ladies of the community, signs of mania in me began to appear. I was witty, talking a mile a minute, fun loving, appearing to have a gay old time. Warning signs! Normally, I am a very serious person and not at all good at teasing or cracking jokes. As Sue recently said to me, "All of us—you, John, and I--are very serious people. We had so much going on in our young lives, how could we be otherwise?" When humor takes over with me, those who know me well say, "Oh no!" Then there is the creative streak. When I'm beginning to enter a hypomanic (just below full-blown mania) state, the creative juices REALLY begin to roll! I can write well, very well, and speak well, too. I was beginning to manifest those signals.

Sue and I were in charge of the music. She was playing the piano. I was going to lead a couple congregational songs and then sing a solo, "When They Ring Those Golden Bells," one of the songs I had sung softly to Dad that last night of his life. When the funeral home director had met with Sue, John and me to plan Dad's funeral, he asked if we had any idea how many people might be attending. We said that outside of the family, probably no more than half a dozen or so. After all, Dad had been gone from Red Oak for many years, and at age ninety and a half, most of his friends were dead. When we arrived at the church, to our great surprise, there were a lot of people. After initial songs and prayers, Sue now welcomed anyone who knew Dad to speak. There was silence. Absolute ethereal, uncomfortable, eternal feeling silence. Just when it appeared nobody was going to speak, an Assembly of God preacher stood up. He stated that when he heard of Dad's death, though he now lived in another part of the state, he knew he was going to come to Dad's funeral. He and his wife were married many years with no children. After all those years, maybe twenty or so, they were blessed with a beautiful baby girl. He told that money was tight. They had no insurance, and Dad came and paid the hospital bill for the birth of the baby. I had never known this. We all knew Dad was a generous person, but it seemed to us he was very selective about his generosity. Dad had never been involved in Pentecostal churches. His sister, Alice, was Pentecostal, and he and she had MANY heated arguments over doctrinal issues. Though Dad was prone to visit various denominations of churches, those with Pentecostal leanings were not among them. So this revelation provided me with a side of Dad I never knew. No one else spoke.

Sue spoke next. She explained that she had left Red Oak when she was eight years old, so many in the audience did not know her. She told that, of her memories of Dad, she fondly remembered their shared love of pinto beans paired with applesauce. Those memories came from the edge of the depression era, so they ate a lot of beans, and, as Sue related, they ate a lot of applesauce, too. Sue didn't speak long.

Now, it was my turn. As I said earlier, I was in a hypomanic state of creativity. These highs are exhilarating. I have read that this is the reason many people refuse to take medication for bipolar disorder. They do not want to miss out on this wonderful euphoria. I've also read that this euphoria is similar to the highs that people get when they experiment with psychedelic drugs—that's why they like to do them. There is no doubt that I was at my best—no way could previous planning been as effective as what I could do impromptu at that moment. I started out speaking with the statement, "I have recently finished reading an autobiography of Billy Graham, and in it, he stated, "Someday you will turn on the television or radio and hear the words 'Billy Graham is dead.' Don't you believe a word of it. I will have only changed addresses." Tim, afterward, in giving one of his rare compliments, told me, "There is nothing you could have used to better connect with that audience than that opening statement."

The family was seated in the center of the church, with friends seated in the aisles on each side. I talked about a more simple time when the birthing and the dying were done at home, with family gathered in a more intimate setting than is often the case today. I talked about my last night with Dad and how I told him he was soon going to join his beloved grandfather about whom he had talked so often with us. Dad seemed to be the favorite grandchild of his paternal grandfather, and for sure this man had a profound influence on Dad. During the early years of their marriage, Granny and Grandpa had lived with these parents, so it's only natural that they would have been so fond of their little grandson. Dad, with voice breaking and tears in his eyes, often told us of the day when he was twelve years old and his grandfather died. With the words, "I don't want to meet my maker with a boozy breath," the grandfather refused a sip of whiskey to help ease him out. As Dad related it, the Grandfather was having a vision that he was in a buggy, and it was gliding across the sky to another destination to join his ancestors. I told those present that my family, behind Dad's back, often joked about someday Dad taking the buggy ride, and during his last night on earth, I talked to Dad about this buggy ride on which he, too, would soon be going. Dad had said that on the day his grandfather died, one by one, each member of the family went into the room to bid the patriarch a final goodbye. When it was Dad's turn, the grandfather asked him to make a promise. He asked Dad to promise him that he would never get drunk and to meet him in heaven. Dad promised. As far as I know, Dad kept the first promise; of course, I can't weigh in on the second one. When I first started speaking, Buddy put his head down in his lap and started quietly sobbing. Before long, handkerchiefs started coming out of pockets and facial tissues started coming out of purses. For most of my talk, I spoke directly to the family, who were sitting there dry-eyed. Later, Linda said to me, "Mother, that was the strangest funeral I have ever attended. Everybody in the church was crying except the family. I don't understand it." I replied, "Linda, I do. I think I understand it very well." Many in that congregation knew Dad. The man who worked in the grocery store when the little girl would come in too ashamed to hold her head up, because, somehow, in a convoluted way, she felt blame for the escapades that had gone on the night before when Dad had been on one of his tears, was there. He, with eyes red from crying, gave me a big hug later. There were others with their own memories of some of the bizarre things Dad had done. I said, "Linda, no, you wouldn't understand. I do." It was though healing was present, not only healing for a family but healing for a little community. Yes, I was told that this funeral, too, was still being discussed many days later. A most wonderful thing happened. After this, when Dad was or is now mentioned, there is no enmity in the tone of voice of anyone in my own family. No one excuses his many flaws. They are sometimes repeated just as a matter of fact, but any trace of bitterness or anger has vanished.

The young, nervous preacher who was conducting Dad's funeral stood up to speak. He had never met Dad but had asked others about him. He hardly knew what to do. Somehow, he felt an obligation to either place Dad in a heaven or hell. Tim, not wanting to be unkind, did tell me later, "Mother, if the preacher had been more experienced, when you finished speaking he would have just said a prayer and closed the service."

That afternoon Aunt Eunice and I were sitting around her kitchen table discussing Dad and the funeral. I asked her, "Aunt Eunice, if Dad hadn't made that promise to his grandfather and kept it, when Dad was on one of his tears, if he had been a drinker, too, what do you think would have happened?" Aunt Eunice, who always so quickly could get to the heart of things and formulate succinctly an answer, said, "We'd all be dead!"

Buddy's brother, Dale, had died on the 8th and Dad had died on the 9th. Buddy, Tim, and Linda flew to Oklahoma on the 10th. Dale's funeral was on the 11th and Dad's funeral was on the 12th. That night we splurged! The late U.S. Senator Robert S. Kerr's luxurious mansion near Poteau had been opened as a Bed and Breakfast Inn.

While we would have been welcome to continue staying with relatives in Red Oak, we all agreed that we would love to stay in Sen. Kerr's beautiful home. What a marvelous treat in a tranquil setting there in those Ouachita Mountains of Eastern Oklahoma! We flew home the next day, the 13th. Back then, I wasn't as adept at catching the first signs of mania as I am now. As the years have gone by, I've gotten better and better at being able to detect signs earlier and earlier. To say I'd had a stressful ten days or so is putting it mildly. As we pulled into our driveway, we were discussing Dad's funeral. I commented that I felt Dad would be so pleased with how everything went. All three of his children were in one accord, sitting together. There was no arguing about his estate as some might have thought that there would be. All had been settled years ago while Dad was alive to supervise and approve it all. Dad would have liked that Sue played the piano and I sang and that we both spoke. He would have even liked the message of the young preacher, with its admonition that all present be prepared for their own death and destiny. I said, "A good case could be made that Dad directed his own funeral." With that comment, there was a huge, collective gasp all around. All thought, "Uh oh! Mother's going OFF!" And they were right.

The Next Day and a Manic Episode

The next morning after our arrival home from Dad's funeral it was clear to me that I was going into a manic episode. I had an empty bottle of medicine with a date on it showing that the prescription had been expired several years. My first thought was to try to get medicine. I knew I needed help. I do not frequent doctors of any kind, but since I had moved to South Carolina, I had been to one for some reason. He practiced in the same clinic where I had taken Mother, so I went there clutching the bottle, begging the receptionist to let me see the doctor to get a refill. She looked at the bottle and then looked at me and said, "There is not a doctor in this building who will give you this medicine. You will need a psychiatrist to prescribe it." I left dejected. I had not been to a psychiatrist since leaving Tennessee and didn't go home and ask a family member to try to help me find one. Remember, my mind was quickly becoming unraveled, so I was not using sound judgment. I decided to go to church to sit in the chapel where it was so peaceful. Perhaps this would calm down my racing mind. It did seem to help, and I struggled through that day.

Recently, I had started a project of writing to friends and family members whom I wanted to thank for helping me in life. Aunt Eunice's husband, Charles Gallagher, was very ill and unable to come to Dad's funeral. While he had not been an important part of my life in my younger years (I don't remember him ever being around for the drama, as Aunt Eunice often was), as I got in my thirties and beyond, I began to cultivate his friendship. Every time we went to Oklahoma, Uncle Charles and I would have good discussions, especially about the royalty business and other things of a financial nature. I had grown to value his opinions and could have told him how much he meant to me when I was in Oklahoma, but I had not done so. I decided to write him a letter and went to the chapel to do this. It was now Tuesday, January 15. I was definitely struggling to keep from going into a full-blown manic episode and spent several hours in the church, not only writing but trying to calm my mind. The letter is very coherent considering the state I was in. This letter became so important to me that I did not want to let it out of my hands, and I started carrying it around in my purse.

By Wednesday, I was not sleeping well at all and got up at 5 a.m. to again go to the church. As I drove, part of the time I was hallucinating that I was driving through walls of fire, a very frightening experience. I was definitely too far gone to exercise the judgment to ask somebody for help, though I carried the empty medicine bottle around in my purse along with the letter to Uncle Charles. I simply did not have the presence of mind to put a stamp on the envelope and go mail the letter. I just kept reading it over and over. I stayed for the morning Mass, and when it was over, I sat down in the lobby/office area and started crying. Somehow with all the people leaving, I was overlooked by the priest and the religious brother who helped conduct the service. Harriet, whom I did not know well at that time, saw me and came to me. As I sat there and began to audibly sob, I tried to tell her about my dad. I can remember her asking me what my dad's name was, and I couldn't get it out. She asked me if it was Frank, as her husband's name was, and I STILL couldn't tell her. Eventually, I was calm enough that she felt she could leave me (she did not know about my mental condition). I then went up to talk to the receptionist and asked to speak with a priest. They were both busy and couldn't see me. She suggested I go to the Urgent Care Center and telephoned for me. I drove myself there and went in still clutching the letter to Uncle Charles and my empty pill bottle. The doctor sent me over to the mental health center, but after sitting there waiting for quite a while, I got up and walked several blocks back to the church to again ask to talk to somebody. By this time, I wanted to read this letter to someone, and, whether I just didn't make this clear or not, the doctor at the Urgent Care, though very kind, had not wanted to listen. I guess the church receptionist talked me into walking back to the mental health center because I did go back. A staff member suggested I call home, and Buddy and Linda soon arrived. We sat there for, again, a long time. There were no psychiatrists on duty, so showing my empty pill bottle did no good there, either. They sent me back to Urgent Care. This time Linda was with me and could talk to the doctor. Perhaps there was a problem finding a psychiatrist with whom I could get an appointment because Linda told the doctor that she knew one in Asheville that might see me. He agreed to see me after 5 p.m. at the end of his day. We met briefly, and he wrote me a prescription for the medicine. I was not assertive and couldn't get across to him, either, how much I wanted to read the letter. By the time we got the prescription filled, I was in a full-blown manic state; my judgment was pretty well gone, and I didn't even want to take the medicine.

It was in this argumentative stage that we arrived home. By that time, I didn't want to listen to anything reasonable. Buddy handles almost any kind of stress by screaming. When I had any mental problems when he was around, he reacted in his normal fashion. He screamed, "You are crazy. I'm going to have you locked in a mental hospital, and you will NEVER get out!" Now, I was definitely in a state where I knew that he had the legal right to sign me in--I wasn't THAT far gone. This statement terrified me!

When Tim was about two, in the mid-sixties, we had gone to the state mental hospital in Oklahoma to visit an uncle of Buddy's. When I reflect on him, I realize he had all the classic symptoms of bipolar disorder, though that word had not been coined back then. He was divorced, and other uncles of Buddy's had periodically had him committed to the mental hospital. After a few months, he would be released into someone's care, and then after a few years, it would happen again. When we went to see him, he was as calm and sensible as anyone, not at all like those around him. As we sat outside at some picnic tables, I looked at the long line of blank faces marching by on the way to the cafeteria for lunch. The picture of seeing those faces with no hope is indelibly imprinted upon my mind.

Yes, Buddy could have had me committed, but I was lucid enough that I replied, "I know that you can have me locked up, but I'll tell you one thing. I WILL eventually get out! But you will NOT have the chance to sign me in; I'll sign myself in." I knew that legally if I signed myself in, I could sign myself out as long as I showed no signs of being a threat to myself or others. I will state at this time that, unlike some with manic-depressive illness, I have never wanted or threatened to commit suicide and have never threatened or wanted to harm anyone. With me, the problem is always the opposite; I'm afraid others want to harm me. I have never, however, been afraid that my children or Buddy would harm me. I stubbornly stated I wanted someone to call an ambulance. I was shifting gears fast, and Buddy's threat prompted me to want to go sign myself into the hospital mental ward. Tim, Buddy, nor Linda could talk me out of my new current plan. No one was willing to call. They were trying to talk me out of this. I wasn't about to take a chance, so I went outside and started hollering, "911." Now, we live in a cove in the mountains, and sounds reverberate with an echo from these mountain walls, so neighbors probably heard my pleas. Linda quickly decided she had better call 911, as I was coming back in to do it myself. The ambulance came, and on the way to the hospital, I had a conversation with Dad that I fully believed he was able to hear. I said, "Dad, I am a chip off the ol' block. You are proud of me, I know. And, thank you, Daddy, for giving me the money so I can pay for all this stuff. This is going to cost a bundle." And, indeed, those few days were expensive, that's for sure.

Tim and Linda followed the ambulance. Even when a person is in a full-blown manic episode, there can be periods where one appears quite normal. I answered all the questions on the psychological test quite well and didn't appear to be very bad at all. After keeping me for a couple hours (still hadn't been able to read the letter to Uncle Charles to anyone), it was decided to dismiss me. I still had the now full bottle of medicine, and on my discharge papers it simply states that I am to take the medicine and get back in contact if my condition worsens. I asked to read the paper I was to sign, and on it, I wrote at the precise line the instructions were given to take the medicine, "if the patient thinks she needs it." I would think that should have been a red flag to the person discharging me, but it was not. Tim and Linda wanted to bring me home, but by then I had decided I wanted to go up to the church (about fifty miles in the opposite direction) where I said all my friends would be praying and waiting for me in the chapel. Tim was quickly losing patience with me, but I kept insisting that I wasn't coming home just yet. He wasn't about to take me to the church, so I told him I would just take a taxi—yes, that was an expensive ride. Linda stayed with me. As we rounded the corner over an hour later, sometime after ten p.m., to my very real surprise, no lights were on in the chapel. If my friends were praying for me, they were certainly not doing it there. I quickly instructed the taxi driver to take me to the friary. The lights were out, but I knocked on the door, asking to see a priest. The elder one came to the door. Linda and I went in, and I tried to explain my situation, again somehow in some bungled way wanting to read the all-important letter. Linda explained my condition to the priest and asked if she could call home and have Tim or Buddy come get me. For some reason, the priest wanted nothing to do with this situation at all, and instead of letting Linda use the phone, he called the police and asked that I be taken to the emergency room. When the policeman arrived, I very willingly got in the car. The policeman said Linda could not ride with us, as she wasn't the one with the problem— it was against the rules. No amount of pleading from me availed. She didn't even know for sure where the hospital was and was left to walk in the middle of the night in the general direction of the hospital. I was certainly lucid enough to be very concerned about this situation, but Linda did arrive safely sometime later and was brought to where I was. After yet another evaluation, a psychiatrist was called. He was less than pleased to be awakened in the middle of the night to come for this call, and his displeasure showed. I kept telling him I didn't want to take my medicine until I had read my letter, because, if I took it, I knew I would very soon go into a sound sleep. I was upset because I'd earlier had to give my purse, with that valuable letter in it, to a nurse. At every medical office, I would repeat in detail the various places I had been sent to that day. Finally, finally, routine questions were dispensed with, and the doctor let me read that all-important letter.

Here is what it said:

Jan. 15, 2002

Dear Uncle Charles,

I wanted to write a letter to tell you how much you mean to me. I know I was just in Red Oak and could have told you in person, and I thought about it, but I guess I'm enough like Dad that I wanted to put it in writing.

You probably don't realize how much you have helped me in life, so I want to tell you. I want to be specific. One of the areas where you have helped me most is in money management. I know that I haven't asked you about specific investments, but I have watched you in your handling of money. You certainly purchase the comforts of life, but nothing in excess. We all know that some of the Gallaghers were very tight. You seem to be the most balanced of all.

I have listened to your conversations. I remember one time you saying that your daddy said, "You need to always have something making money for you while you sleep." I thought that was such a wise way of putting it. I also thought how fortunate to have grown up with such a wise father. That would certainly help you to be so balanced. I also thought about how lucky Charlene is to have such a wise father. She seems so balanced, also.

I feel I've done pretty well in managing money, but I believe I could have done better with a father as wise as you are.

You seem to be balanced in your giving (though, of course, I have no idea what you give), but I just know in my heart that the percentage is okay.

In your daily life, you have taught me by example. Yes, I have been told (and you have said so yourself) that you were pretty wild in your younger days. That is not the side of you I know, though. To me, you have always been stable Uncle Charles, someone I could go to with a problem and get a word of advice.

From all appearances, you have a wonderful family. As you know, in recent years, Charlene and I have grown very close. I have a lot of admiration and respect for her and value her opinion on a wide variety of topics.

My only real close contact with Glenda was on the trip to Idaho in July of 1999. To my delight, I found her to be extremely intelligent and great to talk with. I look forward to many opportunities to get to know her better.

I haven't had much contact with Carla, but she seems very sincere and very sweet.

Lyle—well, Lyle is just easy going ole Lyle. He'll help you out in a pinch, that's for sure, as he did for me by moving my stuff from Okla. to Tenn. back in '76.

I really don't know Curtis or any of your great-grandkids well enough to comment.

That's about it, Uncle Charles. I just wanted you to know that you're kind of like a dad I never had.

I thought about sending this overnight express just in case something happened to you before you got to read it. I don't mind the $10 + that it would cost, but then I thought that you wouldn't want me to be that extravagant. After all, there are times we just have to trust that the right things will happen.

With love,

Beverly

As I look back over this letter, it jumps out how much I was struggling for balance and stability. In my grasping for just that, I used the word balance many times. (Uncle Charles died a couple months later.) Now for the rest of that night's story. We talked only briefly because when I finished reading the letter to the doctor, I asked him if I should take my medicine in front of him then, or wait until I got home. I knew I would go to sleep in the car if I took it immediately. He asked me to take it then, and I did. For four days and nights, I slept most of the hours. On the 21st, I had a follow-up appointment with the psychiatrist in Asheville, and by the 22nd, I was beginning to get back to normal. At this point, I went to the police station to discuss my ride to the hospital and the refusal to let Linda ride. With looking at their reports stating I was very accommodating about everything I was asked to do, and realizing that Linda was put in jeopardy walking alone that night, I was told that the rule would be changed so that officers could make the judgment call regarding letting others ride in the patrol car in such a situation.

Even at this time, fourteen years later, I could give many more details about this manic episode, but in this writing, I have tried to give enough so that someone reading it might get even a faint idea about what it is like. As I was sleeping during the medically induced down phase of this episode, Buddy wrote the following letter (I have left punctuation, etc. as in the original) to Tim and Linda:

Sat. Jan 19, 2002

Tim & Linda

Bev is having problems sleeping. Due to her father's death which has been in progress since July.

I am ashamed that I have not been as understanding as I could have been. On too many occasions I vented my frustration by speaking unkindly and harshly. Just a few kind words would have been such a comfort to her.

In the forty years of marriage I have been the one to threaten a divorce, again unrequited frustration vented on someone dearly loved.

Life would be so empty without her. She has her problems but basically, she is a loving & kind person. In particular for her family. I don't think she knows how to express it in words but she surely does by unselfish actions toward us all. She has served us diligently all our lives. I do not know how to cope but shall try harder than ever before. This has been written for my sake. Writing down one's thoughts helps.

I really do not care about how she wants to pass on the royalties. Especially that from her Father as that, as I have always said, is hers as far as I am concerned to do with as she pleases.

I do believe all we have accumulated together is a 50/50 proposition. She has managed it well and hung on when I might have sold out. I think she fears that even yet. It seems to be a Biggs trait, of my Dad's children anyway.

I am resolved to be more kind loving & understanding toward her. I am sure we shall overcome this as we have overcome much in the past.

Today has been a hard day. I am emotionally drained. I know we have all hurt. Hopefully, it will be a while until we have any more deaths in the family. I'll write more later.

He did not add anything later.

Memories of my Dad – Sue

In 1991 Sue wrote a profile of Dad, and now twenty-five years later she has written her memories of him to be included in this book. Though some of the incidents described are the same, these are her thoughts at age eighty:

MEMORIES OF MY DAD

As far back as I can remember, when I was less than two years of age, I was terrified of my Dad and didn't want anything to do with him. This fear lasted my entire lifetime. And with that much fear, I found it impossible to love him. It was hard enough to forgive him, when I was older, for his subsequent actions.

I was born on the 7th day of April 1936, so I am now quite old, even though my brain thinks young. One of the first memories of my long life occurred when I was about two years old. We were living in Wilburton, Oklahoma, the town where I was born. What I remember was that one of Dad's old hunting dogs, Peggy, had given birth to a litter of puppies that made their home under the house. In that part of Eastern Oklahoma, many houses were built on some kind of pillar so there was space between the house and the ground. The pillars were made of brick, concrete, or some other hard material. There was enough space for me to crawl under the house and drag one of the pups out to play with. I think that it is a real memory and not a story someone has told me because I can remember how it felt—being under that house with all the cobwebs and other spooky things I would cringe from. Dad always had lots of hunting dogs, but Peggy was his favorite. My mother tells that he wanted to name me Peggy, and Mother said she wasn't going to name her daughter after that old bird dog. Instead, she named me Frankie Sue, after my dad.

I never liked that name and went by Sue. No one ever knew what my full name was. My third-grade teacher on my first day in Lincoln School in downtown Oakland (CA), made me aware that I had a stupid name and said from henceforth I was to go by "Sue!" She made me very self-conscious about my name, and I felt as if I was standing before the class bare naked, I was so embarrassed. And so, I never used it. It was one of my most closely guarded secrets.

The next memory happens about the same time. My brother, John, was a baby and breastfeeding. I was older by twenty months and twenty days. I can remember Mother sitting in the rocking chair nursing John, with me standing beside the rocker watching and wishing it was I who was being held instead of Johnnie. In the evening when all four of us gathered in the living room, my dad would holler at me with something like, "You come over here and be Daddy's girl. Come on and sit on my lap." But I was already scared of him, and I'd snuggle ever closer to my mother and refuse to go.

Dad never talked; he yelled. Another time I remember we were at the rodeo, and I wanted in the worst way some of the treats they were peddling, but Dad wouldn't buy me any of them, so I went without the cotton candy, hot dogs, soda pop, and candy I so craved. That was all a bunch of foolishness to my dad. Then would come a lecture about me being "bad" asking for things like that. But then my dad, being the cruel man that he was, liked to see you squirm and be uncomfortable. That trilled him in a strange sort of way.

It was about thirteen miles from Wilburton to Red Oak, and when I was about seven and John was five or six, we moved to Red Oak, or actually to Lodi, a community several miles from Red Oak where my Rider grandparents lived. My mother had a job teaching in the new school, and we lived in the old school house. On the same property slightly downhill sat the new rock schoolhouse that had been built by the WPA. It was constructed of native sandstone, and the grout was white. It was a really beautiful building. It was a one-room school, and Mother taught all grades. The salary was very small, but she could buy groceries to feed us.

This next major memory occurred while we lived in the old school house. The incident happened sometime during the winter months, for I can remember it being cold, so very cold. Mother had heated water to give John and me baths. We had a big galvanized tub for bathing. It must have been Saturday night, for that's when we all bathed in preparation for church on Sunday. I was first in, then John. Dad was out after dark, as he often was, and came home and began fussing with Mother, and he had a gun. He was threatening to shoot all of us and insisting Mom give him a divorce. John and I were standing there covered only by a bath towel when Mom told us, "Run, run and get help." So John and I ran as fast as we could and lost our towels as we ran. We were both terrified and felt that we were running for our lives, and I guess we were. The closest neighbors had a couple boys about my age, and I was ashamed to think they might see me naked. I can remember being so terrified that we'd be shot in the back, or that he would shoot our mother. Well, I've been told that my aunt Eunice, Dad's younger sister, happened to be driving down the road, and when she saw us, stopped her car and told us to get in. She took us home to her house. What happened after that, I can't remember. But I will never forget the terror I felt running through the dark country woods that night with no clothes and barefoot, fearing for my life, but perhaps more fearful of the neighbor boys seeing me naked if we had made it to the nearest neighbors. I was also fearful of us getting bit by a rattlesnake. Snakes were plentiful in Eastern Oklahoma and lived in rocky places.

One of the scariest memories was of the day John and I went off in the car with Dad. Granny cautioned us almost daily to never go alone in the car with Dad. This was probably due to the many threats he had made against our young lives. But he promised he would take us to Wilburton, where he would call and let us talk to our mother, who had gone to California to work. Naturally, with that kind of bait, we couldn't refuse. We both loved our mother and missed her every day. My brother John remembered that Dad had a gun with us inside the telephone booth. I don't remember that. We did get to talk to our mother as he had promised. Unbeknownst to us, he was telling Mother that if she didn't come back to Oklahoma and get us, he was going to shoot us and then kill himself. He sure must have been a sick and confused man at that time. Here he is suing Mother for a divorce, yet wanting her to come back to Oklahoma to live with him.

And then there are his parents, Granny and Grandpa Rider. Granny and Grandpa Rider were pillars of the Lodi/Red Oak community and served their neighbors well. Granny was a midwife and delivered about forty or some odd number of babies all free of charge. She knew quite a bit about medicine and was often called upon to doctor someone, again free of charge. When a member of the community died, Grandpa often made the coffin, and Granny finished it off by lining it with some of her finer cloths. They always raised a garden and planted extra, so they could share with their neighbors. They were good Christians to the core. It seems like, Dad, their oldest child and only son, kept them torn up most of the time with some of his shenanigans. But then Dad did love to see people suffer and squirm.

During World War II, all six of us grandkids went to live with Granny and Grandpa. Our parents were all in California working in the war effort. How they managed to take care of six grandchildren, all under about ten, with no electricity, water, or indoor plumbing, I'll never know. Granny cooked on a wood stove and did her canning on the same stove. She baked fresh bread every day.

We didn't have toys like most kids, but Granny would save her overgrown cucumbers that we could use for cars for the roads we made out of the dusty red dirt in Oklahoma. Grandpa would save his matchboxes for us, and those would also be made into cars. Then we girls had the catalog, Sears or Montgomery Ward, and we would cut paper dolls out of them. This was my favorite pastime. I loved to play paper dolls.

We were always getting into something we shouldn't get in to. Once, we raided Granny's flower beds where she had planted her horseradish. Boy, oh boy, did we ever get into something bad! Another time, we picked wild persimmons before they had ripened, and we were puckered up for a long, long time.

As I said, we didn't have much, but we always had fun. We had several peddlers come by on a regular basis. They all carried penny candy. Well, Granny, being thrifty as she was, always had a penny for each of us, so we could pick out our favorite candy. What a treat!

Another memory of those days is that Granny had an old silent keyboard she let us play with. Bonnie and I loved to play "funerals" and would thump that old keyboard and sing hymns like "Shall We Gather at the River?" or "In the Garden" and "Nothing but the Blood of Jesus." Charlene wasn't as interested in the old keyboard and playing funerals. Granny and Grandpa were staunch Baptist's, and we loved going with them to the Lodi Baptist Church. The Riders were there every time they had a service, including funerals. Grandpa had provided the wood to build this church and donated his labor as well. We also loved to play in the barn, up in Grandpa's hay loft. We loved to jump out of it and land on Grandpa's hay mound. Granny warned us we could land on a pitchfork, but we didn't listen too well. We had a great time living there with them on their farm.

When I was a teenager and visiting in Oklahoma, I remember starting to walk down to Aunt Eunice's and Charlene's house. My dad and some other men, maybe Grandpa, maybe Uncle Charles, I can't remember except they were shooting guns at a target or maybe something on the fence. It was kind of a past time in Southern Oklahoma. Most men liked to shoot. Well, if you don't think it was hard for me to walk out in Granny's yard, past those guys, and on down the road. I felt like screaming, it was so hard. I was afraid Dad would shoot me in the back. Really, I was quite relieved when I arrived at Aunt Eunice's house.

When I would tell my mother that I didn't love my dad, she would try to say that surely I did, after all, he was my blood father. But I knew at a very early age that I didn't love him; I didn't even like him. I just couldn't drum up any feelings of affection toward him. I dreaded spending time with him. We had nothing in common, so there was nothing to even talk about. The only reason I would go to visit him was to spend time with Edith and Beverly.

When I heard that Mom and Dad were getting a divorce, I was one happy eight-year-old girl. I wanted them to divorce. I was happy and glad he was not going to live with us anymore. When Dad wasn't around, I was more comfortable. I had some guilt feelings knowing that I didn't love my dad, but it didn't take away my fear of him. When Mother married Frank Phillips and I had a new step-father, I was very pleased. He was very kind and good to me. He gave me a secure home, and I knew he loved John and me.

In his later years, my dad lived with me for a while in Meadow Vista (CA). Since I had two young grandchildren at the time, I warned them about my dad and some of his strange ways. I cautioned them to tell me immediately should he ever bother them and make them uncomfortable when they were visiting me. I told them that I would believe them no matter what he might tell to the contrary. Sure enough, before he had been there for very long, my granddaughter came and told me that Grandpa was trying to kiss her and get her to sit on his lap. My husband, Butch, was within earshot and heard the story. He went in and got my dad and gave him a good talking to. He told him if he ever bothered either of them, he'd kill him. And I believe he would have.

Dad loved to get up for a midnight snack every evening, so I'd try to keep a home baked cake ready for him every night. He really liked his cake and milk. He liked to crumble a piece of cake into a glass of milk and eat it that way. While Dad lived with me in Meadow Vista, he and I would play dominoes in the evenings. I seldom won. He was much better at dominoes than I. But then he had a good teacher, his father J. Q. Rider, who couldn't be beaten in a game of dominoes. When I'd take my afternoon nap, I'd have to lock my doors. If I didn't, Dad could be in my room leaning over me. I'd wake up scared to death.

I was very happy when Dad fixed up his royalty interests and split them among Beverly, John and me equally. I felt guilty accepting my share because I knew how I felt about him. By this time I also knew that all Dad ever offered or ever gave us were financial things in place of love.

One of the things I asked for when I was a young teen was a cedar hope chest. I had made quite a few things to go in it, and most girls my age had started a chest making things and saving them for when they would be married. Nope, not a chance I'd get one. And my step-mother, Edith, had explained to him that all the young girls wanted one.

Also, in ninth grade, I started typing and asked for a typewriter, so I could practice at home. No again! I got a letter back from him saying that it was a bunch of foolishness—girls learning to type. They'd be better off learning how to keep house, wash, and cook, etc. So, I never got a typewriter. If memory serves me correctly, that was the last thing I ever asked for from my Dad. I never got what I wanted from Dad, only what he wanted to give me. He had two used bikes shipped. In a city like Oakland, it was scary to ride them.

When I was about fourteen, John and I went from Red Oak, Oklahoma, to North Carolina to visit Dad and our other family. Although Edith didn't ever have any spare money, she set aside a quarter every day, so I could walk over to the little café near where their trailer was parked off the highway. That little café served the best chili dogs I had ever eaten, and that's what I bought with my quarter.

Adjoining the café was a small beauty shop. Sometimes I'd drop in there to chat with the patrons and beauty operators. One day some ladies were saying how much Jim's (Dad's boss) children resembled their mother. I knew those boys were not hers and were just visiting for the summer like John and I were. So not having been told that it was a secret, I told the truth to the ladies in the shop. That night Jim came over and hopped all over me for being a gossip and telling tales. His wife was very upset and crying, and boy did he ever chew me out! I tried to say that I was never told that the information I passed on was a big secret. Had I known, I would never have told the ladies. I was not a gossip or a troublemaker. My dad stood by and let Jim yell and berate me and never said a word in my defense. I made up my mind that I was going back to Red Oak as soon as possible. My feelings were really hurt. I also told Dad that would be the last time I ever visited him while I was young. And I never did. Had that happened with Mom and Uncle Frank, they would never have allowed Jim to browbeat me like Jim did. But Dad was afraid to say anything because Jim was his boss!

Also, while I was a young teen, the summer before I started high school, a cousin came to spend a month or so with us. We shopped for clothes and did quite a few fun things. I had a boyfriend at the time, and my cousin didn't have one, but she got to come along anywhere we went. I had started smoking about that time, and my cousin knew it. She went home and told her mother, my aunt. Aunt Alice immediately wrote to Dad about all the worldly, sinful things I was doing. Well, I got a letter from Dad that I've since thrown away but have wished I hadn't. The gist of the letter was that he had a vision. It seems Mother had died and was lying on a cot before God getting her judgment for how she had lived her life. God was condemning her to hell for the way she had raised their children, John and me. Mother didn't want me to respond to that letter, but it made me so irate that I did answer it. I told him quite clearly how I felt about his letter, his vision, and a bunch of other things. We didn't exchange letters after that.

I was a very proud young person, and I was ashamed for people to know that he was my dad. He always was dirty and smelled of B. O. I didn't want people to know he belonged to me.

John loved his dad and pursued him throughout his life.

Sue Rider

January 20, 2016

A Few Travels – The Spice of My Life

Christmas Letters

For well over twenty years, the first Christmas card I received each year was from my beloved math professor at Cumberland University, Lebanon, Tennessee, Dean Jack Howard, who has now passed. He was among the first who encouraged me to write the story of my life. He told me he always saved my Christmas letters, read them over many times during the year, and that they brought him such joy. He asked me to write about my experiences. I decided to choose a few excerpts from some of these letters to share with you. This was one of Dean Howard's favorites, from my 2005 Christmas letter:

Without a doubt, the most memorable experience I had this year took place on our mission awareness trip to Guatemala. We have sponsored Maria for several years now. She, her sister, and her sister's little girl, Daly, and their mother came to see us this year at the CFCA (Christian Foundation for Children and Aging) site in San Lucas Toliman. We are also helping a young mother, Juana. We met Juana on our first trip to Guatemala over two years ago. Her parents could not afford to send her to school. She had quit school after the sixth grade and had married. Her husband was a drunk and beat her badly. In a drunken state one night, he died. Juana had Marvin, then age two, and was pregnant with her little girl, Zulmy Elizabeth. Juana had sought out the director of CFCA and expressed a desire to return to school. As she is not a child or aged person, she doesn't qualify for the CFCA program. The director, however, explained her situation and asked if anybody would be willing to give her a chance. Buddy and I volunteered. We wondered if she, a woman in her twenties, would stick with it, having to go back to school entering the seventh grade. It has been such a blessing to be a part of her life. She not only is sticking with it but is in accelerated classes and is scheduled to graduate next year. (Juana completed a two-year business degree.)

The lovely experience I want to share with you took place in April between Zulmy, then age four and a half, and Daly, then nineteen months. When shopping for gifts for our sponsored persons and their families, I bought two dolls—one for Zulmy and one for Daly. My suitcases quickly got too full, and I didn't seem to have room for both dolls. The suggested ages on the boxes were three years and up, so I decided to leave the doll for Daly behind, and take the bear I had for her.

When we first saw Juana and the children, the children were very shy. I went and got the gifts. When Zulmy saw that doll, her eyes lit up, and she grabbed me before I knew what was happening and gave me a big kiss. She did the same to Buddy. She immediately started patting the doll, bouncing it on her knee and putting it behind her back to carry. She just seemed ecstatic! Through the interpreter, I asked if it were her very first doll. Juana answered that it was. Can any of you imagine the experience of seeing a four and a half-year-old child with her first doll! Buddy immediately said, "It was worth a plane ticket to Guatemala to see that child's eyes light up at the sight of that doll!"

That afternoon, when little Daly and Zulmy, who live about sixty miles apart, met for the first time, Zulmy was playing with her doll. It was apparent that Daly, though only nineteen months, was eagerly eyeing the doll. I was beating myself up because I hadn't left something out of the suitcase and put the extra doll in. Then a beautiful thing happened. With no prompting from anybody, Zulmy reached out to this little stranger and gave her that precious doll. Daly played with it a few minutes, patted and rubbed it; and then, again without any prompting, this little nineteen-month-old girl gave it back to Zulmy. After about fifteen minutes, Zulmy would give it back to Daly, and this sharing continued. It was like there was something innate about all this. I cannot describe the feeling of being in a culture with this kind of love and kindness, where sharing comes so naturally that one appears to be born with the gift.

As much as I sometimes wish I had found room for both dolls, I realize that had I done so, I would have never been able to witness this beautiful example of pure love. It's one thing to share from one's abundance, but quite another to share when you have almost nothing at all. This is such a beautiful Christmas story!

This experience also comes from my Christmas letter of 2005:

Every so often in life, one has an experience where the powers that be arrange our life so that a single moment becomes memorable. Such happened to me this year. When on a trip to South Dakota, we spent a week in Custer, where ancestors on my paternal grandmother's side were early settlers. I had intended to go to the cemetery to try to find her mother, grandparents, and other relative's graves. After a busy sightseeing agenda of the many wonderful things in the area, on the day we were to leave, I still had not done so! Buddy and I hurriedly went to the cemetery. Quickly I saw the graves of the two relatives who had been the witnesses at my grandparent's wedding. I got out of the car to walk around while Buddy drove around to see if, from the car, he could spot the family name on tombstones. There was another lady walking around in the area, also, and I said to her, "I'm looking for Gould's." She said, "I'm looking for Gould's, too. I'm descended from Frank Depot Gould of Elmira, New York." I said, "Well, I'm descended from Frank Depot Gould of Elmira, New York, also." As it turned out, she had already found the graves of my more immediate line of ancestors and took me to them. She, too, had been in Custer for a week but hadn't gone to the cemetery until her last day there. How nice, that just at that moment in time, our lives would converge!

In my 2004 Christmas letter I wrote:

This year, we went on a mission awareness trip to Merida, Mexico, where Tim sponsors a boy, Alejandro. It was such a moving experience, as these trips always are. Alejandro's brother is mentally handicapped. To go to their home and see the poverty they live in is humbling, to say the least. My sister, Sue, sponsors a couple children in Mexico, so she went on the trip, too. Her children and their mother and project director traveled over forty hours and many bus changes from deep in the mountains next to the Guatemalan border to see her. She says the trip has forever changed her life.

There were about twenty of us who rode in a bus each day to remote villages. Some of these villagers only spoke the Mayan language. We would be met at the road and be led in a parade to the village plaza where a fiesta was held in our honor. The experiences are incredible. At one, for an unknown reason, a little girl ran up to me and gave me a big hug, held my hand all the way to the village, and then disappeared. I wondered what had happened to her. Then, at the end of the day, as we were boarding the bus to leave, all at once she appeared with another hug. On another occasion, a little girl slipped up, put her arms around me, and gave me a small heart that said, "I love you." When I think that she could have chosen anyone from the group, but she chose me, I am deeply humbled.

Toward the end of the trip, we all got food poisoning. We had gone to a remote refugee camp for displaced Guatemalans. We were about two hours late getting there. Unknown was the fact that the village had not had their few hours of electricity for the day, and the food had sat out in the hot sun for hours. One by one, everyone started getting sick. Beverly, with the stomach of iron, was last but not least. I was apologizing to Sue for bringing her there. She emphatically said that even if she had known she was going to get sick, she definitely would have still come.

In 2005, my friend, Harriet, and I went on a wonderful trip together led by our parish priest. In an email to Tim and Linda, written June 10, 2005, I described this trip to Italy and Poland:

Our group spent two days in Rome. We went to the four major basilicas plus St. Peter's and the Vatican museums. The ceiling of the Sistine Chapel cleaned is lovely! You and I saw it in its darker days. We went to the general audience with the Pope with the thousands of other people and were directed to sit next to the fence near the Popemobile route in case he took it. Well, it poured rain during the wait until the moment the Pope was to come out. At that point, the sun came out brilliantly. He did make the route, and I was close enough to him to have reached out and touched his hand if he had extended it, but he spent the time waving. When he finished going around and was ready for the speech, it started pouring rain again.

Then we went to Pompeii. It was really nice except for the crowds—just too many! You would like to see it, but definitely in the offseason. It is not worth putting up with crowds just to see leaves on trees and eat in outdoor cafes. We went to the tomb of St. Padre Pio at San Giovanni Rotundo on the east coast of Italy. I thought it was a powerful experience. Padre Pio is known for having exceptional charismatic gifts, including bilocation, levitation, and the ability to read people. (To this day, I remember the extraordinary pull I felt as I walked past his tomb. I personally felt a presence so strong it was hard for me to stand.)

I just loved Poland. I definitely want to go back, again during offseason. May and June are filled with school children seeing the sights. The summer attracts a lot of Europeans. Americans are only beginning to discover the place. Arthur Frommer does not have a guidebook on Poland. How very, very nice. Poland is probably like a Europe that I never saw. It seemed even more like an earlier culture than New Zealand. Things are very cheap. Wonderful full meals for $3 and $4. The people are very unpretentious, not fancy at all. They just seemed genuine. I want to go back—the sooner, the better. However, it will not be on a tour. I would have no qualms about going to Poland and would do it like we used to tour. It is probably more crime free than any of the other European countries. Of course, one has to watch for pickpockets everywhere and be sensible. We were mainly in Krakow, and I would go back and just make that a base. We went to Auschwitz. Everyone should see this, just like every American ought to experience some of the poverty in the world. We needed all day, but had about two hours of the highlights.

I'll close for now and hope this email gets to both of you.

Love,

Mother

The Christmas season of 2009, I wrote:

Last December Buddy and I joined Tim, Mayra, and Eram in Ecuador. We spent a week out at a little fishing village on the Pacific Ocean. This place is like a scene out of an old movie. There was no grocery store--the vegetable truck came around twice a week. Very few people had cars, so walking was a pleasure. The fishing boats were launched by placing logs under the boat, with several people rolling for a pace, then placing another log in front, etc., until the boat finally got out to sea. Our hotel was an old picturesque place ($15 per night) in a beautiful setting. Tim told me it reminded him of a scene in the old Humphrey Bogart classic, "Dark Passage." We did have bathrooms and hot water for showers. We were the only ones there, so the owner was very accommodating. She cooked our meals from the fish Buddy and others caught. The most exciting thing in town was church on Sunday. It was a good place to enjoy our grandson at ten months of age.

In March of this year Bud, Linda, and I went on a "St. Paul's Missionary Journeys" cruise to the Mediterranean. It was a bit early to be cruising the Mediterranean Sea. During the first part, the weather was bad, and we didn't enjoy things very much. We had spent three weeks in Greece thirty years ago. Some say you should hang on to those old memories and not go back. In this case, I agree. In 1979 we rented a car and drove all over the country. Now it is so built up and crowded that we didn't like it. We never got out of the sight of buildings and houses all the way to Corinth. I will never care to go back to Greece.

Turkey was the only part of the trip that I really liked. When we got to Ephesus, it was still rainy and cold. The day we were in port, it was still bad during our morning tour. Buddy decided to stay on the bus, and I didn't blame him. Linda and I decided to take our umbrellas and brave it. We quickly saw we didn't want to stay with the group and hear the speel (I have seldom been on tours and don't do well in those confines). We wanted to strike out on our own and knew we could be back to our bus well within the time frame allotted. Oh, Ephesus is SOOO beautiful. The only other people we saw that were braving the weather was a group of teenagers. They were anxious to practice their English and wanted to talk with us, take our pictures and tell us over and over how beautiful our eyes were (these were such good looking kids—it shows beauty IS in the eye of the beholder). It was such fun interacting with them. Wouldn't you know it—everyone gets back on the bus to head to the ship, and the sun pops out to reveal a glorious day! How I wish we could have headed back out to Ephesus, but the boat sailed at 2 p.m.

Most of the sites in Israel we had seen before. We finished the trip in Egypt. The kids and I had done a very thorough trip there with a small group of fifteen when we lived in Saudi Arabia. At that time, when one approached the pyramids, one could imagine being in a caravan and approaching them from afar. NOW it is wall-to-wall souvenir shops and other buildings. How a country could let this happen is beyond me! There are probably only about two sites where you can even get a picture of the pyramids without all this clutter in the background, and you really have to be positioned to do that. Egypt—another place we shouldn't have gone back to.

We were in Oklahoma this year to celebrate my Uncle Virgil Culberson's 100th birthday. He has a remarkable memory, and I am grateful for the many times over the years that I have been able to sit at his feet and learn so many interesting things about our family and his life for the past one-hundred years. I want to share one of those times. On a visit to him a few years ago, I took Mother's photo album that was filled with pictures taken before I was born. As we sat there and he spoke of the people (many that I didn't know), it was amazing to see his face light up with story after story. At the end of that session, he had talked about most of the people who were in that album. There were a few that he didn't know. That afternoon I went over to the house of an old full-blood Choctaw Indian lady who had been one of Mother's best friends. She started talking about the people in the album. As we turned the pages, I realized there was something remarkable going on. She knew every one of the people that Uncle Virgil didn't know!

Newfound Empowerment

Yesterday, I Felt Well

Yesterday, I felt well, but am not doing as well today. I haven't written in a month now because I've been dealing with some mild problems (I say "mild" because I have not felt I needed medicine) with my bipolar disorder. I thought about writing during this time but just couldn't seem to make myself do it. I decided it would be better to wait until I felt normal before putting words on paper.

On March 31 Buddy had an outburst that I had trouble dealing with. I have previously written about the problems with his tractors and the monetary losses that occurred. As I've written about this previously, I'll only give a brief update now. When Buddy bought the new tractor two years ago on credit and recently sold it, he received $9,000 cash in hand from the sale. He had lost $20,500 in the two years he had owned it. He couldn't seem to find a good tractor like the one he had traded in, but finally found one for $14,000. He asked me to write a check for $10,000 so he could buy this one. I questioned as to why he needed $10,000 rather than $5,000, as he should have had the difference. He quickly got on the defensive and reacted in an angry way. He said he had bought some items to resell. He bought the $14,000 tractor and got it home. A couple days later, I again had a discussion trying to explain to him that our royalty checks have dropped to the point we can no longer spend money so freely. He absolutely blew his top! With eyes filled with venom, he shouted, "I despise you! I detest looking at your face! I want a divorce! The Bible says, 'It's better to live on a housetop than to live with a brawling woman.' You have changed so much! This all started about two years ago when you started running down to Slate and that bunch. You are not the same person I married almost fifty-three years ago. If I'd known you were going to change like this, there is no way I would have married you! We'll just sell this place and go our separate ways!" I was stunned! Buddy has had some rages recently; they seem to get worse with each new one, but no way had any been as destructive as this one.

As I've stated previously, I do not react to outbursts with heated words in return. I know it just adds fuel to the fire, and the main person that would be upset would be me. In a calm, but thorough manner I replied, "Yes, I have changed. I am not the same person you married almost fifty-three years ago, but you are. You haven't changed. I do not regret marrying you because then I wasn't emotionally equipped to even know how to pick out a husband. I'm glad I stayed with you because our children would have never loved another man like they love you, and no other man would have loved them like you do. Even as I have grown over the years, I have known that I still haven't been emotionally equipped to select the right kind of husband for me."

I'm going to make some comments about these last few sentences. What I have said is very true. Earlier I related about unloading on Buddy for sixteen hours, one for each year of our marriage at that time. I realized then that Buddy would not have been the type of person I should have chosen for a husband, but I also realized then that I was not emotionally equipped to choose wisely. If I had chosen divorce and remarried, I would have only jumped from the frying pan into the fire. I would have only chosen somebody that had the same traits—may be expressed differently, but yet still the same. I have previously stated that I feel I often have a gift for seeing things at the time they occur and don't have to wait until hindsight to figure out something. With this gift of perception, I believe I was spared much pain and sorrow. No, Buddy does not have the personality that would have been best for me, but I would have chosen someone with different stripes, yet the same color. It has only been through the writing of the past two years that I feel I am better equipped to choose a companion. In fact, it was on the morning of April 12 after this outburst of Buddy's nearly two weeks before, that I awakened and thought, "Maybe, just maybe, I am now able to see weaknesses and strengths in a person well enough that I could sensibly choose a partner."

The previous week I had finished the letter about how we acquired this beautiful place—what a gift it had been and continues to be. I was nearly in shock with having to deal with the prospect of selling this place and splitting the proceeds because of divorce. I went in and got the letter in the hope that Buddy would read it and appreciate this treasure. As I asked him to read it, he screamed, "Are you just wanting lauds for your writing? Are you just wanting someone to read this and brag about how well you write?" He briefly held the paper and flipped through the three pages, then handed it back to me.

As Buddy continued to rave, I thought of a Bible verse also, "Out of the abundance of the heart the mouth speaketh." I also thought of the American Indians' incorporated values regarding words. The Indian of long ago believed thoughts were powerful, but that the spoken word was even more powerful. They said, "Be careful with words. Once spoken, they go out into the universe and can never be recalled." I believe this sincerely, and from a very early age have tried to practice this. This philosophy has helped me, as I near the age of seventy, not to carry the sorrow of regret for many words hastily spoken.

A few days after his initial outburst, Buddy said to me, "Beverly, the reason I got angry is because the clutch is out on the new tractor, and it costs $2,000 to fix it. I thought you'd be mad because I didn't check it out properly before I bought it."

Buddy studies the Bible almost daily, so I thought to give him an assignment. I asked him to list all the verses in the Bible that talked about how to speak to others. He immediately went to the office and started to work. Presently, he came back with three pages of writing with some verses and studious comments. He completely missed the point that I had hoped to impress! He simply did not see himself in a single verse.

How did I cope? Momentarily after the outburst, I felt a sense of peace. I thought of how I wouldn't have to be concerned about paying the taxes, the insurance, the electricity, the heating costs, etc. for this big house. I thought about how I'd like to pick out a couple acres or so from this farm and build a much smaller house and cut my monthly fixed expenses in half. But then, these thoughts gave way to more troubled ones.

In times of extreme stress, my bipolar illness can be triggered. I always have to live with this reality, and I always will. I've relayed in previous letters how much I believe the past two years of writing have helped me deal with this area of my life as well. I am well aware that many psychiatrists and psychologists believe almost all mental illness is caused by unresolved anger. Some, though, make exceptions for bipolar disorder and schizophrenia. It is well researched that genetics play a major role in both; however, I am prepared, based on my personal experience, to believe that in bipolar, at least, unresolved anger plays a larger role than is currently acknowledged. Pouring out my soul on paper and receiving a cleansing release from anger that I did not know existed has definitely helped me!

It was during this period that I decided to buy a card for myself with the poem, "The Oak Tree," by Johnny Ray Ryder, on the cover. My friend, Linda Brewer Kitchens, had sent me a similar card with this poem years ago when I was going through another of my crises. The poem is about endurance and reaching down to our roots to be able to withstand the batterings that come to us in life.

At the beginning of the inside message I wrote, "TO ME." The message reads:

"Especially now, try to remember that you're stronger than any problem you encounter or any disappointment life will bring. Thinking of you, believing in you, caring for you."

I signed it, "With love, Beverly." I put the date, April 5, 2016, and wrote on the outside of the envelope, Beverly Ann Rider.   Daily, I read the card.

There were some signs of bipolar appearing. I began to lose sleep. Awakening around 3 a.m. each morning is not all bad. It is at this time when I receive a lot of intuitive information about my life and get help in dealing with whatever problem is current. But then this can go on too long, and sleep deprivation becomes crucial to my mental state. If I didn't feel sleepy after about an hour, I would get up and warm a small glass of raw milk which will usually put me back to sleep soon (raw milk still has all its healthful properties—pasteurized or homogenized milk does not have the same effect on me). I would, however, allow myself to stay awake long enough to feel my thoughts were rational, and that I was receiving what was important for me. Too long, and the details can escalate to the point they become irrational and mania begins to take hold.

On a few occasions, I found myself talking with rapid speech to people, also talking with a fair amount of detail in areas that I would not ordinarily reveal. My thoughts were beginning to race, and I would flit to another thought before I could express the previous one—another warning sign. Ah, yes, over the past thirty years, I have become very adept at perceiving the warning signs.

In times of stress, mania is by far the biggest problem for me. I don't usually have any problem with depression until I've had to take medicine to knock me down from my high. This time was different, though, and I will have to watch for this in the future. I was lethargic. I did need to stay in bed a lot, but I was extremely fatigued even after having slept what should have been enough hours. My sister, Sue, would call me daily if I didn't call her. She kept a very close watch on me and was the one that pointed out, "Beverly, you seem to have skipped the mania this time and have gone into depression. I can hear it in your voice. I know this so well because I have experienced it so much myself."

Certainly, I tried to remember to eat at regular times and eat healthy food, but that is something I try to do at any time in order to help keep my bipolar symptoms at bay. Regular sleep, healthy food at regular times, discipline, discipline, discipline. Eternal vigilance. The returns are worth it to me.

Yes, there were the few times when the thoughts came into my brain, "Beverly, there is no one that would ever want you. You have too many problems." But I shoved those thoughts out as soon as I recognized they were appearing. I want to say something here. Even in the past year, I have read works of popular psychologists who have written much that has helped me, but in giving advice on how to select life partners, have advocated just passing people by who have had terrible childhoods. How cruel. I read things like that and just feel crummy. What kind of psychology is that! Maybe that's good advice, but it leaves people like me behind, just out in the dark. Certainly, it's not the positive outlook I want to have!

There is something I better say at this point. In writing all of this, NO WAY am I advocating that others who may have similar challenges to deal with in their mental health choose not to take medicine. I have had to take medicine many times and was quite willing to do so. It's just that when told by competent psychiatrists that there was a ninety-nine percent chance I'd have to be on medication the rest of my life, I hoped to find another way. Certainly, my great-grandfather who declared, "One percent, that's all I need," has been an inspiration to me. Also, I had a father who taught me discipline and REQUIRED it of me. I need to emphasize again that the psychiatrist I saw in Nashville specialized in bipolar disorder, and that he told me I was the only patient he had ever managed who was able to sense when I had an episode coming on and come into his office on my own. I have written this to give some examples of what anyone can do to help themselves, and writing from the depths of one's soul can help. It is not a sign of weakness to admit you need help in any form that is available to you. It is a sign of strength!

More Problems - Then and Now

When Buddy wrote the letter in January 2002 resolving to be more kind toward me, I have no doubt that he meant every word. The resolve, however, melted away very quickly. I have grown tired of writing of problems and was going to quickly skip over some and get on with the ending of this book. Recent circumstances have caused me to rethink this plan. I need to cover things fully not only for the truthfulness of the writing but for my own healing as well. In 2002 Buddy continued to drink heavily and use abusive language toward me. I just did not seem to have the right skills to cope. Instead, I began to have episodes of mania more frequently. Every few months I found myself in the psychiatrist's office and having to go on medication. In professional terminology for those with bipolar, this is rapid cycling. Needless to say, it is not good and is very harmful to the body, especially the brain. My body is very sensitive to medication, and as I've indicated earlier, I never wanted to take it longer than absolutely necessary. This was another of the times I was encouraged to remain on medication all the time, and, yes, for the rest of my life.

Things came to a head at the time of our 40th wedding anniversary in June 2003. Interestingly, it was a sermon that clarified my position. Father A. was relating a story about a mother who had brought a son in for counseling. The mother related the boy's bad language toward her. The boy interrupted with, "I love my mother, but . . ." Father A. said to the boy, "Stop it! No, you don't. That's not love." Something in my brain clicked, "The way Buddy talks to you is not love either." The next week Buddy repeated his oft, "We just need to get a divorce. We don't have anything in common and can't get along." This time, instead of immediately acquiescing to his current whim, I simply said, "Okay."

I didn't say it with any fanfare or heightened tone of voice. I simply said, "Okay." This was the first time I had answered like this. For a few seconds, Buddy was silent, deadly silent. Then he immediately started begging me to change my mind, saying he really didn't want a divorce. Finally, I said, "There are only two ways I'll stay with you. The first is that we both get voice-activated tape recorders, so we can see the interaction of the language you use toward me regularly. The second is that you go to counseling." Now, you may remember what Buddy told me back when I was in therapy after my breakdown when I was forty. He had said that he would die and go to hell before he would let some shrink probe into his demons. Well, I fully expected that he would not be willing at all to meet my second requirement. I was ready to divorce. I choose words carefully and don't say something I am not willing to carry out.

Buddy agreed for me to choose a counselor. I bought six sessions because if one prepaid for five, the sixth one was free. I fully expected we would need many sessions. I went to the first one alone. Buddy and I went together for the second one. I bought the small tape recorders, but before we started wearing them, something with even greater impact happened. We went to a large boat showroom and were at the back of the store looking at boats when a horrible outburst of screaming and cursing was directed at an employee by the owner of the store. There was another couple near us who started walking for the door. Buddy asked me if I wanted to leave, too, and I said, "Yes." As we started toward the door, the owner saw us and came over, asked us to stay, and started talking about how this employee was so incompetent, etc. Buddy said, "I understand," and so we stayed. When we got in the pickup to start home, Buddy turned to me and said, "Would you have rather left?" I said, "Yes." I said nothing further about the incident, but I knew it had been more effective than any tape recording of the two of us could ever be.

That night we were to have our second counseling session together.

I related to the counselor the morning's incident, adding, "If Buddy hadn't been standing right beside me, I would have thought it was he talking. The voice, the tone, and the words were just like Buddy talks to me." Buddy seemed stunned and asked me, "Do I really sound like that?" I said, "Yes, you do." Buddy spoke to the counselor, "It is hard for me to believe that I sound like that, but Beverly always tells the truth. I have never known Beverly to lie to me." Buddy went on to tell the counselor that he never really wanted a divorce but always said that to me to control me. Buddy told him that when he said that, I would always agree with whatever he wanted. Part of this did not surprise me. I had already long ago figured out that with my parents repeatedly separating, filing for divorce, etc. throughout my childhood, this was the last thing I ever wanted to do to my children. I knew why I reacted to this divorce threat the way I did. What I was not just surprised at, but stunned, was that not only did Buddy know what he was doing; he was doing it deliberately—it was premeditated. Buddy confessed quite a few other things, among them that he needed to stop drinking and that he wanted to get back in church.

Buddy didn't go to any more counseling sessions. He said that he didn't need to—that he understood his part in the problems and to go any more would be a waste of time. I was so thrilled with his revelations to the counselor that I agreed. I did go back to one more individual counseling session but didn't feel the need to go further, even though we still had two prepaid ones left. What I didn't realize was that even with all Buddy's admissions and resolves, two counseling sessions were not going to be sufficient to alter a lifetime of inappropriate behavior.

To his credit, Buddy did stop drinking. This was not something I asked him to do. It was something he knew he needed to do. He recognized he could never drink moderately. It would have to be all or nothing for him. The following year he decided to come into the Catholic Church, and we went together for a few years. We had some nice church-related trips together, including study cruises and mission awareness trips to Mexico and Central America. Things were fairly peaceful for a while. It was my initiative to leave the church, but Buddy was anxious to revert back to his earlier fundamentalism and quickly did so.

As Tim and Linda have pointed out, Buddy is like a gambler when it comes to buying and selling tractors. He appears to be addicted, and whether or not he makes money seems to be almost a non-issue. I have related all the problems involved in the purchase of the tractor in March—a tractor that, when the clutch was replaced, seemed so satisfactory for this farm, a tractor that everybody liked and the one that I had certainly invested mental anguish. In July, we found out that Buddy had traded this tractor for two that did not run. He could not tell whether they were good or not because he couldn't even start them. Before he brought them home and had cashed a small check for the difference in the price of our good one, Linda and I begged him to call the man and tell him he wasn't going to complete the deal. After all, I had paid for almost all of this tractor and certainly didn't want him to start trading on that money. Linda and I offered to go to the man, with or without Buddy, and explain to him that Buddy had made a mistake in getting this family tractor involved. The man is an auction dealer, but Buddy had not met him previously. I asked his age. Buddy said he was probably about sixty. I said, "Well, you're about eighty, and I will testify in court if need be about the bad judgment you have been making the past couple years." Buddy went on and on about how the man said that he was a good Christian, and his word was his bond. Buddy, likewise, used the Christian thing to say that he, too, had to stick by his word. Buddy begged to go call the man on the telephone and went outside and used his cell phone to do so. He came back saying the man would not let him out of the deal. This man had told him the bigger tractor only needed a starter, but he didn't want to bother with getting one. Well, Linda and I finally relented due to Buddy's begging about how he needed to keep his word. He got the junk tractors to his mechanic friend, and, as to be expected, the one needing only a starter was junk throughout—head busted, among other things. Both tractors were total pieces of trash! Tim, Linda, and I were all angry that Buddy had refused to let us intervene in his horrible deal. He had traded an approximately $16,000 tractor for $2,500 and two junk tractors!

As he usually does, Buddy jumped on the defense and started screaming at me that he wanted a divorce—the old "we can't agree on anything" syndrome. I agreed. I decided that I'd had enough. I did want a divorce. He immediately started backtracking. I said, instead of getting a lawyer involved now, that we needed to calmly agree on a division of property and get on with it. Buddy screamed that he would "p . . . everything we had away" before he would let me have anything! That did NOT sit well at all with me. These were words I hadn't heard before. Things went from bad to worse. In these writings I've used the words, "a most amazing thing happened," when I've been surprised at my ability to cope with adversity and stress without going into a manic episode, but THIS time an even GREATER thing happened. As the days and nights went by, I WAS sleeping well.   I did NOT even have symptoms that I MIGHT be going into a manic episode! WHAT A NEWFOUND EMPOWERMENT! Oh yes, Buddy, in a non-apologetic way, told me that he didn't really want a divorce—that the reason he said that was to control me. I said, "I know that. You said the same thing to the counselor we went to in 2003." He then started screaming, "I don't remember saying that," but then changed gears with, "I only went to that counselor because that is the only way you said you would stay married."

Relations were strained. I did not back down, but neither did I start exhibiting symptoms of mania. The children noticed this as well. This was NOT the old mother that they knew. She wasn't exhibiting her normal behavior. Buddy started behavior that I never knew existed either. One night I was standing by his recliner chair, and he started taunting me with, "You are going off. You are going crazy." I said, "I most definitely am not. I don't even feel the symptoms that I MIGHT be going off." He kept on—it was like he was trying to goad me into it. This was unconscionable! When I realized what he was doing, on this Friday night I didn't sleep more than two hours. No, it was NOT because I was having symptoms leading to mania. It was because I was lying there in bed pondering why in the world I would even stay in the same house with a man who was actually in some sort of twisted way hoping I would have a manic episode. This was beyond the pale— absolutely appalling! I thought of the times I had been in a manic episode and on horrible medication and was so dizzy and nauseated that I would fall down in the floor trying to get from the bed to the bathroom. I would call the doctor and tell him that my body was telling me that "it didn't want this medication—it was rejecting it." The doctor has said, "Well, keep on taking it and maybe your body will adjust." I had no enemies of whom I was aware, but I would be on the downside of one of these horrible episodes and think, "I wouldn't wish this off on my worst enemy!" And to think my own husband seemed to be wishing that he could see this behavior in me. That week he continued with taunts, "You are going crazy. You might not think so, but you are." When I told Linda this, she said, "Yes, Dad came up to my house and said, 'Your mother is going crazy.'" Linda told me that she replied, "Well, if I lived in the same house with a man who changes his mind as often as you do, I'd go crazy, too!" As Linda so aptly pointed out, "Dad has lost his last measure of control. Threatening you with divorce is not working any longer." His last card to play in trying to control me was using the bipolar episodes.

So, as you can see, July and August have been harsh, but very revealing months for me. Now, I do not wish to go overboard on my newfound self-empowerment, but I am simply unwilling to tolerate this previous lifestyle any longer. I have been methodically getting some financial things in order—things that would make a divorce less traumatic from that standpoint. Buddy seems to know that I mean business. It doesn't matter that Buddy will be eighty years old in October and that I turned seventy at the end of May. I don't intend to spend the remainder of my good years, however many they may be, living like I have the first 70. Even before you said it to me, Dr. Slate, I have always believed that "the best is yet to be." I have always believed that everything that happened to me in life was for a purpose—something I would be using to help me in the next stage of my life. I have said earlier in these writings that I didn't, as most people seem to do, have to wait to see why something happened.   Most people will say, "If I knew then what I know now," I would do such and such. Previously I have said that all my life I seemed to have a gift to see the purpose in things as they were happening. I could see the good immediately. I didn't have to wait until later.

At one point during August, Buddy screamed, "You have just hidden behind mental illness," and in the middle of that sentence, as if in parenthesis, added, "I know you couldn't help it, but . . ." The words sounded VERY HARSH, but I immediately thought, "Yes, maybe that IS what I've done! When I told Linda what her dad said, without missing a beat, she said, "Well, HE hides behind religion!" To deal with stress by retreating into episodes of mental illness would be from my deepest unconscious, that's for sure, but, nevertheless, I thought of the conversation with Dr. C way back when I was forty—the one where I emphatically told him to not ever say to me again that I caused all of this.

Bipolar is supposed to be a genetic, brain chemical problem. In my own case, I wouldn't try to deny that at all. It certainly runs in my family in every generation of which I know.   After over two years of digging deep into my soul and pouring out on paper buckets of tears for years of grief, I feel that this writing has helped me to overcome my problems more than any other single thing I've ever done. I feel a wholeness and have a sense of confidence that I've never felt nor had in my entire life. That's a great way to be at age seventy!

The Stock From Whence I Came

Those I Knew

It has always been my intention to write about those that I knew and then do another chapter about those I didn't know. They are the stock from whence I came.

MOTHER

Mother was born on the Choctaw Indian Reservation about three miles south of Wilburton, Oklahoma. She had no birth certificate and for most of her life thought she was born in 1909. When she applied for social security, she gave that year and stated the sources for this date. Among them was the information that she had been baptized in the Catholic Church. At the time of her birth, the priest at the church in Hartshorne, Oklahoma, served several areas, and on the books there it was written that she had been baptized in 1908. Those were the records that the government accepted, and they paid her a lump sum for the year she could have been receiving social security.

Soon after Mother started the ninth grade in school, her father, who was a coal miner, had a severe stroke and was bedfast for many years. Mother had to quit school at that time and go to work to help support her family. She went to work as a waitress at the Green Frog Restaurant in Wilburton, each day walking the three miles back and forth from her home.

Mother's relationship with her father seems to have been very good. She always spoke fondly of him. She never spoke unkindly about her mother, but when I asked Uncle Virgil about her parents, this was his reply, "Eram was a fine, soft-spoken man. I thought a lot of him, but I didn't think much of the old lady." From what I gathered, Maggie was a bossy, controlling woman. Mother grew up in deep poverty, but then so did all of her friends and neighbors. Her childhood friends remained her friends for life, and I knew several of them. If anybody gave her anything, she treasured it, and I still have some of those little gifts. She never forgot a kindness toward her.

When the dust bowl came in the thirties, Mother was one of the Okies who eventually made their way to California. John Steinbeck's *Grapes of Wrath* was Mother's story, too. When World War II changed the face of the American worker, Mother worked as a welder in the shipyards. I have an 11" x 14" commemorative photo that the Kaiser Company presented to her, in which she and the other employees are pictured with the ship they had built.

The following story illustrates both the mores of our country at the time as well as my mother's character. One Christmas season Mother was riding the bus from California back to Oklahoma. Somewhere in Kansas, the bus broke down, and all of the passengers were taken to a hotel to spend the night. There was a black lady on the bus, and she was not only denied a room but also was not allowed to go in for a meal. Mother went in and bought sandwiches for both of them. While all of the other passengers enjoyed their beds in a warm place, amid the lady's entreaties to the contrary, Mother sat with her outside on a park bench in front of that hotel for all of that cold, windy night.

It was August 1942, while they were both living in California, that Mother first married Dad. Before their first child was born in October 1943, Dad had taken her back to her parents' home in Oklahoma and had taken up with the woman who became his third wife. Mother was in her thirties, pregnant with a first child, out on an Indian reservation with no medical care at all. When it came time for the birth, Mother was having trouble, and, eventually, a doctor was brought in from town. He took the baby with forceps and injured its skull in the process. He was a perfectly formed baby boy, and for almost a week Mother cradled her little baby until he died. I was told by others, and Mother has even told me this herself, that she was so scarred by the circumstances that she never wanted to have another child. Granny, Dad's mother, lived about twenty miles away. Granny told me that when she got word of the death, she got a ride into town and caught a bus to Wilburton. She paid for the baby's casket and funeral and bought a little heart-shaped tombstone for him. Even this year a relative told me it was always felt that Dad had great responsibility for the baby's death.

Dad's third wife did not stay with him but for a few months until she was getting a divorce. Work was available in California, and Mother went back. It was very common for the people in Eastern Oklahoma to be going back and forth between California, and Dad was working there when he and Mother married again. When she was about seven months pregnant with me, he took her back to Oklahoma, telling her that he figured that she would die this time and that he didn't want the expense of shipping her body back. Today when I read about modern studies that have shown the importance of the baby in the womb having a peaceful environment and how emotions are transferred, I shudder to think what mine must have been. This time she was taken to a doctor who told her that she would require more expertise than he felt he had, and Dad did take her to McAlester where there was a hospital and a more experienced doctor. There I was born.

Yes, Mother let people run over her and abuse her, but thankfully, she did have a bottom line. When people say you should choose your battles, for sure, Mother let others win most of them. Many times during this writing I have been asked by relatives, "Have you written yet about how your mother saved the royalty?" This is what happened. In spite of Dad's brilliance in acquiring the mineral interest in the locations that he chose, he could do some of the dumbest things. Once, some lawyers at a bank in Holdenville, Oklahoma, became acquainted with Dad and talked to him about setting up a trust, making them the trustees. They appealed to his desire to divide his estate equally among his children, but it was an awful document that would have given them complete power to buy and sell and make any business decisions. If Mother and Dad had signed that document, it is most likely there soon would have been nothing left for Mother and Dad, let alone his children. I still have a copy of this trust, and it is clearly stated that we would have no legal recourse at all if we disagreed with anything the trustees did. Mother read it and understood quite well enough even the legal language to see the royalty could quickly be gone forever. She refused to sign the document. Dad, in his usual abusive way, ranted and raved at her. He had become convinced he should let these lawyers handle everything. He threatened Mother with divorce, and that is another time that one was filed. We were living in Alabama at the time, but he took Mother back to Oklahoma and left her. She still refused to sign.

Mother was greatly attached to my children, and we were living in trailers side by side, with Dad and Buddy both working at Brown's Ferry Nuclear Plant. Mother hated to be away from the children, but she stood her ground. When the months turned into summer, I let both of the children stay with her until school started in the fall. Dad, as usual when divorce was spoken of, did not support Mother financially. Mother was in her sixties. Granny was working at an Indian boarding school helping care for the children, and she got Mother a job there. In the meantime, Dad would make trips back to Oklahoma to harass Mother into signing these papers. This whole episode dragged on for over a year, and the divorce was granted. In the divorce decree, Mother was given half of everything they owned, including half the royalty. So, Dad's desire to have his children share equally in his estate was torn asunder. I would have inherited Mother's half! Dad may have won all the battles with Mother in the over thirty years that he had known her, but he lost the war. He and Mother reconciled, and the divorce was set aside. Sue, John, and all the relatives know that even though Dad is the one who acquired the royalty, we would have all had NOTHING if Mother, at great personal pain to her, hadn't had a bottom line and stood her ground.

Mother was a doormat, that's for sure. But she was also much more than that. She was a deeply kind person. Anytime, anywhere, when my mother's name is mentioned among those that knew her, the first words that come from their mouths are, "what a kind person she was!" If she had any strong opinions, she seldom voiced them and certainly did not try to impose them on others. Perhaps I can best capture the kind of person that she was by retelling the nicest compliment I ever heard given about my mother. Many years ago my sister and I were visiting with some people, and the conversation evolved to stepmothers and their negative image. When asked her experiences having a stepmother, Sue started to say some nice things about my mother, paused in trying to express her feelings, and then summed them up by saying, "You know how the Catholic Church makes saints out of people? Well, Edith is the kind of person that they would make a saint."

DAD

Later, I am going to let Dad tell his story in his own words.

GRANNY

In her older years Dad's mother, Myrtle Laura, my granny, kept a little airbrushed plaque on her living room wall that stated, "I can't say much for my first childhood, but I'm having a helluva time in my second!" In a nutshell, that describes Granny. And what a first childhood she had! She was the eldest child of seven, all born about two years apart. They lived in Newcastle, Wyoming, a young, raw, Western town on the frontier, the town of her birth. When she was about thirteen years old, on a bitterly cold winter night, she opened a bedroom door and found a blood-soaked father who had shot himself in the head. Her father was still breathing. She has often told me of running barefoot through the snow in her nightgown with the drops of her father's blood on her gown tainting the snow red. She was running to her grandparent's house for help. Even in her eighties, with tears streaming down her face, Granny has sat in her rocking chair and told me this story. The country doctor arrived. Granny remembered so vividly the doctor standing by the bed and turning to her mother and saying, "There's a ninety-nine percent chance he won't live." At this point, her father gathered enough strength to raise his head and say, "One percent, that's all I need!" This is not a flawed, frightened memory of a young girl's brain. The country doctor kept a journal that is now in a museum in Newcastle, and in his journal, he gave this account. Personally, I have not been to the museum and seen the journal, but there are family members who have.

Yes, I've heard this story often from Granny, because she always said, with words clothed in a touch of remorse and guilt, "Beverly, your dad is just like my dad. I marked him!" Her dad, Jack, did recover sufficiently enough to leave town, and his granddaughter, Hazel, whom I visited this summer in Idaho, told me, "He left and went back to his people." With desertion and pressure from her family and local townsmen who threatened to take her children from what they felt was harm's way, Eva Viola, Granny's mother, divorced Jack. In 1909 Eva took the children, following her parents, and moved to southern Missouri, where she met and married a widower with a young son. They had six more children. Granny went to work for a neighbor as a house girl, cooking, cleaning and caring for an elderly family member in that household. It was there that she met one of their sons, John Quincy Rider, who had recently returned from working on the Silverton Railroad that goes from Durango to Silverton, Colorado, and married him. She was fifteen, and he was twenty-seven. They married in August 1910, and Dad was born the following July. After her father had left the family, she only saw him one more time. As she often told it, she and Grandpa were continuing to live with his parents, and one day his mother came in and told her there was a man in the yard who wanted to see her. As she came toward the door, Granny recognized him and started screaming. Grandpa's parents couldn't understand why she was screaming that he was her father, and she didn't want to see him, and they insisted she come out on the porch. When her father saw that she truly wanted nothing to do with him, he walked away. Granny said that the scene with him walking down the road was the last time she ever saw her dad. She was pregnant with my dad at the time, and when she would tell me, "Your dad is like he is because I marked him," she was just repeating the folk wisdom of the day, an "old wife's saying," if you will. Today, I have no doubt that those who track the baby in the womb with advanced technology and monitor their responses to various stimuli, would agree with her feeling as expressed in her words, "I marked him!"

How can I put on paper words to capture the spirit of my grandmother? I can only make a feeble attempt. Perhaps I will start with a story that I believe illustrates her character. Grandpa died in 1960 when Granny was sixty-five years old. Granny wanted to move to town, so she sold their farm and got enough money to build a small two-bedroom house. The contractor she hired left town owing a portion of the lumber bill to the local building supply store. Though she had already paid the contractor, she was considered responsible for this lumber bill. There wasn't enough money after building her house to pay this debt. Granny learned to drive a car when she was in her sixties. She got a job taking care of children at an Indian boarding school thirty-five miles away and drove day in and day out and worked and paid that bill!

It was from Granny that I learned to respect the dead and to respect graves. When I was a little girl, Granny often took me up on the hillside across from their house and showed me the graves of a mother and father and their children. She would talk about the horrible flu that broke out in 1918, the pandemic that killed an estimated twenty to fifty million people worldwide, and tell me that these graves represented only a small number of the people who died. She said this particular family had come through in a wagon and were on their way to make a new start in a new place. One by one they came down with the flu, and she and Grandpa took care of them until they died. Granny and Grandpa knew none of their relatives to contact, so Grandpa made their coffins, Granny made their grave clothes, and they buried the family on their own land. In a local history book, *The Annals of Red Oak*, author Flossie Chaudoin, in writing about the flu, states, "Since the Riders did not take it, they spent their days and nights taking care of the sick. Myrtle would take care of them during the day, cooking food, giving medicine, washing clothes, or whatever else needed to be done and John would stay with them at night and care for them. Many people died from this flu, and those that didn't have it were afraid to go into a house where anyone did. But the Riders kept right on. Mr. Rider made caskets for the ones that passed away and Mrs. Rider made their clothes."

Granny always wanted to be on the television program, *"I've Got a Secret."* She was a midwife to sixty-five babies, and wrote to the TV show personnel her secret, "I'm sixty-five years old and have washed and dressed sixty-five new-born babies," but she was not chosen.

Granny was always out for a good time. She tried to make every job fun! She was an expert seamstress and sewed for the public. Someone would come with a catalog and show Granny a picture. She would grab some newspaper or a brown paper sack and with scissors in hand start cutting out the pattern. She made a lot of ladies' dresses for fifty cents, charging a quarter for a child's. I have a complete Miss Revlon doll wardrobe from the fifties that Granny made, including a fur coat, swimsuit, and more. The tiny little tucks and carefully made bows on the dresses seem almost impossible to make. I still have the Miss Revlon pattern that she used to make the clothes. She made everything on the pattern but one thing, and that was the bride's dress. Bridal dolls were popular at that time, but I never wanted one. I remember how badly Granny wanted to make that dress. She even begged me to let her make it, but I said, "No, I don't want it."

Granny absolutely loved to travel! People laugh to this day about her saying that one time someone came by and wanted to know if she wanted to go to Ft. Smith, Arkansas—a big shopping treat back in the fifties. She wasn't dressed properly but said it taught her a lesson. From that day, she got up, dressed and fixed herself nicely for the day—just in case somebody came by and offered her a trip somewhere. She was proud of the fact that for her 75th birthday year, she traveled by public bus coast to coast and stuck her feet in both the Atlantic and Pacific Oceans by visiting her daughter in California and me in Florida. Her daughter took her to Mexico, and other relatives drove her to Canada from their home in Washington State. Buddy often says that around our house, one better not mention the word, "Go," or I'll have my bags packed. I just say, "Well, I come by it honestly!"

As I put these words on paper, I realize that perhaps it is from Granny that I place such importance in contacting my family and friends on a regular basis. We cousins call each other at least monthly, visit when we can, make an effort to attend funerals, etc. In my acquaintance with others, this closeness even seems a bit out of the ordinary. I've had people say to me that maybe I do this because I'm an only child, but those who have siblings do the same thing. By the time Granny and Grandpa moved to Oklahoma in 1917, her family had left Missouri and moved back to Wyoming and South Dakota, with many of them later moving to Idaho. Granny was the one who was isolated, but most summers, even when I was a child, she made a trip back West for a lengthy visit with her family. When I was in Idaho this summer, I was told stories of how Granny would arrive by bus after an arduous trip from Oklahoma, and be ready, with a smile on her face and a spring in her step, to go immediately to the orchards to begin picking cherries and other fruit.

One day, years after Granny had died, Aunt Eunice and I were talking about her, and Aunt Eunice said, "Beverly, Mama was not always the jovial person that you knew. She was very different when we were growing up." I can only imagine that was very, very true.

A most delightful thing happened to me in Idaho this July when I visited with Granny's niece and nephew, Hazel and Floyd. Floyd's wife, Joan, gave me a gorgeous wool coat that my grandmother had made for her the summer of 1966, exactly fifty years ago. Granny would have been seventy-one when she made it. It is a deep rose color and looks of the Jackie Kennedy era, that's for sure. It fit me perfectly. I can tell you that as I tried it on, chills covered my whole body. My relatives there laughingly said that every time I wore it, Granny would be telling me which street to go down, where to turn, etc. What a treasure!

GRANDPA

My grandfather, John Quincy Rider, was born near Marquette, Kansas, in 1883. When I was a child, his sister, Aunt Frances, used to show me a picture of him with the family standing in front of the sod house that was their home. (Sod houses were typical prairie homes for settlers.) Their parents had left Missouri to try homesteading in Kansas. I've been told that the father went on ahead, the mother coming later. As a pioneer mother, she had to bury three little ones out of her six children.

At first, things seemed to be going well, and the father borrowed money against his farm to buy another farm. With the wind, the droughts, and the grasshopper plagues, he nearly lost the original farm. He did manage to save the farm but decided to sell out and return to Missouri. Grandpa never forgot the family shared fear of the threat of losing their farm. Because of these childhood experiences, my grandpa never wanted to owe money. He, even in Oklahoma, was not like the surrounding farmers who borrowed seed money for crops with the plan to pay it back when the harvest came in. Grandpa paid cash for his seeds. Grandpa always said, "If you can't pay for it, you can't afford it." I agree with Grandpa! In 1950 he and Granny built a very nice farmhouse for the era and area in which they lived, one of the nicest in the community, and I can assure you that not one cent was owed on it the day they moved in. Grandpa was very good in mathematics and used this ability to construct excellent buildings. He was known for his well-kept orchard and a fine herd of livestock. Grandpa never drove a car, and I can remember as a child riding in the wagon with him and Granny into town on Saturdays for Trades Day.

Grandpa was a very serious man. He seldom smiled. I never remember him telling a joke. He was a rock-solid pillar of the community, the kind of person who was wanted for a school board member. He was known for his sound thinking and often people would seek him out for counsel because of his good judgment. I never heard him say ill of others, nor did I ever meet anybody who had. His words were few. He was a deep thinker.

Grandpa had been reared a Methodist. When he and Granny moved to Oklahoma, I have been told he hitched up the wagon and team each Sunday and drove the family the four or so miles to the Methodist church in town. When a church was built in the local farming community where they lived, Grandpa contributed lumber cut from his farm. The church was incorporated as a Baptist church, and Grandpa and the family attended, but he didn't wish to join as a member because he did not hold to some of the Baptist beliefs. Granny has told me many times the story about how she talked to him and pointed out that she wanted to join the church there in the community. Still, Grandpa refused. One Sunday she told him she was joining whether he came in or not. Grandpa did not give an answer. She said she went forward to join, looked around, and he was standing behind her. So, Grandpa could hold his beliefs, but he could also compromise. Grandpa definitely was not a controlling husband. He was not the boss who would say, "Father knows best and that's the end of that." Granny and Grandpa were very different in temperament, but in my entire life, I never heard them have an argument.

When I was young, when I'd go to the grocery store wearing something I'd made, people would often say, "You're just like your granny!" I always wanted them to say, "You're just like your grandpa," but nobody ever did. As I have finished writing about my grandpa, it has just now struck me that I DO have certain characteristics that he had. When people often say certain things about the way that I am, they don't know that these traits are just like Grandpa's!

GRANDMA MENDENHALL

Perhaps I need a segment entitled, "Those I Barely Knew." Grandma Mendenhall, Granny's mother, would fit better there. When I was small, she lived in Idaho, but Dad definitely made it a priority to go see her on occasion. She was a woman of large frame, very strong, and a very hard worker. After her marriage ended with Jack, she worked as a cook in a sawmill camp to put food on the table for her children. In addition, she also took in laundry. She was known as an excellent cook. Many of her grandchildren remember the wonderful smells that came from her kitchen from freshly baked bread and the pies that would be lined up cooling on the window sill. A hard worker needs to eat heartily. On a visit there, I remember her saying one morning, "I always have my first pancake without syrup and then have syrup on the second one." This would be followed by oats and then meat and eggs and bread.

The thing I remember most about Grandma Mendenhall was the deep port wine stain that covered almost half her face. This was not some faint color, but a deep, thick, purple area that even had large bumps on it. How often I've thought of what that young girl had to overcome because of her looks. For the males who attached so much importance to a person's outward so-called beauty, they sure passed up a treasure in her!

When speaking of her to my grandson and others, I always say that Laura Ingalls Wilder's *Little House Books* are my great-grandmother's story, too. Eva Viola Gould was born in the big woods of Muskegon, Michigan, in 1880. She traveled with her pioneer family in a covered wagon to the West, staying a few years in Kearney, Nebraska, then later moving on to Newcastle, Wyoming Territory, when the town was only six months old. She attended school the first day school was held in Newcastle. As an adult, she moved to southern Missouri, just as Laura did. She, unlike Laura, though, returned to the West –Wyoming and South Dakota. In 1946 she moved to Nampa, Idaho. She loved to travel, so I got the wanderlust from my great-grandmother, too. She lacked a couple months being eighty-nine years old when she passed away during a visit to a son in Montana.

Those I Never Knew

One hundred and two passengers set sail on the Mayflower, and of that number, fifteen were my direct ancestors—all on Grandpa's side of the family. When I sign a guest book in museums in Massachusetts, giving a person the honor of listing someone from their Pilgrim heritage, I like to put Mary Chilton. Tradition says young Mary was the first female to set foot on the famous Plymouth Rock. History records that her father, James, the oldest passenger at sixty-four years, was the victim of a brutal assault in Leiden, Holland, over religious beliefs. He lay near death, and it is felt that this incident strengthened the resolve of the Pilgrims to leave Holland and set sail to the New World where they could practice their beliefs without fear. James signed the Mayflower Compact, but never got to set foot on the land, as he died on the boat while it was still anchored off Cape Cod. The mother, Susanna, died the first year also, leaving Mary an orphan at thirteen. Mary did not remain a Puritan. She married John Winslow, who became a merchant and shipbuilder, providing Mary and their ten children a life of luxury in Boston. A portrait of John's brother, Edward, seen so often in books, hangs in Pilgrim Hall Museum at Plymouth, Massachusetts. It was painted from life and is the only true picture of a Pilgrim known to exist.

One day about two years ago, I was searching on Amazon for a book, and a popup came on the screen advertising a book entitled *The Mayflower Pilgrims*. The title seemed unrelated to what I was searching for, but since I knew I had ancestors who had come on the Mayflower, I was intrigued. I ordered the book, and when it arrived, can you imagine my delight to find that the author was a retired college professor, Dr. David Beale, who lived not far from me in Greenville, South Carolina. WOW! Was I ever excited! What a wonderful book it is! It has been my source for some of these comments. Yes, I have had the privilege of meeting with Dr. Beale and his wife. As we sat and visited, I was mesmerized by his detailed accounts of my ancestors from their days in Holland to their lives in the founding days of our country. He spoke of them as if they were old friends. He has even led tours to the sites in Holland and England connected with the Pilgrims. He told me he has many files on these people, and that I was welcome to use them if I wanted to write a book about particular ancestors of mine! If I ever write another book, perhaps this will be the subject matter.

For my generation, my sister Sue has been the family member who has been interested in continuing the genealogical research of our family. Fortunately, there were others of our lineage who in an earlier time were interested in family history, so we have some neat stories to go along with dates and places of births, marriages, and deaths. Sue has done a thorough job building on those who wrote before and has worked on this project for many years. I have no desire to reinvent the wheel but will give a brief synopsis of some of those with whom we share a drop of blood. We are directly descended from Charlemagne, again on Grandpa Rider's side. On Granny's side, we had several kinfolk who were involved in the Salem Witch Trials. Some were the accused and others were the accusers. Some of them are characters in *The Crucibles*, Arthur Miller's famous play about this period. Grandpa was directly descended from Martin Luther's brother (Martin Luther's line itself ended many years ago). One Benjamin Rider, a direct ancestor of Grandpa's, spent the winter at Valley Forge and was a personal bodyguard to General Washington.

In 2002 Buddy and I took a motorhome trip on the Oregon Trail, spending six weeks experiencing sites connected to this famous route. While parked in Kearney, Nebraska, I saw a brochure for a pageant that was being held that weekend in Ash Hollow State Historical Park, a couple hundred miles west. It was a local fundraiser, complete with a chuck wagon meal and a play incorporating songs that were popular in that era. Readings would be taken from several diaries of those who were on the trail. This event had not been in any of the travel guides I had studied prior to our trip. I had planned a few more days around Kearney, but quickly changed my mind and said to Buddy, "Let's head out for Ash Hollow and go to this event." It was on Granny's side of the family that I had ancestors who felt the call of the Far West. I knew that a brother of my direct ancestor and most of his family had died on the trail. In fact, I had purposely taken a copy of a letter with me on this trip that had been written by a surviving daughter, Sarah Ann, to her eldest sister, Sophia, who with her husband had settled in Iowa. In keeping with my desire in this book to use letters when I can, letting people tell their own story, I asked permission of Irene Tunnell, a family historian in Granny's line who lives in Newcastle, Wyoming, to use this letter and story. It is taken from her book, *Freel O'Friel Cousins and Kin*. It is as follows:

Ash Hollow—June 23, 1852
140 Miles from Fort Laramie

Dear Uncle—

I find here a station for the purpose of conveying letters to the states and I hasten to inform you of our travels and the incidents pertaining thereto. First of all I would mention the sickness we have had and I am sorry to say the deaths. First of all Francis Freel died June 4, 1852, and Maria Freel followed on the 6th. Next was Polly Carsner, who died on the 8th, and Amos Freel next, he died on the 9th, and LaFayette Freel soon followed, he died on the 10th. Elizabeth Freel, wife of Amos, died the 11th, and her baby died the 17th. So you see we have had a sad affliction on our short journey. You see we have lost seven persons in a few short days, all died of cholera. Although I know this will be a sad epistle of news to send you, still I feel it a duty to let you know how matters are progressing, and thank God, we are all well, and likely to do well for we have had no sickness since the baby died. Please allow Sophia Parkinson to read this letter when you have perused it and let all of our good friends know of our affliction. We have had very good luck with our teams, and have prospered well except for the sickness and deaths.

And I would say a word about traveling and tell it to all of your friends that may think of coming on this vast prairie, it is this, do not as you value your lives, ever drink water out of the springs or sunken wells, on the side of the road or anywhere else. Always use the Platte River water and you will have no sickness. Even if you have to go a mile or two miles, do it rather than drink out of these cursed pit holes of death. For it is nothing else than that caused all our sickness.

We didn't know anything about it, and as the water is generally good and pleasant to drink, we thought we were using the best. So remember this and, as I said before, advise our friends to do the same. I have no time to write at present, for we are stopping our teams in the middle of the road, for the purpose of writing this, so good-bye for the present.

George Kisor and Ann Kisor (Sarah Ann Freel)

That letter was taken to Sophia Parkinson and put into her hands without comment. Perhaps she should have been warned in some way, but she was so delighted to see this first letter from the distant members of the family that she felt no premonition. She started to read with joy, caught her breath at the first mention of death, then quickly read on until she came to the name of her mother. The letter fluttered to the floor as Sophia fell in a faint. When she was revived, she tried not to believe. Only gradually did she come to accept the unhappy facts. The only one who had cholera and survived was little Martha Elon Freel, 9 years old. Many years later she told her granddaughter about it—she had refused all other food but insisted on eating the rose hips that she had gathered.

Buddy and I had gone to the event on Saturday night. The next morning I decided to get out the letter I had brought. Though I was aware of the contents, I had not bothered to pay attention to the date nor from where it was written. As I opened the letter, chills went up and down my body, for it had been written exactly 150 years ago that day and from the place where I was reading it!

Andrew Jackson Philips

Granny's father died in 1938 in Lodgegrass, Montana, on the Crow Indian Reservation. Some of my relatives have gone to Montana and visited Jack's grave. It was in 2013 that I thought it was way past time that I honor him, too. It was July, but some of the graves still had artificial flowers on them from Memorial Day. I had been told the general area in the cemetery where the grave was located. When I got to that section and got out of the car to start looking for names, no graves there were decorated, but I saw in the distance a grave with a single red rose that the wind had blown onto the tombstone. The thought immediately came to me, "I bet that is going to be the grave." I walked straight there, and indeed it was.

If it were not from writing this book and inquiring from elderly members of our family, I might have been guilty of perpetuating a myth about my great-grandfather. I knew he only had one leg and knew it had been cut off by a train. I had always assumed that he had been drunk (yes, I knew he was a drinker) and had maybe even passed out on a railroad track at a most inopportune time. No one of my generation knew any different, and we even have a photo of him with the one leg. This summer when I asked Hazel Hardy, Granny's niece who lives in Nampa, Idaho, about the accident, she told me that wasn't the case at all. He had gone to South Dakota to visit his mother. Not having much money, he was "riding the rails," as it was called, catching freight cars as the hobos did. In Edgemont, South Dakota, on his way back home, it was raining; and as he grabbed the handles on a freight train, he slipped on the wet rails and fell under the train, cutting his leg off. Hazel had personally talked to her grandmother Eva about him. Hazel also told me that her grandmother said, "He was not a bad man. He just loved the drink."

Of those I never knew, this great-grandfather is probably the one who has had the greatest influence on my life. When the psychiatrist said to me there was a ninety-nine percent chance I would have to be on medication the rest of my life, it was because of him that I would say, "One percent, that's all I need!" At so many times in my life, some of which I've related in these writings, I feel an overwhelming presence envelop me with words of wisdom for direction in my life, and yes, sometimes words of comfort. It is often not just a feeling of one presence, but of many—sometimes a room full. Sometimes an event happens or I receive special help in a situation, and I feel it's because of him. Stranger even yet, there are times when I'm outside, even in town, I have one of these events or feelings, and a direct inspiration comes to me. I look down, and there will be a crow feather at my feet. It is always newly dropped, sparkling clean, the shape in pristine condition. I've started collecting these and keep them in a box on my bedside table. It doesn't happen often, but it did happen after a very helpful event as recently as two months ago. It only happens at those most special and needful times.

Dad, In His Own Words

Dad often voiced that he would like to write a book—that he felt a lot of people would like to hear about his experiences, dreams, visions, etc. I have a lot of Dad's writing. Yes, I have letters that he wrote about dreams where he saw me and others in hell, screaming because of the fire. I could use some of them to help Dad tell his story, but I have decided not to do so. To begin with, I don't see how they could help others or even help me. I feel no need to embarrass Dad by exposing some of these writings. I do have some, however, that would allow Dad to express some of his experiences. One is a document that he filed in the District Court in Latimer County, Oklahoma, in December 1985, when he was suing an oil company over a business problem. It was I who typed this document. As Dad talked, I tried to stay true to what he was saying to me. The contents I have heard many times— the stories of his grandfather's death, the experience of the feeling he had to get from under the car that fell, how he acquired the truck and welding machine after World War II, the fire at his garage, and how he acquired the first piece of mineral interest. Dad was always consistent in these stories. He never changed anything in the retelling.

Dad's tells some of the stories of his life in the first half of the document, so that is the only part I am including. The remainder, though in great detail and in his own words, is about his perceived wrong with the oil company. The property was sold through the Indian Department in Muskogee, Oklahoma, with their approval, as all Indian land had to be sold.

This is Dad's story in his own words:

STATE OF OKLAHOMA,
COUNTY OF LATIMER.

FRANK E. RIDER
Plaintiff,

-vs-

ARKANSAS-LOUISANA GAS CO., et al.,
and
AMOCO PRODUCTION COMPANY, et al.,
Defendants.

PETITION FOR TRIAL

Comes now the plaintiff, representing himself in this case, and making known to the Court that by reasons thereof set forth in this document, plaintiff asks that this case be set for trial by jury at the earliest convenience of the Court.

DATED this 18th day of December 1985.

FRANK E. RIDER
Plaintiff

This is Frank Rider. I'm telling you some of the experiences I have had with the Almighty Creator and how he has led me and directed me and talked to me. You know, this may seem foolish to a lot of people, but it is the truth, so help me God and keep me steadfast. I was a young boy, and my grandfather was a very fine devoted Christian, and he talked to me and showed me and tried to teach me about what a beautiful place heaven was and how he longed to go home. That was his home—homesick for heaven. Then, next on down through the years when I was just a small lad, maybe four or five or six years old (I think I was six), he passed away. On his deathbed, they had gotten the doctors and told them they had done all for him that they could do. The doctor told the folks to get him some whiskey, and my aunt talking to one another and discussing this told him that Dad wouldn't appreciate it. He wouldn't have it that way. They finally decided if that was the doctors' orders, that is what they'd have him do. So, they got him some whiskey and fixed a toddy just like they were told. We were all standing around watching him. When he took his glass (he had been taking his medicine perfectly), my aunt gave him this and said, "Here Dad, here is your medicine." He took this cup up and got it within about six inches of his nose, and he smelled it was whiskey. He set it down just as calmly, and said, "Frances, what's going on here?" She told him, and started crying, and said, "Dad, that's the doctor's orders." He told her, "Well, don't call the doctor anymore. I'm going to meet my Saviour and I'm ready to meet him, and I'm not going to meet him with a boozy breath." Then a couple days later he called them all to his bed. He knew he was passing on and going on to heaven, and he had a long talk with each one of them. He bid them all goodbye and talked to them, and I was the last one that talked to him. He said, "Frank, would you promise me one thing?" I said, "What's that, Grandpa?" He said, "Grandpa's going to die. He's going to heaven." He said, "I am not going to be here to talk to you anymore. I'm going on home. I'm on the road home. It feels like I'm in the buggy just floating through the clouds." He said, "Won't you make me one promise before I get home?" I said, "Yes, Grandpa, I'll do anything you want me to do." And he said, "Don't ever get drunk and meet me in heaven." He went ahead describing and said, "You know, I just feel like I'm in the clouds floating." He said to me, "Do you see that city over there?" and he kind of pointed to the wall. That was a long time before there was any television or anything. He said, "Do you see that city here, the arch over the gate, the buildings shining with gold?" I said, "No, Grandpa, I don't see anything." He said, "You've got to look for it to see it." He said, "Look for it." Then I was concentrating and looking, and it just seemed like I could see him in an old buggy there and as he talked with me and was telling me about his going home and wanted me to meet him in heaven. He kept talking along that line. "I saw this vision that he was talking about where the streets were paved with gold and the big arch over the road where the street was going into the city. It looked like I saw him just go through the gate. As he went through, he said, "It's finished. I'm home." Big tears came trembling down his cheeks, as he said, "It's finished. I'm home. Goodbye." You know, then in a few minutes, my aunt went over to the bed and touched his arm and screamed and threw up her arms and said, "It's finished. He's dead. He's gone." They all started mourning and weeping. I could feel that he didn't want us to mourn, that he wanted us to meet him in that beautiful city some day, and that's my desire to meet him over in that beautiful city where the streets are paved with gold, and where the buildings are made out of diamonds and precious stones.

Here is another vision I've had. Tom Lucas was preaching at Lodi schoolhouse. They held church at the school, and he was holding a revival meeting. He preached a sermon on hell, and that was so real that I could see a vision of a lake of fire, and he preached about the rich man and Lazarus. He had a good sermon on hell. I saw that vision. There was a voice spoke to me and told me that if I didn't come forward that night that was going to be my last opportunity. He also preached in the sermon about the spirit of God wouldn't always strive with man, and it had been striving with me for some time to repent and start a new life and make a public profession.

About the next thing that was revealed to me was a few years later. I was under a T-model Ford car, and I had the front axle and front springs out from under it and was tightening the rod bearings on it, and I had a hoist holding this car up and a rope tied on to the side holding the car up. I was sitting straight up under the car working on it. There was a voice told me to get out from under there, and I started to get out and look around to see what was happening. I was there by myself. Then I thought, "What's wrong with me?" I had a kind of funny feeling. I just wondered if I was going crazy or something. Then I set there and started to go back working on the rod bearings, tightening the nuts or something. Then it spoke to me again and said, "Get out from under there." I kind of hesitated there for a few minutes. I just said, "What's wrong with me?" I started back to working on it again and it seemed like something grabbed me by the shirt collar and throwed me out or pushed me out, just shoved me out from under it and said, "I said, get out!" I didn't anymore than get straightened up till that car fell. That board came off of it that the rope was tied to with that rope block and let that car fall right down there. If I'd been sitting under there, I'd have been mashed. It would have killed me instantly.

There are several things that have happened in my lifetime. It's a mystery. In other words, everything about God is a mystery. None of it is understandable. We can't understand God's plan and God's way of doing things. It's all a mystery. I thank him for being a mysterious God. You know, God is a merciful God, and God is a loving God, even though he'd warned me and talked to me these times and I'd seen these visions, I backslid and went back to living like the devil wanted me to. I had divorced a family and ran off and married again. This woman that I married, she took me for everything that I had. I had paid off her home, fixed it up and then after that I couldn't figure out why God was dealing with me like I was, and I tried to repent along about that time. I never could get any satisfaction or anything. I started going to church. Then she quit me and sued me for a divorce after she got everything she could out of me. I was so depressed, and I was trying to live right. I went up to the mountains and prayed, got on top of Red Oak mountain up there, on the tip-top. I lay down and prayed on my stomach. I couldn't believe there was a God. It came to that stage that I just very near was there, and I told God that he was going to have to come to me and talk to me, that I had lived on faith as long as I could. I was going to have to see. As I was living there, I looked up and there was an image sanding out in front of me, and I talked to this image, and I started questioning him. I said, "God, why have you done me this way?" And He said, "Why accuse me? I haven't wronged you. It was this woman that mistreated you and abused you and wronged you. I haven't wronged you. Why accuse me?" Well, that was just as simple and clear as could be. I even told Him that if He didn't come and appear that I was going to perish—that I couldn't live on faith anymore, that I had to have some more evidence. I said, "You said in Your Word that it wasn't Your will that any perish, and if I couldn't talk to You, I was going to perish." Then after this happened, I came to my senses and woke up. I was just kind of in a dream-like state. It was the winter time when this all happened. The trees weren't bloomed out or had any leaves on them or anything, but when I came to my senses and all, I looked around, and the trees had green leaves and were beautiful. Well, you know, there's a lot of things that are a mystery, that I don't understand, but I thank God that he is merciful, and that he forgave me and all.

Then after I got all over this again, I went back and remarried and started to try to live right and do right. I was broke. About that time the war was over and everybody had lost their job or just about, that were on construction work. I had lost mine, and we got down to where we had $1.50 one Sunday, and we needed some milk. We went to church, and I told Edith, "Well, you give fifty cents, and I'll give fifty cents." She said, "Well, we can't do that. We only have a dollar and a half, and we need some milk." I said, "Well, we'll give fifty cents a piece and we'll get that milk," and I said, "If we starve to death and all, and heaven is like the Good Book says it is, we'd be better off in heaven than we would on this earth." She agreed to it, so we gave this dollar and spent this fifty cents, and we were broke the next morning. I went down to the Union Hall to see about a job. The line was filled up, there was a long line, and I was nearly to the end of the line. The business agent saw me down at the far end, and he called me and wanted me to come in to his office, and he sent me out on a job and said, "This will just be for one day, but you won't lose your place if you'll go out and take it." You had to sign up and you were on a list. You had a number that you went to work on. I went out there and took that job for that day. He paid me that evening and wanted me to work a half hour overtime. I worked this half hour overtime. He paid me for that and then wanted me to work another half hour overtime, so I worked that other half hour, and he told me to come back the next morning, and he would have my check ready and pay me two hours show-up time for coming after it. Well, I went after my check the next morning, and he said, "Mr. Rider, I want you to work for me today." So, I worked that day. That evening he had his check ready again. He wanted me to work that evening again, so I worked that evening, and he wanted me to come back after my check the next morning—this overtime check. So, I came back the next morning, and he wanted me to work the next day. He came around, and he kind of had tears in his eyes and tells me, "Something tells me that you're a good man and that you will make me a good hand, and you're on steady now." The next job after that, he made me superintendent on the job. When I quit and went back to pipelining, he told me that if I ever wanted a job, to just look him up, and he would make a place for me. That first morning, that Monday morning after we'd given the last dollar we had, we got a letter out of the mail, or a couple. She'd got two or three unemployment checks. I got a couple. That proves to me that God can do miracles.

Then, I had ordered a welding machine; I had gotten a priority to get a welding machine. At that time during the war, you had to have a priority to buy anything like that, so I got this priority to buy this welding machine. They had ordered for me, and it had come in, but I didn't have but around $260, if I'm not mistaken. Then, I started down to the place where I bought this welding machine. I was going down to tell them I couldn't get it. I thought I could borrow the money at the bank at home. They wrote me a nice letter and told me that it was a violation of the law for them to loan money out of the state. I was in

California. That kind of hurt me, and I just thought he was putting me off or something. I started on down to the place to tell them I couldn't get it, that they could sell it to somebody else, that I had a priority for it, but I didn't have the money to buy it. I started by the Bank of America there, and something told me to go in there and get the money, and I kind of stopped a little bit, and said, "Oh, I couldn't get a dime in there." I started on, and something just kind of stopped me and told me to, "Go in there and do what I tell you to, and I'll give you the money." I could hardly believe it. I started to go again, and it seemed like someone just shoved me in the door and told me to, "Do what I tell you to, and you'll get the money." I went in the bank. The teller looked at me and said, "Could I do anything for you?" I said, "Well, I guess. I'd like to see the president of the bank." She said, "Just who are you?" I said, "Frank Rider." She said, "Do you have an appointment with him?" I told her, "No." She said, "I'm afraid it's going to be impossible for you to see the president of the bank." Then she said, "Just a minute, and I'll call his office and see if he will see you." She called, and he said that he had a client in there and it would be a few minutes, to send me on up and have him wait in the waiting room. So when he got through with the client, he came to the door and greeted me and shook hands, and said, "What could I do for you?" I told him, "Well, probably there's not one thing that you'd do for me, but there's a lot you could do for me." He said, "Well, what's your trouble?" I said, "Well, I've been like the prodigal son. I wasn't as fortunate as he was, though. I had wasted all my money in riotous living. I didn't have any money and didn't have any friends, or seem to. I'd bought a welding machine and truck and had a priority to get them, and I didn't have the money to pay for them. Something just told me to come in here." Big tears were running down his cheeks, and he said, "Mr. Rider, You're a Christian." I said, "I haven't told you I'm a Christian." He said, "I know you are. Something is telling me on the inside that you are and to let you have the money." He wanted to know how much I needed. I told him that I didn't have any idea how much it was. I just ordered it. He wanted to know where I was getting it. He called up and told them I'd be up after it, and to let me sign a note up there, and he would take care of it. Therefore, I got the money, and I got this pickup in just about a week's time. Now, that proves to me that the Lord is all-powerful and can do all things. So, I took that welding machine and truck and got a job on the pipeline, and I made some good money, and it wasn't long until I was back on my feet again.

Then I came home for a while, and I put in a welding shop there in Red Oak. I'd bought a new paint gun and a trailer and could travel around spray painting. I painted a few barns and houses and ran a garage and welding shop and was doing pretty well. I had traded for a motion picture outfit, and I bought a PA system for religious work. I got about a pickup load of film with it. The guy that had this motion picture outfit showed it around at these army camps, putting up little shows. I got all of this nasty, filthy film, and I wanted to get a bunch of religious film and show it around churches, etc. and thought I could help the Lord that way. He laid it on my heart and wanted me to put out this screen out back of the shop and advertise that PA system all over town that there was a free show back of this shop where I was. I rebelled and wouldn't do it. I had about 500 gallons of paint, I believe, in the shop, had a couple barrels of turpentine and linseed oil, and paint thinner, about three barrels in all. I believe I had two or three drums of oxygen there by it. I had painted a car. I was figuring on selling this motion picture outfit. There was supposed to be a guy to look at it that day. I had locked up the shop, and I had cleaned a carburetor.

There was a can of gasoline where I'd cleaned it, and the papers I had torn off of this car. There was a construction outfit there that wanted a piece of stuff welded. I told him I wouldn't weld it for him. I had this motion picture outfit all set up, and I was going to sell it to a guy that day, or the next day. I wouldn't do it, and he said they just had to have it and kept on. Finally, I started to weld it for him. I didn't even open up the building, just went in the front door and left the doors closed. I welded this piece for him or was going to. It was a big thick piece, and it took a lot to burn it and V it out, cut it out to make a bevel so you could make a good weld. I started to kick the paper out the door, and I kicked this can of gasoline over into that paper and into that film, and I lost everything I had. The building burned up and two or three buildings there right adjoining me. That's what a person gets for rebelling against God. He's going to punish his children if they don't do what he tells them to. That's the punishment I got for doing that. Then I was down broke again.

I went back to work and got started again and began to get on my feet. I went down to Norris to church. I had about $200 or $300. That was all I had, and I didn't have a job either at that time. Something came over me, and I was supposed to give them $100 to help with this revival meeting down at this little country church. Well, I gave this $100, and as I was coming home that night, driving back towards Red Oak, it looked like a big fire right where this Rider gas well is. It looked like such a big fire I thought the world was coming to an end, it was such a bright light. A lot of times they flare these wells when they test them; they light up the whole country when they do that. They do that mostly in just a new field. Then going on home, kind of a voice spoke to me and said, "Frank, get this property here. I'm going to make it available for you." It said, "It's going to be worth something one of these days." Well, it wasn't but just a short time until this property was for sale, and it was through the Indian Department in Muskogee. This particular land was owned by an Indian lady. The day of the sale I put a sealed bid in at Muskogee, and I got the land. That is how I got ahold of this track of land, and I felt like the Good Lord wanted me to have it, so I felt good over it, and I still feel good over it.

It was just a short time after that that they began to lease land for drilling oil and gas wells, and there were two or three that tried to lease this from me. There was one person that offered more than any of the rest would give. They were trying to lease this for $1 an acre and $2 an acre, then $5 an acre. They went ahead and were leasing property like this.

At this point in the document, after giving this background, Dad begins to talk about the reasons he has brought the lawsuit, so I will end the narrative here.

Dear Mother

November 20, 2016

Dear Mother,

As I near the close of the book I have written about my life, I wanted to write a letter to you. I had a shell about me for a large portion of my life. There was a lot that I didn't talk about—to you or anyone else. As I reflect on things where I should have said, "I'm sorry," two things stand out in my mind. One occurred when I was eight years old, and we were living in Kansas. We had moved nearly every month from the beginning of the school year until we went back to Red Oak. You had had all of your teeth pulled due to having gum disease and was awaiting dentures. I was embarrassed by this and didn't want you to check me into the new school on the first day. I told you I wanted Owana (Dad's boss's wife) to check me in. You sensed why, and I know you were hurt. Though we didn't ask Owana to check me in, I never did tell you that I was sorry I had done that. You even brought this incident up once in a while later in life, and I still never said, "I'm sorry." This comes to my mind quite often. You did not have the advantages I have had. I have my teeth cleaned regularly and even had some gum work done to clear up the same problem you had. At seventy, I have never had a single cavity and have healthy gums as a result of having advantages you never had. I am really sorry that I hurt your feelings that day so very long ago. I wasn't a child who talked back to you nor to Dad, so, thankfully, I don't have many regrets about unkind things spoken.

The second thing that I feel I owe you an apology for occurred when you were getting dementia. You always wanted to help, but you had reached the stage that there wasn't a lot you could truly help with in the kitchen. I remember one day I was having some company for supper, and you wanted to do something. As I tried to think of something you could truly do to help, I handed you a sack of potatoes and asked you to peel some potatoes. I don't remember whether it was a five-pound sack or a ten-pound sack. What I do remember with deep regret is that I got busy doing other things and looked around, and you had peeled the whole sack of potatoes! Without thinking first, I scolded you for peeling all of them by saying rather sharply, "Mother, I didn't want the whole sack peeled." I can still see the crestfallen look on your face, and when I do, it makes me very sad. I don't remember what I then said to you, but it wasn't enough to erase the sorrow I have about the incident. You were always so quick with work. You could have a whole sack of potatoes peeled in the same time it would take me to peel only a few.

Linda told me that when I had the breakdown in 1986 that you would sit up at the trailer and cry with deep remorse, saying that you should have gotten me away from Dad. You took the burden on yourself that my breakdown was completely your fault. I hope that now you understand that it wasn't. It is true that when I was a little child, you would often say you were going to take me and go back to California and get a job in a restaurant, and we would get away from Dad. Yes, sometimes I wished that you would and wondered why you would never follow through. It was while I was in therapy that I realized I shouldn't blame you, even secretly. I did reach a breakthrough and truly forgave you. I realize that you, as most parents, were doing the best you could as you went along. You knew that you could not provide much for me financially. I'm sure that was very much on your mind.

Granny used to beg you to put a little something aside every week to have a little nest egg in case Dad threw one of his fits. When you came back from Oklahoma to Alabama, you did just that, but you used a thousand dollars to buy us that little pop-up tent camper. The kids and I had such fun with it. We went on many trips. I don't think I ever thanked you properly. I want to tell you that Buddy and I looked at a small Lazy Daze motorhome the same size as our first one. The lady who had it for sale had had it custom made and had had a lot of fun in it. She was asking $20,000. It wasn't exactly like the plan I thought I wanted, plus it really needed a lot of cleaning, and I decided to give it a pass. A few months later, on your birthday, Mother, I was sitting at the computer thinking about that little pop-up tent camper that you bought for the kids and me when the telephone rang. It was the lady who had the little motorhome for sale. She asked if I would be interested in buying it for $10,000. Wow! I could do quite a bit of cleaning for $10,000! Mother, I said this was your birthday, but I had this wonderful feeling that it was a gift from you to us! When I went to insure it, the agent said the loan value (not the wholesale price, but the loan value) was $23,000! It's even a teal and cream color, my very favorite of all the Lazy Daze colors!

I could go on talking about other times when your presence has been so very real, but I'm most grateful for the comforting dream the night that Tim had earlier in the day got the troubling diagnosis about his severe eye problem. Eram was born that morning, and it seemed as though you were back and forth between here where Tim and I were and Ecuador where the birth took place. I can't even begin to describe how real your presence seemed as that dream unfolded. It seemed that being between both places almost instantly was something you could do so effortlessly. I was in such a state of shock about Tim's eye diagnosis and yet relieved that Eram was born safely. You were overjoyed at his birth, and it did seem as if you were watching over us all. I received the courage to face the days ahead.

Mother, there were so many times when I was small that you would say, "I know I am very strong. I know I am very strong to be able to withstand all I have gone through." I will confess. I didn't feel you were strong. I viewed you as very weak. Now that I have written this book, I understand. Yes, I agree that you were very strong to have not cracked under everything that happened to you. You were strong, Mother, but you lacked the courage to change your situation. I can identify with that. When I wanted so badly to seek professional help to become a more whole person, Buddy said, "No, solve your own problems. You are the strongest person I ever knew." I may have appeared to be strong, Mother, but I wasn't as strong as you were. For sure, Mother, to speak out for myself, as badly as I wanted to change, I, too, did not have the courage.

Love from your daughter,

Beverly

Dear Dad

January 31, 2017

Dear Daddy,

When I tell people that I'm closing out my book by writing a letter to you, a lot of them chuckle and wonder out loud if I'm really going to let you have it with both barrels. I quickly assure them that is not the case at all. I simply want to write a second letter, a sequel to the one I wrote to you for your 85th birthday. This is not to accuse you of anything or drag up things that you would refuse to acknowledge, anyway. This is a letter to tell you some of the things I appreciate about you that I didn't put in the other one. Yes, there will be some things in it about you that are very troubling to me. Perhaps getting them on paper will be beneficial to me as have been so many of the things I've previously written.

Daddy, when I mailed the previous letter, I thought you would reply by calling me. If you couldn't use the telephone well, there were plenty of people who would have been glad to help. I waited and waited for your call, but it never came. When Sue went up to Idaho for your birthday, she told me that when she arrived you were sitting on the front porch. She commented on what a pretty shirt you were wearing, and you said, "Beverly got it for me." She said you never wanted to pull it off. When someone took it to launder it, you threw a big fit. It seemed to have been missing a day or so, and you never let anyone have any peace until it was found. She told me you said I had written you a letter, but that you did not show it to her.

When I visited you later, after you were in California with Sue for a few months and then in a nursing home there, you never one time asked how Mother was. I even wondered if maybe your mind was the reason you never asked about her until once a nurse was coming down the hall, and you said to me, "That nurse looks like your mother did when she was young." Daddy, year after year as I took care of Mother, never one time did you inquire as to how she was. That seems almost unconscionable to me.

Yes, when I was even very young, you did everything that you seemed to want to do. You bought yourself an airplane. You bought the finest photography equipment—items that would have been the envy of professionals. You built a darkroom on a two-wheeled luggage trailer, furnished it with the latest developers and enlargers, and had Mother tow it around behind our car as we moved from place to place. You bought professional music recording devices and made phonograph records and later eight-track tapes for people. Yet we had a little trailer with no bathroom, and in the winter you didn't want to hook up water in some of the places we lived because it was too hard to keep it from freezing. I can remember Mother carrying buckets of water and washing our clothes on a rub board.

When Sue has said that when you died maybe we should donate your brain to science, it was not a joke. She was serious. What a paradox you have been. When I was about nine or ten, and we were living somewhere in New Mexico or Arizona, you came in from work one night and told us about the Indians out near the job site dancing for rain. Every night for about a week you came in and talked about this. I can still see your expression as you came in the door one night so happy because it had started raining. As you started talking about it, it was as though something welled up inside you, and you got that contorted look on your face as if you were trying to hold back tears (Sue knows that look well, too). You were, however, unable to hold back your relief and joy that it was raining. Most people would have called that pagan. Most of the time you would have, too, and would have gone on and on about religion, and that there was only one straight and narrow path. But you didn't that time, Daddy.

You used to have the same expression come upon you when you talked about your grandfather, Granny's dad. You were so proud of the fact that he was a good baseball player and have often talked about how he played with his peg leg and was so good even playing with only one real leg. When you talked of him, it was as though he was an important part of you. Daddy, it was only when I was writing about him in this book that I realized you never got to see that grandfather in your entire life.

Once when we were living in Tennessee, you hired Tim and Linda to dig potatoes. Tim was a teenager by then, with Linda not far behind. They dug potatoes for most of the day. When they were finished, you pulled out two dollars. They were not impolite—just disappointed. They did not take the money. Later that day Tim was up at the trailer with you and Mother, and he came home telling me some of the interesting things you had talked about and wondered if I'd ever heard these stories. I had not. You told about remembering the move from Missouri to Oklahoma in 1917. You traveled by rail and your dad had rented a whole train car, which you said was called an immigrant car. You and Granny and Grandpa and Alice and baby Eunice rode in the car with the animals. Grandpa had brought some sheep to try sheep farming, which ended up not being suited to the climate in Oklahoma. He also brought a cow and chickens. Tim said it was all so interesting, and he listened attentively. When you finished, you pulled out a $20 bill and tried to pay him for listening to you. He did not take it, of course, but Tim commented to me about how sad that was. He added that he wished you would talk about more of those kinds of things instead of always wanting to talk about religion. Daddy, we all got SO sick of you always talking about religion, religion, religion, and trying to cram it down everybody's throat!

Daddy, one of the things I appreciate about you is that whenever you divided property among Sue, John and me, each time you tried to make it as fair a division as possible. Oh yes, sometimes it came with strings attached, and you made threats about giving one's part to a TV evangelist or whatever, but in the end, each time we all got something as close as possible to equal value.

One of the things I've thought about as I've written this book is the confidence you had in me when I was just a young teenager. When I learned to type in the tenth grade, you took me around with our little Royal portable typewriter in tow and let me type the deeds to mineral interests and leases you would buy. You told me to be very careful—that the legal land descriptions with all the SW ¼'s and NW ½'s, etc. had better be exactly right, or the whole thing would be considered void. Daddy, I don't remember you checking a single one. You told me how it needed to be done properly and never considered that I would do otherwise. I wouldn't trust my own children like this even now! I would be checking and double checking. I can tell you this, though. When the properties did become very valuable, I used to get very nervous knowing that lawyers for the oil companies were combing through these documents with a fine tooth comb. I used to worry a bit that if something was found to be wrong, Sue and John would blame me.

While I'm on the subject of mineral interest, I want to tell you that some of my most embarrassing moments involving you occurred when I typed lawsuits for you, and we went to file them. I can remember standing on the second floor of the courthouse and wishing the floor would open up, and I could sink to the basement and below. I had the same feeling when we were in church during testimony portions of the service. I never liked these testimony meetings and felt people were just bragging about how special they were—how much God loved them above others. You used to sit there for a long time, and I would be hoping that you weren't going to get up. When it looked like everybody had had their say, you usually would rise. You never gave the standard testimony, though. You would start out by stating that the Lord had sent you to warn the people about the oil companies and how they were going to cheat people out of their land and mineral interest. You would go on and on and on with the warnings and then ask for people to meet you after church for more details. Those were the times when, again, I wished the floor would open up, and I could just sink down into the earth.

Daddy, there have been many discussions about you and whether you even had the capacity to love. Sometimes members of your family have had to search the depths of their minds to find answers. I have a box of letters from Tim and Linda, along with replies, to you and Mother and to Buddy and me at various periods beginning in 1976, when Buddy first went to Saudi. These were written from assorted places depending on what our situation was at the moment. I want to quote a portion of one Linda wrote to her dad in 1976, just before she turned nine (spelling and punctuation are hers):

Dear Arab,

How are you?

We are in Calif. now. I left my Pooh bear at Sue's. Went about 100 miles to get it. I cryed terrible you can ask Mom aboat it. . . .

All that I tell you is secret except what you wante to tell.

Love, Linda Biggs

Perhaps to a child, it just seemed like a hundred miles, but Sue could hardly believe you would drive any child back anywhere because he or she was crying for a stuffed bear. She noted that you certainly wouldn't have done that for her or John or me. When I asked Linda today for permission to use part of this letter, it brought this event to her mind—something that had been buried in the recesses of her memory. Dad, sometimes we have to grasp at straws to find what I would like to believe is the real you.

It was on the way home from this same trip that after a long weary day, I asked you to take the toll road through the Kentucky mountains, but you wouldn't because you didn't want to pay the toll. When I offered (not in a smart manner) to pay the toll, you turned around to the back seat and slapped me in the face. I said nothing. Daddy, I have taken so many degrading incidents from you and others in my life that respect for me has suffered. I certainly have not been a good example for my children.

When we were living in Tennessee, I remember the day you came to my house and started telling me about coming from a place where Buddy was drunk and people were making fun of him. You asked me to divorce him. This coming from YOU, Daddy, the daddy that told me I could date no others? I will tell you that long before this incident I realized I made my own choices about my marriage. But the very nerve, Daddy!

It seems to me that even as a child I believed the Indian teaching that words are powerful. Once spoken, they go out into the world, and you can never take them back. As I stated in the letter to Mother, I don't consciously remember many words that I regret speaking. There was one dramatic incident that I do want to talk to you about, though. In pondering over this incident that I created, I have sometimes wondered if I should have spoken to you as I did. I always conclude that, yes, every word needed to be spoken as carefully as it was, but maybe the whole thing should have been done in complete privacy instead of in front of Mother and Tim and Linda. Maybe the outcome would have been different. I am referring to the time that I had come home from Abu Dhabi to find that Mother was supposed to go to the hospital for surgery, and you were refusing to take her. I was livid, but I controlled my emotions as I calmly asked you to sit down. I started in on you. Part of my reasoning, at least I thought, was to show my support to Mother, but maybe it was a whole lot more complicated than that. I started talking to you and naming some of the atrocious things you had done in your life—many of which happened before I was even born. After all, living in Red Oak, population 500, where everybody knew more about a person than you ever wanted them to know, I was told plenty about you. Soon after I started talking, you closed your eyes and became motionless. I would name something, then stop periodically and ask you to blink your eyes if you loved me. You kept them tightly closed. I would talk about other horrible things and ask you to nod your head if you loved me. You would not move. This went on and on with me talking about something and then asking you to move your finger or make some other gesture if you loved me. You remained motionless. I guess this didn't last more than 30 minutes or so, but it seemed like an eternity, probably for you as well as for me. By the time I finished, I wondered if you even heard me, but you silently got up and walked out. Everyone was silent. Linda was twelve. Tim was fifteen. As I said earlier, I could never bring myself to regret a single word, but I did wonder if I should have used an audience. I'm still not sure, Dad. Soon after beginning this book, Sue and I had a phone discussion about the money you had left all of us and the effect it had on our relationship toward you. I was relaying part of this conversation to Linda, and she said, "Mother, all YOU ever wanted from Grandpa was for him to say, 'I love you.'"

Love from your daughter,

Beverly

Some Closing Thoughts

It was my Christmas letters that first prompted friends to encourage me to write a book. It seemed fitting to close this book with an excerpt from my Christmas letter for this past year. I wrote it on Christmas Day, 2016:

> My big project of writing my autobiography, which I have been working on for 2 ½ years, is nearing completion. As I have gone along, it has been reviewed by my college psychology professor and is now also being reviewed by an English professor, under whom I had a speech class in college. It has always been my intention to have it printed, but am now told that should be my last choice—that it is good enough for publication. We shall see. Regardless of what happens, it has been a tremendous healing experience for me—more than I ever dreamed possible. In fact, I am happy to report that even though I've had some very stressful situations this past year, I didn't even have the symptoms, nor even feel like they were coming on, for my bipolar disorder. Perhaps it's out of line to use the word miracle, but it sure seems like that for me. When I began this project I had no idea it would do so much.

A well-loved verse penned by Robert Browning says,

"Grow old along with me!

The best is yet to be,

The last of life,

for which the first was made."

We often hear the first two lines quoted, and I believe them for sure, but the lines that speak most deeply to my soul are,

"The last of life, for which the first was made."

We are all the sum total of our life's experiences. With these experiences we receive gifts. What gifts have I been given that I may use to help others? Chief among them, may I have the gift of discernment to use these gifts wisely in whatever the future holds—the last of life, for which the first was made.

Appendix

DIFFERENT PLACES I HAVE LIVED

These are the places I have lived and the approximate amounts of time spent in each. This list is from the one prepared from Mother's memory an afternoon we spent together when I asked her for the information. I have moved 134 times to 102 different towns. Prior to marriage, I moved 109 times, living in 84 different towns in 25 states. After marriage, I moved 25 times to 19 different towns in 6 additional states and 2 foreign countries.

1. Born in McAlester, Oklahoma - May 28, 1946
2. Red Oak, Oklahoma – lived 5 months
3. Tuscola, Illinois – 2 months
4. Wilburton, Oklahoma – 2 months
5. Casa Grande, Arizona – 2 weeks
6. Rodeo, California – 3 months – had 1st Birthday
7. Vallejo, California – 2 weeks
8. Oakland, California – 2 months
9. Antioch, California – 2 weeks
10. Fontana, California - 2 weeks
11. Bakersfield, California – 2 weeks
12. Portersville, California – 2 weeks
13. Avena, California – 1 month
14. Galena, California – 1 month
15. Richmond, California – 2 months
16. Oakland, California - 1 month
17. Kennewick, Washington – 3 months

18. Richland, Washington – 1 month
19. Martinez, California – 2 weeks
20. Oakland, California – 1 month
21. Ft. Lupton, Colorado – 2 months – had 2nd Birthday
22. Pierce, Colorado – 1 month
23. Cheyenne, Wyoming – 2 months
24. Newcastle, Wyoming – 2 months
25. Casper, Wyoming – 3 months
26. Red Oak, Oklahoma – 3 months
27. Cortez Dam, Wyoming – 3 months
28. Pocatello, Idaho – 3 months – had 3rd Birthday
29. Worland, Wyoming – 1 month
30. Newcastle, Wyoming – 1 month
31. Lusk, Wyoming – 2 months
32. Newcastle, Wyoming – 1 month
33. Casper, Wyoming – 2 months
34. North Kansas City, Missouri – 4 months
35. Sapulpa, Oklahoma – 3 weeks
36. Shelby, North Carolina – 1 month – had 4th Birthday
37. Mt. Holly, North Carolina – 1 month
38. Salisbury, North Carolina – 1 month
39. Lexington, North Carolina – 1 month
40. Stokesdale, North Carolina – 1 month
41. Madison, North Carolina – 1 month
42. Gaffney, South Carolina - 2 months
43. Lynchburg, Virginia – 3 weeks
44. Gaffney, South Carolina – 1 month
45. Memphis, Tennessee – 1 month
46. Wharton, Texas – 1 month
47. Red Oak, Oklahoma (Christmastime) – 1 month
48. Clinton, Tennessee – 1 month
49. Kingston, Tennessee – 1 month

50. Union City, Tennessee – 1 month
51. Dyersburg, Tennessee – 1 month
52. Monroe, Louisiana – 2 months
53. Tulsa, Oklahoma – 1 month – had 5th Birthday
54. Birmingham, Michigan – 1 month – started kindergarten
55. Red Oak, Oklahoma – 2 months – kindergarten
56. Boise City, Oklahoma – 1 month
57. Dumas, Texas – 4 months
58. Red Oak, Oklahoma – 2 months
59. Dodge City, Kansas – 1 month
60. Warrensburg, Missouri – 1 month
61. Red Oak, Oklahoma – 2 weeks – had 6th Birthday
62. Kingsley, Iowa – 1 week
63. Booneville, Missouri – 2 months
64. Red Oak, Oklahoma – started 1st grade
65. Kevil, Kentucky - 9 months –
    finished 1st grade and had 7th Birthday
66. Red Oak, Oklahoma – 2 months – started 2nd grade, went 6 weeks
67. Midland, Texas – 2 months – 2nd grade
68. Eunice, New Mexico – 2 months – 2nd grade
69. L Platte, Nebraska – 2 months – 2nd grade
70. Wilburton, Oklahoma - 2 months –
    finished 2nd grade at Red Oak
71. Fergus Falls, Minnesota – 2 months – had 8th Birthday
72. Lyons, Kansas – 1 month – started 3rd grade
73. Newton, Kansas – 1 month – 3rd grade
74. Hutcheson, Kansas – 1 month – 3rd grade
75. Greensburg, Kansas – 1 month – 3rd grade
76. Red Oak, Oklahoma – 5 months – finished 3rd grade
77. Fruita, Colorado – 2 months – started 4th grade, went one week
78. Moab, Utah - 2 months – 4th grade
79. Independence, Kansas – 2 months – 4th grade

80. Lamesa, Texas – 4th grade

81. Aztec, New Mexico – 2 months – finished 4th grade

82. Perry, Iowa – 2 months

83. Edmond, Oklahoma – 2 months – started 5th grade, went 1 month, skipped to 6th grade

84. Fremont, Nebraska – 1 month – 6th grade

85. Red Oak, Oklahoma – 2 weeks – 6th grade

86. Gallup, New Mexico – 2 months – 6th grade

87. Holbrook, Arizona – 6 weeks – 6th grade

88. Winslow, Arizona – 6 weeks – 6th grade

89. Palmdale, California – 3 months – went 6 weeks in 6th grade, finished last of June

90. Winslow, Arizona – 1 month - started 7th grade

91. Red Oak, Oklahoma – 1 month – 7th grade

92. Iola, Kansas – 6 weeks – 7th grade

93. Chanute, Kansas – 6 weeks – 7th grade

94. Independence Kansas – 6 weeks – 7th grade

95. Red Oak, Oklahoma – 3 months – finished 7th grade

96. Mt. Vernon, Illinois – 2 months

97. Belleville, Illinois – 2 weeks

98. Paxton, Illinois – 1 month – started 8th grade

99. St. Anne, Illinois – 3 months – 8th grade

100. Lowell, Indiana – 2 months - 8th grade

101. Red Oak, Oklahoma – 3 months - finished 8th grade

102. Mendota, Illinois 1 month

103. Galena, Illinois – 6 weeks

104. Mendota, Illinois – 2 weeks

105. Freeport, Illinois – 1 month

106. Elgin, Illinois – 2 ½ months – started 9th grade, went 9 weeks

107. Red Oak, Oklahoma – finished 9th grade

108. Clear Lake, Wisconsin – 6 weeks

109. Red Oak, Oklahoma – 10th, 11th, and 12th grades

Note: I changed schools 38 times, attending 29 different schools in 13 states. I married June 15, 1963, in Red Oak, Oklahoma, one month after graduating high school, two weeks after my 17th birthday. We left after a few months for a job in Marshall, Illinois.

110. Marshall, Illinois – 6 weeks

111. Red Oak, Oklahoma – 3 ½ years

112. Beloit, Wisconsin – 1 week

113. Fond du Lac (Eden), Wisconsin – 4 ½ months

114. Red Oak, Oklahoma – 4 months

115. Oklahoma City, Oklahoma – 2 weeks

116. Eufaula, Oklahoma – 6 weeks

117. Springdale, Arkansas – 6 weeks

118. Red Oak, Oklahoma – 7 months

119. Fernandina Beach, Florida – 6 months

120. White Springs, Florida – 2 months

121. Athens, Alabama – 8 months

122. Homestead, Florida – 2 months

123. Athens, Alabama – 4 years - August 1971 – August 1975

124. Newcastle, Oklahoma – 10 months

125. Castalian Springs, Tennessee – 14 months

126. Udhailiyah, Saudi Arabia – 8 months

127. Abqaiq, Saudi Arabia – 1 year

128. Castalian Springs, Tennessee – 6 months

129. Abu Dhabi, United Arab Emirates – 15 months

130. Castalian Springs, Tennessee – from January 1981 –1995, with exceptions noted

131. Oswego, New York – Bud lived Jan – July. 1985; I spent 2 ½ months

132. Columbus, Mississippi – Bud lived 3 weeks in August 1985; I spent 1 week.

133. Lakewood, New Jersey – Bud lived several months in 1985; I spent 1 month.

134. South Carolina - 1995 - Present

COUNTRIES WHERE I HAVE BEEN

1. United States
2. Canada
3. Mexico
4. Iceland
5. Luxembourg
6. France
7. Switzerland
8. Italy
9. Germany
10. Liechenstein
11. England
12. Scotland
13. Wales
14. Spain
15. Morocco
16. The Netherlands
17. Saudi Arabia
18. Republic of Ireland
19. Northern Ireland
20. Egypt
21. United Arab Emirates
22. Jordan
23. Oman
24. Qatar
25. Belgium
26. Greece
27. Norway
28. Sweden
29. Denmark
30. Austria
31. Australia
32. New Zealand
33. Ecuador
34. Guatemala
35. Portugal
36. Andora
37. Poland
38. Cayman Islands
39. Honduras
40. Belize
41. Panama
42. Israel
43. Turkey
44. Bahamas

Epilogue

Just when you thought the story was done, you turned the page and another had begun.

I am recovering from a manic-depressive episode that has lasted for most of the month of December. What a wake-up call for me! I was preparing for a revised printing of my manuscript, changing the format a bit and doing some tweaking. When I wrote some closing thoughts in February 2017 and the preface in June 2018, I truly believed that the writing had been so cathartic that I was leaving that part of my life behind, too. Such was not to be. Yes, I have accepted that bipolar disease will always be a part of me. I will always have to be ever vigilant. And that's okay.

My first thoughts concerning the book were that I could leave out a few sentences that I had written in the last page of the manuscript and in the preface, and be done with it. I quickly knew that for those of you who had faithfully read and stayed with me to the end, this would not be fair. My husband's dramatic mood swings within minutes are evidence that his dementia is progressing. I was caught off guard and began to develop manic signs. After about a week, the depressive part began. This is not an "I am sad" type depression. Coming down from a high leaves one emotionally flat, extremely fatigued, and irritable. And it seemed like this would never go away.

For me, I can go to bed for as much rest as I need. There are many out there who are not so lucky. They have to try to go to work each morning and keep on plugging on. I ordered some books on managing bipolar— books that have recently been published. I read some each day, and this is so helpful. Knowledge is power. I bought the physicians' desk reference book on bipolar and am studying this, also. I want to know as much about this illness as I can learn. Perhaps it will not only help me, but maybe there will be opportunities to help others from what I glean from books as well as my own experiences.

Yes, I have challenges ahead, and I want to be proactive. I want to use the gifts I have been given in this latest experience to enjoy life, for I do believe that "the best is yet to be."

Beverly Ann Rider
January 4, 2019